THE
GOLEM
AND THE
DJINNI

THE
GOLEM
AND THE
DJINNI

HELENE WECKER

blue door

Blue Door
An imprint of HarperCollins*Publishers*
77–85 Fulham Palace Road,
Hammersmith, London W6 8JB

First published in Great Britain by Blue Door 2013
1

Copyright © Helene Wecker 2013

Helene Wecker asserts the moral right to
be identified as the author of this work

A catalogue record for this book is
available from the British Library

HB ISBN: 978-0-00-748017-3
TPB ISBN: 978-0-00-748016-6

Book design by William Ruoto

Printed and bound in Great Britain by
Clays Ltd, St Ives plc

MIX
Paper from
responsible sources
FSC C007454
FSC
www.fsc.org

FSC™ is a non-profit international organisation established to promote
the responsible management of the world's forests. Products carrying the
FSC label are independently certified to assure consumers that they come
from forests that are managed to meet the social, economic and
ecological needs of present and future generations,
and other controlled sources.

Find out more about HarperCollins and the environment at
www.harpercollins.co.uk/green

For Kareem

THE
GOLEM
AND THE
DJINNI

I.

The Golem's life began in the hold of a steamship. The year was 1899; the ship was the *Baltika*, crossing from Danzig to New York. The Golem's master, a man named Otto Rotfeld, had smuggled her aboard in a crate and hidden her among the luggage.

Rotfeld was a Prussian Jew from Konin, a bustling town to the south of Danzig. The only son of a well-to-do furniture maker, Rotfeld had inherited the family business sooner than expected, on his parents' untimely death from scarlet fever. But Rotfeld was an arrogant, feckless sort of man, with no good sense to speak of; and before five years had elapsed, the business lay before him in tatters.

Rotfeld stood in the ruins and took stock. He was thirty-three years old. He wanted a wife, and he wanted to go to America.

The wife was the larger problem. On top of his arrogant disposition, Rotfeld was gangly and unattractive, and had a tendency to leer. Women were disinclined to be alone with him. A few matchmakers had approached him when he'd inherited, but their clients had been from inferior families, and he'd turned them away. When it became clear to all what kind of businessman he really was, the offers had disappeared completely.

Rotfeld was arrogant, but he was also lonely. He'd had no real love affairs. He passed worthy ladies on the street, and saw the distaste in their eyes.

It wasn't very long before he thought to visit old Yehudah Schaalman.

Stories abounded about Schaalman, all slightly different: that he was a disgraced rabbi who'd been driven out of his congregation; that he'd been possessed by a dybbuk and given supernatural powers; and even that he was over a hundred years old and slept with demon-women. But all the stories agreed on this: Schaalman liked to dabble in the more dangerous of the Kabbalistic arts, and he was willing to offer his services for a price. Barren women had visited him in the dead of night and conceived soon after. Peasant girls in search of men's affections bought Schaalman's bags of powders, and then stirred them into their beloveds' beer.

But Rotfeld wanted no spells or love-potions. He had something else in mind.

He went to the old man's dilapidated shack, deep in the forest that bordered Konin. The path to the front door was a half-trampled trail. Greasy, yellowish smoke drifted from a chimney-pipe, the only sign of habitation. The walls of the shack slouched toward a nearby ravine, in which a stream trickled.

Rotfeld knocked on the door, and waited. After some minutes, he heard a shuffling step. The door opened a hand's width, revealing a man of perhaps seventy. He was bald, save for a fringe. His cheeks were deeply furrowed above a tangled beard. He stared hard at Rotfeld, as though daring him to speak.

"Are you Schaalman?" Rotfeld asked.

No answer, only the stare.

Rotfeld cleared his throat, nervous. "I want you to make me a golem that can pass for human," he said. "And I want it to be female."

That broke the old man's silence. He laughed, a hard bark. "Boy," he said, "do you know what a golem is?"

"A person made of clay," Rotfeld said, uncertain.

"Wrong. It's a beast of burden. A lumbering, unthinking slave. Golems are built for protection and brute force, not for the pleasures of a bed."

Rotfeld reddened. "Are you saying you can't do it?"

"I'm telling you the idea is ridiculous. To make a golem that can pass for human would be near impossible. For one thing, it would need some amount of self-awareness, if only enough to converse. Not to mention the body itself, with realistic joints, and musculature . . ."

The old man trailed off, staring past his visitor. He seemed to be considering something. Abruptly he turned his back on Rotfeld and disappeared into the gloom of the shack. Through the open door Rotfeld could see him shuffling carefully through a stack of papers. Then he picked up an old leather-bound book and thumbed through it. His finger ran down a page, and he peered at something written there. He looked up at Rotfeld.

"Come back tomorrow," he said.

Accordingly, Rotfeld knocked again the next day, and this time Schaalman opened the door without pause. "How much can you pay?" he demanded.

"Then it can be done?"

"Answer my question. The one will determine the other."

Rotfeld named a figure. The old man snorted. "Half again, at the very least."

"But I'll have barely anything left!"

"Consider it a bargain," said Schaalman. "For isn't it written that a virtuous woman is more precious than rubies? And her virtue"—he grinned—"will be guaranteed!"

Rotfeld brought the money three days later, in a large valet case. The edge of the nearby ravine was newly disfigured, a piece the length of a man scooped away. An earth-stained spade leaned against a wall.

Schaalman opened the door with a distracted look, as though interrupted at a crucial moment. Streaks of mud crusted his clothing and daubed his beard. He saw the valet case and grabbed it from Rotfeld's hand.

"Good," he said. "Come back in a week."

The door slammed shut again, but not before Rotfeld had caught a glimpse inside the shack, of a dark figure laid out in pieces on a table—a slender trunk, rough limbs, and one curled hand.

"What do you prefer in a woman?" Schaalman asked.

It was the following week, and this time Rotfeld had been allowed inside. The shack was dominated by the table that Rotfeld had glimpsed before, and the young man couldn't help sneaking glances at its burden: a human-shaped form, draped with a sheet. He said, "What do you mean, what do I *prefer?*"

"I'm creating a woman for you. I assumed you'd want some say in the matter."

Rotfeld frowned. "I like an attractive figure, I suppose—"

"Not her physical aspects, not yet. Her temperament. Her personality."

"You can *do* that?"

"Yes, I believe that I can," the old man said with pride. "At least, I can steer her toward certain proclivities."

Rotfeld thought hard. "I want her to be obedient."

"She'll already be obedient," Schaalman said, impatient. "That's what a golem is—a slave to your will. Whatever you command her, she'll do. She won't even wish otherwise."

"Good," Rotfeld said. But he was perplexed. Having put aside appearance and obedience, he had little idea what else he wanted. He was about to tell Rotfeld to do whatever he thought best—but then, in a burst of memory, he recalled his younger sister, the only girl he'd ever truly known. She'd been full of curiosity, and a burden to their mother, who could not stand her always underfoot and asking questions. In one of the few generous acts of his life, young Otto had taken her under his wing. Together they'd spent whole afternoons wandering through the woods, and he'd answered her questions about anything and everything. When she'd died at age twelve, drowned in a river on a summer afternoon, he'd lost the only person in his life who'd ever really mattered.

"Give her curiosity," he told Schaalman. "And intelligence. I can't stand a silly woman. Oh," he said, inspiration warming him to his task, "and make her proper. Not . . . lascivious. A gentleman's wife."

The old man's eyebrows shot up. He'd expected his client to request motherly kindness, or an eager sexual appetite, or else both; years of manufacturing love spells had taught him what men like Rotfeld thought they wanted in a woman. But curiosity? Intelligence? He wondered if the man knew what he was asking for.

But he only smiled and spread his hands. "I'll try," he said. "The results may not be as precise as you might wish. One can only do so much with clay." Then his face darkened. "But remember this. A creature can only be altered so far from its basic nature. She'll still be a golem. She'll have the strength of a dozen men. She'll protect you without thinking, and she'll harm others to do it. No golem has ever existed that did not eventually run amok. You must be prepared to destroy her."

The task was finished the night before Rotfeld left for the docks at Danzig. He made his final trip to Schaalman's leading a dray-cart loaded with a large wooden crate, a modest brown dress, and a pair of women's shoes.

Schaalman appeared not to have slept for some time. His eyes were dark smudges, and he was pale, as though drained of some essential energy. He lit a lamp that hung above the worktable, and Rotfeld caught his first true glimpse of his intended.

She was tall, almost as tall as Rotfeld himself, and well proportioned: a long torso, breasts that were small but firm, a sturdy waist. Her hips were perhaps a bit square, but on her it seemed correct, even appealing. In the dim light he spied the dark shadow between her legs; he glanced away from it as though disinterested, aware of Schaalman's mocking eyes, and the pounding of his own blood.

Her face was wide and heart shaped, her eyes set far apart. They were closed; he could not tell their color. The nose was small and curved under at the tip, above full lips. Her hair was brown and had a slight wave, and was cut to brush her shoulders.

Tentative, half-believing, he placed a hand on her cool shoulder. "It looks like skin. It *feels* like skin."

"It's clay," said the old man.

"How did you do this?"

The old man only smiled, and said nothing.

"And the hair, and eyes? The fingernails? Are they clay too?"

"No, those are real enough," Schaalman said, blandly innocent. Rotfeld remembered handing over the case of money, and wondering what sort of supplies the old man needed to buy. He shivered and decided not to think about it again.

They dressed the clay woman and carefully lifted her heavy body into the crate. Her hair tangled about her face as they arranged her, and Rotfeld waited until the old man's back was turned before gently smoothing it into place again.

Schaalman found a small piece of paper and wrote on it the two necessary commands—one to bring her to life, and one to destroy her. He folded the paper twice, and placed it in an oilskin envelope. On the envelope he wrote COMMANDS FOR THE GOLEM, and then handed it to Rotfeld. His client was eager to wake her, but the old man was against it. "She might be disoriented for a time," he said. "And the ship will be too crowded. If someone realized what she was, they'd throw you both overboard." Reluctantly, Rotfeld agreed to wait until they reached America; and they nailed the lid on the crate, sealing her away.

The old man poured them each a finger of schnapps from a dusty bottle. "To your golem," he said, raising his glass.

"To my golem," Rotfeld echoed, and downed the schnapps. It was a triumphant moment, marred only by his persistent stomachache. He'd always had a delicate constitution, and the stress of the last few weeks had ruined his digestion. Ignoring his stomach, he helped the old man lift the crate into the dray-cart, and then led the horse away. The old man waved after the departing Rotfeld, as though seeing off a pair of newlyweds. "I wish you joy of her!" he called, and his cackle echoed through the trees.

The ship set sail from Danzig, and made its stop in Hamburg without incident. Two nights later Rotfeld lay in his narrow bunk, the oilskin envelope labeled COMMANDS FOR THE GOLEM tucked away in a pocket. He felt like a child who'd been given a present and then instructed not to open it. It would have been easier if he could've slept, but the pain in his stomach had grown into a lump of misery on the right side of his abdomen. He felt slightly feverish. The cacophony of steerage surrounded him: a hundred diverse snores, the hiccupping sobs of babies, an occasional retch as the ship rode from swell to trough.

He turned over, squirming against the pain, and reflected: surely the old man's advice was overcautious. If she was as obedient as promised, there'd be no harm in waking her, just to see. Then he could command her to lie in the crate until they reached America.

But what if she didn't work properly? What if she didn't wake at all, but only lay there, a lump of clay in the shape of a woman? It struck him for the first time that he'd seen no proof that Schaalman could do what he'd promised. Panicked, he fished the envelope from his pocket, withdrew from it the scrap of paper. Gibberish, meaningless words, a jumble of Hebrew letters! What a fool he'd been!

He swung his legs over the side of his bunk, and fetched a kerosene lamp off its nail. Pressing a hand to his side, he hurried through the maze of bunks to the stairwell and down to the hold.

It took him nearly two hours to find the crate, two hours of picking his way through stacks of suitcases and boxes bound with twine. His stomach burned, and cold sweat dripped into his eyes. Finally he moved aside a rolled-up carpet, and there it was: his crate, and in it his bride.

He found a crowbar, pried the nails from the crate, and yanked off the lid. Heart pounding, he pulled the paper from his pocket, and carefully sounded out the command labeled *To Wake the Golem*.

He held his breath, and waited.

Slowly the Golem came to life.

First to wake were her senses. She felt the roughness of wood under her fingertips, the cold, damp air on her skin. She sensed the movement of the boat. She smelled mildew, and the tang of seawater.

She woke a little more, and knew she had a body. The fingertips that felt the wood were her own. The skin that the air chilled was her skin. She moved a finger, to see if she could.

She heard a man nearby, breathing. She knew his name and who he was. He was her master, her entire purpose; she was his golem, bound to his will. And right now he wanted her to open her eyes.

The Golem opened her eyes.

Her master was kneeling above her in the dim light. His face and hair were drenched with sweat. With one hand he braced himself on the edge of the crate; the other was pressed at his stomach.

"Hello," Rotfeld whispered. An absurd shyness had tightened his voice. "Do you know who I am?"

"You're my master. Your name is Otto Rotfeld." Her voice was clear and natural, if a bit deep.

"That's right," he said, as though to a child. "And do you know who *you* are?"

"A golem." She paused, considering. "I don't have a name."

"Not yet," Rotfeld said, smiling. "I'll have to think of one for you."

Suddenly he winced. The Golem didn't need to ask why, for she could feel it as well, a dull ache that echoed his. "You're in pain," she said, concerned.

"It's nothing," Rotfeld said. "Sit up."

She sat up in the crate, and looked about. The kerosene lamp cast a feeble light that roamed with the ship's rocking. Long shadows loomed and retreated across stacks of luggage and boxes. "Where are we?" she asked.

"On a ship, crossing the ocean," Rotfeld said. "We're on our way to America. But you must be very careful. There are many people on this ship, and they'd be frightened if they knew what you were. They might even try to harm you. You'll need to lie here very still until we reach land."

The ship leaned sharply, and the Golem clutched at the edges of the crate.

"It's all right," Rotfeld whispered. He lifted a shaking hand to stroke her hair. "You're safe here, with me," he said. "My golem."

Suddenly he gasped, bent his head to the deck, and began to retch. The Golem watched with chagrin. "Your pain is growing worse," she said.

Rotfeld coughed and wiped his mouth with the back of his hand. "I told you," he said, "it's nothing." He tried to stand, but staggered, and fell to his knees. A wave of panic hit him as he began to realize that something was truly wrong.

"Help me," he whispered.

The command struck the Golem like an arrow. Swiftly she rose from her crate, bent over Rotfeld, and lifted him as though he weighed no more than a boy. With her master in her arms, she wove her way around the boxes, up the narrow staircase, and out of the hold.

A commotion broke out at the aft end of steerage. It spread down the deck, waking the sleepers, who grumbled and turned over in their bunks. A crowd began to grow around a cot near the hatch, where a man had collapsed, his face gray in the lantern-light. A call threaded its way from row to row: was there a doctor nearby?

One soon appeared, in pajamas and an overcoat. The crowd parted for him as he made his way to the cot. Hovering next to the sick man was a tall woman in a brown dress who watched, wide eyed, as the doctor undid the young man's shirt and pulled it back. Carefully the doctor prodded Rotfeld's abdomen, and was rewarded with a short scream.

The Golem lunged forward and snatched the man's hand away. The doctor pulled back, shocked.

"It's all right," the man on the cot whispered. "He's a doctor. He's here to help." He reached up, and clasped her hand.

Warily the doctor felt Rotfeld's abdomen again, one eye on the woman. "It's his appendix," he announced. "We must get him to the ship's surgeon, quickly."

The doctor grabbed one of Rotfeld's arms and pulled him to standing. Others rushed to help, and together the knot of men moved through the hatch, Rotfeld hanging half-delirious at its center. The woman followed close behind.

The ship's surgeon was the sort of man who did not appreciate being roused in the middle of the night, especially to cut open some nameless peasant from steerage. One look at the man writhing weakly on his operating table, and he wondered if it was worth the trouble. Judging by the advanced state of the appendicitis and the high fever, the appendix had likely already burst, flooding the man's belly with poisons. The surgery alone might finish him off. After delivering their burden, the foreigners who'd brought the man had hovered by the hatchway, unsure of themselves, and then left without a word of English.

Well, there was nothing for it. He'd have to operate. He called down for his assistant to be roused and began laying out his instruments. He was searching for the ether jar when suddenly the hatch was wrenched open behind him. It was a woman, tall and dark-haired, wearing only a thin brown shift against the cold Atlantic air. She rushed to the side of the man on the table, looking near panicked. His wife or sweetheart, he supposed.

"I suppose it's too much to ask that you speak English," he said; and of course she only stared, uncomprehending. "I'm sorry, but you can't stay here. No women permitted in the surgery. You'll have to leave." He pointed at the door.

That, at least, got through: she shook her head vehemently and began to expostulate in Yiddish. "Look here," the surgeon began, and took her elbow to steer her out. But it was as though he'd grabbed hold of a lamppost. The woman would not move, only loomed over him, solid and suddenly gigantic, a Valkyrie come to life.

He dropped her arm as though it had scalded him. "Have it your way," he muttered, disconcerted. He busied himself with the ether jar, and tried to ignore the bizarre presence behind his shoulder.

The hatch opened again, and a young man fell in, looking roughly wakened. "Doctor, I'm—good lord!"

"Never mind her," the surgeon said. "She refuses to leave. If she faints, so much the better. Quick now, or he'll die before we can open him up." And with that, they etherized their patient and set to work.

If the two men had known the powerful struggle taking place inside the woman behind them, they would've deserted the surgery and run for their lives. Any lesser creation would have throttled them both the moment their knives touched Rotfeld's skin. But the Golem recalled the doctor in the hold, and her master's assurance that he was there to help; and it had been that doctor who'd brought him here. Still, as they peeled back Rotfeld's skin and hunted through his innards, her hands twisted and clenched uncontrollably at her sides. She reached for her master in her mind, and found no awareness, no needs or desires. She was losing him, bit by bit.

The surgeon removed something from Rotfeld's body and dropped it in a tray. "Well, the damned thing's out," he said. He glanced over his shoulder. "Still on your feet? Good girl."

"Maybe she's simple," muttered the assistant.

"Not necessarily. These peasants have iron stomachs. Simon, keep that clamped!"

"Sorry, sir."

But the figure on the table was struggling for life. He inhaled once, and again; and then, with a long, rattling sigh, Otto Rotfeld's final breath left his body.

The Golem staggered as the last remnants of their connection snapped and faded away.

The surgeon bent his head to Rotfeld's chest. He took up the man's wrist for a moment, then gently placed it back. "Time of death, please," he said.

The assistant swallowed, and glanced at the chronometer. "Oh two hundred hours, forty-eight minutes."

The surgeon made a note, true regret on his face. "Couldn't be helped," he said, his voice bitter. "He waited too long. He must have been in agony for days."

The Golem could not look away from the unmoving shape on the table. A moment ago he'd been her master, her reason for being; now he seemed nothing at all. She felt dizzy, unmoored. She stepped forward and touched a hand to his face, his slack jaw, his drooping eyelids. Already the heat was fading from his skin.

Please stop that.

The Golem withdrew her hand and looked at the two men, who were watching in horrified distaste. Neither of them had spoken.

"I'm sorry," said the surgeon finally, hoping she would understand his tone. "We tried our best."

"I know," said the Golem—and only then did she realize that she'd understood the man's words, and replied in the same language.

The surgeon frowned, and shared a glance with his assistant. "Mrs. . . . I'm sorry, what was his name?"

"Rotfeld," said the Golem. "Otto Rotfeld."

"Mrs. Rotfeld, our condolences. Perhaps—"

"You want me to leave," she said. It wasn't a guess, nor was it a sudden understanding of the indelicacy of her presence. She simply *knew* it, as surely as she could see her master's body on the table, and smell the ether's sickly fumes. The surgeon's desire, his wish for her to be elsewhere, had spoken inside her mind.

"Well, yes, perhaps it would be better," he said. "Simon, please escort Mrs. Rotfeld back to steerage."

She let the young man put his arm about her and guide her out of the surgery. She was shaking. Some part of her was still casting about, searching for Rotfeld. And meanwhile the young assistant's embarrassed discomfort, his desire to be rid of his charge, was clouding her thoughts. What was happening to her?

At the door to the steerage deck, the young man squeezed her hand guiltily, and then was gone. What should she do? Go in there, and face all those people? She put her hand on the door latch, hesitated, opened it.

The wishes and fears of five hundred passengers hit her like a maelstrom.

I wish I could fall asleep. If only she would stop throwing up. Will that man ever quit snoring? I need a glass of water. How long until we reach New York? What if the ship goes down? If we were alone, we could make love. Oh God, I want to go back home.

The Golem let go of the latch, turned, and ran.

Up on the deserted main deck, she found a bench and sat there until morning. A chill rain began to fall, soaking her dress, but she ignored it, unable to focus on anything except the clamor in her head. It was as though, without Rotfeld's commands to guide her, her mind was reaching out for a substitute and encountering the ship's worth of passengers that lay below. Without the benefit of the bond between master and golem, their wishes and fears did not have the driving force of commands—but nonetheless she heard them, and felt their varying urgencies, and her limbs twitched with the compulsion to respond. Each one was like a small hand plucking at her sleeve: *please, do something.*

The next morning, she stood at the railing as Rotfeld's body was lowered into the sea. It was a blustery day, the waves white-tipped and choppy. Rotfeld's body hit the water with barely a splash; in an instant the ship had left it behind. Perhaps, the Golem thought, it might be best to hurl herself overboard and follow Rotfeld into the water. She leaned forward and peered over the edge, trying to gauge the water's depth; but two men hurriedly stepped forward, and she allowed herself to be drawn back.

The small crowd of onlookers began to disperse. A man in ship's livery handed her a small leather pouch, explaining that it held everything that had been on Rotfeld's person when he died. At some point a compassionate deckhand had placed a wool coat about her shoulders, and she tucked the pouch into a pocket.

A small knot of passengers from steerage hovered nearby, wondering what to do about her. Should they escort her below decks, or simply leave her be? Rumors had circled the bunks all night. One man insisted that she'd carried the dead man into steerage in her own two arms. Then there was the woman who muttered that she'd seen Rotfeld at Danzig— he'd made himself conspicuous by berating the deckhands for not taking care with a heavy crate—and that he'd boarded the ship alone. They remembered how she'd grabbed at the doctor's hands, like a wild animal. And she was simply *odd*, in a way they couldn't explain even to themselves. She stood far too still, as if rooted to the deck, while those around her shivered in the cold and leaned with the ship. She hardly blinked, even when the ocean mist struck her face. And as far as they could tell, she hadn't yet shed a single tear.

They decided to approach her. But the Golem had felt their fears and suspicions and she turned from the rail and walked past them, her stiff back a clear request for solitude. They felt her passing as a slap of cold, grave-smelling air. Their resolve faltered; they left her alone.

The Golem made her way to the aft staircase. She passed steerage and continued down to the depths of the hold: the one place in her short existence where she hadn't felt herself in peril. She found the open crate and climbed into it, then drew the lid into place above her. Muffled in darkness, she lay there, reviewing the few facts of which she was certain. She was a golem, and her master was dead. She was on a ship in the middle of the ocean. If the others knew what she was, they would be afraid of her. And she had to stay hidden.

As she lay there, the strongest of the desires drifted down to her from the decks above. A little girl in steerage had misplaced her toy horse, and now wailed for it, inconsolable. A man traveling second class had been three days without a drink, trying to make a fresh start; he paced his tiny cabin, shaking, fingers knotted in his hair, unable to think about anything except a glass of brandy. Each of these, and many others, pulled at her in turn, rising and falling. They urged her to climb out of the hold, to help in some way. But she remembered the suspicions of the passengers on the foredeck, and stayed in the crate.

She lay there the rest of the day and into the night, listening to the boxes around her shift and groan. She felt useless, purposeless. She had no idea what to do. And her only clue to where they were going was a word that Rotfeld had spoken. *America*. It might mean anything.

The next morning, the ship awoke to warmer weather and a welcome sight: a thin line of gray between ocean and sky. Passengers drifted to the deck, watching westward as the line thickened and stretched. It meant all their wishes granted, their fears forgotten, if only for the moment; and down in the hold the Golem felt an unexpected and blissful relief.

The constant thrum of the ship's propellers quieted to a purr. The ship slowed. And then came the distant sound of voices, yelling and cheering. Curiosity made the Golem rise at last from her crate, and she emerged onto the foredeck, into the noonday sun.

The deck was crowded with people, and at first the Golem didn't see what they were waving at. But then, there she was: a gray-green woman standing in the middle of the water, holding a tablet and bearing aloft a torch. Her gaze was unblinking, and she stood so still: was it another golem? Then the distance became clear, and she realized how far away the woman was, and how gigantic. Not alive, then; but the blank, smooth eyes nevertheless held a hint of understanding. And those on deck were waving and shouting at her with jubilation, crying even as they smiled. This, too, the Golem thought, was a constructed woman. Whatever she meant to the others, she was loved and respected for it. For the first time since Rotfeld's death, the Golem felt something like hope.

The ship's horn sounded, making the air vibrate. The Golem turned to go back down to the hold, and only then did she glimpse the city. It rose, enormous, at the edge of an island. The tall, square build-ings seemed to move between each other, dancing in rows as the ship drew closer. She glimpsed trees, piers, a harbor alive with smaller craft, tugs and sailboats that skimmed the water like insects. There was a long gray bridge that hung in a net of lines, stretching east to another shore. She wondered if they would go under it; but instead the great ship turned westward and pulled in closer to the docks. The sea became a narrow river.

Men in uniform walked up and down the foredeck, shouting. *Go collect your belongings*, they said. *We'll dock soon at New York, and you'll be taken to Ellis Island by ferry. Your luggage in the hold will be delivered to you there.* Not until she'd heard these messages repeated half a dozen times did the Golem realize that the men were speaking in different languages, and that she understood every single one of them.

Within minutes the deck had been cleared of passengers. She moved into the shadow of the wheelhouse, and tried to think. She had no possessions save the coat she'd been given; its dark wool was grow-ing warm in the sunlight. She felt inside the pocket and found the little leather satchel. There was that, at least.

A trickle of passengers reemerged from the stairway, and then a general flood, all dressed for travel and carrying their bags and suitcases. The uniformed men began to shout again: *Form an orderly line. Be ready to give us your name and nationality. No pushing. No crowding. Mind your children.* The Golem stood apart, unsure. Should she join them? Find somewhere to hide? Their minds clamored at her, all wanting only a speedy trip through Ellis Island and a clean bill of health from the inspectors.

One of the uniformed men saw the Golem standing alone and hesitant, and walked toward her. A passenger intercepted him, put a hand to his shoulder, and began to talk in his ear. It was the doctor from steerage. The ship's man was carrying a sheaf of papers, and he flipped through them, searching. He frowned and stepped away from the doctor, who melted back into line.

"Ma'am," the officer called, looking straight at the Golem. "Come here, please." All around them went quiet as the Golem approached. "You're the one whose husband died, is that correct?"

"Yes."

"My condolences, ma'am. It's probably just an oversight, but you don't seem to be on the manifest. May I see your ticket?"

Her ticket? She had none, of course. She could lie, and say she'd lost it, but she'd never lied before and didn't trust herself to do it well. She realized that her only options were to remain silent, or to tell the truth.

"I don't have a ticket," she said, and smiled, hoping that would help.

The officer sighed wearily and placed a hand around the Golem's arm, as though to prevent her from running away. "You'll have to come with me, ma'am."

"Where are we going?"

"You're going to sit in the brig until we get the passengers sorted, and then we'll ask you a few questions."

What should she do? There was no way to answer their questions without exposing herself. Already everyone was staring. Alarmed, she turned in the man's insistent grip, looking for some sort of escape. They were still under way, fording the middle of the river, smaller ships gliding to either side. Beyond the busy piers, the city gleamed invitingly.

The officer gripped her arm harder. "Ma'am. Don't make me force you."

But he didn't want to force her, she saw. He didn't want to deal with her at all. More than anything, the officer wished she would just disappear.

The edge of a smile lifted the Golem's mouth. Here, finally, was a desire she could gratify.

With a flick of her elbow, she broke from the startled officer and ran to the railing. Before anyone could even shout out, she vaulted the edge, arced out into the shimmering Hudson, and sank like a stone.

A few hours later, a stevedore smoking a cigarette on the corner of West and Gansevoort saw a woman walk past from the direction of the river. She was soaking wet. She wore a man's woolen jacket and a brown dress that clung immodestly to her body. Her hair was plastered to her neck. Most astonishing was the thick, brackish mud that covered her skirt and shoes.

"Hey, miss," he called out to her, "you go for a swim?"

The woman gave him a strange smile as she went by. "No," she said. "I walked."

2.

In the neighborhood of Lower Manhattan called Little Syria, not far from where the Golem came ashore, there lived a tinsmith by the name of Boutros Arbeely. Arbeely was a Maronite Catholic who'd grown up in the bustling village of Zahleh, which lay in the valley below Mount Lebanon. He had come to adulthood at a time when it seemed every man under the age of thirty was leaving Greater Syria to seek his fortune in America. Some were spurred on by missionaries' tales, or by relatives who'd made the journey and whose letters home now arrived thick with banknotes. Others saw a chance to elude the army conscription and punishing taxes demanded by their Turkish rulers. In all, so many left that in some villages the markets fell silent, and the grapes on the hillsides were left to burst on the vines.

Arbeely's late father had come from a family of five brothers, and over the generations their land had been divided and redivided until each brother's parcel was so small it was hardly worth the effort of planting. Arbeely himself made barely a pittance as a tinsmith's apprentice. His mother and sisters kept silkworms to bring in extra money, but still it wasn't enough. In the general rush to America, Arbeely saw his chance. He bid his family farewell and boarded a steamship bound for New York, and soon had rented a small smithing shop on Washington Street, at the heart of the growing Syrian neighborhood.

Arbeely was a good and conscientious worker, and even in New York's crowded marketplace his goods stood out as quality for the price. He made cups and plates, pots and pans, household tools, thimbles, candlesticks. Occasionally a neighbor would bring him something to repair, a damaged pot or a twisted door hinge, and he would return it in better shape than when it was new.

That summer Arbeely received an interesting request. A woman named Maryam Faddoul came to the shop with an old, battered, yet rather lovely copper flask. The flask had been in Maryam's family as long as she could remember; her mother, who'd used it for olive oil, had given it to Maryam when she'd sailed to America. "So you'll always have a piece of home with you," her mother had said.

With her husband Sayeed, Maryam had opened a coffeehouse on Washington Street, which quickly became a thriving hub of the neighborhood. One afternoon, while surveying her bustling kitchen, Maryam decided that the flask, while still beloved, had grown a bit too pockmarked and worn. Would it be possible, she asked Arbeely, to repair a few of the dents? And perhaps restore the polish?

Alone in his shop, Arbeely examined the flask. It was about nine inches high, with a round, bulbous body that tapered to a thin neck. Its maker had decorated it with a very precise and detailed band of scrollwork. Instead of the usual repeating pattern, the loops and whorls threaded through their neighbors seemingly at random, before joining up with themselves again.

Arbeely turned the flask around in his hands, fascinated. Clearly it was old, older perhaps than Maryam or her mother knew. Copper was rarely used on its own anymore, owing to its softness; brass and tin were much more durable and easier to work. In fact, given its likely age, the flask didn't seem as battered as perhaps it should have been. There was no way to determine its provenance, for it had no forger's stamp on its bottom, no identifying mark of any kind.

He examined the deep dents in the scrollwork, and realized that correcting them would lead to visible seams between the new work and the old. Better, he decided, to smooth out the copper, repair the flask, and then rework the entire design.

He wrapped a sheet of thin vellum around the base, found a stick of charcoal, and took a rubbing of the scrollwork, careful to catch every mark of the maker's awl. Then he secured the flask in a vise, and fetched his smallest soldering iron from the fire.

As he stood there, his iron poised above the flask, a strange feeling of foreboding stole over him. His arms and back turned to gooseflesh. Shivering, he put down the iron, and took a deep breath. What could possibly be bothering him? It was a warm day, and he'd eaten a hearty breakfast. He was healthy, and business was good. He shook his head, took up the iron again, and touched it to the scrollwork, erasing one of the loops.

A powerful jolt blasted him off his feet, as though he'd been struck by lightning. He flew through the air and landed in a heap beside a work-table. Stunned, ears ringing, he turned over and looked around.

There was a naked man lying on the floor of his shop.

As Arbeely stared in amazement, the man drew himself to sitting and pressed his hands to his face. Then he dropped his hands and gazed around, eyes wide and burning. He looked as though he'd been chained for years in the world's deepest, darkest dungeon, and then hauled roughly into the light.

The man staggered to his feet. He was tall and well built, with handsome features. Too handsome, in fact—his face had an eerie flaw-lessness, like a painting come to life. His dark hair was cropped short. He seemed unconscious of his nakedness.

On the man's right wrist was a wide metal cuff. The man appeared to notice it at the same time as Arbeely. He held up his arm and stared at it, horrified. "Iron," he said. And then, "But that's impossible."

Finally the man's glance caught Arbeely, who still crouched next to the table, not even daring to breathe.

With a sudden terrible grace, the man swooped down upon Ar-beely, grabbed him around the neck, and lifted him clean off the floor. A dark red haze filled Arbeely's sight. He felt his head brush the ceiling.

"Where is he?" the man shouted.

"Who?" wheezed Arbeely.

"The wizard!"

Arbeely tried to speak but could only gargle. Snarling, the naked man threw him back to the ground. Arbeely gasped for air. He looked around for a weapon, anything, and saw the soldering iron lying in a pile of rags, gently smoldering. He grabbed its handle, and lunged.

A blur of movement—and then Arbeely was stretched out on the floor again, this time with the iron's curved handle pressed at the hollow of his throat. The man knelt over him, holding the iron by its red-hot tip.

There was no smell of burning flesh. The man didn't so much as flinch. And as Arbeely stared aghast into that too-perfect face, he could feel the cool handle at his throat turn warm, and then hot, and then hotter still—as though the man were heating it somehow.

This, Arbeely thought, *is very, very impossible.*

"Tell me where the wizard is," the man said, "so I can kill him."

Arbeely gaped at him.

"He trapped me in human form! Tell me where he is!"

The tinsmith's mind began to race. He looked down at the soldering iron, and remembered that strange foreboding he'd felt before he touched it to the flask. He recalled his grandmother's stories of flasks and oil lamps, all with creatures trapped inside.

No. It was ludicrous. Such things were only stories. But then, the only alternative was to conclude that he'd gone mad.

"Sir," he whispered, "are you a djinni?"

The man's mouth tightened, and his gaze turned wary. But he didn't laugh at Arbeely, or call him insane.

"You are," Arbeely said. "Dear God, you *are*." He swallowed, wincing against the touch of the soldering iron. "Please. I don't know this wizard, whoever he is. In fact, I'm not sure there are any wizards left at all." He paused. "You may have been inside that flask for a very long time."

The man seemed to take this in. Slowly the metal moved away from the tinsmith's neck. The man stood and turned about, as though seeing the workshop for the first time. Through the high window came the noises of the street: of horse-drawn carts, and the shouts of the paperboys. On the Hudson, a steamship horn sounded long and low.

"Where am I?" the man asked.

"You're in my shop," Arbeely said. "In New York City." He was trying to speak calmly. "In a place called America."

The man walked over to Arbeely's workbench and picked up one of the tinsmith's long, thin irons. He gripped it with a look of horrified fascination.

"It's real," the man said. "This is all real."

"Yes," Arbeely said. "I'm afraid it is."

The man put down the iron. Muscles in his jaw spasmed. He seemed to be readying himself for the worst.

"Show me," he said finally.

Barefoot, clad only in an old work shirt of Arbeely's and a pair of dungarees, the Djinni stood at the railing at Castle Gardens, at the southern tip of Manhattan, and stared out across the bay. Arbeely stood nearby, perhaps afraid to draw too close. The shirt and dungarees had come from a pile of old rags in the corner of Arbeely's workshop. The dungarees were solder-stained, and there were holes burned into the shirtsleeves. Arbeely had had to show him how to do up the buttons.

The Djinni leaned against the railing, transfixed by the view. He was a creature of the desert, and never in his life had he come so close to this much water. It lapped at the stone below his feet, reaching now higher, now lower. Muted colors floated on its surface, the afternoon sunlight reflecting in the ever-changing dips of the waves. Still it was hard to believe that this was not some expert illusion, intended to befuddle him. At any moment he expected the city and water to dissolve, to be replaced by the familiar steppes and plateaus of the Syrian Desert, his home for close to two hundred years. And yet the moments ticked away, and New York Harbor remained stubbornly intact.

How, he wondered, had he come to this place?

The Syrian Desert is neither the harshest nor the most barren of the Arabian deserts, but it is nevertheless a forbidding place for those who do not know its secrets. It was here that the Djinni was born, in what men would later call the seventh century.

Of the many types of djinn—they are a highly diverse race, with many different forms and abilities—he was one of the most powerful and intelligent. His true form was insubstantial as a wisp of air, and invisible to the human eye. When in this form, he could summon winds, and ride them across the desert. But he could also take on the shape of any animal, and become as solid as if he were made of muscle and bone. He would see with that animal's eyes, feel with that animal's skin—but his true nature was always that of the djinn, who were creatures of fire, in the same manner that humans are said to be creatures of earth. And like all his brethren djinn, from the loathsome, flesh-eating *ghuls* to the tricksterish *ifrits*, he never stayed in any one shape for very long.

The djinn tend to be solitary creatures, and this one was more so than most. In his younger years, he'd participated in the haphazard rituals and airborne skirmishes of what could loosely be called djinn society. Some minor slight or squabble would be seized upon, and hundreds of djinn would summon the winds and ride them into battle, clan against clan. The gigantic whirlwinds they caused would fill the air with sand, and the other denizens of the desert would take shelter in caves and the shadows of boulders, waiting for the storm to pass.

But as he matured, the Djinni grew dissatisfied with these diversions, and took to wandering the desert alone. He was inquisitive by nature—though no one thing could hold his attention for long—and rode the winds as far west as the Libyan Desert, and east to the plains of Isfahan. In doing so, he took more of a risk than was sensible. Even in the driest desert a rainstorm could strike with little warning, and a Djinni caught in the rain was in mortal danger. For no matter what shape a Djinni might assume, be it human or animal or its own true shape of no shape at all, it was still a living spark of fire, and could easily be extinguished.

But whether luck or skill guided his path, the Djinni was never caught out and roamed wherever he would. He used these trips as opportunities to search for veins of silver and gold, for the djinn are natural metalsmiths, and this one was unusually adept. He could work the metals into strands no thicker than a hair, or into sheets, or twisted ropes. The only metal he could not touch was iron: for like all his kind, he held a powerful dread of iron, and shied away from rocks veined with ore in the way a man might recoil from a poisonous snake.

One can wander far and wide in the desert without spying another creature of intelligence. But the djinn were far from alone, for they had dwelt as neighbors with humans for many thousands of years. There were the Bedouin, the roving tribes of herdsmen who scratched out their perilous existence on what the desert had to offer. And there were also the human cities far to the east and west, which grew larger every year, and sent their caravans through the desert between them. But neighbors though they were, both humans and djinn harbored a deep distrust of each other. Humankind's fear was perhaps more acute, for the djinn had the advantage of invisibility or disguise. Certain wells and caves and rock-strewn passes were considered habitations of the djinn, and to trespass was to invite calamity. Bedouin women pinned amulets of iron beads to their babies' clothing, to repel any djinn that might try to possess them, or carry them away and turn them to changelings. It was said among the human storytellers that there had once been wizards, men of great and dangerous knowledge, who'd learned to command and control the djinn, and trap them in lamps or flasks. These wizards, the storytellers said, had long since passed from existence, and only the faintest shadows of their powers remained.

But the lives of the djinn were very long—a djinni's lifespan might last eight or nine times the length of a human's—and their memories of the wizards had not yet faded to legend. The elder djinn warned against encounters with humans, and called them conniving and perfidious. The wizards' lost knowledge, they said, might be found again. It was best to be cautious. And so interactions between the two races mostly were kept to the occasional encounter, usually provoked by the lesser djinn, the *ghuls* and *ifrits* who could not keep themselves from mischief.

When young, the Djinni had listened to the elders' warnings and taken heed. In his travels he'd avoided the Bedouin, and steered clear of the caravans that moved slowly across the landscape, bound for the markets of Syria and Jazira, Iraq and Isfahan. But it was perhaps inevitable that one day he should spy upon the horizon a column of some twenty or thirty men, their camels loaded with precious goods, and think, why should he not investigate? The djinn of old had been incautious and fool-hardy in allowing themselves to be captured, but he was neither. No harm would come from merely observing.

He approached the caravan slowly and fell in behind at a safe distance, matching their pace. The men wore long, loose robes of many layers, all dusty with travel, and covered their heads with checked cloth against the sun. Snatches of their conversations carried to the Djinni on the wind: the time to their next destination, or the likelihood of bandits. He heard the weariness in their voices, saw the fatigue that hunched their backs. These were no wizards! If they'd had any powers they would magic themselves across the desert, and save themselves this endless plodding.

After a few hours the sun began to lower, and the caravan passed into an unfamiliar part of the desert. The Djinni remembered his caution, and turned back toward safer ground. But this glimpse of humankind had only inflamed his curiosity. He began to watch for the caravans, and followed them more and more often, though always at a distance; for if he drew too close, the animals would grow nervous and skittish, and even the men would feel him as a wind at their backs. At night, when they came to rest at an oasis or caravanserai, the Djinni would listen to them talk. Sometimes they spoke of the distances they had to travel, their pains and worries and woes. Other times they spoke of their childhoods, and the fireside tales their mothers and aunts and grandmothers had told them. They exchanged well-worn stories, boasts of their own or of the warriors of ages past, kings and caliphs and wazirs. They all knew the stories by heart, though they never told them the same way twice and quibbled happily over the details. The Djinni was especially fascinated at any mention of the djinn, as when the men told tales of Sulayman, the human ruler who seven hundred years before had yoked the djinn to his rule, the first and last of the human kings to do so.

The Djinni watched, and listened, and decided they were a fascinating paradox. What drove these short-lived creatures to be so oddly self-destructive, with their punishing journeys and brutal battles? And how, at barely eighteen or twenty years of age, could they grow to be so intelligent and cunning? They spoke of amazing accomplishments, in cities such as ash-Sham and al-Quds: sprawling markets and new mosques, wondrous buildings such as the world had never seen. Djinn-kind, who did not like to be enclosed, had never attempted anything to compare; at most the homes of the djinn were bare shelters against the rain. But the Djinni grew intrigued by the idea. And so he selected a spot in a valley and, when he was not chasing caravans, began to build himself a palace. He heated and shaped the desert sands into curving sheets of opaque blue-green glass, forming walls and staircases, floors and balconies. Around the walls he wove a filigree of silver and gold, so that the palace appeared to be netted inside a shining web. He spent months making and unmaking it according to his whim, and twice razed it to the ground in frustration. Even when whole and habitable, the palace was never truly finished. Some rooms sat open to the stars, their ceilings confiscated to serve as floors elsewhere. The web of filigree grew as he found veins of metal in the desert rocks, and then all but vanished when he ransacked it to gild an entire hall. Like himself, the palace was usually invisible to other beings; but the men of the desert would sometimes glimpse it from a distance, as the last rays of the evening sun struck it and set it ablaze. Then they would turn, and spur their horses faster— and not until many miles had passed, and they were safe within sight of their own cooking fires, would they dare to look back again.

The shadows were growing longer at Castle Gardens, yet still the Djinni could not tear his eyes from the harbor. Once, when quite young, he'd come across a small pool in an oasis. In the manner of youth everywhere determined to test their limits, he took on the shape of a jackal, waded into the pool up to his haunches, and stood there as long as he dared, the chill seeping up through his paws and into his limbs. Only when he thought his legs might collapse did he leap back out again. It was the closest he'd ever come to death. And that had only been a very small pool.

It would take almost no effort to vault the railing, to fall or leap in. Only a minute or two of immersion, and he would be extinguished.

Nauseated, he dragged his eyes away. Steamers and tugboats chugged by, leaving their spreading wakes behind. At the horizon, the fading light picked out an undulating line of land. On an island in the middle distance there stood an enormous statue in the shape of a woman, made of what looked to be some greenish metal. The scale of the statue was boggling. How many rocks must have been melted, how much raw metal collected, to create her? And how did she not break through the thin disk of land, and fall into the sea?

According to Arbeely, this bay was only the smallest part of an ocean whose vastness defied comprehension. Even in his native form he could never have hoped to cross it—and now that native form was lost to him. He'd examined the iron cuff thoroughly, hoping to find some overlooked weakness, but there was none. Wide but thin, it fit close to his wrist, and was hinged on one side. The setting sunlight gave a dull sheen to the clasp with its pin. He couldn't budge the pin, no matter how hard he pulled. And he knew, without even trying, that Arbeely's tools would be no match for it.

He closed his eyes and attempted for the hundredth time to change form, straining against the cuff's enchantment. But it was as though the ability had never existed. And even more astonishing, he had no recollection of how it had come to be on his wrist.

Along with their longevity, the djinn were blessed with prodigious, near-eidetic memories, and the Djinni was no exception. To him, a human's powers of recollection would seem only a dubious patchwork of images. But the days—weeks? longer?—that preceded capture, and the event itself, were concealed from his mind by a thick haze.

His last clear memory was of returning to his palace after tracking an especially large caravan, with close to a hundred men and three hundred camels. He'd followed them eastward for two days, listening to their conversations, slowly getting to know them as individuals. One camel driver, a thin, older man, liked to sing quietly to himself. The songs told of brave Bedouin men on swift horses, and the virtuous women who loved them; but the man's voice carried a sadness even when the words did not. Two guards had discussed a new mosque in the city of ash-Sham, called the Grand Mosque, apparently an immense building of stunning beauty. Another young guard was soon to marry, and the others all took turns joking at his expense, telling him not to worry, they would hide outside his tent on his wedding night, and whisper what to do. The young guard retorted by asking why he should trust *their* advice on women; and his tormentors responded with fantastic tales of their own sexual prowess that had the entire company howling with laughter.

He'd followed them until at last on the horizon he spied a low band of green. It was the Ghouta, the oasis fed by the river that bordered ash-Sham. Reluctantly he'd slowed his pace and watched until the caravan became a thin wedge on the horizon, a spear-point piercing the Ghouta. The green belt might appear benign, but even the Djinni was not so rash as to travel into it. He was a djinn of the desert, and in the Ghouta's lush fields he would be out of his element. There were stories of creatures there that didn't take kindly to wayward djinn, and would trick them into the river, holding them under until they were extinguished. He decided to exercise caution for once and return home.

The journey back had been long, and by the time he reached his palace a strange loneliness had settled over him. Perhaps it had to do with the caravan. He'd grown used to their conversation, their songs and stories; but he had no part in them, he merely overheard. Perhaps it had been too long since he'd sought out his own kind. He decided he would leave off chasing caravans, and go to the habitations of his clan, and dwell among them for a time. Perhaps he'd even seek out female companionship, a djinniyeh who might desire his attentions. He'd arrived at his palace at sunset, making plans to leave again in the morning—and there his memories ended.

After that, only two images penetrated the haze. In the first, a man's brown, gnarled hands clamped the iron cuff across his wrist, and with this image came the impression of searing cold and bottomless fear, a djinn's natural reaction to iron—but how, he wondered, did he not feel it now? And then, the second image: a man's leathered face, lips cracked and grinning, the bulging yellow eyes glowing in triumph. *Wizard*, the memory told him. But that was all; and in the next instant he was sprawled, naked and bound, on the floor of Arbeely's shop.

Except that it had not been only an instant. Apparently he'd been trapped in the flask for over a thousand years.

It was Arbeely who'd managed to calculate that figure, while searching for clothes for his naked guest. He'd pressed the Djinni for anything he could remember from the world of men, something that might narrow down the year of his capture. After a few false starts, the Djinni had recalled the caravan guards talking of the Grand Mosque, the new building in ash-Sham. "They'd said that inside the mosque was the head of a man, but not his body," he said. "It made no sense to me. I might have misunderstood."

But Arbeely assured the Djinni that he'd heard correctly. The head belonged to a man called John the Baptist, and the mosque was now known as the Umayyad Mosque—and it had stood in the city of ash-Sham for over a thousand years.

It didn't seem possible. How could he have been trapped for that long? Rare was the djinn that lived more than eight hundred years, and he himself had been nearing two hundred when he began to chase the caravans. But not only was he still alive, he felt no older than before. It was as though the flask had not only contained his body, but also paused him in time. He supposed that this way, a wizard could extend the usefulness of his captive for as long as possible.

The flask now sat on a shelf in Arbeely's shop. Like the iron cuff, it revealed nothing of its maker. Arbeely had shown him the partially erased pattern of scrollwork around its base—apparently a sort of magical stopper that had kept him sealed inside. *But how did you fit in there with the olive oil?* Arbeely had asked, a puzzle not nearly as interesting to the Djinni as how he'd allowed himself to be captured and bound to human form in the first place. Perhaps the wizard had followed him to the djinn habitations, or laid some sort of trap. He wondered if the wizard had treated him like one of Sulayman's slaves, forcing him to build pleasure palaces and slaughter enemies at his command. Or had the wizard simply cast him aside, like an enticing trinket that, once acquired, loses its appeal?

Of course, the man would be dead by now. The wizards of legend had been powerful indeed, but still mortal. The yellow-eyed man had long since gone to dust. And whatever enchantment he'd placed upon the Djinni, his death had not lifted it. The thought came, crawling, hideous: he might be trapped like this forever.

No. He pushed the thought away. He would not accept defeat so easily.

He looked down at the iron railing, then gripped it with both hands, concentrating. He was near exhaustion; the confinement in the flask had apparently destroyed his strength—but even so, within a few moments the metal was glowing a dull red. He tightened his grip and then let go, leaving behind an outline of his fingers pressed into the railing. No, he wasn't helpless. He was still a djinn, one of the most powerful of his kind. And there were always ways.

He was beginning to shiver, but he ignored it. Instead he turned and gazed up at the city that rose from the water's edge, the enormous square buildings that reached far into the heavens, their windows set with perfect panes of glass. As fantastical as cities like ash-Sham and al-Quds had seemed from the caravan men's tales, the Djinni doubted that they'd been half so wondrous or terrifying as this New York. If he must be marooned in an unknown land, surrounded by a deadly ocean, and constrained to one weak and imperfect form, at least he'd ended up somewhere worth exploring.

Arbeely stood a few feet away, watching the glow of the iron railing fade beneath the Djinni's hands. It still seemed impossible that this could be happening while the rest of the city went about its business, unchanged and unknowing. He wanted to grab the nearest passerby and shout: *Look at this man! He isn't a man at all! See what he's done to the railing!* He supposed that if he wanted to be hauled off to the lunatic asylum, there were worse ways to go about it.

He looked out across the bay, trying to see it through the Djinni's eyes. He wondered how he himself would feel, to wake up and discover that over a thousand years had passed. It would be enough to drive anyone mad. But the Djinni only stood straight-backed and grim, staring at the water. He didn't look like a man about to run amok. The dirty, too-small clothes he wore clashed ludicrously with his figure and features, hanging from him as though in apology. He turned his back to the water and gazed at the buildings massed at the park's edge. It was only then that Arbeely noticed that the Djinni was shaking from head to toe.

The Djinni took a step from the railing. His knees buckled, and he fell.

Arbeely lunged and caught him before he hit the ground, and hoisted him to his feet, "Are you ill?"

"No," the Djinni muttered. "Cold."

They made their way back to the shop, Arbeely half-supporting, half-carrying his new acquaintance. Once inside, the Djinni stumbled to the banked forge and collapsed, leaning against its scorching side. The borrowed work shirt smoldered where it touched the metal, but he didn't seem to notice. He closed his eyes. After a while his shaking stopped, and Arbeely decided he'd fallen asleep.

The man sighed and looked about. There was the copper flask, sitting on the shelf, but he didn't want to think about it for the moment. He needed an easy task, something quiet and calming. He found a teakettle with a hole in the bottom, brought to him by a local restaurant owner. Perfect: he could patch a teakettle in his sleep. He cut a patch from a sheet of tin plate, heated both kettle and patch, and set to work.

Occasionally he glanced at his guest, and wondered what would happen when he woke. Even silent and unmoving, the Djinni carried a strange air about him—as though he were not quite real, or else the only real thing in the room. Arbeely supposed that others would sense it as well, but he doubted they'd ever guess at its meaning. The young mothers of Little Syria still tied iron beads around their babies' wrists and made gestures to ward off the Evil Eye, but out of tradition and fond superstition more than true fear. This new world was far removed from the tales of their grandmothers—or at least so they'd thought.

Not for the first time he wished he had a confidant, someone with whom he could share even the most outrageous secret. But in the tightly knit community, Boutros Arbeely was something of an outsider, even a recluse, happiest at his forge. He was terrible at idle chitchat, and at wedding banquets could be found sitting alone at a table, examining the stamp-marks on the cutlery. His neighbors greeted him warmly on the street, but never lingered long to talk. He had many acquaintances, but few close friends.

It had been no different in Zahleh. In a family of women he'd been the silent, dreaming boy-child. He'd discovered smithing by lucky accident. Sent to run an errand, he'd stopped in front of the local forge and watched, fascinated, as a sweating man hammered a sheet of metal until it became a bucket. It was the transformation that enthralled him: useless to useful, nothing to something. He returned over and over to watch until the smith, exasperated with being spied upon, offered to take on the boy as an apprentice. And so smithing came to fill Arbeely's life, to the near exclusion of all else; and though he supposed in a vague way that someday he'd find a wife and start a family, he was content with things as they were.

But now, glancing at his guest's prone form, he felt a premonition of lasting change. It was the same as when he'd been seven years old and heard his mother's rising wail through the open window as she learned of her husband's death, killed by bandits on the road from Beirut. Now as then, he sensed the threads of his life scattering and rearranging before this new and overwhelming thing that had landed among them.

"What is that you're doing?"

Arbeely jumped. The Djinni hadn't moved, but his eyes were open; Arbeely wondered how long he'd been watching. "I'm patching a teakettle," he said. "Its owner left it on the stove too long."

The Djinni inclined his head toward the kettle. "And what metal is that?"

"It's two metals," said Arbeely. "Steel, dipped in tin." He found a scrap on the table and held it out to the Djinni, pointing out the layers with his fingernail. "Tin, steel, tin. You see? The tin is too soft to use on its own, and with steel there's the problem of rust. But together like this, they're very strong, and versatile."

"I see. Ingenious." He sat up straighter, and held out his hand to the teakettle. "May I?" Arbeely handed him the kettle, and the Djinni peered at it, turning it over in his now-steady hands. "I assume the difficulty lies in thinning the edges of the patch without exposing the steel."

"That's it exactly," said Arbeely, surprised.

The Djinni laid his hand over the patch. After a few moments, he began to carefully rub the patch around its edges. Arbeely watched, dumbfounded, as the outline of the patch disappeared.

The Djinni handed the teakettle back to Arbeely. It was as though the hole had never been.

"I have a proposition for you," said the Djinni.

Spring rains can come on suddenly in the desert. On the morning after the Djinni returned from following the caravan to the Ghouta, the skies clouded over, releasing first a thin patter of raindrops, and then a respectable downpour. The dry riverbeds and gullies began to run with water. The Djinni watched the rain sluice down the walls and crenellations of his palace, irritated at the inconvenience. He had planned to depart for the djinn habitations at first light, but now he would have to wait.

And so he roamed his glass halls, examining the metalwork and making idle changes here and there to pass the time. His thoughts returned to the men of the caravan, their conversations and jests. He remembered the old man's songs about the Bedouin, and wondered if the men in them had truly been so brave, the women so beautiful. Or were they only invented legends, the details altered and exaggerated over time?

For three days the rains came and went, three days of infuriating confinement. If the Djinni had been able to go outside, and chase himself to the ends of the earth, then his growing obsession with the world of men might have dissipated, and he might have gone to visit the djinn habitations of his youth, as planned. But when the clouds exhausted themselves and the Djinni at last emerged to a newly washed landscape, he found that all thoughts of returning to his own people had vanished with the rains.

3.

The Golem was not even a few hours in New York before she began to long for the relative calm of the ship. The din of the streets was incredible; the noise in her head was worse. At first it nearly paralyzed her, and she hid under an awning as the desperate thoughts of the push-cart vendors and paperboys rode ahead of their shouting voices: *the rent is due, my father will beat me, please somebody buy the cabbages before they spoil.* It made her want to slap her hands over her ears. If she'd had any money, she would've given it all away, just to quiet the noise.

Passersby glanced her up and down, taking in her staring eyes, the dirty and disheveled dress, the ludicrous men's coat. The women frowned; some of the men smirked. One man, weaving drunk, grinned at her and approached, his thoughts bleary with lust. To her surprise she realized this was one desire she had no wish to fulfill. Repulsed, she dashed to the other side of the street. A streetcar came rattling around the corner and missed her by a hair. The conductor's curses trailed her as she hurried away.

She wandered for hours, through streets and alleys, turning corners at random. It was a humid July day, and the city began to stink, a pungent mix of rotting garbage and manure. Her dress had dried, though the river silt still clung to it in flaking sheets. The woolen coat made her even more conspicuous as the rest of the city sweltered. She too was hot, but not uncomfortable—rather, it made her feel loose-limbed and slow, as though she were wading through the river again.

Everything she saw was new and unknown, and there seemed to be no end to it. She was frightened and overwhelmed, but an intense curiosity lay beneath the fear, leading her on. She peered inside a butcher's shop, trying to make sense of the plucked birds and strings of sausages, the red oblong carcasses that hung from hooks. The butcher saw her and started to come around the counter; she gave him a quick, placating smile, and walked on. The thoughts of passersby flew through her mind, but they led to no answers, only more questions. For one thing, why did everyone need money? And what exactly *was* money? She'd thought it merely the coins she saw exchanging hands; but it was so ubiquitous in both fear and desire that she decided there was a larger mystery to it, one she had yet to decipher.

She skirted the edge of a fashionable district, and the shop windows began to fill with dresses and shoes, hats and jewelry. In front of a milliner's she stopped to gaze at an enormous, fantastical hat on a pedestal, its wide band bedecked with netting and fabric rosettes and a gigantic, sweeping ostrich plume. Fascinated, the Golem leaned forward and put one hand on the glass—and the thin pane shattered beneath her touch.

She jumped back as a rain of shards tumbled from the window and scattered onto the sidewalk. In the shop, two well-dressed women stared out at her, hands over their mouths.

"I'm sorry," the Golem whispered, and ran away.

Afraid now, she hurried through alleys and across busy thoroughfares, trying not to blunder into pedestrians. The neighborhoods shifted around her, changing block to block. Grubby-looking men and indignant shopkeepers shouted at one another, airing grievances in a dozen languages. Children dashed home from shoeshine stands and games of stickball, thinking eagerly of supper.

A sort of mental exhaustion began to set in, dulling her thoughts. She headed eastward, following the tips of the shadows, and found herself in a neighborhood that bustled with less chaos and more purpose. Shopkeepers were rolling up their awnings and locking their doors. Bearded men walked slowly next to each other, talking with intensity. Women stood chatting on corners, string-tied packages in their arms, children pulling at their skirts. The language they spoke was the same one she'd used with Rotfeld, the language she'd known upon waking. After the day's riot of words, hearing it again was a small, familiar comfort.

She slowed now, and looked around. Next to her a tenement stoop beckoned; she'd seen men and women, young and old, sitting on such stoops all day. She tucked her skirts beneath herself and sat down. The stone was warm through her dress. She watched people's faces as they came and went. Most were tired and distracted, occupied with their own thoughts. Men began to arrive home from their shifts, exhaustion on their faces and hunger in their bellies. She saw in their minds the meals they were about to tuck into, the thick dark bread spread with schmaltz, the herring and pickles, the mugs of thin beer. She saw their hopes for a cooling breeze, a good night's sleep.

A loneliness like fatigue pulled at her. She couldn't sit on the stoop forever, she must move on; but for the moment, it felt easier to stay where she was. She rested her head against the brick of the balustrade. A pair of small brown birds was pecking in the dust at the bottom of the stoop, unconcerned by the tramping feet of passersby. One of the birds fluttered up the steps and landed next to the Golem. It prodded at the stone with its sharp beak, then turned sideways and hopped onto the Golem's thigh.

She was surprised but managed to hold perfectly still as the bird perched in her lap, bobbing and pecking at the remains of the riverbed silt that still dusted her skirt. Thin, hard feet scratched at her through the fabric. Slowly, very slowly, she extended a hand. The bird hopped onto her palm and stood there, balanced. With her other hand she stroked its back. It sat patiently as she felt its soft sleek feathers, the tiny fluttering heartbeat. She smiled, fascinated. It tilted its head and looked at her with a round unblinking eye, then pecked once at her fingers, as though she were simply another patch of earth. For a moment they regarded each other; and then it gathered itself and flew away.

Startled, she turned to track its path—and saw an elderly man watching her from the shadow of a grocer's cart. Like her, the man was dressed in a black wool coat despite the heat. A white fringe peeked out from underneath the hem. He wore a white beard, neatly trimmed, and his face beneath his hat was a net of deep lines. He watched her calmly, but the thought she heard was tinged with fear: *could she be what I think she is?*

Hurriedly the Golem stood and walked away, not looking back. Ahead of her was a crowd of men and women, passengers from the Second Avenue Elevated. She tried to lose herself among them, following the main part of the crowd as small groups splintered away at corners and doorways. At last she ducked into an alleyway, then dared to look out. The man in the black coat was nowhere to be seen.

Relieved, she emerged from the alley and continued east. Now the air smelled of the sea again, of salt and coal smoke and engine grease. The shops were mostly closed, and the pushcart vendors were packing up their suspenders and cheap trousers, their pots and pans. What would she do once night fell? Find a place to hide, she supposed, and wait for morning.

A stab of reflected hunger struck her. A scrawny, dirt-stained boy was loitering on the sidewalk ahead, eyeing a nearby vendor who stood sweating over his cart. As she watched, a man in shirtsleeves approached the vendor and gave him a coin. The vendor plucked up a sheet of waxed paper, dipped into his cart, and emerged with a doughy disk the size of his fist. The man bit into it as he walked toward the Golem, fanning the steam from his mouth. The boy's hunger rose, desperate and all-consuming.

If the boy were not starving, if the man had not passed so near—if, most of all, her experiences that day had not drained her so—she might have controlled herself, and walked away. But she was not so lucky. The boy's visceral plight had transfixed her. Didn't he need the meal more than the man did?

No sooner had she formed this thought than her hand reached out, plucked the man's meal from his grasp, and handed it to the boy. In the next moment he was running away down the street, as fast as his legs could carry him.

The man grabbed her arm. "What did you mean by that?" he snarled.

"I'm sorry," she began, about to explain; but the man was red-faced and furious. "You thief!" he shouted. "You'll pay for that!"

Others were beginning to notice. An older woman stepped to the man's side. "I saw the whole thing," she said, glaring at the Golem. "She stole your knish and gave it to the boy. Well, girl? What do you have to say for yourself?"

She looked around, bewildered. Men and women were forming a crowd around her, eager to see what would happen. "Pay up," someone called.

"I don't have any money," she said.

A hard laugh ran through the crowd. They wanted her to be punished; they wanted her to pay. They were flinging their angry desires at her like stones.

Panic filled her—and then, strangely, it ebbed away. She felt as though time was slowing, stretching. Colors grew sharper, more focused. The low sun seemed bright as noon. *Fetch a policeman*, someone called, and the words were slurred, elongated. She closed her eyes, feeling as though she were on the edge of an abyss, teetering, about to fall.

"That won't be necessary," said a voice.

Instantly the crowd's attention shifted—and the Golem felt the abyss recede. Relieved, she opened her eyes.

It was the old man in the black coat, the one who'd been watching her. He was coming quickly through the onlookers, concern on his face. "Will this pay for your knish?" he asked, and handed the man a coin. Then, slowly, as though not to startle her, he placed a hand on the Golem's arm. "Come with me, my dear," he said. His voice was quiet, but firm.

Did she have a choice? It was either he, or the crowd. Slowly she stepped toward the old man, away from her accuser, who stood frowning at the coin.

"But this is too much," her accuser said.

"Then do something good with the rest," replied the old man.

The crowd began to disperse, some clearly feeling they'd been robbed of entertainment. Soon it was just the two of them, together on the sidewalk.

He regarded her again as he had in the cart's shadow. Then he leaned forward, and seemed to sniff the air around her. "As I thought," he said, a touch regretful. "You're a golem."

Shocked, she took a step back, ready to run. "No, please," he said. "You must come with me, you can't be wandering the streets like this. You'll be discovered."

Should she try to lose him again? But then, he had just saved her; and he seemed neither angry nor accusatory, only concerned. "Where will you take me?" she asked.

"My home. It's not far from here."

She didn't know if she could trust him—but he was right, she couldn't keep wandering forever. She decided she must trust him. She must trust *someone*.

"All right," she said.

They began to walk back the way she had come. "Now tell me," the old man said, "where is your master?"

"He died at sea, two days ago. We were crossing from Danzig."

The man shook his head. "How unfortunate," he said. Whether he referred to Rotfeld's death, or the larger situation, she wasn't certain. "Is that where you lived, before this?"

"No, I wasn't alive," she said. "My master didn't wake me until the crossing, just before he died."

That surprised him. "You mean to say you're only two days old? Extraordinary." He rounded a corner, and the Golem followed. "And how did you make it through Ellis Island, on your own?"

"I was never there. An officer on the ship tried to question me, because I had no ticket. So I jumped into the river instead."

"That showed quick thinking on your part."

"I didn't want to be discovered," she said.

"Just so."

They walked on, back the way the Golem had come. The sun had long since ducked behind the buildings, but the sky still shone, brassy and thick with the day's heat. Children began to emerge from the tenements again, looking for one last adventure before bedtime.

The man was quiet as they walked. She realized she didn't even know his name, but she hesitated to ask—he was lost in his thoughts. She could feel the questions circling in his mind, all with herself at their heart: *what should I do with her?* And in one brief flash, she saw an image of herself struck down, turned to a formless heap of dirt and clay in the middle of the street.

She halted, stock-still. But instead of panic, she only felt a deep weariness. Perhaps it would be for the best. She had no place here, no purpose.

He'd noticed she was no longer at his side and doubled back, concerned. "Is something wrong?"

"You know how to destroy me," she said.

A pause. "Yes," he said, guarded. "I have that knowledge. Few do, these days. How did you know this?"

"I saw it in your mind," she said. "You considered it. For a moment, you wanted it."

Confusion furrowed his brow—and then he laughed, without mirth. "Who made you?" he asked. "Was it your master?"

"No," she replied. "I don't know my maker."

"Whoever it was," he said, "was brilliant, and reckless, and quite amoral." He sighed. "You can feel others' desires?"

"And fears," she said. "Since my master died."

"Is that why you stole that knish, for the boy?"

"I didn't mean to steal," she said. "He was just . . . so very hungry."

"It overwhelmed you," he said, and she nodded. "We'll have to address that. Perhaps with training . . . Well, that can wait, for now. We must deal with more practical matters first, such as finding you clothing."

"Then—you won't destroy me?"

He shook his head. "A man might desire something for a moment, while a larger part of him rejects it. You'll need to learn to judge people by their actions, not their thoughts."

A moment's hesitation; and then she said, "You're the only one to speak kindly to me since my master died. If you think it best to destroy me, I'll abide by that decision."

Now he looked shocked. "Have your few days been so difficult? Yes, I see they must have been." He put a comforting hand on her shoulder; his eyes were dark but kind. "I'm Rabbi Avram Meyer," he said. "If you'll allow it, I will take you under my protection, and be your guardian. I'll give you a home, and whatever guidance I can, and together we'll decide what course is best. Do you agree?"

"Yes," she said, relieved.

"Good." He smiled. "Now, come with me. We're almost there."

Rabbi Meyer's building was a tenement like all the others, its hard facade stained with dirt and smoke. The lobby was dark and close, but well kept; the stairs creaked with protest beneath their feet. The Golem noticed that her companion's breathing grew labored as they ascended.

The Rabbi's rooms were on the fourth floor. A narrow entryway led to a cramped kitchen with a deep sink, a stove, and an icebox. Socks and underclothes hung above the sink, drying. More laundry sat in piles on the floor. Dirty dishes lay jumbled together on top of the stove.

"I wasn't expecting company," said the Rabbi, embarrassed.

The bedroom was large enough only for its bed and a wardrobe. Beyond the kitchen was a small parlor, with a deep, worn sofa of green velvet set beneath a large window. Next to it was a small wooden table, with two chairs. A large collection of books lined one side of the room, their spines cracked and faded. More books were stacked in haphazard piles about the room.

The Rabbi said, "I don't have much, but it's enough. Consider this your home, for the time being."

The Golem stood in the middle of the parlor, not wishing to dirty his sofa with her dress. "Thank you," she said.

And then, she caught sight of the window. The sky was darkening, and the gas lamps in the parlor were bright enough to create a reflection. She saw the image of a woman, superimposed against the neighboring building. One hand fluttered up slightly from her side, then lowered; the woman in the window did the same. She stepped closer, fascinated.

"Ah," said the Rabbi quietly. "You haven't seen yourself yet."

She studied her own face, then ran a hand through her hair, felt the thin strands stiff with river water. She gave it an experimental tug. Would it grow, or remain forever the same length? She ran her tongue over her teeth, then held out her hands. Her nails were short and square. The nail on the left index finger had been set a bit off center. She wondered if anyone beside herself would ever notice.

The Rabbi watched her examine herself. "Your creator was quite gifted," he said. But he couldn't keep a hint of disapproval from his tone. She looked back down to her fingertips. Nails, teeth, hair: none of these features were made of clay.

"I hope," she said, watching her own mouth move, "that no one was harmed in my making."

The Rabbi smiled sadly. "So do I. But what's done is done, and you are not to be blamed for your own creation, whatever the circumstances.

Now, I must go find you some clean clothes. Stay here, please—I'll be back shortly."

Alone, she watched her reflection for a little while longer, thinking. What if the Rabbi had not come when he had? What would have happened? She'd been standing inside the angry crowd's circle, feeling the world fall away, as though she were about to cross a threshold into— what? She didn't know. But in that moment, she'd felt calm. Peaceful. As though all worries and decisions were about to be lifted from her shoulders. Remembering, she shivered with a fear she didn't understand.

It was growing late, and most of the shops were closed; but the Rabbi knew that a few would still be open near the Bowery, willing to sell him a woman's dressing gown and a few pairs of underclothes. He could barely afford the expense: besides his small pension from his former congregation, his only income came from teaching Hebrew to young boys studying to become *bar mitzvot*. But it must be done. Warily he crossed the raucous thoroughfare, avoiding the paths of drunken men, and the eyes of the women who stood beneath the Elevated, waiting for custom. On Mulberry he found a clothing store still open, and bought a woman's shirtwaist and skirt, a dressing gown, slips and drawers, and stockings with garters. After a moment's hesitation, he added a nightgown to the pile. She wouldn't need it for sleeping, of course, but the selection of women's things had overwhelmed him; and besides, she couldn't simply wear a dressing gown with nothing on beneath it. The clerk frowned at his coat and fringe, but took his money quickly enough.

He carried the string-wrapped package back across the Bowery, thinking. It would be difficult, living with someone who sensed one's desires. If he wasn't careful, he'd fall to chasing his own mind, trapped in the maddening game of *don't think about that*. He'd have to be completely honest and unabashed, and hide nothing. It wouldn't come easy. But any misplaced courtesy would do her a disservice. The larger world would not be so accommodating.

There would be consequences to his actions, to his sheltering of her: he had known this from the moment he'd recognized her nature and decided not to destroy her. Childless, retired, a widower for close to ten years, Rabbi Avram Meyer had planned for himself a quiet old age and an uneventful death. But the Almighty, it seemed, had planned otherwise.

In a nondescript tenement hallway, Boutros Arbeely opened a door and stepped back to allow his guest admittance. "Here it is. My palace. I know it's not much, but you're welcome to stay here until you find a place of your own."

The Djinni gazed inside with alarm. Arbeely's "palace" was a tiny, dim room barely large enough for a bed, a miniature armoire, and a half-moon table pushed up against a dingy sink. The wallpaper was pulling away from the wall in thick ripples. The floor, at least, was clean, though this was something of a novelty. In honor of his guest, Arbeely had kicked all his laundry into the armoire and leaned against the door until it shut.

Eyeing the room, the Djinni felt a claustrophobia so strong he could barely bring himself to enter. "Arbeely, this room isn't fit for two inhabitants. It's barely fit for one."

They'd been acquainted for little more than a week, but already Arbeely had realized that if their arrangement was to work, he'd have to curb his irritation at the Djinni's offhand slights. "What more do I need?" he said. "I spend all my time at the forge. When I'm here, I'm asleep." Gesturing to the walls, he said, "We could string a sheet across, and bring in a cot. So you don't have to sleep in the shop anymore."

The Djinni looked at Arbeely as though he'd suggested something insulting. "But I don't sleep in the shop."

"Then where have you been sleeping?"

"Arbeely. I don't *sleep.*"

Arbeely gaped; for he hadn't realized. Every evening when he left the shop, the Djinni would still be there, learning to work the delicate tinplate. And each morning, on returning, he'd find the Djinni hard at work again. Arbeely kept a pallet in the back room, for the nights when he was too tired to drag himself to his bed; he'd simply assumed that the Djinni was using it. He said, "You don't sleep? You mean, not at *all*?"

"No, and I'm glad of it. Sleep seems like an enormous waste of time."

"I like sleeping," Arbeely protested.

"Only because you tire."

"And you don't?"

"Not in the way you do."

"If I didn't sleep," Arbeely mused, "I think I'd miss the dreams." He frowned. "You do know what dreams are, don't you?"

"Yes, I know what dreams are," the Djinni said. "I can enter them."

Arbeely paled. "You *can*?"

"It's a rare ability. Only a few clans of the highest djinn possess it." Again Arbeely noted that casual, matter-of-fact arrogance. "But I can only do so in my true form. So there's no need to worry, your dreams are safe from me."

"Well, even so, you're more than welcome—"

Irritated, the Djinni cut him off. "Arbeely, I don't want to live here, awake or asleep. For now, I'll stay in the shop."

"But you said—" Arbeely paused, not wanting to go on. *I'll go mad if you keep me caged here for much longer*, the Djinni had said, and it had stung. Their plan required that the Djinni be kept out of sight until Arbeely had taught him enough to pass as a new apprentice; but this meant that the Djinni was forced to stay hidden in the back of the shop during the day—a space nearly as small as Arbeely's bedroom. Arbeely understood that the Djinni chafed at the restriction, but he'd been hurt by the implication that he was the Djinni's jailor.

"I suppose I would feel odd if I had to stay in a room all night and watch a man sleep," Arbeely conceded.

"Exactly." The Djinni sat down on the edge of the bed, and looked around once more. "And really, Arbeely, this place is terrible!"

His tone was so plaintive that Arbeely started laughing. "I don't mind it, really," he said. "But it isn't what you're used to."

The Djinni shook his head. "None of this is." Absentmindedly he rubbed the cuff on his wrist. "Imagine," he said to Arbeely, "that you are asleep, dreaming your human dreams. And then, when you wake, you find yourself in an unknown place. Your hands are bound, and your feet hobbled, and you're leashed to a stake in the ground. You have no idea who has done this to you, or how. You don't know if you'll ever escape. You are an unimaginable distance from home. And then, a strange crea-ture finds you and says, 'An Arbeely! But I thought Arbeelys were only tales told to children! Quick, you must hide, and pretend to be one of us, for the people here would be frightened of you if they knew.'"

Arbeely frowned. "You think I'm a strange creature?"

"You miss my point entirely." He lay back on the bed and stared at the ceiling. "But yes. I find humans strange creatures."

"You pity us. In your eyes, we're bound and hobbled."

The Djinni thought for a moment. "You move so slowly," he said.

Silence hung between them; and then the Djinni sighed. "Arbeely, I promised I wouldn't leave the shop until you felt the time was right, and I've kept that promise. But I meant what I said before. If I don't find some way to regain my freedom, even a degree of it, I believe I'll go mad."

"Please," Arbeely said. "Just a few more days. If this is going to work—"

"Yes," the Djinni said, "yes, I know." He stood and walked to the window. "But in all of this, my one consolation is that I've landed in a city the likes of which I never could have imagined. And I intend to make the most of it."

Warnings flooded Arbeely's mind: the inadvisability of wandering strange streets at night, the gangs and cutthroats, the bawdy houses and stews and opium dens. But the Djinni was looking out the window with an air of hungry longing, across the rooftops to the north. He thought again of the Djinni's image of himself, bound and hobbled.

"Please," he only said. "Be careful."

After the stifling confines of Arbeely's bedroom, the tinsmith's shop seemed almost cavernous in comparison. Alone, the Djinni sat at the workbench, measuring out solder and flux. He had to be careful with the solder; his hands were warm enough that it tended to melt if he held it too long. Arbeely had patiently demonstrated how to spread the solder along a joint, but when it came time for the Djinni to try, the solder had run from the plate in a river of droplets. After a few more tries he'd begun to improve, but it strained every ounce of his patience. He longed to simply meld the seams with his fingers, but that would ruin the point of the exercise.

It galled him, though, to curtail the one ability he had left. Never before had he truly appreciated how many of his powers were lost to him outside his native form. If he'd known, he might've spent more time exploring them, instead of simply chasing after caravans. The ability to enter dreams, for example, was something he'd barely ever used.

Like all their other attributes, this ability varied wildly among different types of djinn. In the lesser *ghuls* and the *ifrits*, it manifested as a crude possession, performed mostly for amusement, trickery, or petty revenge. The possessed human would become little more than a poorly handled puppet until the Djinni grew tired and abandoned the game. Many of the possessed were permanently damaged; some even perished from the shock. In the worst cases, the Djinni would become trapped in the human's mind. When this happened, it was almost a certainty that both human and Djinni would go insane. If the human was very lucky, a shaman or minor magician might be on hand to drive the possessor from its prey. Once, the Djinni had encountered one of his lesser brethren soon after it had been forced from a human in this way. The burning, twisted thing had been perched on a stunted tree, babbling and howling as the branches smoldered around it. The Djinni had observed it with a mixture of pity and distaste, and avoided the tree by a wide distance.

The Djinni's own abilities were nothing so blunt as wholesale possession. In his native form he could insinuate himself into a mind painlessly, and observe it without being noticed. But he could only do so when the subject lay in the realm of sleep, its mind open and unguarded. He'd tested this ability only a few times, and only on lesser animals. Snakes, he learned, dreamed in smells and vibrations, their tongues darting to sample the air, their long bodies pressed close to the dirt. Jackals dreamed in yellows and ochers and fragrant reds, reliving their kills as they slept, their limbs and paws churning at the air. After a few such experiments, he'd mostly left off the practice: it was mildly amusing, but it tended to leave him confused and disoriented as he readjusted to his own formless form and regained his sense of self.

He'd never tried to enter a human's mind. The dreams of men were said to be slippery and dangerous, full of shifting landscapes that could trap a djinni and hold him fast. A wizard, the elders warned, could snare a djinni in his mind, trick it into a dream-labyrinth and force it into servitude. They'd made it seem like a reckless folly even to consider it. Likely they'd overstated the danger, but still he'd refrained, even when the caravan men had collapsed in sleep at the end of a day's journey.

Would he have risked it, if he'd known the ability would be taken from him? Perhaps; but he doubted he would've gained much from the experience. And in a sense, he reflected as he measured out yet more solder, the loss mattered little. He was now spending more than enough time with humans to account for the difference.

In the Syrian Desert, the last of the spring rains soaked into the hill-sides. Delicate blossoms unfurled among the rocks and thistles, dotting the valleys with yellow and white.

The Djinni floated above the valley, enjoying the view. The rain had rinsed the dust from his palace, and now every inch sparkled. Had he thought to leave this behind, to go back to the djinn habitations? What-ever for? This was where he belonged: with his palace and his valley, the warm spring sun and the fleeting wildflowers.

But already his mind was racing ahead to his next encounter with humans. There was, he knew, a small encampment of Bedouin nearby. He'd spied their sheep-flocks and their fires from a distance, their men traveling on horseback, but until now he'd avoided them. He wondered, how did their lives differ from those of the caravan-men? Perhaps, instead of finding another caravan to follow, he would turn his wanderings to-ward their encampment. But should he remain content with observing them from a distance, when a much more intimate option lay available to him?

Movement below him caught his eye. As though drawn by his musings, a young Bedouin girl had appeared on the ridge at the valley's edge. Alone save for her small flock of goats, she walked the ridge with a sprightly energy to match the freshness of the day.

An impulse struck him. Descending to the parapets of his palace, he reached out and touched the blue-white glass.

The girl on the ridge froze in amazement as, for a moment, the Djinni's palace appeared sparkling before her eyes.

The Djinni watched the girl sprint excitedly back the way she'd come, driving her goats before her. He smiled, and wondered what a girl such as she might dream about.

4.

Slowly, over days and weeks, the Golem and Rabbi Meyer learned how to live with each other.

It wasn't easy. The Rabbi's rooms were small and cramped, and the Rabbi had grown used to his solitude. Not that living cheek by jowl with a stranger was a new experience—when he'd first come to America he'd boarded with a family of five. But he'd been younger then, more adaptable. In recent years, solitude had become his one indulgence.

As he'd predicted, the Golem quickly sensed his discomfort. Soon she developed the habit of positioning herself as far from him as possible, as though trying to leave without leaving. Finally he sat her down and explained that she shouldn't go elsewhere simply because he was in the room.

"But you want me to," she said.

"Yes, but against my own will. My better self knows that you may sit or stand wherever you wish. You must learn how to act according to what people say and do, not what they wish or fear. You have an extraordinary window into people's souls, and you'll see many ugly and uncomfortable things, much worse than my wishing you to stand somewhere else. You must be prepared for them, and learn when to discount them."

She listened, and nodded, but it was more difficult for her than he realized. To be in the same room with him, knowing he wanted her elsewhere, was a small torture. Her instinct to *be of use* tugged at her to leave, to get out of his way. To ignore it was akin to standing in the path of an oncoming streetcar, trying not to move. She would start to fidget, or would break things by accident—the handle of a drawer ripping away as she grasped it, the hem of her skirt tearing as she pulled at the fabric. She'd apologize profusely, and he would tell her it meant little; but his dismay was hard to suppress, and it only made matters worse.

"It would be better if I had something to *do*," she said finally.

At once the Rabbi saw his mistake. Without thinking, he'd given the Golem the worst life possible: that of idleness. And so he relented and allowed her to take over the cleaning of the rooms, which until then he'd insisted on doing himself.

The change—both in the Golem, and in the Rabbi's abode—was instantaneous. With a task to perform, the Golem could lose herself inside it and begin to ignore the distractions. Each morning she would scrub the dishes from breakfast and tea, and then take up the rag and attack the stove, removing a few more layers of the persistent grime that had built up in the years since the Rabbi's wife had died. Then she'd make the Rabbi's bed, folding the corners of the sheet tight against the sagging frame. Any dirty clothes in the hamper—save for his undergarments, which he steadfastly refused to let her clean—were carried to the kitchen sink and washed, then hung to dry. The clothes from the day before were taken down and ironed, folded, and put away.

"I can't help but feel I'm taking advantage of you," said the chagrined Rabbi, watching her stack his dishes in the cupboard. "And my students will think I've hired a maid."

"But I like doing the work. It makes me feel better. And this way I can repay you for your generosity."

"I wasn't looking for payment when I offered to take you in."

"But I want to give it," she said, and went on stacking dishes. Eventually the Rabbi decided to reconcile himself to the situation, defeated by necessity and the lure of freshly ironed trousers.

When they spoke to each other, they spoke quietly. The tenement was noisy, even at night, but the walls were thin, and the Rabbi's neighbors would be all too intrigued by the sound of a young woman's voice. Fortunately, she had no need to visit the shared water closet in the hall. Once a day she washed herself in the kitchen while the Rabbi sat in his bedroom or at the table in the front room, occupying his mind with study and prayer.

It was hardest when one of the Rabbi's students would come over for his lesson. A few minutes beforehand, the Golem would go to the bedroom and crawl underneath the Rabbi's bed. Soon would come the knock at the door, the scrape of the parlor chairs against the floorboards, and the Rabbi's voice: *so, have you studied your portion?*

There was barely enough room under the bed for the Golem. It was narrow and hung so low that the brass springs almost brushed her nose. To lie still and silent in such an enclosed space was no easy task. Her fingers and legs would begin to twitch, regardless of how much she tried to relax. Meanwhile, a small army of wants and needs would make their way to her mind: from the boy and the Rabbi, both of whom would give anything for the clock to go faster; from the woman in the room below, who lived in a constant torment of pain from her hip; from the three young children next door, who were forced to share their few toys, and always coveted whatever they didn't have—and, at a more distant remove, from the rest of the tenement, a small city of strivings and lusts and heartaches. And at its center lay the Golem, listening to it all.

The Rabbi had advised her to concentrate on her other senses to drown out the noise; and so the Golem would press her ear to the floor and listen to water gurgling through the pipes, mothers scolding their children in blistering Yiddish, the banging of pots and pans, arguments, prayers, the whirr of sewing machines. Above it all, she heard the Rabbi teaching the boy to chant his portion, his hoarse voice alternating with the boy's young, piping one. Sometimes she would chant silently along, mouthing the words, until the boy left and she could come out again.

The nights were almost as difficult. The Rabbi went to bed at ten and did not wake until six, and so for eight hours the Golem was alone with the vague, dreaming thoughts of others. The Rabbi suggested reading to pass the time; and so, one night, she pulled a volume from the Rabbi's shelves, opened it at random, and read:

> . . . Cooked victuals may be put on a stove that was heated with straw or stubble. If the stove was heated with the pulp of poppy-seed or with wood, cooked victuals may not be put upon it, unless the coals were taken out or covered with ashes. The students of Shammai say: victuals may be taken off the stove, but not put back upon it. The students of Hillel permit it.
>
> The schoolmen propounded a question: "As for the expression

'shall not be put,' does it mean 'one shall not put it back,' but if it has not been taken off, it may be left there?"

There are two parts to our answer . . .

She closed the book and stared at the leather cover. Were all books like this? Daunted and a bit irritated, she spent the rest of the night looking out the window, watching the men and women walk by.

In the morning she told the Rabbi of her attempt at reading. Later that day he went out to run errands, and brought her back a flat, thin package. Inside was a slender book, with a gaily illustrated cover. A large ship, populated with animals, floated at the crest of a gigantic wave. Behind the ship, a band of colors curved a half circle, its apex brushing the clouds above.

"This is a better start for you, I think," the Rabbi said.

That night, the Golem was introduced to Adam and Eve, and Cain and Abel. She learned about Noah and his Ark, and the rainbow that was the sign of God's covenant. She read of Abraham and Isaac on the mountain, the near sacrifice and its aftermath. She thought it all very strange. The stories themselves were easy to follow; but she wasn't sure what she was supposed to *think* of these people. Had they actually existed, or had they been invented? The tales of Adam and Noah said they lived to be many hundreds of years old—but wasn't this impossible? The Rabbi was the oldest person she'd met in her brief life, and he was far short of a century. Did this mean that the book told lies? But the Rabbi was always so careful to say only the truth! If these were lies, then why had the Rabbi asked her to read them?

She read the book three times through, trying to understand these long-ago people. Their motives, needs, and fears were always at the surface, as easy for her to grasp as those of a man passing by. *And Adam and Eve were ashamed, and hid to cover their nakedness. And Cain grew jealous of his brother, and rose up and slew him.* How different from the lives of the people around her, who hid their desires away. She recalled what the Rabbi had said: to judge a man by his actions, not his thoughts. And judging by the actions of the people in this book, to act on one's wishes and desires led, more often than not, to misdeed and misfortune.

But were all desires wrong? What about the hungry boy for whom she'd stolen the knish? Could a desire for food be wrong if one were starving? A woman down the hall had a son who was a peddler, in a place called Wyoming. She lived in wait of a letter from him, some sign to let her know that he was alive and safe. This too seemed right and natural. But then, how was she to know?

In the morning, when the Rabbi asked her what she'd thought of the book, she hesitated, searching for the right words. "Were these real people?"

He raised an eyebrow. "Would my answer change your understanding of them?"

"I'm not sure. It's just that they seem too *simple* to be real. As soon as a desire arose, they acted on it. And not small things, like 'I need a new hat' or 'I want to buy a loaf of bread.' Large things, like Adam and Eve and the apple. Or Cain killing Abel." She frowned. "I know I haven't lived very long, but this seems unusual."

"You've watched children playing in the street, haven't you? Do they often ignore their desires?"

"I see what you mean," she said, "but these aren't stories about children."

"I believe they are, in a way," said the Rabbi. "These were the world's first people. Everything they did, every action and decision, was entirely new, without precedent. They had no larger society to turn to, no examples of how to behave. They only had the Almighty to tell them right from wrong. And like all children, if His commands ran counter to their desires, sometimes they chose not to listen. And then they learned that there are consequences to one's actions. But tell me, now—I don't think you found reading an enjoyable way to pass the time."

"I tried to enjoy it!" she protested. "But it's hard to sit still for so long!"

The Rabbi sighed inwardly. He'd hoped that reading would be a good solution, even a permanent one. But he saw now it was too much to ask of her. Her nature wouldn't allow it.

"If only I could walk outside at night." Her voice was a quiet plea.

He shook his head. "That isn't possible, I'm afraid. Women out alone at night are assumed to be of poor moral character. You'd find yourself prey to unwanted advances, even violent behavior. I wish it were otherwise. But perhaps it is time," he said, "for us to venture outside during the day. We could take a walk together, after I've seen my students. Would that help?"

The Golem's face lit with anticipation, and she spent the morning cleaning the already spotless kitchen with renewed focus and zeal.

After the last student had come and gone, the Rabbi outlined his plan for their walk. He would leave the tenement alone, and she would follow five minutes later. They'd meet a few blocks away, on a particular corner. He gave her an old shawl of his wife's, and a straw hat, and a parcel to carry, a few books he'd wrapped in paper and tied with string. "Walk as though you have an errand and a purpose," he said. "But not too quickly. Look to the women around you for example, if need be. I'll be waiting." He smiled encouragingly, and left.

The Golem waited, watching the clock on the mantel. Three minutes passed. Four. Five. Books in hand, she stepped into the hall, closed the door, and walked out onto the noon-bright street. It was the first she'd left the Rabbi's rooms since coming to live with him.

This time she was more prepared for the assault of wants and wishes, but their intensity still took her aback. For a wild moment she wanted to flee back into the building. But no—the Rabbi was waiting for her. She eyed the incessant traffic, the streams of pedestrians and hawkers and horses all moving past one another. Gripping the parcel as if it were a talisman, she took a last quick glance up and down the street, and set off.

Meanwhile the Rabbi stood on his corner, waiting nervously. He too was having difficulty mastering his thoughts. He'd considered tailing the Golem, to make certain she didn't fall into trouble—but it would be far too easy for her to discover his mind, focused on her as it was, and he couldn't risk, or bear, to lose her trust. And so he'd done what he'd said he would, and went to the corner and waited. It was a test for himself as well, he decided—to see if he could let her go, and live with the knowledge that she was out there in the world, beyond his control.

Fervently he hoped they both would pass the test, for their current arrangement was growing hard to bear. His guest was undemanding, but nevertheless she was a constant and uncanny presence. He longed for the unabashed luxury of sitting alone at his table in his undershirt and shorts, drinking tea and reading the newspaper.

And there were other, more urgent considerations. In the bottom drawer of his dresser, hidden beneath his winter clothing, lay a draw-string bag that he'd found in the pocket of her coat. Inside the bag was a man's billfold with a few notes, an elegant silver pocket watch—its works now hopelessly corroded—and a small oilskin envelope. The words COMMANDS FOR THE GOLEM were written on the envelope in spindly and uneven Hebrew. It held a roughly folded square of paper that, happily or not, had survived the journey to shore. He'd read the paper; he knew what it contained.

In the tumult of her arrival in New York, the bag's existence had evidently fallen from her mind. But it was her property, and all that was left of her erstwhile master; he felt obscurely wrong in keeping it hidden. But then, if a child had landed at Ellis Island carrying a pistol in his pocket, would it not be right to confiscate it? For now, at least, he was resolved to keep the envelope safely out of her sight.

In the meantime, though, it had set his mind working. He'd assumed that there were only two solutions to the predicament of the Golem: either destroy her, or do his best to educate her and protect her. But what if there was a third way? What if he could, in essence, discover how to bind a living golem to a new master?

As far as he knew, this had never been done before. And most of the books—and the minds—that might once have helped him were long gone. But he was loath to discount the possibility. For now, he would see to the Golem's education as best he could until she could live on her own. And then, he would set to work.

But now he put those thoughts aside—for he'd spied a familiar figure coming toward him, tall and straight, walking carefully with the crowd. She'd seen him too, and was smiling, her eyes alight. And now he was smiling back, a bit dazed by the surge of pride he'd felt at the sight of her, like a bittersweet weight on his heart.

Far across the Atlantic, the city of Konin in the German Empire bustled on as usual, barely altered by the departure of Otto Rotfeld. The only real change came when the old furniture shop was leased by a Lithuanian and turned into a fashionable café; all agreed that it improved the neighborhood immensely. In truth, the only resident of Konin who gave much thought to Rotfeld was Yehudah Schaalman, the reviled hermit who had built the man a golem. As the weeks turned to months, and Rotfeld's submerged body gave itself over to the currents and sea creatures, Schaalman would sit evenings at his table, drinking glasses of schnapps and wondering about the unpleasant young man. Had he found success in America? Had he woken his clay bride?

Yehudah Schaalman was ninety-three years old. This fact was not common knowledge, for he had the features and bearing of a man of seventy and, if he wished, could make himself appear younger still. He had survived to this old age through forbidden and dangerous arts, his considerable wits, and a horror of death that drove all else before it. One day, he knew, the Angel of Death would at last come for him, and take him to stand before the Books of Life and Death, there to listen to the recitation of his transgressions. Then the gate would open, and he would be cast into the fires of Gehenna, there to be punished in a length and manner to fit his misdeeds. And his misdeeds had been many, and varied.

When he was not selling love charms to foolish village girls or untraceable poisons to hollow-eyed wives, Schaalman bent every scrap of his will to his dilemma: how to indefinitely postpone the day of the Angel's arrival. And so he was not, as a rule, a man given to idle reverie. He did not waste his time speculating about every customer who sought his services. But then why, he asked himself, had this hapless furniture maker captured his attention?

Yehudah Schaalman's life had not always been this way.

As a boy, Yehudah had been the most promising student that the rabbis had ever seen. He had taken to study as though born for no other purpose. By his fifteenth year it had become common for Yehudah to argue his teachers to a standstill, weaving such supple nets of Talmudic argument that they found themselves advocating positions exactly opposite to the ones they'd believed. This agility of mind was matched only by a piety and devotion to God so strong that he made the other students seem like brazen heretics. Once or twice, late at night, his teachers murmured to one another that perhaps the wait for the Messiah would not be as long as they had expected.

They groomed him to become a rabbi, as quickly as they could. Yehudah's parents were delighted: poor, barely more than peasants, they had gone without to provide for his education. The rabbinate began to debate where to send the boy. Would he do the most good at the head of a congregation? Or should they send him on to university, where he could begin to teach the next generation?

A few weeks before his ordainment, Yehudah Schaalman had a dream.

He was walking on a path of broken stones through a gray wilderness. Far ahead of him, a featureless wall stretched across the horizon and reached high into the heavens. He was exhausted and footsore; but after much walking Yehudah was able to discern a small door, little more than a man-shaped hole, where the path met the wall. Suddenly full of a strange, fearful joy, he ran the rest of the way.

At the door he paused, and peered inside. Whatever lay beyond was shrouded in mist. He touched the wall: it was painfully cold. He turned around and found that the mist had swallowed the path, even up to his own feet. In the whole of Creation, there was only himself, the wall, and the door.

Yehudah stepped through.

Mist and wall disappeared. He was standing in a meadow of grasses. The sun shone down and bathed him in warmth. The air was thick with scents of earth and vegetation. He was filled with a great peace unlike any he had ever known.

There was a grove of trees past the meadow, golden-green with sunlight. He knew there was someone standing inside the grove, just beyond his sight, waiting for him to arrive. Eagerly he took a step forward.

In an instant the sky darkened to storm-black. Yehudah felt himself seized and held. A voice spoke in his head:

You do not belong here.

Meadow and grove disappeared. He was released—he was falling—

And then he was on the path again, on his hands and knees, surrounded by broken stones. This time, there was no wall, or any other landmark to travel toward, only the stones leading through the blasted landscape to the horizon, with no hint of respite.

Yehudah Schaalman awoke to darkness and the certain knowledge that he was somehow damned.

When he told his teachers he was leaving and would not become a rabbi, they wept as though for the dead. They pleaded with him to explain why such an upright student would forsake his own purpose. But he gave no answer, and told no one of the dream, for fear that they would try to reason with him, explain it all away, tell him tales of demons who tormented the righteous with false visions. He knew the truth of what he'd dreamed; what he didn't understand was *why*.

And so Yehudah Schaalman left his studies behind. He spent sleepless nights combing through his memories, trying to determine which of his sins had damned him. He hadn't led a spotless life—he knew he could be proud and overeager, and when young he had fought bitterly with his sister and often pulled her hair—but he had followed the Commandments to the best of his ability. And were not his lapses more than compensated by his good deeds? He was a devoted son, a dutiful scholar! The wisest rabbis of the age thought him a miracle of God! If Yehudah Schaalman was not worthy of God's love, then who on earth was?

Tormented by these thoughts, Yehudah packed a few books and provisions, said farewell to his weeping parents, and struck out on his own. He was nineteen years old.

It was a poor time to be traveling. Dimly Yehudah knew that his little shtetl lay inside the Grand Duchy of Posen, and that the duchy was a part of the Kingdom of Prussia; but to his teachers these were mundane matters, of little consequence to a spiritual prodigy such as Yehudah, and had not been dwelled upon. Now he learned a new truth: that he was a naive, penniless Jew who spoke little Polish and no German, and that all his studies were useless. Traveling the open roads, he was beset by thieves, who spied his thin back and delicate looks and took him for a merchant's son. When they discovered that he had nothing to steal, they beat him and cursed him for their troubles. One night he made the mistake of asking for supper at a well-to-do German settlement; the burghers cuffed him and threw him to the road. He took to loitering on the outskirts of the peasant villages, where at least he had a chance of understanding what was said. He longed to speak Yiddish again, but he avoided the shtetls entirely, afraid of being drawn back into the world he had fled.

He became a laborer, tilling fields and tending sheep, but the work didn't suit him. He made no friends among his fellows, being a thin and ragged Jew who spoke Polish as though it dirtied his mouth. Often he could be seen leaning on his spade or letting the bull walk away with the plow as he ruminated once more on his past sins. The more he reflected, the more it seemed to him that his entire life was a catalog of misdeeds. Sins of pride and laziness, of anger, arrogance, lust—he'd been guilty of them all, and no counterweight could balance the scale. His soul was like a stone shot through with brittle minerals, sound in appearance but worthless at heart. The rabbis had all been deceived; only the Almighty had known the truth of it.

One hot afternoon, while he reflected in this way, another field-worker scolded him for laziness; and Yehudah, in the depths of his gloom and forgetting his Polish, responded with a more insulting an-swer than he'd intended. The man was upon Yehudah in an instant. The others gathered around, glad to finally see the arrogant boy receive his comeuppance. Flat on his back, nose gushing with blood, Yehudah saw his adversary crouched above him, one fist pulled back to strike again. Behind him rose a circle of jeering heads, like a council of demons sitting in raucous judgment. In that moment, all the heartache, resent-ment, and self-loathing of his exile contracted to a hard point of rage. He sprang up and barreled into his attacker, knocking him to the ground. As the others watched in horror, Yehudah proceeded to pummel him remorselessly about the head and was on the verge of gouging out one of his eyes when finally someone grabbed him in a bear hug and pulled him away. In a frenzy, Yehudah twisted and bit until the man let him go. And then Yehudah ran. The local constables stopped chasing him at the edge of town, but Yehudah kept on running. He had nothing now but the clothes on his back. It was even less than he'd started with.

He ceased pondering his roster of sins. It was clear now that the corruption of his soul was an elemental fact. That he had avoided capture and jail did not console him: for now he began to dwell on the greater judgment, the one that lay beyond.

He left off fieldwork and instead wandered from town to town, searching out odd jobs. He stocked shelves, swept floors, cut cloth. The pay was meager at best. He began to pilfer for survival, and then to steal outright. Soon he was stealing even when there was no need. In one village he worked at a mill, filling the flour sacks and taking them into town to be sold. The local baker had a daughter with bright green eyes and a shapely figure, and she liked to linger while he unloaded the sacks of flour in her father's storeroom. One day he dared to brush his fingers across her shoulder. She said nothing, only smiled at him. The next time, emboldened and inflamed, he beckoned her into a corner and grabbed clumsily at her. She laughed at him, and he ran from the storeroom. But the time after that, she did not laugh. They copulated atop the shifting sacks, their mouths thick with flour dust. When it was over, he climbed off her, neatened himself with shaking hands, called her a whore, and walked away. At the next delivery she did not respond to his advances, and he slapped her across the face. When he returned to the mill, her father was waiting for him, along with the police.

For the crimes of rape and molestation, Yehudah Schaalman was sentenced to fifteen years in prison. Two years had passed since his dream; he was now twenty-one years old.

And so the third phase of his education began. In prison, Schaalman hardened and turned clever. He learned to be always on his guard, and to size up each man in a room as a possible opponent. The last traces of his old gentleness vanished, but he couldn't disguise his intellect. The other inmates thought him a laughingstock—a skinny book-learned Jew, locked up with murderers! They called him "Rabbi," at first jeeringly; but soon they were asking him to settle disputes. He accepted, and handed down pronouncements that married Talmudic precision with the strict moral code of the prison yard. The inmates respected his judgments, and eventually even the wardens were deferring to him.

Still he kept to himself, holding himself apart from the hierarchy of the prison and its gangs. He had no toadies, kept no corrupt guard in his pocket. The others thought him squeamish, afraid to dirty his hands, but he could see who held the real power, and it was himself. He was the definitive arbiter of justice, fairer than the courts. The inmates hated him for it, but they left him alone. In this manner Schaalman survived for fifteen long years, unharmed and untouched, nursing his bitterness and anger while the prison seethed around him.

At thirty-five he finally emerged and discovered that he would've been safer if he'd stayed behind bars. The countryside was aflame. Tired of the theft of their lands and their culture, the Poles of the duchy had risen up against their Prussian occupiers, only to be drawn into a military battle they had no hope of winning. Prussian soldiers roamed from village to village, stamping out the last of the resistance, looting the synagogues and Catholic churches. It was impossible to travel unnoticed. A group of Prussian soldiers came upon Schaalman on the road and beat him for sport; and then, even before his wounds had closed, a gang of Polish conscripts did the same. He tried to find work in the villages, but he bore the invisible mark of the prison now, in his hard features and his calculating eye, and no one would have him. He stole food from storehouses and stable feed-buckets, slept in fields, and tried to stay out of sight.

And so it was that one night, in a filthy camp at the edge of a field, starving and nearly mad with fear of death, Schaalman awoke from a gray dreamless sleep to see a strange light on the horizon, a pulsing, red-orange glow that grew as he watched. Still in that realm between sleep and waking, Schaalman stood and, taking no notice of his few belongings on the ground, began to walk toward it.

A furrow had been plowed down the middle of the field, making a highway that pointed straight at the light. He stumbled over clods of earth, barely conscious and dizzy with hunger. It was a warm, windy night, and the grain rippled in the breeze, a million small voices whispering his secrets.

The glow brightened, and stretched higher into the sky. Above the whispering of the field he heard voices: men shouting to one another, women crying out in anguish. The scent of woodsmoke reached his nose.

The field fell away behind him, and the ground began to slope upward. The glow now stretched across his vision. The smoke had turned acrid, the screams louder. The slope steepened until Schaalman was on his hands and knees, dragging himself upward, at the edge of his strength and beyond the boundaries of reason. His eyes were shut against the effort, but the red-orange light still floated before him, compelling him to keep moving. After what seemed an unutterable distance, the hill began to level, until Schaalman, sobbing with exhaustion, perceived that he had reached the crest. With no strength left even to lift his head, he collapsed into a fugue deeper than sleep.

He woke to a clear sky, a gentle breeze, and a strange clarity of mind. His hunger was extreme, but he felt it at a remove, as though someone else were starving and he merely observed. He sat up and looked around. He was in the middle of a clearing. There was no sign of the hill; the ground was flat in every direction. There was nothing to tell him which direction he had come, or how to return.

Before him lay the charred ruins of a synagogue.

The grass around the structure had singed along with it, carving a black circle into the ground. The fire had burnt the walls down to the foundation, leaving the sanctuary open to the elements. Inside, fallen beams jutted from twin columns of blackened pews.

Carefully he stood and crossed into the burnt circle of grass. He paused at the place where the door would have been, then stepped across the threshold. It was the first time in seventeen years that he'd entered a house of worship.

Not a living thing stirred inside. An eerie quiet hung over all, as though even the sounds of the outside world, the rustlings of bird and grass and insect, had been muffled. In the aisle, Schaalman picked up a handful of woody ash and sifted it between his fingers—and realized that the synagogue couldn't have burned only the night before, for these ashes were as cold as stone. Had it all been a dream? Then what had led him here?

Carefully he walked the rest of the way up the aisle. A few spars from the ceiling blocked his path. He put his hands to them, and they crumbled to splinters.

The lectern was singed but still whole. There was no sign of the ark or its scroll; presumably they had been either saved or destroyed. The remains of prayer books lay scattered near the dais. He lifted from the ground a browned half-page, and read a fragment of the Kaddish.

Behind the dais was a space that had once been a small room, likely the rabbi's study. He stepped over the half-wall that remained. Burnt papers littered the floor in drifts. The rabbi's desk was a seared oblong hulk of wood in the middle of the room. A drawer was set into its front. Schaalman grasped the handle, and the fitting came away in his hand, lock and all. He wormed his fingernails into the crack that lay between the drawer and the desk, and broke the face to smithereens. He reached inside the exposed drawer, and withdrew the remains of a book.

Carefully he placed it atop the desk. The book's spine had peeled away from the body, so that it could not properly be said to be a book any longer, but rather a sheaf of singed papers. Scraps of leather clung to the cover. He lifted the cover away, and placed it aside.

The book had darkened from the edges inward, leaving only an island of undamaged writing on each page. The paper itself was as thick as rag, and the writing was of a spidery hand that held forth in an old-fashioned, declamatory Yiddish. With growing wonder he lifted each page, his fingers cold and trembling. Broken snippets of text ran together before his eyes:

> . . . a sure charm against fever is the recitation of the formula discovered by Galen and augmented by . . .
>
> . . . should be repeated forty-one times for highest efficacy . . .
>
> . . . aid in good health after a fast, collect nine branches from a nut-tree, each branch bearing nine leaves . . .
>
> . . . to make one's voice sweet to others, direct this exhortation to the Angel of . . .
>
> . . . increase of virility, mix these six herbs and eat at midnight, while reciting the following Name of God . . .

. . . speak this Psalm to ward away demonic influence . . .

. . . of a golem is permissible only in times of deepest danger, and care must be taken to ensure . . .

. . . repeat the demon's name, removing one letter with each iteration, until the name has dwindled to one letter, and the demon will dwindle likewise . . .

. . . to negate the ill effect that results from a woman passing between two men . . .

. . . this sixty-lettered Name of God is especially useful, though it is not to be uttered during the month of Adar . . .

Page after page, the secrets of long-dead mystics laid themselves before him. Many were irredeemably lost save for a few brief words, but some were whole and undamaged, and others were tantalizingly close to complete. This was the knowledge forbidden to all but the most pious and learned. His teachers had once hinted that wonders such as these would someday be his; but they'd denied him even the briefest glimpse, saying he was still far too young. To utter a charm or an exorcism or a Name of God without purity of heart and intention, they'd said, would be to risk one's soul to the fires of Gehenna.

But for Schaalman, the fires of Gehenna had long been a foregone conclusion. If that was to be his end, then he would make the most of the meantime. Some influence, divine or demonic, had led him to this place, and had placed unutterable mysteries in his hands. He would take that power, and he would use it to his own ends.

The papers lay crisped and quietly crackling beneath his fingers. In the distant dizziness of his hunger, he could swear he felt them vibrate like a plucked string.

5.

After a few more days of nervous coaching, Arbeely decided that the time had come to introduce the Djinni to the rest of Little Syria. The plan he'd devised to do so relied on the very woman who was, in a sense, responsible for the Djinni's new life in Manhattan: Maryam Faddoul, the coffeehouse proprietress, who'd brought Arbeely a copper flask in need of repairing.

The Faddouls' coffeehouse was famous for having the best gossip in the neighborhood, a distinction due entirely to the female half of its management. Maryam Faddoul's great gifts in life were a pair of guileless brown eyes and an earnest desire for the happiness and success of all her acquaintances. Her sympathetic nature made her a popular audience for the airing of grievances; she agreed wholeheartedly with every opinion and saw the wisdom in every argument. "That poor Saleem," she might say, "it's so obvious how much he loves Nadia Haddad! Even a blind goat could see it. It's such a shame that her parents don't approve."

And then a customer might protest, "But, Maryam, only yesterday her father was here, and you agreed with him that Saleem was still too young, and not yet ready to be a good provider. How can both be right?"

"If all our parents had waited until they were ready to marry," she'd reply, "then how many of us would be here?"

Maryam was a master at the beneficial application of gossip. If a businessman was drinking coffee and smoking a narghile, and bemoaning the smallness of his shop—business was booming, if only he had space for larger orders!—Maryam would appear at his side, refill his cup with an easy tilt of her wrist, and say, "You should ask George Shalhoub if you can take over his lease when he moves away."

"But George Shalhoub isn't moving."

"Is that so? Then it must have been some other Sarah Shalhoub I talked to yesterday. Now that her son is going to work in Albany she can't stand the thought of being away from him, so she is trying to convince George that they must go as well. If someone hinted they were willing to take the lease off his hands, then George might find himself much more willing." And the man would hurriedly settle the bill and head out the door in search of George Shalhoub.

All the while, Sayeed Faddoul would be watching from the small kitchen, a smile in his eyes. Another man might grow jealous of his wife's attentions, but not him. Sayeed was a quiet man—not awkward, as Arbeely could be, but possessed of a calm and steady nature that complemented his wife's heartfelt vivacity. He knew that it was his presence that let Maryam be so free; an unmarried woman, or one whose husband was less visible, would be forced to rein in her exuberance, or else risk the sorts of insinuations that might damage her name. But everyone could see that Sayeed was proud of his wife and was more than content to remain the unobtrusive partner, allowing her to shine.

At last Arbeely set his plan into motion. A message boy was dispatched to the Faddouls, alerting Maryam that her flask had been repaired. Accordingly she arrived that afternoon, still dressed in her apron and bringing with her the dark smell of roasted coffee. As always, Arbeely's heart squeezed at the sight of her, a not unpleasant ache, as if to say, *Ah well.* Like many of the men of the neighborhood, he was a little bit in love with Maryam Faddoul. What luck to be that Sayeed, her admirers thought, to live always in the light of her bright eyes and understanding smile! But none would dream of approaching her, even those who regarded the conventions of propriety as obstacles to be overcome. It was clear that Maryam's smile shone from her belief in the better nature of those around her. To demand more of that smile for themselves would only serve to extinguish it.

"My dear Boutros!" she said. "Why don't I see you at the coffee-house more often? Please tell me business has doubled and you must work night and day, because that is the only excuse I'll accept."

Arbeely blushed and smiled, and wished he were not so nervous. "Business *has* been good, actually, and I have more work than I can handle alone. In fact, I must introduce you to my new assistant. He arrived a week ago. Ahmad!" he called toward the back room. "Come meet Maryam Faddoul!"

The Djinni emerged from the storeroom, ducking his head to clear the threshold. In his hands he held the flask. He smiled. "Good day, madam," he said, and offered the flask to her. "I'm very pleased to meet you."

The woman was plainly astounded. She stared at the Djinni. For a moment, his eyes darting between them, Arbeely's fears were lost in a sudden flush of envy. Was it only the Djinni's good looks that caused her to stare like that? No, there was something else, and Arbeely had felt it too, at their calamitous first encounter: an instant and compelling magnetism, almost instinctual, the human animal confronting some-thing new, and not yet knowing whether to count it as friend or foe.

Then Maryam turned to Arbeely and swatted him across the shoul-der.

"Ow!"

"Boutros, you're horrible! Hiding him from everyone, and not say-ing a word! No announcement, no welcome—he must think us all ter-ribly rude! Or are you ashamed of us?"

"Please, Mrs. Faddoul, it was at my request," the Djinni said. "I fell ill during the crossing, and was bedridden until a few days ago."

In an instant the woman's indignation turned to concern. "Oh, you poor man," she said. "Did you cross from Beirut?"

"No, Cairo," he said. "In a freighter. I paid a man to hide me on board, and it was there I became ill. We docked in New Jersey, and I was able to sneak away." He spoke the learned story easily.

"But we could have helped you! It must have been so frightening, to be sick in a strange country, with only Boutros for a nursemaid!"

The Djinni smiled. "He was an excellent nursemaid. And I had no wish to be a burden."

Maryam shook her head. "You mustn't let pride get the better of you. We all turn to each other here, it's how we make our way."

"You are right, of course," the Djinni said smoothly.

Her eyebrows arched. "And our secretive Mister Arbeely, how did you meet him?"

"Last year I passed through Zahleh, and met the smith who taught him. He saw that I was interested in the craft, and told me about his apprentice who had gone to America."

"And imagine my surprise," interjected Arbeely, "when this half-dead man knocks on my door and asks if I am the tinsmith from Zahleh!"

"This world works in strange ways," Maryam said, shaking her head.

Arbeely studied her for signs of skepticism. Did she really believe this concocted story? Many Syrians had traveled odd and winding paths to New York—on foot through the forests of Canada, or fording box-laden barges out of New Orleans. But hearing their tale spoken aloud, Arbeely felt it was too remarkable for its own good. And the Djinni had none of the pallor or weakness of one who had been seriously ill. In fact, he looked like he could swim the East River. Too late to change it now, though. Arbeely smiled at Maryam, and hoped the smile looked natural.

"And are you from near Zahleh?" Maryam asked.

"No, I am Bedouin," the Djinni replied. "I was in Zahleh to deliver my sheepskins to market."

"Is that so?" She seemed to look him over again. "How astonishing you are. A Bedu stowaway in New York. You must come to my coffee-house, everyone will want to meet you."

"I would be honored," the Djinni said. He bowed to Maryam and returned to the back room.

"Such a story," Maryam murmured to Arbeely as he saw her to the door. "Obviously he has the endurance of his people, to have made it here. But still, I'm surprised at you, Boutros. You might have had better sense. What if he'd died in your care?"

Arbeely squirmed in very real embarrassment. "He was adamant," Arbeely said. "I didn't want to go against his wishes."

"Then he placed you in a very difficult position. But then, the Bedouin are certainly proud." She shot a glance at him. "Truly, he is Bedu?"

"I believe so," Arbeely said. "He knows very little of the cities."

"How odd," she said, almost to herself. "He doesn't seem . . ." She trailed off, her face clouding; but then she came back to herself. Smiling at Arbeely, she thanked him for the repair. Indeed, the flask was much improved; Arbeely had smoothed away the dents, restored the polish, and then reproduced the patterned band down to the tiniest awl-mark. She paid and left, saying, "By all means, you must bring Ahmad to the coffeehouse. No one will speak of anything else for weeks."

But going by the immediate flood of visitors to Arbeely's shop, it grew clear that Maryam had not waited for their visit; rather, in her enthusiastic manner, she had spread the story of the tinsmith's new Bedouin apprentice far and wide. Arbeely's own little coffeepot bubbled constantly on the brazier as the entire neighborhood filed in and out, eager to meet the newcomer.

Thankfully, the Djinni performed his part well. He entertained the visitors with tales of his supposed crossing and ensuing illness, but never spoke so long that he risked tangling himself in his story. Instead he painted in broad strokes the picture of a wanderer who one day decided, on little more than a whim, to steal away to America. The visitors left Arbeely's shop shaking their heads over their strange new neighbor, who seemed protected by the accidental good fortune that God granted to fools and small children. Many wondered that Arbeely would take on an apprentice with such meager credentials. But then, Arbeely was considered a bit strange himself, so perhaps it was a case of like attracting like.

"Besides," said a man at the coffeehouse, rolling a backgammon piece between his fingers, "it sounds like Arbeely saved his life, or close to it. The Bedouin have rules about repaying such debts."

His opponent chuckled. "Let's hope for Arbeely's sake that the man can actually work a smith!"

Arbeely was heartily glad when the flood of visitors lowered to a trickle. Besides the pressure of maintaining their story, he'd spent so much time entertaining his neighbors that he'd fallen far behind on business. And it seemed that each visitor had brought along something that needed mending, until the shop was crammed full of dented lamps and burned pots. Many of the repairs were strictly cosmetic, and it was clear that their owners had been moved more by a sense of neighborly support than actual need. Arbeely felt grateful and a little bit guilty. To look at the rows of damaged items, one would think Little Syria had been struck by a plague of clumsiness.

The Djinni found the attention amusing. It wasn't hard to keep his story consistent; most of the visitors were too polite to press him overmuch for details. According to Arbeely, there was a certain glamour to the Bedu that would work in his favor. "Be a bit hazy," Arbeely had told him as they prepared their plan and rehearsed their stories. "Talk about the desert. It'll go over well." Then he'd been struck by a thought: "You'll need a name."

"What would you suggest?"

"Something common, I would think. Oh, let's see—there is Bashir, Ibrahim, Ahmad, Haroun, Hussein—"

The Djinni frowned. "Ahmad?"

"You like it? It's a good name."

It was not so much that he liked it, as that he found it the least objectionable. In the repeated *a*'s he heard the sound of wind, the distant echo of his former life. "If you think I need a name, then I suppose it's as good as any."

"Well, you'll definitely need a name, so Ahmad it shall be. Only please, remember to answer to it."

The Djinni did indeed remember, but it was the only aspect of Arbeely's plan that made him uncomfortable. To him the new name suggested that the changes he'd undergone were so drastic, so pervasive, that he was no longer the same being at all. He tried not to dwell on such dark thoughts, and instead concentrated on speaking politely, and maintaining his story—but every so often, as he listened to the chatter of yet more visitors, he spoke his true name to himself in the back of his mind, and took comfort in the sound.

Of all the people whom Maryam Faddoul told about the newcomer, only one man refused to take interest: Mahmoud Saleh, the ice cream maker of Washington Street. "Have you heard?" she told him. "Boutros Arbeely has taken a new apprentice."

Saleh made a noise like "hmm" and scooped ice cream from his churn into a small dish. They were standing on the sidewalk in front of Maryam's coffeehouse. Children waited before him, clutching coins. Saleh reached out a hand, and a child placed a coin in his palm. He pocketed the coin and held out the ice cream dish, careful to avoid looking at the child's face, or Maryam's, or indeed at anything other than his churn or the sidewalk. "Thank you, Mister Mahmoud," the child said—a courtesy due, he knew, only to the presence of Maryam. There was a rattle as the child took a spoon from the cup tied to the side of his tiny cart.

"He's a Bedouin," Maryam said. "And rather tall."

Saleh said nothing. He spoke little, as a rule. But Maryam, practically alone among the neighborhood, wasn't perturbed by his silence. She seemed to understand that he was listening.

"Did you know any Bedu in Homs, Mahmoud?" she asked.

"A few," he said, and held out his hand. Another coin; another dish. He'd tried to avoid the Bedu who lived on the outskirts of Homs, close to the desert. He'd thought them a grim people, poor and superstitious.

"I never knew any," Maryam mused. "He's an interesting man. He says he stowed away as if for a lark, but I sense there's more. The Bedu are a private people, are they not?"

Saleh grunted. He liked Maryam Faddoul—in fact, it could be said that she was his only friend—but he wished she would stop talking about the Bedu. Along that path lay memories he did not wish to revisit. He checked the churn. Only three servings of ice cream were left. "How many more?" he asked aloud. "Count off, please."

Small voices sounded: *one, two, three, four, stop pushing, I was here first, five, six.*

"Numbers four through six, please come back later."

There were groans from his would-be customers, and the sound of retreating footsteps. "Remember your places in line," Maryam called after them.

Saleh served the remaining children and listened as they returned the flimsy tin dishes to their place on the cart, atop the sack of rock salt.

"I ought to go back inside," Maryam said. "Sayeed will be needing my help. Good day, Mahmoud." Her hand squeezed his arm briefly—he caught a glimpse of her frilled shirtwaist, the dark weave of her skirt—and then she was gone.

He counted the coins in his pocket: enough for ingredients for another batch. But it was late in the afternoon, and a film of clouds had formed across the sun. In the time it would take him to buy milk and ice and then mix the ice cream, the children would no longer be so eager. Best to wait until tomorrow. He tied down the contents of his cart and began his slow trudge up the street, head bowed, watching his own feet as they moved, black shapes against a field of gray.

It would've come as a great shock to his neighbors to know that the man they called Ice Cream Saleh, or Crazy Mahmoud, or simply *that strange Muslim who sells ice cream*, had once been Doctor Mahmoud Saleh, one of the most respected physicians in the city of Homs. The son of a successful merchant, Saleh had grown up in comfort, free to pursue his studies and then his profession. In school, his excellent marks won him entrance to the medical university in Cairo, where it seemed the entire field was transforming as he watched. An Englishman had discovered that one could avoid postsurgical gangrene simply by dipping the surgical instruments into a solution of carbolic acid. Another Englishman soon established an irrefutable link between cholera and unsanitary drinking water. Saleh's father, who'd heartily supported his studies, grew angry when he learned that in Cairo his own son was dissecting corpses: did Mahmoud not understand that on the Day of Judgment these desecrated men would be resurrected unwhole, their bodies opened and organs exposed? His son drily replied that if God was so literal in his resurrections, humanity would be brought back in a state of decay so advanced that the marks of dissection would seem minor in comparison. In truth he'd had his qualms as well, but pride kept him from saying so.

After completing his studies, Saleh returned to Homs and established a practice. His patients' living conditions continually dismayed him. Even the most affluent families had little notion of modern hygiene. Sickrooms were kept closed, the air poor and stifling; he flung open the windows, ignoring the protests. Sometimes he even encountered a patient who'd been burned on the arm or chest, a thoroughly discredited practice meant to draw out ill humors. He would dress the wound and then berate the family, describing to them the dangers of infection and sepsis.

Though sometimes it seemed he waged an impossible battle, Doctor Saleh's life was not without its joys. His mother's half-sister approached him regarding her daughter, whom he'd watched mature into a young woman of beauty and gentle character. They were married, and soon they had their own daughter, a darling girl who would stand her little feet on Saleh's and make him walk her about the courtyard, roaring like a lion. Even when his father died, and was lowered into the grave next to his mother, Saleh took comfort in knowing that the man had been proud of him, despite their differences.

And so it went, the years passing quickly, until one evening, a wealthy landowner came to the door. He told Saleh that the Bedouin family who tended his lands had a sick girl. Instead of a doctor, they'd brought in an old healer woman without a tooth in her head, who was using the most outlandish of folk remedies to try to cure her. The man couldn't stand to see the child suffer and said that if Saleh agreed to examine her, he would pay the fee himself.

The Bedouin family lived in a hut at the edge of the city, where the carefully tended farmland gave over to scrub and dust. The girl's mother met Saleh at the door. She was dressed heavily in black, her cheeks and chin tattooed in the style of her people. "It is an *ifrit*," she said. "It needs to be cast out."

Saleh replied that what the girl needed was a proper medical examination. He told her to fetch him a pot of boiled water, and went into the hut.

The girl was in convulsions. The healer woman had scattered handfuls of herbs about the room and now sat cross-legged next to the girl, muttering to herself. Ignoring her, Saleh tried to hold the girl down long enough to peel back one of her eyelids—and succeeded just as the old woman finished her incantation and spat three times upon the ground.

For a moment, he thought he saw something in the girl's eye leaping toward him—

And then the thing was inside his head, scrabbling to get out—

Unbearable pain seared through his mind. All went dark.

When Saleh came to, there was foam on his lips and a leather strap in his mouth. He gagged and spat it out. "To keep you from biting off your tongue," he heard the healer say, in a voice that sounded hollow and distant. He opened his eyes—and saw kneeling above him a woman whose face was thin and insubstantial as onionskin, with gaping holes where her eyes should have been. He screamed, turned his head, and vomited.

The landowner fetched one of Saleh's colleagues. Together they loaded the half-conscious man into a cart and took him back home, where the doctor could conduct a thorough examination. The evidence was inconclusive: perhaps a bleeding in the brain, or a latent condition that had somehow been triggered. There was no way to be certain.

From then on, it was as though Saleh had stepped away from the world. An unreality permeated all his senses. His eye could no longer measure distances: he would reach for something and it would be no-where near his grasp. His hands shook, and he couldn't properly hold his instruments. Occasionally a fit would overtake him, and he would fall down and froth at the mouth. Worst of all, he could no longer look at a human face, be it man's or woman's, stranger or beloved, without succumbing to nauseated terror.

Weeks and months passed. He tried to return to medicine, listening to complaints and making simple diagnoses. But he couldn't disguise his malady, and his remaining patients disappeared. The family adapted a more frugal lifestyle, but within months, their savings were gone. Their clothes grew shabbier and the house fell into disrepair. Saleh spent his days alone in a shaded room, trying to consult medical texts he could barely read, searching for an explanation.

His wife became ill. She tried to hide it at first but then turned feverish. Saleh sat by helplessly as his former colleagues offered their aid. Still she worsened. One night, burning and delirious, she mistook Saleh for her long-dead father and begged him for ice cream. What could he do? There was a churn sitting in a cupboard, purchased during more extravagant days. He rolled it into the kitchen and washed the dirt and dust away. His daughter's chickens had laid that morning. Sugar they still had, as well as salt and ice, and milk from a neighbor's goat. Laboriously he set out the supplies, moving slowly lest he fumble and spill. He smashed the ice with a hammer, then beat together the eggs and sugar and goat's milk. He added the ice and rock salt, and packed the mixture around the inside of the churn. He wondered, when had he learned this? Certainly he'd watched his wife make ice cream, as a treat for their daughter and her friends, but he'd never paid any particular attention. Now it was as though he'd done it all his life. He fixed the lid on the churn and turned the crank around and around. It felt good to work. The mixture began to stiffen. A clean sweat broke on his forehead and in his armpits. He stopped when it felt right to do so.

He returned to the bedroom with a small dish of ice cream and found that his wife had descended into chills. He set the dish aside and held her shaking hand. She did not return to consciousness, and died as dawn was breaking. Saleh hadn't recognized the beginnings of the death throes, and thus hadn't been quick enough to wake their daughter to say good-bye.

The next afternoon, Saleh sat alone in the kitchen as his wife's sisters prepared her body. Someone came in and knelt next to him. It was his daughter. She wrapped her arms around him. He closed his eyes so that he could remember how he used to see her, her dark hair and bright eyes, the sweet freckles on her cheek. Then she noticed the churn.

"Father," she said, "who made the ice cream?"

"I did," he said. "For your mother."

She did not remark on the strangeness of this, only dipped two fingers inside the churn, then brought them to her mouth. Her red-rimmed eyes blinked in surprise.

"It's very good," she said.

After that, there was little question as to his path. He needed to support himself and his daughter. The house was sold, and his wife's brother's family took them in; but they were not wealthy people, and Saleh had no wish to strain their charity. And so, with a white cloth wrapped around his head to keep away the sun, Doctor Mahmoud became Ice Cream Saleh. Soon he was a common sight in the streets of Homs, lugging the churn on a small wheeled cart garlanded with a string of bells, calling out *Ice cream! Ice cream!* Doors would open and children would come running, clutching coins; and he would keep his head averted so as not to see the light filtering through their bodies, and the bottomless holes in their eyes.

Soon Saleh was one of the most successful ice cream sellers in the neighborhood. Partly this was due to the ice cream itself. All agreed that what made his ice cream superior to others was its smooth texture. Other sellers would use too much ice, and the cream would freeze too quickly, becoming gritty and harsh. Or they might not churn it enough, and the children would be left with a disappointing, half-melted soup. Saleh's, though, was perfect every time. But his success also developed from his tragic story—*there goes Ice Cream Saleh, did you know he was once a famous physician*—and for the children it was an exercise in suspense. Would Ice Cream Saleh fall down in the street today, and foam at the mouth? They were always disappointed when he did not, though the ice cream was a consolation. When a fit did overtake him, he'd try to warn the children: "Don't be frightened," he would say, the words slurring in his ears. And then his vision would go dark, and he would enter another world, one of hallucinations, whispered words, and strange sensations. He could never remember these visions when he woke, his face in the dust, the children invariably having fled.

He spent years wandering the streets in this way, footsore and hoarse, his hair gone to silver. What money he could spare was put aside for his daughter's future, as they could no longer count on a generous bride-price. How surprised they were, then, when a local shopkeeper approached Saleh with an offer that was more than he'd dared hope for. Saleh's daughter, the man said, had impressed him as a rare example of filial piety, and such a woman was all he desired as a wife and mother of his children. No one seemed to think much of him—he was known mostly for his unsolicited opinions on the failings of his neighbors—but he made a good living and didn't seem cruel.

"If God gave me one wish," Saleh said to his daughter, "I would tell Him to set the princes of the world before you and say, 'Choose, whichever one you like, for none is too wealthy or too noble.'" He kept his eyes closed as he spoke; it had now been eight years since he had looked at his own daughter.

She kissed his forehead and said, "Then I thank God you cannot have your wish, for I hear that princes make the worst of husbands."

The marriage contract was signed that summer. Less than a year

later she was dead: a hemorrhage during childbirth, and the baby stran-
gled in the canal. The woman attending the birth had not been able to
save either of them.

Her aunts prepared her body for burial, just as they'd prepared her
mother, washing and perfuming her and wrapping her in the five white
sheets. At the funeral, Saleh stood in the open grave and received his
daughter into his arms. Pregnancy had enlarged and softened her body.
Her head rested on his shoulder, and he gazed down at the covered landscape of her face, at the ridge of her nose, the hollows of her eyes. He laid
her on her right side, facing the Qaba. The shroud's perfume blended
oddly with the clean, sharp smell of damp clay. He knew the others were
waiting for him, but he made no move to climb out. It was cool and quiet
there. He reached out and drew his fingers across the jagged wall, feeling
with his distant senses the ridges left by the gravedigger's spade, the clay
slick and gritty between his fingers. He sat down beside his daughter's
body, and would have stretched out next to her except that he was then
hauled out of the grave by his armpits, his son-in-law and the imam having decided to cut short the spectacle before it grew any worse.

That summer he had fewer customers, though the weather was as
hot as ever. He could hear parents murmuring to their children as they
passed, *no, dearest, not from Mister Saleh*. He understood: he was no longer
merely tragic, but cursed.

He could not pinpoint how the idea first came to him, to take the
last of his money and go to America, but when it did he embraced it
quickly. His wife's family thought he'd finally fallen into insanity. How
would he survive in America on his own, when he barely could make his
way through Homs? His son-in-law told him that there were no mosques
in America, and he would not be able to pray properly. Saleh replied only
that he had no need of prayer, as he and God had parted company.

None of them understood his purpose. America was not meant to
be a new beginning. Saleh had no wish to survive. He would take his
ice cream churn across the sea, and there he would die, from sickness
or starvation or perhaps even sheer accident. He would end his life away
from the pity and the charity and the stares, in the company of strangers
who only knew what he was, not what he had once been.

And so he left, in a steamship out of Beirut. He spent the wretched voyage breathing the miasma of close air in the steerage deck, listening to the coughing of the passengers and wondering what he would contract. Typhoid? Cholera? But he emerged unscathed, only to suffer the humiliating interview and examination at Ellis Island. He'd given two young brothers his last bit of money to say he was their uncle, and they kept their word, promising the immigration clerk that they would support Saleh and keep him from indigence. He passed the medical exam only because the doctor could point to nothing physically wrong with him. The brothers took him to Little Syria, and before the disoriented Saleh could protest they had found him a place to live. It cost only a few pennies a week: a tiny room in a damp cellar that smelled of rotting vegetables. The only light came from a small grate, high on the wall. The young men took him around the neighborhood and showed him where he could buy milk and ice, salt and sugar. Then they purchased sacks full of peddling notions, wished him good luck, and left town for a place called Grand Rapids. That evening Saleh found in his pockets two dollars in change that had not been there before. After weeks of seasickness and exhaustion, he didn't even have the strength to be angry.

And so once again he became Ice Cream Saleh. The streets of New York were more crowded and treacherous than Homs, but his route was smaller and simpler, a narrow loop: Washington Street south to Cedar, then Greenwich north to Park, and back to Washington Street again. The children learned just as quickly as their Homs cousins to put the coin in his outstretched hand, and never to look into his eyes.

One sweltering afternoon, he was scooping ice cream into his small tin bowls when he felt a soft hand touch his elbow. Startled, he turned and glimpsed a woman's cheekbone. Quickly he looked away. "Sir?" a voice said. "I have water for you, if you'd like. It's so hot today."

For a moment he considered refusing. But it was indeed incredibly hot, a humid oppression like none he'd ever known. His throat felt thick, and his head ached. He realized he didn't have the strength to refuse. "Thank you," he said finally, and held out one hand toward the direction of her voice.

She must have appeared puzzled, for he heard a child's voice say, "You'll have to give him the glass, he never looks at anyone."

"Oh, I see," the woman said. Carefully she placed the glass of water in his hand. The water was cool and clean, and he drank it down. "Thank you," he said again, holding the glass out to her.

"You're welcome. May I ask, what is your name?"

"Mahmoud Saleh. From Homs."

"Mahmoud, I'm Maryam Faddoul. We're standing in front of my coffeehouse. I live upstairs with my husband. If you're in need of anything—more water, or a place to sit out of the sun—please, come in."

"Thank you, madam," he said to her.

"Please call me Maryam," she said, and there was a friendly smile in her voice. "Everyone does."

After that day, Maryam would often come out and speak with him and the children, whenever his slow trudge took him past her shop. The children all seemed to like Maryam: she took them seriously, remembered their names and the details of their lives. When Maryam was at his side he was inundated with customers, not just children but their mothers as well, and even merchants and factory workers returning home at the end of a shift. His route was a fraction of what it had been in Homs, but he sold just as much ice cream, if not more. In a way it was exasperating: he hadn't come to America to succeed, but it seemed that America would not let him fail.

Now, with his churn in tow, he considered Maryam's news of the Bedouin apprentice as he passed Arbeely's shop. He'd never gone in, only felt the wave of heat from the open door. For a moment he considered it. Then, irritated at memories, he resolved to give no more thought to Maryam's news but only watched the dark shapes of his feet as they moved inexorably toward his cellar home.

In the Syrian Desert, the three days of rain came to an end. The waters soaked into the earth, and soon green shoots were carpeting the lowlands, spreading up the sides of the hills. For the Bedouin tribes, these brief days were of great significance: a chance to turn their animals out to pasture and let them eat their fill, before the days grew hotter and the new growth died away.

And so it happened that one morning a Bedouin girl named Fadwa al-Hadid drove her small flock of goats out to the valley near her family's encampment. Singing softly to herself and switching the straying goats with a thin branch, she crested a small ridge—and there, glinting in the valley, was an enormous palace made entirely of glass.

She goggled at it for a moment before deciding that it was, indeed, truly there. Bursting with excitement, she gathered her goats, ran them back to the encampment, and rushed into her father's tent shouting about a shining palace that had suddenly appeared in the valley.

"It must have been a mirage," said her father, Jalal ibn Karim al-Hadid, who was known to his clan as Abu Yusuf. Her mother, Fatim, simply snorted and shook her head, and went back to nursing her youngest. But the girl, who was fifteen, stubborn, and headstrong, dragged her father from the tent, pleading with him to go look at the palace with her.

"Daughter, you simply can't have seen what you thought you saw," said Abu Yusuf.

"Do you think me a child? I know a mirage when I see one," she insisted. "And it stood as real before me as you do now."

Abu Yusuf sighed. He knew that look in his daughter's eye, that blazing indignation that defied any attempt at reason. Worse, he knew it was his own fault. Their clan had been fortunate of late, and it had made him indulgent. The winter had been mild, and the rains had come on time. His brothers' wives had both born thriving sons. At the turning of the year, as Abu Yusuf had sat warm in the glow of the fires and watched his clan as they ate and played and squabbled around him, he'd told himself that perhaps finding a husband for Fadwa could wait. Let the girl have one more year with her family, before sending her away. But now Abu Yusuf wondered if his wife was right: perhaps he had coddled his only daughter beyond reason.

"I don't have time to argue about nonsense," he told her sharply. "Your uncles and I are taking the sheep to pasture. If there's a magical palace out there, we'll see it. Now go and help your mother."

"But—"

"*Girl, do as I say!*"

He rarely shouted. She drew back, stung. Then she turned and ran into the women's tent.

Fatim, who'd heard it all, came in after her and clucked her tongue at her daughter. Fadwa sniffed and avoided her eyes. She sat herself in front of the low table where the day's dough was rising and began to rip the dough to pieces and pound them flat, using rather more force than necessary. Her mother sighed at the noise, but said nothing. Better the girl exhaust herself than stay a simmering nuisance all morning.

The women cooked and milked and mended as the sun traced its familiar path through the sky. Fadwa bathed her little cousins, and endured their howls and recriminations. The sun set, and still the men were not yet returned. Fatim's expression began to darken. Bandits were rare in their valley, but even so, three men and a large herd of sheep would make an easy target. "Enough of that," she snapped at Fadwa, who was struggling to clothe a squirming boy. "I'll do it, since you can't. Go and sew your wedding dress."

Fadwa obeyed, though she'd rather do just about anything else. She was no good at fine stitching, she had little patience for it; she could weave well enough, and mend a tent as quick as Fatim, but embroidery? Little stitches arranged just so? It was dull work, and it made her go cross-eyed. More than once Fatim had looked over her daughter's progress and commanded her to rip it all out again. No girl of hers, she declared, would be married in such a sloppy dress.

If it were up to Fadwa, she would toss the dress into the cooking fire and sing loudly as it burned. Life in her clan's encampment grew more stifling with each day, but it was nothing compared with her terror at the idea of marriage. She knew she was a spoiled child; she knew her father loved her, and wouldn't be so harsh as to choose a husband who was cruel or stupid simply to make a good alliance. But anyone could be fooled, even her father. And to leave everyone she had ever known, and live with a strange man, and lie beneath him, and be ordered about by his family—was it not like dying, in a way? Certainly she wouldn't be Fadwa al-Hadid anymore. She'd be someone else, another woman entirely. But there was nothing to do about it: she would marry, and soon. It was as certain as the sunrise.

She looked up at a joyful cry from her mother. The men were coming into camp, driving the sheep before them. The sheep stumbled against one another, drowsy from full bellies and a long journey. "A good day," one of Fadwa's uncles called. "We couldn't ask for better grazing."

Soon the men were sitting down to their dinner, tearing at the bread and cheese. The women served them and then retired to their tent to eat what was left. With her husband safely home, Fatim's mood improved; she laughed with her sisters-in-law and cooed over the baby at her breast. Fadwa ate silently, and gazed across at the men's tent, at her father's solid back.

Later that night, Abu Yusuf drew his daughter aside. "We went by the place you spoke of," he told her. "I looked hard, but I saw nothing."

Fadwa nodded, dejected but unsurprised. Already she herself had begun to doubt it.

Abu Yusuf smiled at her downturned face. "Have I told you about the time I saw an entire caravan that wasn't there? I was about your age. I was out with my sheep one morning, and saw a gigantic caravan come marching down through a pass in the hills. At least a hundred men, coming closer and closer. I could see the men's eyes, even the breath from the camels' noses. I turned and ran back home, to make them come see. And I left my sheep behind."

Fadwa's eyes widened. This was a carelessness she wouldn't have believed of him, even as a boy.

"By the time I returned with my father, the caravan was gone without a trace. And most of my sheep had vanished as well. It took all day to hunt them down, and some had gone lame from the rocks."

"What did your father say?" She was almost afraid to ask. Karim ibn Murhaf al-Hadid had died many years before Fadwa was born, but stories of his severe character were legend in the tribe.

"Oh, at first he said nothing, only whipped me. Then, later, he told me a tale. He said that once when he was a little boy, playing in the women's tent, he looked out and saw a strange woman dressed all in blue. She was standing just beyond the camp, smiling at him, and holding out her hands. He could hear her calling, asking him to come and play. The girl who was supposed to be watching him had fallen asleep. So he followed the woman out into the desert—alone, in the middle of a summer afternoon."

Fadwa was astonished. "And he lived!"

"It was a near thing. They didn't find him for hours, and by then his blood was boiling. It was a long time before he was well again. But he said he would have sworn on his father's name that the woman was real. And now"—he smiled—"you will have a story to tell *your* children, when they come running to you and swear that they saw a lake of clear water in a dry valley, or a horde of djinn flying across the sky. You can tell them of the beautiful shining palace you knew to be there, and how your cruel and terrible father refused to believe you."

She smiled. "You know I won't say that."

"Perhaps, perhaps not. Now"—he kissed her forehead—"finish your chores, child."

He watched as she turned back toward the women's tent. His smile faltered, then faded. He had not been honest with his daughter. The tales of the caravan and his father's misadventure were true enough—but earlier that day, driving the sheep along the ridge, he had, for the briefest of moments, been blinded by a shining vision of a palace in the valley below. A blink, and it had disappeared. He'd stared at the empty valley for a long time, telling himself that the sunlight must strike the eye in a particular way at this spot, creating the illusion. Nevertheless, he was shaken. As his daughter had said, it had been no vague, wavering mirage—he'd seen impossible details, spires and battlements and glittering courtyards. And standing a little ways from the open gate, the figure of a man, staring up at him.

6.

It was almost the end of September, but the summer heat lingered without mercy. At midday the streets thinned, and pedestrians congregated under the awnings. The brick and stone of the Lower East Side soaked up the day's heat and released it again at sundown. The rickety staircases that ran up the backs of the tenements became vertical dormitories as residents dragged their mattresses onto the landings and made camp on the rooftops. The air was a malodorous broth, and all labored to inhale it.

The High Holy Days were near unendurable. The synagogues sat half-empty as many chose to pray at home, where they might at least open a window. Red-faced cantors sang to a few miserable devout. At Yom Kippur, the Sabbath of Sabbaths, not a few congregants fainted where they stood, the prescribed fast having worn away the last of their strength.

For the first Yom Kippur since he became a bar mitzvah, Rabbi Meyer did not fast. Though the elderly were exempted from fasting, the Rabbi had been loath to give it up. The fast was meant to be the culmination of the spiritual work of the High Holy Days, a cleansing and purifying of the soul. This year, however, he had to admit that his body had grown too frail. To fast would be a mark against him, a sin of vanity and a refusal to accept the realities of aging. Hadn't he once counseled his congregants against this very misdeed? Nonetheless he took no pleasure from his lunch on Yom Kippur, and could not escape the feeling that he was guilty of something.

He was comforted that at least there was plenty to eat—for, to pass her time, the Golem had taken up baking.

It had been the Rabbi's idea, and he scolded himself for not thinking of it earlier. The notion came to him when he stopped at a bakery one morning and glimpsed a young man at work in the back, rolling and braiding dough for the Sabbath challahs. Loaf after loaf took shape underneath his hands. His quick, automatic movements spoke of the years he'd spent in this very spot, at this very task; and in that moment he seemed to the Rabbi almost a golem himself. Golems did not eat, of course—but why should that keep a golem from becoming a baker?

That afternoon, he brought home a heavy, serious-looking English volume, and gave it to the Golem.

"*The Boston Cooking-School Cook Book*," she read, nonplussed. She cracked the tome with trepidation—but to her surprise the book was simple, sober, and clearly written. There was nothing here to confuse her, only patient and consistent instruction. She repeated the names of the recipes to the bemused Rabbi, in English and then in Yiddish, and was astonished when he declared many of them completely alien to him. He had never eaten finnan haddie—a type of fish, apparently—or gnocchi à la romaine, or potatoes Delmonico, or any of a host of complicated-sounding egg dishes. She declared that she would cook a meal for him. Perhaps a roast turkey with sweet potatoes and succotash? Or lobster bisque followed by Porterhouse steaks, with strawberry shortcake for dessert? The Rabbi hastily explained, not without regret, that these dishes were too extravagant for their household—and besides, lobsters were *treyf*. Perhaps she should start small, and work upward from there. There was nothing he liked more, he said, than a fresh-baked coffee cake. Would that do for a beginning?

And so the Golem ventured alone out of the tenement, and went to the grocer's at the corner. With money from the Rabbi she bought eggs, sugar, salt, and flour, a few different spices in twists of paper, and a small package of walnut meats. It was the first time she had been truly alone, out in the city, since her arrival. She was growing more accustomed to the neighborhood; she and the Rabbi had taken to walking together a few afternoons a week, the Rabbi having decided that the Golem's need to experience the world far outweighed whatever gossip might result. Still, he kept a close eye on her at all times. He'd begun to have a recurring nightmare of losing her in a crowd, seeking her in a growing panic, and finally glimpsing her tall form in the middle of a mob shouting for her destruction.

The Golem would sense these nightmares, of course, not as clearly as waking thought, but clear enough to know that the Rabbi was afraid for her, and afraid of her as well. It saddened her deeply, but she tried not to think on it. To dwell on his fears, and her own loneliness, would do no one good.

She baked the coffee cake, following the directions with fervent exactitude, and was successful in her first attempt. She was pleasantly surprised at the ease of the chore, and at the almost magical way that the oven transformed the thick batter into something else entirely, something solid, warm, and fragrant. The Rabbi ate two slices with his morning tea and declared it one of the best cakes he'd ever tasted.

She went out and bought more ingredients that afternoon. The next morning, the Rabbi awoke to find a bakery's worth of pastries on the parlor table. There were muffins and cookies, a phalanx of biscuits, and a towering stack of pancakes. A dense, strongly spiced loaf was something called gingerbread.

"I had no idea one could bake so much in an evening!" He said it lightly, but she saw his dismay.

"You wish I hadn't," she said.

"Well"—he smiled—"perhaps not so much. I'm only one man, with one stomach. It would be a shame to let this all turn stale. And we must not be so exorbitant, you and I. This is a week's worth of food."

"I'm so sorry. Of course, I didn't think—" Shame filled her, and she turned from the table. She'd been so proud of what she'd done! And it had felt so good to work, to spend all night in the kitchen measuring and mixing, standing before the little oven that spilled its heat into the already sultry room. And now she could barely look at her handiwork. "I do so many things wrongly!" she burst out.

"My dear, don't be so hard on yourself," the Rabbi said. "These concerns are all new to you. I've been living with them for decades!" A thought came to him. "Besides, none of this need go to waste. Would you be willing to give some of it away? I have a nephew, Michael, my sister's son. He runs a hostel for new immigrants, and has many mouths to feed."

She wanted to protest: she'd made these for the Rabbi, not for strangers. But she saw that he was offering her a gracious way to salvage her mistake, and that he hoped she would take it.

"Of course," she said. "I'd be happy to."

He smiled. "Good. In fact, let's take them together. It's time you had a conversation with someone besides a butcher or grocer."

"You think I'm ready?"

"Yes, I do."

Excited, nervous, she struggled to stand still. "Your nephew. What sort of man is he? What should I say to him? What will he think of me?"

The Rabbi smiled and raised his hands, as though to hold back her tide of questions. "First, Michael is a good boy—I should say a good man, he's nearing thirty. I respect and admire his work, though we don't see eye to eye. I only wish—" He paused, but then remembered that the Golem would certainly see some part of it. Better to explain, than leave her with a vague, confusing picture. "We used to be closer, Michael and I. My sister died when he was young, and my wife and I brought him up. For many years, he was as close as a son. But then—well, certain things were said between us. A sadly typical argument between the old and the young. The damage was never quite repaired. We see each other less often, now."

There was more to it, the Golem saw—not an evasion on the Rabbi's part, but an unspoken depth of detail. Not for the first time she felt the vast chasm of experience between them: he, who had lived for seven decades, and she, with barely a month's worth of memories.

"As for what you shall say to each other," the Rabbi continued in a lighter tone, "it needn't be a long conversation. You can explain what the different pastries are, at least. No doubt he will ask you where you come from, and how long you've been in the city. Perhaps we should rehearse a story. You can tell him you're a young widow from near Danzig, and that I'm acting as your social worker. Close enough to the truth, in a manner of speaking." He smiled, but with a hint of sorrow; and she knew he was telling her something he didn't quite believe.

"I'm sorry," she said. "You shouldn't have to lie to your nephew. Not for my sake."

The Rabbi was silent for a moment. Then he said, "My dear, I am

beginning to realize that there are many things that I will need to do—
that I *must* do, for your sake. But they are my decisions. You must allow
me to regret a small lie made in the service of a larger good. And you
yourself must learn to become comfortable doing the same." He paused,
and then said, "I don't yet know if you'll ever be able to live a normal life,
among others. But you must know that to do so, you would have to lie to
everyone in your acquaintance. You must tell no one your true nature,
ever. It is a burden and a responsibility that I wouldn't wish on anyone."

A heavy silence fell.

"It had occurred to me," the Golem said finally. "Perhaps not as
clearly as that. I think I didn't want to believe it."

The Rabbi's eyes were wet; but when he spoke his voice was steady.
"Perhaps with time, and practice, it will become easier. And I will help
you, as best I can." He turned away, whisked a hand over his eyes; when
he turned back, he was smiling. "But now, let us talk of something more
cheerful. If I'm to introduce you to my nephew, I must tell him your
name."

She frowned. "I don't have one."

"My point exactly. It's far past time that you were named. Would
you like to choose a name for yourself?"

She thought a moment. "No."

The Rabbi was taken aback. "But you must have a name."

"I know." She smiled. "But I'd like you to choose it for me."

The Rabbi wanted to object: he'd hoped that the act of choosing
a name would help her toward independence. But then he admonished
himself. She was still like a child in so many ways, and one did not expect a child to name itself. That honor fell to the parent. In this, she had
grasped the meaning of the thing better than he.

"Very well," he said. "I've always liked the name Chava for a girl. It
was my grandmother's name, and I was very fond of her."

"Chava," the Golem said. The *ch* was a soft and rolling sound in the
back of the throat, the *ava* like a spoken sigh. She repeated it quietly to
herself, testing it while the Rabbi looked on, amused.

"Do you like it?" he asked.

"Yes," she said, and she did.

"Then it's yours." He raised his hands over her, and closed his eyes. "Blessed One who protected our forefathers and led us out of bondage, watch over your daughter Chava. May her days be marked by peace and prosperity. May she be an aid, a comfort, and a protector to her people. May she have the wisdom and courage to see her way forward on the path that you have laid before her. Be this the will of the Almighty."

And the Golem whispered, "Amen."

All things considered, it was not one of Michael Levy's better days.

He stood behind his paper-strewn desk with the harried air of a man reacting to a dozen crises at once. In his hand was a letter informing him, with regret, that the ladies who volunteered to clean on Sundays would no longer be doing so; their Ladies' Workers League had schismed and then dissolved, and with it their Charitable Action Committee. Ten minutes earlier, the head housekeeper had informed him that a number of that week's residents had arrived with dysentery, and they were going through bed linens at an alarming rate. And, as always, there was the almost physical pressure of the nearly two hundred new immigrants who bunked in the dormitories that hung above his head. And as long as they were under his roof, Michael was responsible for their welfare.

The Hebrew Sheltering House was a way station where men fresh from the Old World could pause, and gather their wits, before jumping headfirst into the gaping maw of the New. All were allowed to stay five days at the Sheltering House, during which they were fed and clothed and given a cot to sleep on. At the end of those five days they had to depart. Some moved in with distant relatives, or took the peddler's path; others were recruited by the factories and slept in filthy flophouse hammocks for five cents a night. When he could, Michael tried to steer the men away from the worst of the sweatshops.

Michael Levy was twenty-seven years old. He had the sort of pink, wide-cheeked face that was cursed to perpetual youth. Only his eyes showed the years: they were deeply lined and shadowed, by reading and fatigue. He was taller than his uncle Avram, and something of a scarecrow, the result of never slowing down and eating a proper meal. His friends liked to joke that with his ink-stained cuffs and tired eyes he looked more like a scholar than a social worker. He would reply that it was only fitting, as his work was more of an education than a classroom could ever offer.

There was pride, and defensiveness, in his answer. His teachers, his aunt and uncle, his friends, even his all-but-absent father: all had expected him to go to university. And they'd been shocked and dismayed when young Michael announced his plan to dedicate himself to social work, and the betterment of the lives around him.

"Of course that's all good and noble," a friend told him. "Which one of us isn't committed to the same thing? But you've got a first-rate mind—use *that* to help people. Why let it go to waste?" The friend in question wrote for one of the Socialist Labor Party papers. Every week his name ran above a moving paean to the Working Man, each turning on a scene of brotherly solidarity that he'd happened to witness— usually, conveniently enough, on the day before his deadline.

Michael stood firm, if somewhat wounded. His friends wrote their articles, they went to marches and listened to speeches, they debated the future of Marxism over coffee and strudel—but Michael heard an airy emptiness in their rhetoric. He didn't accuse his friends of taking an easy road, but neither could he follow them. He was too honest a soul; he had never learned to deceive himself.

The only one who understood was his uncle Avram. It was the other change in Michael's life that the Rabbi couldn't countenance.

"Where is it written that a man must turn his back on his faith to do good in the world?" the Rabbi had asked, staring in horror at his nephew's bare head, at the neat sideburns where sidelocks had once hung. "Who taught you this? Those philosophers you read?"

"Yes, and I agree with them. Not with everything, maybe, but at least that as long as we keep to our old beliefs, we'll never find our place in the modern world."

His uncle laughed. "Yes, this wonderful modern world that has rid us of all ills, of poverty and corruption! What fools we are, not to cast our shackles aside!"

"Of course there's much that still needs changing! But it does no good to chain ourselves to a backward—" He stopped. The word had slipped from his mouth.

His uncle's expression grew even darker. Michael saw he had two options: recant and apologize, or own what he'd said.

"I'm sorry, Uncle, but it's how I feel," said Michael. "I look at what we call faith, and all I see is superstition and subjugation. *All* religions, not just Judaism. They create false divisions, and enslave us to fantasies, when we need to focus on the here and now."

His uncle's face was stone. "You believe me to be an instrument of subjugation."

The instinct to protest was on his lips—*of course not! Not you, Uncle!*—but he held back. He didn't want to add hypocrisy to his list of offenses.

"Yes," he said. "I wish I felt otherwise. I know how much good you've done—how could I forget all those visits to the sick? And the time the Rosens' store burned down? But good deeds should come from our natural instinct toward brotherhood, not from tribalism! What about the Italians who owned the butcher's shop next to the Rosens? What did we do for *them*?"

"I can't take care of everyone!" snapped the Rabbi. "So perhaps I'm guilty of only looking after my own kind. That too is a natural instinct, whatever your philosophers might say."

"But we must grow beyond it! Why reinforce our differences, and keep ancient laws, and never know the joy of breaking bread with our neighbors?"

"Because we are Jews!" his uncle shouted. "And that is how we live! Our laws remind us of who we are, and we gain strength from them! You, who are so eager to throw away your past—what will you replace it with? What will you use to keep the evil in Man from outbalancing the good?"

"Laws that apply to everyone," said Michael. "That put all men on equal footing. I'm no anarchist, Uncle, if that's what worries you!"

"But an atheist? Is *that* what you are now?"

He could see no way around it. "Yes, I think I am," he said, looking away to hide from the pain in his uncle's eyes. For a long, miserable time after, Michael felt he might as well have struck the man across the face.

They'd been slow to reconcile. Even now, years later, they only saw each other once a month or so. They kept to cordial small talk and avoided opinions on painful subjects. The Rabbi congratulated Michael on each success and spoke consoling words at his defeats—which were many, for Michael's job was far from easy. When the previous supervisor, who'd insisted on only taking money from Jewish Socialist groups, had quit, the Sheltering House was weeks away from shuttering for lack of funds. Michael was invited to accept the position and saw for himself the many dozens of men in their dormitories. The weave of their clothes, the cut of their beards, and their vaguely bewildered air all marked them as fresh from the boat. These were the most vulnerable of the immigrants, most likely to be duped or swindled. He reviewed the House's ledgers, which were in chaos. He accepted the position, then swallowed his pride and went to the local congregations and Jewish councils, begging for lifeblood. In exchange, advertisements for Sabbath services were posted on the notice board in the hallway, next to the announcements of party meetings.

He still believed what he'd told his uncle. He attended no synagogue, said no prayers, and hoped that one day all men would lose their need for religion. But he knew that sweeping change only happened slowly, and he understood the value of pragmatism.

The Rabbi saw the religious advertisements when he visited, but said nothing. He too seemed to regret the rift between them. They were practically each other's only relations—Michael's father having long since decamped for Chicago, leaving behind a dozen frustrated creditors—and in a neighborhood of sprawling families, Michael felt it keenly. So when the Rabbi came knocking on his office door that afternoon, Michael was truly glad to see him.

"Uncle! What brings you here?" The men embraced, a bit formally. Michael had grown used to his own uncovered head, the lack of fringe beneath his vest; but he still felt naked in the man's presence. Then he caught sight of the woman in the door's shadow.

"I'd like you to meet a new friend," said the Rabbi. "Michael, this is Chava. She's newly arrived in New York."

"I'm pleased to meet you," the woman said. She was tall, taller than him by an inch or two. For a moment she seemed a dark and looming statue; but then she moved forward into the room, and was merely a woman in a plain shirtwaist, holding a cardboard box.

Michael realized he was staring; he caught himself. "Likewise, of course! How long have you been here?"

"Only a month." She gave a small embarrassed smile, as if apologizing for her recent arrival.

"Chava's husband died on the voyage," his uncle said. "She has no family in America. I've become her social worker, after a fashion."

Michael's face fell. "My God, how terrible. I'm so sorry."

"Thank you." It was a whisper.

There was a moment of silence, awkward with the weight of her revealed widowhood. Then the woman seemed to notice the box in her hands. "I made these," she said, a bit abruptly. "They were meant for your uncle, but I made too many. He suggested I bring them to you, and you could give them to the men who live here." She held out the box to Michael.

He opened it, unleashing a heavenly scent of butter and spices. The box was full of pastries, all different kinds: butter-horns, almond macaroons, spice cookies, sweet buns, gingersnaps. "You made *all* of these?" he said, incredulous. "Are you a baker?"

The woman hesitated, but then smiled. "Yes, I suppose I am."

"Well, the men will certainly appreciate these. We'll make sure everyone gets a piece." He closed the box, fighting temptation. The almond macaroons in particular were making his mouth water; they'd been his favorite since childhood. "Thank you, Chava. This will be a great treat for them. I'll take them straight to the kitchen."

"You should try a macaroon," she said.

He smiled. "I will. They're my favorite, actually."

"I—" She seemed to catch hold of herself, then said, "I'm glad."

"Chava," the Rabbi said, "perhaps you might wait for me in the parlor."

The woman nodded. "It was a pleasure to meet you," she said to Michael.

"And you as well," he replied. "And thank you, truly. On behalf of all the men."

She smiled, and withdrew into the hallway. For such a tall woman, she moved quite silently.

"My God, what a tragedy for her!" Michael said when she was out of earshot. "I'm surprised she stayed in New York, instead of going back home."

"There was little there for her," said his uncle. "In a way, she had no choice."

Michael frowned. "She isn't living with *you*, is she?"

"No, no," his uncle said quickly. "She's staying with a former congregant, for now. An old widow. But I must find her a more permanent living situation, and a job as well."

"That shouldn't be difficult. She seems capable, if quiet."

"Yes, she's very capable. But at the same time she's almost painfully innocent. It makes me afraid for her. She'll need to learn how to protect herself, to live in this city."

"At least she'll have you to look out for her."

His uncle smiled grimly. "Yes. For now."

An idea had been forming in Michael's mind; finally he gave it his attention. "You say you're looking for a job for her?"

"Yes. Not a sweatshop, if I can help it."

"Are you still in touch with Moe Radzin?"

"We're cordial enough to say hello on the street, I suppose." He frowned. "You think there might be a job for Chava at Radzin's?"

"I was just there yesterday. The place was in chaos, and Moe was having fits. One of his assistants ran off to God knows where, and another is leaving to take care of her sister." He smiled and pointed at the box. "If those taste as good as they look, then the bakery could use her. You should go talk to him."

"Yes," the Rabbi said slowly. "It's a possibility. But Moe Radzin . . ."

"I know. He's just as sour and unhappy as ever. But he's fair, at least, and generous when he wants to be. The House gets all our bread from him, at discount. And his employees seem to respect him. Well, except for Thea."

The Rabbi snorted. Thea Radzin was a formidable complainer, the sort of woman who began conversations with a list of her ailments. Among her husband's female employees she worked as a matchmaker in reverse, listing their defects to any man who showed an interest.

Michael pressed on, feeling obscurely that if he could help his uncle, some of his guilt would be unburdened. "There are worse bosses than Moe Radzin. And perhaps he'll feel some obligation to treat Chava well, if he knows you're watching out for her."

"Perhaps. I'll speak to him. Thank you, Michael." He squeezed his nephew's shoulder; and Michael, with a burst of concern, saw that his uncle had never looked so worn and tired, not even when dealing with the stresses of a congregation. He had always worked himself far too hard. And now, instead of resting, he'd taken the welfare of a young widow upon himself. Michael wanted to suggest that there were any number of women's groups that could look after her. But the Jewish women's charities, he knew, were even more strapped than the men's.

He said good-bye to his uncle and sat back at his desk. Even with his misgivings about his uncle's health, the brief glimpse of the woman had intrigued him. She'd seemed quiet and shy, but the way she'd looked at him had been unnerving. She'd stared directly into his eyes, unblinking, a deep and candid gaze. He understood what his uncle meant about her needing to protect herself, but at the same time Michael felt it was *he*, not she, who had been laid bare.

The Sheltering House's parlor was surprisingly spacious, running the length of the dim front hall. The Golem stood in the corner next to a dilapidated wing chair. It was now midmorning, and many of the men in the dormitories had left already, to look for work or a place to pray. But close to sixty remained, and the weight of their worrying minds pressed down on the Golem from above. It reminded her powerfully of her first night, on the *Baltika*, how the passengers' fears and desires had been amplified by the strange surroundings. These were the same wild hopes, the same apprehensions. It hadn't been as bad in Michael's office; she'd been too focused on the challenge of speaking to a stranger, and not giving herself away.

She was beginning to fidget. How much longer would the Rabbi be? Against her will she glanced up at the ceiling. Up there was hunger, loneliness, fear of failure, and loud wishes for success, of home, of a gigantic platter of roast beef—and one man who stood in line for the W.C., wanting only a newspaper to read while he waited . . .

She glanced at the parlor table. An issue of *Forverts* lay there, waiting to be claimed.

"No," she said to herself, louder than she had meant. She left the parlor and began to pace the long, dim corridor. Her hands gripped her elbows. She would knock on Michael's door, tell the Rabbi they needed to leave, that she didn't feel well—

To her relief, the office door opened, and the Rabbi and Michael stepped out, saying a few last words to each other. The Rabbi saw the Golem's strained expression, and his good-bye grew more hurried. At last they were walking down the dark wooden hall to the rectangle of sunlight at its end.

"Are you all right?" asked the Rabbi when they were on the street.

"The men," she began, and found she couldn't go on: her thoughts were too quick, too choppy. She struggled to relax. "They all want so much," she got out at last.

"Was it too much for you?"

"No. Nearly. If we'd stayed."

The silent clamor of the Sheltering House faded behind her, was swallowed into the diffuse buzz of the city. Her mind began to slow. She shook out her fingers, feeling the tension ebb. "There was a man, upstairs," she said. "He wanted a newspaper. I saw one in the parlor, and nearly brought it to him."

"That would have been quite a surprise for him." He tried to speak lightly. "You were able to hold back, though."

"Yes. But it was difficult."

"You are improving, I think. Though you nearly gave yourself away, with the macaroons."

"I know." She cringed at the memory, and the Rabbi smiled. "Chava," he said, "it's a cruel irony that you have the most difficulty precisely when those around you are on their best behavior. I suspect you would find it much easier if we all cast politeness aside, and took whatever we pleased."

She considered. "It would be easier, at first. But then you might hurt each other to gain your wishes, and grow afraid of each other, and still go on wanting."

Approval raised his eyebrows. "You're becoming quite the student of human nature. Do you think you have improved enough to go out regularly on your own—say, to hold down a job?"

Apprehension clutched at her, mingled with excitement. "I don't know. I'm not sure *how* I would know, except through trying."

"Michael tells me that Radzin's Bakery is looking for new workers. I know Moe Radzin from years ago, and I thought I might try to get you a position there. I should be able to secure an interview with him, at least."

"A bakery?"

"It would be hard work, and long hours surrounded by strangers. You'd have to take constant care."

She tried to imagine it: working all day with her hands, in an apron and a starched cap. Stacking the neat rows of loaves, their brown undersides still dusty with flour, and knowing that she had made them.

"I'd like to try," she said.

7.

On a warm Saturday in September, the Djinni stood at the back of a crowded rental hall and watched as a man and woman were united in the Maronite Catholic sacrament of marriage. Despite the palpable joy of the other onlookers, he was not in the best of moods.

"Why should I go, when I don't even know them?" he'd asked Arbeely that morning.

"You're part of the community now. You'll be expected at these things."

"I thought you said I should maintain some distance, while I'm still learning."

"Distance is one thing. Rudeness is another."

"Why is it rudeness if I don't know them? And I still don't understand the purpose of a wedding. What could possibly induce two free beings to partner only with each other for the rest of their existence?"

Here, the conversation had deteriorated. Arbeely, flustered and aghast, tried to defend the institution, bringing forth every argument he could think of: paternity and legitimacy, marriage's civilizing influence, the need for chastity in women and fidelity in men. The Djinni scoffed at each of these, insisting that the djinn had no such preoccupations, and he saw no need why men and women should either. To which Arbeely said that it was just the way it was, regardless of what the Djinni thought, and he must attend the wedding and try to keep his opinions to himself. And the Djinni replied that of all the creatures he'd ever encountered, be they made of flesh or fire, none was quite as exasperating as a human.

At the front of the hall, the bride and groom knelt as the priest swung a censer back and forth above them. The bride, eighteen years old, was named Leila but called Lulu, a name that suggested a sauciness not at all evident in the small and shyly smiling girl. Her bridegroom,

Sam Hosseini, was a round and friendly man, well known in the community. He had been one of the first Syrian merchants to settle on Washington Street, and his imported-goods store was a neighborhood mainstay, attracting clients from far beyond its borders. Over the years he'd become quite prosperous, and was generous in helping his neighbors, so few begrudged him his success. As the priest intoned the service, Sam beamed with happiness and cast occasional glances down at Lulu, as if to confirm his great luck.

The ceremony ended, and everyone walked to the Faddouls' coffeehouse for the wedding banquet. The café tables were covered with platters of kebabs and rice and spinach-and-meat pies, and ribbon-tied bags of sugared almonds. Women crowded one side of the coffeehouse, eating and chatting. On the other side, men poured *araq* into each other's glasses and traded news. Sam and Lulu sat at their own small table in the middle, receiving congratulations, looking dazed and happy. A gift table near the door held a growing collection of boxes and envelopes.

But the Djinni was not among the crowd. He was in the alley behind the coffeehouse, sitting cross-legged on an abandoned wooden crate. The atmosphere in the wedding hall had been oppressive, humid with sweat and incense and perfume, and he was still irritated by what he saw as a pointless ceremony. He had no wish to be cooped up in the coffeehouse with dozens of strangers. Besides, the day had turned beautiful; the sky between the buildings was a pure blue, and a meandering breeze cleared the smell of refuse from the alley.

From his pocket he pulled a handful of gold necklaces, purchased from a shabby storefront on the Bowery. Arbeely had taken him there, saying it was the only place he knew of to purchase gold inexpensively; but he had seemed uncomfortable and frowned at the low prices, later remarking that he was certain they'd been stolen. They were of middling workmanship—the links were not entirely uniform, and the chains hung in an uneven sort of way—but the gold was of good quality. The Djinni gathered them into one palm and cupped his hands around them to melt them, and then began idly to shape the metal. When his hands stilled, he was holding a miniature golden pigeon. With a thin, pointed wire he added a few details—the suggestion of feathers, pinprick eyes—

and then surrounded the bird with a filigree cage. It felt good to work with his hands, instead of the crude tools that Arbeely insisted he use when someone might be watching.

The alleyway door of the coffeehouse opened. It was Arbeely. "There you are," the man said. A small plate and a fork were in his hands.

Irritated, the Djinni said, "Yes, here I am, enjoying a moment of solitude."

A flash of hurt passed over the man's face. "I brought you a piece of the *kinafeh*," he said. "It's about to run out. I was worried you wouldn't get any."

Guilt pricked vaguely at the Djinni. He knew Arbeely was doing much to help him, but it made him feel oppressed and beholden, and it was hard to keep from lashing out. He slipped the caged bird into his pocket and accepted the proffered plate, which held a square of something heavy-looking, with brown and cream-colored layers. He frowned. "What exactly is this?"

Arbeely grinned. "The closest thing to heaven on earth."

The Djinni took a cautious bite. The act of eating was still difficult. Not the mechanism itself—chewing and swallowing were simple enough actions, and the food burned to nothingness inside him. But he'd never tasted anything before, and had been taken completely by surprise at his first experiences of flavor. The sensations of sweet and savory, salt and spice, were arresting, even overwhelming. He'd learned to take the food in small bites and chew slowly. Even so, the *kinafeh* was a shock. Sweetness burst across his tongue, and thin strands of dough crunched between his teeth, the sound echoing deep in his ears. A creamy tartness made his jaw tighten.

"Do you like it?" asked Arbeely.

"I don't know. It's . . . startling." He took another tentative bite. "I think I like it."

Arbeely looked around the alley. "What are you doing out here, anyway?"

"I needed a moment of quiet."

"Ahmad," Arbeely said—and the Djinni cringed at the name, his but not his—"I understand, really. God knows, I'm the same way at these things. But we don't want people to think you're a recluse. Please, come in and say hello. Smile once or twice. For me, if not yourself."

Reluctantly, the Djinni followed Arbeely back to the party.

Inside, the tables had been pushed to the edges of the room, and a group of men was dancing in a fast-moving ring, their arms about each other's shoulders. The women crowded around them, cheering and clapping. The Djinni stood out of their way, in the back of the room, and observed the bride through breaks in the crowd. Of all the people at the wedding, she was the one who'd caught his interest. She was young and pretty, and clearly very nervous. She barely touched the food in front of her but smiled and spoke with the well-wishers who approached their table. Next to her, Sam Hosseini ate like a starving man, and stood to greet everyone with hugs and handshakes. She listened to her new husband talk, and looked up at him with obvious fondness; but occasionally she would glance about, as if looking for reassurance. The Djinni remembered what Arbeely had told him, that she was only a few weeks in America, that Hosseini had proposed to her on a visit home. And now, the Djinni reflected, she was in a new place, on unsure footing, surrounded by strangers. Like himself, in a way. A shame, that according to Arbeely she now belonged to this man only.

The bride was still scanning the room. The dancing men spun to one side, and she saw the Djinni regarding her. He held her in his gaze for a long moment. Then she looked away; and when she greeted the next guest there was color high in her cheeks.

"Ahmad, would you like coffee?"

He turned, startled. It was Maryam. She carried a tray of tiny cups, each full of thick, cardamom-scented coffee. She wore her customary hostess's smile, but her eyes carried an edge of warning. Clearly she'd seen his interest. "So you can drink to their happiness," she said.

He lifted a cup from her tray. "Thank you."

"Of course," she replied, and moved on.

He eyed the diminutive cup of coffee. Liquid in such a small amount would not hurt him, and it smelled interesting enough. He downed it all at once, as he'd seen the others do, and nearly choked. It was incredibly bitter; drinking it felt like an assault.

He winced and set the cup on a table. He'd had enough of human revelry for one day. He searched out Arbeely in the crowd, caught the man's eye, and pointed at the door. Arbeely held up one hand, as if to say, *wait a moment*, and indicated the newlyweds' table.

But the Djinni did not want to congratulate the happy couple. He was in no mood to speak words he didn't feel. As Arbeely tried to wave him over, the Djinni moved through the crowd, left the stifling coffeehouse, and went out into the city.

The Djinni walked north along Washington Street, wondering if he'd ever be truly alone again. At times the desert had felt too empty for him, but this opposite extreme was harder to bear. The street was no less crowded than the coffeehouse had been. Families thronged the sidewalks, all taking advantage of the warm weekend afternoon. And where there were not humans there were horses, a standstill parade of them, each attached to a cart, each cart carrying a man, each man yelling at the others to clear out of his way—all in a myriad of languages that the Djinni had never before heard but nonetheless comprehended, and now he was coming to resent his own seemingly inexhaustible resources of understanding.

He was not walking aimlessly; he had a destination in mind. A few days earlier, Arbeely had shown him a map of Manhattan and offhandedly pointed out a long, green hole in the island's middle. "Central Park," Arbeely had said. "It's immense, nothing but trees and grass and water. You'll have to see it someday." Then the tinsmith had moved on to other topics, such as where to catch the Elevated, and which neighborhoods to avoid. But that long, open expanse of green had caught the Djinni's attention. He had only to find an Elevated platform on Sixth Avenue; and the Elevated, it seemed, would take him there.

At Fourteenth he turned east, and the crowd began to change character. There were fewer children, and more men in suits and hats. In the streets, elegant carriages mixed with dray-carts and delivery wagons. The buildings were changing as well, growing taller and wider. At Sixth Avenue a narrow ribbon of metal ran high above the street. He watched as a string of metal boxes ran along the ribbon, sending sparks into the street below. Through the train's tiny windows he caught glimpses of men and women, their faces placid as they rushed by.

He climbed a stairway to a platform, gave the ticket seller a few coins. A train soon arrived, squealing horribly as it halted. He boarded it and found a seat. More and more passengers entered the car, until the seats were all taken and the stragglers were forced to press together in the aisles. The Djinni shuddered as the car filled past what seemed possible.

The doors closed and the Elevated strained forward. He'd thought it might feel like flying, but he was soon disabused of that notion. The train vibrated as though to shake the teeth from his head. Buildings flashed past so close to the window that he recoiled. He debated getting off at the next stop and walking the rest of the way, but the other passengers seemed to chide him with their nonchalance. He clenched his jaw and watched the streets grimly as they sped past.

Fifty-ninth Street was the end of the line. He descended the staircase, feeling a bit sick. It was late in the afternoon, and the sky was clouding over, turning to a gray-white sheet.

Across from the station rose a wall of greenery. A high iron fence ran along it, as though to hold back something wild. There was a wide gap in the middle of the fence, and Sixth Avenue disappeared inside, curving around and out of sight. A steady stream of pedestrians and carriages came and went. He crossed the street and passed inside.

Almost immediately the sounds of traffic faded away, were replaced by a descending hush. A grove of trees edged the path on both sides, turning the air cool and heavy. Gravel crunched under his shoes. Open carriages ambled past, the horses' hooves beating a pleasant rhythm. Smaller paths broke away from either side of the carriage road, some wide and paved, others little more than dirt tracks overhung with lush vegetation.

Soon the shading grove came to an end, and the land opened into a vast swath of rolling lawn. The Djinni stopped, stunned by the vivid sea of green. Trees bordered its far edges, shielding the city from view. In the middle of the lawn, a herd of plump, dusky-white sheep stood peacefully together, eating lazy mouthfuls of grass. Benches lined the road, and here and there people sat, in pairs or threes or the occasional solitary gentleman—though women were never alone in public, he had noticed this—and watched the carriages go by.

He stepped off the path and walked about in the grass for a few moments, feeling the earth give and spring back. He bounced on the balls of his feet, unaware of the smile that rose to his lips. Briefly he considered abandoning the path altogether, and walking the length of the lawn, perhaps without his shoes; but then he spied a small sign staked into the ground that read PLEASE STAY TO THE PATH. And indeed, a few passersby were frowning at him in admonishment. He thought the rule absurd but had no wish to be noticed. So he stepped back onto the path, vowing to return at night, when hopefully he could do as he liked.

The carriage road branched away east, and the Djinni followed its curve over a pretty wooden bridge. Through a copse of tall trees he spied a long, straight path of shining gray-white. He left the road to investigate, and the gray-white path revealed itself as a broad promenade of flagstone, lined with high, arching trees. There were more people here than on the carriage path, but the scale of the space was so grand that he took little notice of the crowd. Children ran past, and one boy's hoop went rolling away from him, tilting across the Djinni's path. Startled, he plucked it from the stones and gave it back to the boy, who ran to catch up with his fellows. The Djinni continued on, wondering about the function of the hoop.

Eventually the broad walk descended into a tunnel that cut beneath a carriage road. On the other side of the tunnel, a broad plaza of red brick curved along the shore of a pond. In the middle of the plaza he saw what he took at first for an enormous winged woman, floating above a foaming cascade of water. No, not a woman—a sculpture of a woman, perched atop a pedestal. The water flowed into a wide, shallow basin at her feet, and then into a pool that stretched almost the width of the plaza.

He walked to the pool's edge and watched the fountain, entranced. He'd never thought to see water sculpted this way, in sheets and streams that changed constantly. It wasn't as frightening as the giant expanse of New York Harbor, but still he felt a not quite pleasant thrill. A fine spray struck his face, a smattering of tiny needles.

Serenely the woman hung above him. In one hand she carried a slender stem of flowers; with the other she reached out, gesturing to he knew not what. Her wings stretched behind her, wide and curved. A human woman, with the inhuman power of flight—but if Arbeely was to be believed, wouldn't they be frightened by such a woman? And yet the artist had sculpted her with reverence, not fear.

There was movement next to him: a young woman, standing nearby, watching him. He glanced at her, and she quickly turned her head, pretending to study the fountain as well. She wore a dress of dark blue that cinched tightly at the waist, and a large hat with a rolled brim, adorned with a peacock feather. Her brown hair was gathered in ringlets at the nape of her neck. By now the Djinni had seen enough of human costumes to know that everything about her spoke of wealth. Strangely, she seemed to be alone.

She glanced back at him, as if unable to help herself, and their eyes met. Hers darted away again. But then she smiled, as though conceding defeat, and turned to face him.

"I'm sorry," she said. "You seemed so entranced by the fountain. But it was rude of me to stare."

"Not at all," he replied. "I'm indeed entranced. I've never seen anything like this before. Can you tell me, who is the woman with the wings?"

"She's called the Angel of the Waters. She blesses the water, and all who drink it are healed."

"Healed? Of what?"

She shrugged her shoulders, a gesture that made her seem even younger than he'd thought. "Of whatever ails them, I suppose."

"And what," the Djinni asked, "is an angel?"

This question made her pause. She glanced him over again, as if reassessing him. Likely she'd already noticed the inferior cut of his clothing, and the accent in his English—but this question must have implied a strangeness not evident in his appearance.

She said, "Well, sir, an angel is a messenger of God. A heavenly being, higher than Man, but still a servant."

"I see." In fact, her words made little sense to him, but he sensed that pressing her further would be a mistake. He'd have to ask Arbeely. "And this is what angels look like?"

"I suppose," she said. "Or perhaps, this is one way of picturing them. It all depends on what you believe."

They stood, not quite together, gazing at the fountain.

"I've never seen anything like her," he said. He felt he must speak again, or risk the girl drifting from him.

"You must be from *very* far away, if your country has no angels," she said.

He smiled. "Oh, but there are angels in my land. I only didn't know what was meant by the word."

"But your angels aren't like her?" She nodded at the woman who hovered above them.

"No, not like her. In my land, the angels are made of an everlasting fire. They can change form to whatever suits their mood, and appear to men's eyes in that form, as the whirlwind appears in the dust that it carries."

She was listening, her eyes on him. He went on. "The angels in my land serve no one, neither higher than themselves nor lower. They roam where they wish, led only by their whims. When they encounter one another, they will sometimes react with violence, or else passion; and when they encounter humans"—he smiled down into her staring eyes—"the results are often the same."

She glanced away hotly. For a few moments there was only the sound of the water and others' conversations. "Your land," she said finally, "sounds like a savage place."

"It can be, at times."

"And in your land, is it considered proper to talk this way to a woman in a public park?"

"I suppose not," he said.

"Or perhaps the women of your land are different, that you would be so free with them."

"No, they are not so very different," he said, amused. "Though until now I would have said that they surpass those here in both beauty and pride. And now, I find my assumptions are shaken."

Her eyes went wide. She drew breath to answer him—and he wanted dearly to hear whatever she would say—but suddenly she glanced to her left, and took a step away from him. An elderly woman in a stiff black dress and a veiled hat was approaching. The young woman, with effort, restored her features to neutrality.

"Thank you for waiting, dearest," said the old woman. "There was a terrible line. You must have thought I'd deserted you."

"Not at all. I've been enjoying the fountain."

The old woman looked darkly over the girl's head at the Djinni, and then whispered something to her companion.

"Of course not," the young woman replied, barely audible. "Auntie, you know I would never. He only tried to ask me a question, but I couldn't understand. I don't think he speaks English."

She darted a quick, pleading glance at him: *please don't betray me.* Amused, he dipped his head a fraction, the ghost of a nod.

"The impertinence," the older lady muttered, narrowing her eyes at the Djinni. She spoke more loudly now, assuming he wouldn't understand, though of course her tone was plain. "I'm sorry, Sophia, I never should have left you alone."

"Really, Auntie, it's of no concern," the young woman said, embarrassment in her voice.

"Promise not to speak a word of this to your parents, or I won't hear the end of it."

"I promise."

"Good. Now let's take you home. Your mother will be beside herself if you aren't ready in time."

"I can't stand these parties, they're so wearisome."

"Don't say that, my dear, the season's just starting."

The older woman took her companion's arm—Sophia, she had called her. Sophia glanced up at the Djinni. It was clear she wanted to say something, but couldn't. Instead she allowed the older woman to escort her from the fountain, across the expanse of red brick. They ascended the staircase to the carriage drive, and then they were gone from sight.

Quickly he dashed across the terrace, startling those in his path. He took the stairs two and three at a time. Near the top he paused. Keeping

out of sight, he watched from below as the two women approached a gleam-
ing, open-topped carriage that waited on the drive. A man in livery opened
the passenger door for them. "M'lady. Miss Winston."

"Thank you, Lucas," said the young woman as he helped her into
the carriage.

The man climbed onto his high perch and flicked the reins, and the
carriage rolled smoothly away down the drive. The Djinni watched the
carriage until it curved past a grove of trees and disappeared.

He considered. It was late in the day, and growing cold. The sky
was still overcast, and edging on threatening. Now would be the time
to turn south and retrace his steps. No doubt Arbeely was wondering
where he was.

But the young lady had intrigued him. Moreover, the dark, aimless
longings that had surfaced at the wedding party had returned, and he
was not in the habit of denying his own impulses. Arbeely, he decided,
could wait for him a few minutes longer.

He had little to go on, only her name, but in the end it was almost absurdly easy to discover where Sophia Winston lived. He accomplished
it by traveling eastward to the edge of the park, alongside the path her
carriage had taken; and then, once he was through the gate and again on
the city streets, asking the first man who passed by.

"Winston? You mean Francis Winston? You must be joking." The
man he'd stopped was large and jowly, and dressed like a laborer. "He's
in that new mansion at Sixty-second. Big heap of white bricks, as big as
Astor's. Can't miss it." He pointed north with a meaty finger.

"Thank you." The Djinni strode off.

"Hey!" the man yelled after him. "What you want with the Winstons, anyhow?"

"I'm going to seduce their daughter," the Djinni called back, and the
man's roar of laughter followed him up Fifth Avenue.

He found the Winston residence easily, just as the man had said.
It was an enormous three-story limestone palace, topped by dark gables
that rose to high peaks. The house was set back from the street, behind a
swath of neatly trimmed grass and a spike-topped iron fence that ran the

length of the sidewalk. It hadn't yet acquired the thick patina of grime that clung to its neighbors, and it wore this newness with a quiet self-satisfaction.

At the front of the house was an enormous lamp-lit portico. The Djinni walked past it, and turned the corner, following the iron fence. Lights blazed in the tall windows beyond. He could see figures moving about inside, silhouetted behind drapery. At the back corner of the house, a thick hedge stretched out to meet the sidewalk, and the iron fence became an imposing brick wall, shielding the grounds behind the mansion from passing eyes.

The Djinni eyed the fence. The bars were strong, but not especially thick. He eyed the distance between them. Two, he decided, would be enough. He wrapped a hand around each of the bars, and concentrated.

Sophia Winston sat disconsolate in her bedroom, still in her dressing gown, hair damp from the bath. The guests would be arriving in less than an hour. As her aunt had predicted, Sophia's mother was in one of her states, careening about the house like a loose parakeet, issuing orders to every servant within earshot. Her father had retreated to the library, his usual foxhole. Sophia wished she could join him, or else help put her brother George to bed. But George's governess disliked Sophia's "interference," saying it undermined her authority. And if Sophia's mother found her mooning over travel journals in the library, there would be a row.

Sophia was eighteen years old, and she was lonely. As the daughter of one of the richest and most prominent families in New York—indeed, in the country—it had been made clear to her, in ways both subtle and overt, that she was expected to do little more than simply exist, biding her time and minding her manners until she made a suitable match and continued the family line. Her future unrolled before her like a dreadful tapestry, its pattern set and immutable. There would be a wedding, and then a house somewhere nearby on the avenue, with a nursery for the children that were, of course, mandatory. She'd spend interminable summers in the country, traveling from estate to estate, playing endless games of tennis, chafing under the strain of being constantly a guest in someone else's home. Then would come middle age, and the expected taking-up of a cause, Temperance or Poverty or Education—it did not matter so long as it was virtuous and uncontroversial, and furnished opportunities for luncheons with dowdy speakers in severe dress. Then old age and decrepitude, the slow transformation into a heap of black taffeta in a bath chair, to be displayed briefly at parties and then put out of sight; to spend her last days sitting bewildered by the fire, wondering where her life had gone.

She knew she would not fight this fate. She didn't have the stomach for prolonged family strife, nor the fortitude to make her own way in the world. And so, to escape, she turned to fantasies of rebellion and adventure, fueled by the volumes in her father's library, journals that ignited her mind with tales of exotic lands and ancient civilizations. She dreamed of riding on horseback with a Mongol tribe, or floating down the Amazon to the heart of the jungle; or strolling, in linen tunic and trousers, through the colorful street-markets of Bombay. The necessary privations of such travels, such as lack of proper beds or running water, were no matter, for in these dreams they were conveniently forgotten.

Recently she'd glimpsed an article on the late Heinrich Schliemann, and his discovery of the lost city of Troy. All of Schliemann's colleagues had insisted that the city was only a Homeric myth, that Schliemann was chasing a fantasy. But Schliemann had triumphed. The article was accompanied by a photograph of a beautiful dark-eyed woman, arrayed like a warrior-queen in ancient jewelry found at the site. She was Schliemann's Greek-born wife, who had assisted him at the excavation; and when Sophia read that this woman's name was also Sophia, she felt a bitter pang, as though her own best destiny had passed her over. If only it had been Sophia Winston draped in ancient jewelry, Sophia Winston standing at the dig with her intrepid husband, gazing down upon the golden face of Agamemnon!

She could lose herself in these fantasies for hours. She'd been drifting in and out of one that very afternoon, during the walk in the park, to distract herself from her aunt's acid-tongued gossip, and her dread of the impending party. At the time, the strange man at the fountain had seemed to materialize from out of the daydream: a tall and handsome foreigner who spoke to her in perfect English. Now, in the familiar light of her bedroom, she cringed to remember their conversation. He'd made her feel flustered and young, and far out of her depth.

Reconciling herself to the night ahead, she sat before the mirror and began to brush out her hair. Her maid had already laid out her gown, a new wine-red silk. She had to admit that she was looking forward to wearing it; the season's new fashions were quite flattering to her figure.

Something moved at the edge of her vision. She turned, startled. A man was standing on her balcony, just beyond the French doors, peering in through the glass.

She jumped up and nearly screamed, clutching her dressing gown to her neck. The man raised his hands and looked at her pleadingly, plainly asking her not to raise an alarm. She squinted at the glass, past her own thin reflection, and realized: it was him, the man from the park.

She goggled. How had he gotten onto the grounds? Her room was on the second floor—had he scaled the wall, and then climbed across the balconies? She hesitated a moment, then picked up the lamp and stepped toward the French door, the better to see him. He watched as she approached. Through the distortions of the glass he seemed almost impossibly still. She paused a few feet from the door, debating. She could still scream.

The man smiled, and extended an arm. An invitation—to talk?

Heart pounding, she fetched a shawl and stepped out onto the balcony. The night air was chill, and smelled of rain. She did not close the door behind her but drew the shawl tightly about herself. "What are you doing here?"

"I came to apologize," he said.

"To *apologize*?"

"I fear I offended you earlier."

"You're trespassing on our property and invading my privacy, in order to apologize?"

"Yes."

"I could scream. I could have you arrested."

He acknowledged this with silence. They stared at each other, across the few feet that separated them.

Finally she relented. "All right. I suppose that if you risk so much to apologize, then it is only fair that I offer forgiveness. So, there. You are forgiven. You may go now."

He nodded once, bowed to her, and then, in the most graceful movement that Sophia had ever seen, placed one hand on the balustrade and vaulted up onto it. He looked across to the next balcony, and she realized he was readying himself to jump.

"Wait!" she cried.

He froze, wobbling slightly, and put a hand out to steady himself; and she shuddered to think she might have killed him.

"I'm sorry," she said, "it's only—I just want to know—what is your name?"

There was a moment when he seemed to consider the question, and then he said, "Ahmad."

"Ahmad," she repeated. "Where are you from?"

"You would know it as Syria."

"*I* would know it as Syria? What do *you* know it as?"

"Home," he said.

He stood nonchalantly above her on the wide balustrade, not seeming to notice the two-story drop beneath him. Again she felt that creeping sense of unreality, as though he'd merely stepped from a tale. As though none of this were truly happening.

"Ahmad. Will you tell me something? And for pity's sake, come down from there before you fall."

He smiled and jumped back down to the balcony. "What shall I tell you?"

"Tell me what it's like where you're from. Where did you live?"

She'd expected him to name a city, but instead he said, "In the desert."

"The desert! Isn't that dangerous?"

"Only if one isn't careful. The desert is wild, but not impassable."

"I've seen pictures," she said, "in my father's journals. But I'm sure they don't do it justice."

Both started at a sudden noise. Someone was knocking at her bedroom door. The man crouched, as though about to spring to the balustrade again.

"Wait," she whispered.

Softly she crept back into the bedroom. She lay down on her bed, mussing the sheets so it would look as though she'd been asleep. "One moment," she called, and then hung her head upside down and shook it vigorously, disheveling her hair and hopefully bringing a flush to her cheeks. She rose from the bed, adopted an air of listless ill health, and opened the door.

A maid stood in the doorway, with an armful of linens. She took in the sight of Sophia still in her dressing gown and shawl, and her eyes widened with alarm. "Miss Sophia, your mother says the guests will be here in a half hour."

"Maria, I'm afraid that I'm not feeling well," Sophia said. "I have a terrible headache. Will you please tell my mother that I must have a rest first, and then I promise I'll come down to the party?"

"What?" cried a voice. Both women flinched as Julia Hamilton Winston, one of the most formidable doyennes of New York society, came charging down the hall in a billowing blue gown, her hair still tied in curling rags.

"Mother," Sophia pleaded as the woman advanced on them, "I'm really not feeling well. I'm sorry."

"This is nonsense. You were well enough at dinner."

"It came on suddenly, my head is pounding."

"Then take an aspirin," her mother snapped. "I've certainly suffered through enough parties with headaches and morning sickness and any number of illnesses. You are far too soft, Sophia. And too eager to shirk your responsibilities."

"Please," she said. "Just a half hour, that's all I'm asking. If I can sleep a bit, I'll feel better. And I'm afraid if I stand up much longer I'll be sick."

"Hmm." Her mother placed a hand on Sophia's forehead. "Well, you do feel a bit warm." She took her hand away and sighed, her face still registering distrust. "Half an hour only. Do you understand? And then I'll have Maria drag you from your bed."

"Yes, Mother. Thank you."

She closed the door and listened as the women's steps retreated down the hall, then went out once more to the balcony. He was where she had left him, wearing an expression of amusement.

"Very skillful," he said. "Do you do that often?"

She blushed in the dark. "My mother and I tend to disagree," she said. "We're very different people. We want different things from our lives."

"And what is it," he asked, "that you want from your life?"

She did not move but made herself meet his eyes. She would not blush again, she told herself; she would not look away. "Why did you come here? Truly, I mean. None of this nonsense about apologies."

"Because you intrigue me, and you are beautiful," he said.

She did blush at that, and turned, and placed more distance between them. "You are rather more direct than most men."

"And that displeases you?"

"No. Not as such. But I'm not accustomed to it." She sighed. "To tell the truth, I am very sick indeed of men who are not direct. And tonight this house will be full of them." She glanced over at him again. "Your home, in the desert. Will you tell me more?"

"One can travel the desert for days, months, years, and never meet another soul," he said quietly. "Or, if you wish, you can seek out the company of the desert peoples, or attempt to trace the ways of those creatures who don't wish to be seen, such as the djinn—although that," he said with a secret smile, "is rather more difficult. If somehow you gained the power of flight, you could travel with the birds, the hawks and kestrels. Like them, you could sleep as you flew." He paused. "Now I will ask *you* a question. Why will your house be full of men who aren't direct?"

She sighed. "Because I'm coming of age to marry. And because my father is very, very wealthy. They'll all be looking to make an advantageous match. They'll compliment my good looks and my opinions. They'll ask my friends about my tastes, and then affect them as their own. I'm about to become the quarry in a hunt, and it isn't even *me* they want. I'm simply a means to an end."

"Are you so certain about that? If a man tells you that you're beautiful, do you doubt his sincerity?"

She hesitated, then took a deep breath and said, "I suppose it depends on the man."

They were drawing closer to each other. The cypress trees that edged the garden were tall enough to screen out much of their surroundings; if she was very still, and kept her head at a certain angle, it was as though she was not in New York at all, but in a garden on the Mediterranean coast. The faint noises of the street behind them were the wash of a distant surf. The man beside her was a complete stranger. He could be anyone.

She could feel her allotted seconds ticking away. He was waiting, patient and careful, watching her. She shivered.

"Are you cold?" he asked.

"Aren't you?"

"I'm rarely cold." He glanced through the French door into the bedroom but didn't ask whether she would be more comfortable indoors. Instead he only drew closer to her, and slowly—so slowly that she would have had plenty of time to protest, to draw back, if this wasn't what she wanted—placed a hand on her waist.

At his touch, a blossom of warmth filled the pit of her stomach and spread outward. She could feel the heat of his hand through the layers of her dressing gown and shawl. Her eyes drifted shut. At last she stepped closer, and brought her face up to meet his.

Later she would reflect that he did not remark upon her forwardness, or ask her if this was what she truly wanted, or any of the other seemly protests that a man might make to absolve himself of responsibility. At one point he'd seemed about to pick her up and carry her through the door to her bed, but she'd shaken her head *no*, not wishing to leave the night and the shadowed garden, terrified that in the too-familiar room of her childhood she would lose her nerve. And so their tryst took place in a darkened corner of the balcony, a granite wall cold at her back. She wrapped the ends of her shawl about them both, pulling him close. His hands seemed to be everywhere at once, his lips hot on her skin, raining kisses upon her neck, the hollow of her throat. As her excitement grew, so did the dread of losing this moment, of returning to her life and having to endure the consequences; and so when at last the stars burst behind her eyelids and her entire body turned to fire, it was a fierce sadness as well as joy that made her bury her head in his shoulder and stifle a cry.

Finally she was able to stand on her own feet again. She felt his gentle fingers in her hair, his lips resting at her forehead. She could not look up at him. Tears gathered in her eyes. If she didn't move, if she held perfectly still, she would be able to keep time from tumbling forward—

The knock came again at her bedroom door.

"I must go," she whispered, and broke from him and fled.

The next day, the society columns in the city papers proclaimed the Winstons' soiree a memorable triumph. And indeed, it had been one of those rare evenings in which, through chance combinations of guests and wine and conversation, an honest vivacity takes hold, and it seems that no other house in the city could be as full of lively cheer and good feeling. But the true surprise of the night had been the newly arresting presence of the daughter of the house. Until then, the general opinion of Sophia Winston had been that she was lovely enough, but that she didn't try. Her dreaming, disengaged air, her lack of an inner circle of friends, were taken as snobbishness. Among her peers were many girls who came from wealth but who, for reasons of inheritance or business, were not as secure in their futures as Sophia. And so they resented her for what they saw as an ostentatious disinterest in the game of romantic calculation that they themselves were forced to play.

But on this night, in full view of the city's finest, Sophia Winston appeared transformed. She entered late, descending the grand staircase before hundreds of guests. There was a high color in her cheek, a marvelous complement to her close-fitting burgundy gown. And although her air of disinterest hadn't entirely disappeared, it was changed to a much more becoming distraction, as though she were waiting for someone who might appear at any moment. A number of the young men in attendance noticed her truly for the first time, and began to think that it might not be so terrible to marry for money. Sophia's mother saw the new consideration in their eyes and could not have been more pleased.

As for Sophia herself, she spent the evening in a daze of excitement, guilt, and rising disbelief at what she'd allowed to happen. It might all have been a dream, except for the insistent memory of her body. Thinking about it made her feel dizzy and panicked, so she pushed it to the furthest corner of her mind; but in the middle of a conversation it would come rushing back, making her blush and stammer and then ask the nearest young man if he might fetch her an ice.

By the end of the evening she was exhausted. She stood dutifully with her parents as the last guests drifted away into the night, and then retreated upstairs. She didn't expect him to still be there, but she was gripped anew by nervousness as she entered her bedroom.

The balcony was dark and empty. The rain that had threatened all day was falling at last, in a steady patter upon the garden.

Something glinted from the railing. Atop the polished granite sat a miniature golden pigeon, asleep in its filigree cage.

The rain transformed the city. It washed the filth from the sidewalks and reflected the gas lamps in puddles of clear water. It drummed on the taut awnings, and cascaded from gutters and overhangs into the near-empty streets. Midnight had long since come and gone, and even those with nowhere to go had taken shelter, in basement dives and the dark corners of tenement hallways.

The Djinni ran alone through the streets of New York.

He didn't need to be in danger. At any moment he could simply duck into a doorway and wait for the storm to end. But he wanted, more than anything, to keep running. He resolved that he would run until he reached Washington Street, or until his strength gave out, whichever came first.

After Sophia had left him, he'd spent some time standing on her balcony, contemplating the garden below, feeling a peace tenuous enough that he did not care to examine it too closely. Noises from the party drifted upward from the ballroom. On another night he might be tempted to investigate the opulent mansion while its inhabitants were busy in other rooms; but he sensed he'd tested his luck enough for one evening. On a whim he withdrew the golden birdcage from his pocket, and placed it on the balustrade where Sophia would surely find it. Why not? He had no special attachment to it, and it was a worthy gift, even for the daughter of such a wealthy home. Then, descending the way he'd come, he made his way to the street and turned south. Reaching the Elevated, he discovered that it had ceased operation for the night. He would have to walk the entire way back.

No matter. He was in a fine mood, and he would not tire from mere walking.

Then the rain began. At first it felt slightly invigorating, altogether different from the frightening prospect of total immersion. But then it started to rain harder, each drop striking him like a tiny blow, and he realized he'd underestimated the distance to Washington Street. He began to walk more quickly, and then to jog; and soon he was running into the rain, a grimace on his face that might have signified pleasure or pain. The rain struck his bare skin with a faint sizzle. If those few unlucky paupers and policemen still outdoors had taken the time to look, they would have seen a man running swiftly, silently, with wisps of steam streaming behind him.

Faster and faster he ran, cutting west and then south again. He began to feel a slow creeping enervation, a delicious laziness that whispered to him, telling him to simply lie down and let the rain painlessly take him. But he fought down the impulse and ran on, thinking of Arbeely's shop, and the ever-warm forge.

At last he found Washington Street, and raced past the deserted market at Fulton. The rain did not let up. His smooth gait became a stagger, and once he almost fell to his knees, but still he kept on. With the last of his strength, he ran the final blocks to Arbeely's shop.

Sam and Lulu's banquet had long since ended. With the plates cleared and the Faddouls' coffeehouse restored to its usual cheerful order, Arbeely had gone back to the forge to work, and to distract himself from his concern over the Djinni's disappearance. He felt faintly ridiculous, fretting like a mother hen. As afternoon stretched to evening, his concern became irritation, and then anger, and finally, when the rain began, out-right fear. He convinced himself that wherever the Djinni was, he was not so foolish as to be outside in a storm.

The door to the shop crashed open. The Djinni tumbled across the threshold and down the short flight of stairs, landing facedown on the floor.

"My God!" Arbeely ran to his side. The Djinni was unmoving. Curls of steam rose from his clothing. In a panic, Arbeely grabbed him by the shoulders and flipped him over.

The Djinni's eyes opened, and he grinned weakly up at his em-ployer. "Hello, Arbeely," he croaked. "I've had the most wonderful eve-ning."

8.

With the arrival of October, the summer weather departed for good. The leaves in Central Park barely had a chance to turn before they fell, to be raked by the gardeners into sodden heaps and carted away. A gray sky filled the gutters with cold, unending drizzle.

The busy corner of Allen and Delancey Streets, where Radzin's Bakery stood, was a moving patchwork of grays and browns. Pedestrians in shawls and overcoats trampled piles of garbage, their backs rounded against the wind. Greasy smoke rose from barrels on the edge of the street, where ragpickers and errand boys warmed their hands before moving on. But inside Radzin's the atmosphere was altogether different. The cold wind ended at the door, held back by a constant heat from the two enormous ovens at the rear of the shop. While their customers arrived stamping their feet and shivering, Moe Radzin worked the ovens in shirtsleeves and an apron, perspiration darkening his broad back. In the middle of the shop stood two large wooden tables perpetually coated with flour, where Thea Radzin and her assistants rolled and braided and kneaded and mixed. The display counter at the front of the bakery stretched nearly the width of the shop and was packed with ryes and wheat loaves and dinner rolls, sweet pastries and macaroons, and honey-sweet strudels stuffed with raisins. General opinion held that Radzin's bread was good enough for the price, but that their pastries were the best in the neighborhood.

The bakery lived by its daily rhythm. At five o'clock each morning, Moe Radzin unlocked the front door and swept the ashes from the ovens, laid new coals, and coaxed them to life. Thea arrived at five-thirty, along with their children, Selma and little Abie, who stumbled about, half-asleep. They uncovered the dough that had been rising overnight, punched it down, and set about shaping the day's first loaves. At six the assistants arrived: young Anna Blumberg, and Chava, the new girl.

Anna Blumberg was a source of some consternation to her employers. A tailor's daughter, she had left Cincinnati at sixteen and traveled alone to New York. She'd had vague plans of joining the Yiddish theater and becoming the next Sara Adler, but the city itself had been the real draw; and after two unsuccessful auditions she'd shrugged, given up, and looked about for a job. The Radzins had taken her on, and she'd become fast friends with the other two assistants. It was a major blow for Anna when the young women had left, one so soon after the other.

As far as Moe Radzin was concerned, the departures were a mixed blessing: it left him shorthanded, but he no longer had to endure the girls' constant gossip and flirtations. So when Radzin's old rabbi had come to see him soon after, along with a tall, solemn-looking greenhorn girl carrying a plate of homemade pastries, he wasn't sure whether to count this new development as blessing or curse.

Radzin was a man not given to the benefit of the doubt. He looked from the girl to the Rabbi, and decided that Meyer's story was at least partly a lie. The girl did seem to be in financial straits—her clothing was cheap and ill fitting, and she wore no jewelry at all—but the dead husband, he decided, was a fiction, or else beside the point. Most likely this was the Rabbi's impoverished mistress. But then, what did it matter? Men had their needs, even holy men. More to the point, if he hired her, the Rabbi would owe him a favor. And besides, her pastries were excellent.

Soon it became clear that the girl was quite a find. She was a dedicated worker and seemed never to tire. At first they had to remind her to take the occasional break. "We aren't slave drivers, dear," Thea Radzin told her on the first day, after the girl had worked for six hours without pause. The girl had smiled, embarrassed, and said, "I'm sorry. It's only that I enjoy the work so much, I don't want to stop."

Mrs. Radzin, usually so quick to find fault with her husband's hires, adored her from the start. Thea was a tough-skinned woman with a sentimental core, and the young widow's story played strongly to her sensibilities. One night Moe Radzin made the mistake of voicing his suspicions regarding the girl's relationship with the Rabbi, and in response his wife had blistered his ears with her opinion of his cynicism, his distrust, and, from there, his character in general. After that, Radzin kept his theories to himself. But even he had to admire the girl's unflagging energy. At times her hands seemed to move impossibly quickly, shaping rolls and twisting pretzels with uncanny precision, so that each was a mirror image of its neighbors. He'd had plans to fill the other empty position, but within days of the new girl's appearance the bakery was turning out its usual complement of goods. One less worker meant there was more space to move around, and they were saving nearly eleven dollars a week in salary. Radzin decided that his former assistants had been wasting even more time than he'd thought.

Only Anna refused to be won over. She'd been thrown into depression when her confidantes had left, and now this new girl seemed to think she was good enough to replace both of them. Of course the girl's story was wonderfully tragic, but even that dimmed in the face of her awkward silence and ostentatious diligence. Anna watched her work and knew that she herself was now the one who didn't measure up.

Anna would've been pleased to know that the Golem wasn't nearly so certain of herself as she appeared. Passing as human was a constant strain. After only a few weeks she looked back on that first day, when she'd worked six hours without stopping, and wondered how she could have been so careless, so naïve. It was all too easy for her to be caught up in the rhythm of the bakery, the thumps of fists on dough and the ringing of the bell over the door. Too easy to match it, and let it run away with her. She learned to make a deliberate mistake once in a while, and space the pastries a bit more haphazardly.

And then there were the customers, who kept their own rhythms and added their own complications. Each morning at six-thirty a small crowd would already be waiting for the bakery to open. Their thoughts pulled at the Golem as she worked: longings for the beds they had just vacated, and the warm arms of sleeping lovers; dread of the day before them, the bosses' orders and the back-breaking labor. And running below it all, the simple anticipation of a nice warm bun or a bagel, and maybe a sugar cookie for later. At lunchtime came the patrons in search of onion-studded bialys or thick slices of bread. Kerchiefed women with babies in tow would pause at the window outside, wondering what to buy for supper. Errand boys came in clutching hard-earned pennies, and left with macaroons and slices of honey cake. Young men and women courted each other slyly in line, casually mentioning a dance that a union group or *landsmanschaft* was putting on: *if you aren't doing anything maybe you can stop by; well, I'm awfully busy tonight, Frankie, but then maybe I will.*

The Golem heard all of it, their words and needs and desires and fears, simple and complex, helpless and easily solved. The impatient customers were the worst, the harried mothers who wanted only a loaf of bread and a quick escape before the children began howling for cookies. A few times the Golem even stepped away from her table toward these women, drawn to fetch whatever they wanted so they would leave. But then she'd catch herself, and stretch her fingers out and draw them in again—in the way that another woman might take a deep breath—and remind herself to be more careful.

Anna and Mrs. Radzin took turns seeing to the customers. Mrs. Radzin in particular was a model of efficiency at the counter, chatting quickly with them—*hello Mrs. Leib, is it challah for you today, and your mother, is she better, oh the poor dear, do you want with poppy seeds or without?* She filled orders almost without looking, monitoring the glass case as its contents dwindled, and anticipating what would need resupplying in the afternoon. After ten years at the bakery, the woman had a near-perfect sense of what would be popular on a given day and what wouldn't.

Anna, on the other hand, could barely remember what was on offer, let alone which items were running low. Her talents lay in a completely different direction. She'd discovered that standing behind a counter was, in its own way, as satisfying as being onstage. She had a smile for everyone, and complimented the women and admired the men, and made funny faces at the children. The Golem noticed how the customers' moods improved when Anna was at the till, and felt her own burst of envy. How did the girl do it? Was it a learned skill, or did it come to her naturally? She tried to imagine herself chatting and laughing with a roomful of strangers, completely at her ease. It seemed an impossible fantasy, like a child wishing for wings.

Thea Radzin had decreed that before the Golem could work at the counter she must learn the baking itself, and so for the first few weeks she was spared a turn at the register. But inevitably the afternoon came when Mrs. Radzin was out on an unexpected errand, and Anna had to visit the water closet; and Mr. Radzin turned from the ovens, gesturing at her with his chin. *Go on.*

She approached the register gingerly. She knew, in theory, what to do. The prices were all clearly posted, and there was no question of whether she could handle the numbers: she'd discovered she could tell at a glance how many cookies were on a baking sheet, or the value of a random handful of coins. It was the talking that frightened her. She imagined making some terrible, unforgivable mistake, and running away to hide under the Rabbi's bed.

At the front of the line was a stout woman in a knitted shawl, who stood scanning the rows of loaves. Over a dozen people were clustered behind her, their faces all turned toward the Golem. For a moment she quailed; but then, with an effort, she pulled her attention away to focus on the woman in the shawl. Immediately she knew the order as if the woman had said it out loud: *a rye bread, and a slice of strudel.*

"What would you like?" she asked the woman, feeling faintly ridiculous, since the answer was so plain.

"A loaf of rye," the woman said.

The Golem hesitated, waiting for the second half of the order. But the woman said nothing. "And perhaps some strudel?" she asked finally.

The woman laughed. "You caught me looking, did you? No, I have to watch my figure. I'm not the slip of a thing I used to be."

A few of the other customers were smiling now. Embarrassed, the Golem fetched the rye. Apparently she could assume nothing—even a desire as simple as a bakery order.

She gave the woman the rye, and made change for her nickel. The woman said, "You're new here, aren't you? I've seen you working in the back. What's your name?"

"Chava," said the Golem.

"Green as grass, aren't you? Don't worry, you'll be an American soon enough. Don't work this one too hard, Moe," she called to Mr. Radzin. "She doesn't look it, but she's delicate. I can tell these things."

Radzin snorted. "Delicate my foot. She can braid a dozen challahs in five minutes."

"Really?" The woman's eyebrows raised. "Then you'd better treat her well, hadn't you?"

He snorted again but made no other reply.

The woman smiled kindly. "Take care, Chavaleh." And she left, carrying her rye.

A heavy satchel slung across his back, Rabbi Meyer walked slowly up Hester Street toward his home, ignoring the dirty puddles that threatened to drown his shoes. It was late afternoon, and the cold and damp had taken on a wintry edge. He'd developed a cough when the weather turned, and now it nagged at him as he climbed his staircase. More troubling, he'd begun to experience strange moments of vertigo, when it seemed as though the ground had disappeared beneath him and he was spinning through the air. It would last only a few seconds, but it left him trembling and exhausted. His strength was ebbing away exactly when he needed it most.

His rooms were empty and chill, the sink stacked with dishes. Now that the Golem was living at a boardinghouse a few blocks away, all had returned to its former neglect. How quickly he'd grown used to a woman's presence. He felt oddly bereft now, going to bed each night without seeing her at her solitary post on the couch, gazing out the window at the passersby.

And yet. Time and again he wondered if he'd made a terrible error in judgment. Lately he'd spent nights lying awake and imagining what might happen, if through his carelessness the Golem harmed someone or was discovered. He pictured a mob descending on the Lower East Side and turning Jewish families out onto the street, looting synagogues and pulling old men about by their beards. It would be the very sort of pogrom they'd thought they'd left behind.

In these moments, submerged in his terrible thoughts, he was tempted to go to her boardinghouse and destroy her.

It would be easy to do: a single phrase, spoken aloud. Few still had the knowledge, and it was only by sheerest chance that he'd learned it. His yeshiva had been home to an ancient Kabbalist, half-mad and steeped in lore. The old man had taken a liking to sixteen-year-old Avram and adopted him as a sort of secret pupil, showing him mysteries that the other rabbis would occasionally hint at but dared not touch. Young Avram had been too excited by his special status to consider whether the knowledge might come to be a burden, instead of a gift.

In one of his final lessons, the old man gave Avram a lump of brownish red clay and bade him construct a golem. Avram shaped the clay into an approximation of a man six inches tall, with sausage-shaped arms and legs, and a round dull head with pinprick eyes and a shallow slash for a mouth. The old rabbi gave Avram a scrap of paper on which was written a brief phrase. Avram said the words, his heart pounding. Instantly the dark little thing sat up, looked around, and then stood and began to walk briskly about the tabletop. Its limbs bent oddly, without benefit of joints. Avram had made one leg too long, and the little golem moved with a lurching swagger, like a sailor newly ashore. It gave off a not-unpleasant whiff of freshly turned earth.

"Command it," the old rabbi said.

"Golem!" said Avram, and the doll-like thing pulled instantly to attention. "Jump up and down three times," Avram said. The golem executed three small hops, reaching about an inch off the table. Avram grinned with excitement. "Touch your head with your left hand," he said, and the golem did so, a toy soldier saluting its commander.

Avram cast about for something else for the golem to do. In a corner near the desk, a brown spider sat lazily spinning a web between two discarded bottles. "Kill that spider," he said, pointing.

The golem leapt off the desk and fell to the floor. It picked itself up and scampered to the corner. Avram followed it, holding a candle aloft. The spider, sensing the golem's approach, tried to scramble away; but the golem was on top of it in a dark blur, scattering the bottles and smashing the spider with its crude fist. Avram watched his creation attack the spider again and again until it was little more than a damp mark on the yeshiva floor. And still the golem went on attacking.

"Golem, stop," Avram said in a thin voice. The golem glanced up briefly, but then resumed smearing the spider's remains into the ground. "*Stop*," he repeated in a louder voice, but now the golem didn't even look at him. Avram felt a rising panic.

Silently the old rabbi passed him another slip of paper, with another phrase. Gratefully he took it and read it aloud.

The little golem burst apart in midswing. A small shower of dirt rained down among the bottles and the dead spider. Then, blessed silence.

"Once a golem develops a taste for destruction," the old rabbi said, "little can stop it save the words that destroy it. Not all golems are as crude or stupid as this one, but all share the same essential nature. They are tools of man, and they are dangerous. Once they have disposed of their enemies they will turn on their masters. They are creatures of last resort. Remember that."

He'd thought about his crude golem for a long time afterward, haunted by the image of the small creature in its frenzy of violence. Had he done wrong to animate it in the first place? How much did a spider's life count for in the eyes of God? He'd trod on spiders all his life; why did this death feel so different? He had atoned for both golem and spider at Yom Kippur that year, and for years afterward. Gradually, his everyday slights toward kin and colleagues had crowded the incident from his prayers, but he'd never been able to dismiss it entirely. In that room, he had commanded life and death, and later he'd wondered why the Almighty had allowed him to do so. But the purpose of the lesson became clear on the day when the Rabbi spied, walking through Orchard Street's riotous crowd, a tall woman in a wool coat and a dirty dress, who carried in her wake the scent of freshly turned earth.

No matter how much he was tempted, he knew that he couldn't destroy her. She was an innocent, and not to blame for her own existence. He still believed this, no matter how much his fear tried to convince him otherwise. It was the real reason why he had named her Chava: from *chai*, meaning life. To remind himself.

No, he could not destroy her. But perhaps there was another way.

He sat at the parlor table, opened the leather satchel, and withdrew a stack of books and loose papers. The books were old and time-eaten, their spines and bindings cracking. The loose papers were covered with notes in the Rabbi's own hand, copied from those books that had been too fragile to move. He'd spent the morning—had spent weeks of mornings, now—walking from synagogue to synagogue, making excuses to drop in on old friends, fellow rabbis he hadn't seen in years. He took tea, inquired after their families, listened to stories of fading health and congregational scandals. And then, he asked for a small favor. Would he be able to spend a few minutes in his friend's private library? No, there was no particular book he was looking for—just a question of interpretation, a particularly thorny issue that he meant to solve for a former congregant. A matter of some delicacy.

It raised their suspicions, of course. As rabbis they'd all seen every sort of conundrum that a congregation could throw at them, and there were few problems that couldn't be discussed in confidence, as a hypothetical if nothing else. Rabbi Meyer's request suggested something else, something disturbing.

But they acquiesced and left their offices to give their friend some time alone; and when they returned, he was gone. A note left folded on a desk or chair would inform them that he'd remembered an appointment, and must apologize for leaving so suddenly. Also, he'd found an interesting book that shed some light on his situation, and had been so bold as to borrow it. He would return it, the note assured them, within a few weeks. And when the rabbis searched their bookcases for the missing book, invariably—and to little surprise—they found that he'd taken the most dangerous volume they owned, the one they'd always meant to destroy but never quite could. Often the book had been hidden, but the Rabbi had managed to find it anyway.

It made them all deeply uneasy. What could Meyer possibly want with that knowledge? But they said nothing, to a man. There was desperation in Meyer's evasions and near-thefts, and they began to feel a guilty relief that he hadn't brought them into his confidence. If the book could help, so be it. They could only pray that whatever problem Meyer was facing would be taken care of as soon as possible.

The Rabbi put water on to boil for his tea, and prepared a meager supper: challah and schmaltz, a bit of herring, a few half-sour pickles, a drop of schnapps for later. He was not particularly hungry, but he would need the strength. He ate slowly, clearing his mind, preparing himself. And then he set the dishes aside, opened the first book, and began to work.

At six o'clock Thea Radzin turned the sign in the bakery window from OPEN to CLOSED. The dough for the next morning's loaves was set out to rise, the tables wiped down, the floor swept clean. The leftover goods were put aside, to be sold at cut rate the next day. At last the Radzins, Anna, and the Golem all filed out the back door and went their separate ways.

The Golem's boardinghouse was a creaking clapboard building that had somehow evaded demolition. It sat incongruously among Broome Street's modern tenements, an old lady sandwiched between hulking toughs. The Golem opened the front door quietly, went past the damp and faded parlor, and headed upstairs. Her room was on the second floor, facing the street. It was no larger than the Rabbi's parlor, but it was her own, a fact that made her excited, proud, and lonely all at once. There was a narrow bed, a small writing desk, a cane-bottomed chair, and a tiny armoire. She would have preferred to do without the bed, since she had no need of it, but a room without a bed would certainly raise questions.

For the room she paid seven dollars per week. To any other working girl with her salary, this would have been near impossible. But the Golem had no other expenses. She bought no food, and never went out, except to the bakery, and to visit the Rabbi once a week. Her only other expenditure had been to fill out her wardrobe. She now owned a few changes of shirtwaist and skirt, along with a dress of plain gray wool. She'd also bought a full complement of ladies' undergarments, and, when the weather turned cold, a woolen cloak. For these expenses, as well as the burden of washing them that fell to her landlady, she felt obscurely guilty. She had no real *need* for any of it. The cloak especially was for show. She felt the October cold and damp, but it didn't bother her; it was merely another sensation. The cloak, on the other hand, scratched at her neck and trapped her arms. She would have been happier to walk down the street in only her shirtwaist and skirt.

All of the boardinghouse tenants received a small breakfast each morning, left outside their door: a cup of tea, two slices of toast, and a boiled egg. The tea she poured into the water-closet sink when no one was around. The toast and boiled egg she wrapped in a piece of waxed paper and gave to the first hungry child she passed on her way to the bakery. She didn't have to do this; she had discovered that she could, in fact, eat. On one of her last nights at the Rabbi's, curiosity and boredom had overcome her lingering trepidation, and she decided to ingest a small piece of bread. She'd sat at the table staring at it, building courage, and then carefully placed it in her mouth. It sat on her tongue, strangely heavy. Moisture welled up around it. It tasted like it smelled, only more so. She opened and closed her mouth, and the bread grew damp and broke into smaller pieces. It seemed to be working, but how could she be sure? She chewed until there was nothing left but a paste, then gathered it all to the back of her mouth and worked her throat to swallow. The bread slid down her throat, encountering no resistance. She stayed at the table for hours, slightly nervous with the anticipation of *something*. But to her slight disappointment, the night passed without incident. The next afternoon, however, she felt a strange cramp in her lower abdomen. Hesitant to leave—the halls were crowded with neighbors, and the Rabbi was out on an errand—she fetched a large bowl from the kitchen, then bunched up her skirts, pulled down her underclothes, and expelled into the bowl a small amount of mashed bread, seemingly unaltered by its journey. When the Golem later excitedly described to the Rabbi what had happened, he turned a bit red and congratulated her on her discovery, and then asked her not to do it again.

The act of eating proved useful at the bakery, as she learned to make adjustments based on taste, and to eat a pastry occasionally as the others did. But it was hard not to feel each prop—the cloak and the toast and the quickly eaten pastries—as a small pang, a constant reminder of her otherness.

It was early evening still. An entire night stretched before her. She opened her armoire, and removed her gray dress. From beneath her bed she withdrew her small sewing box and scissors. Settling herself in the cane chair, she began to pick the dress apart at the seams. Within minutes it had become a small heap of fabrics. The buttons she laid carefully on the desk, to save for last. She had devised this occupation soon after coming to the boardinghouse, when she'd spent an evening so dull that she'd resorted to counting things to pass the time. She'd counted the tassels on her lamp shade (eighteen) and the number of boards in the floor (two hundred forty-seven), and had opened the armoire in search of more things to count, when her gaze fell on the dress. She removed it from the armoire and studied how it was made. It seemed simple enough: the large panels that connected at the seams, the darts that shaped the bosom. Her sharp eyes took in each element, and then she set to work, uncreating and then creating it again.

It was a pleasant occupation, sewing. She reconstructed the dress slowly, making it last, her stitches as short and even as a machine's. When she finished it was almost four in the morning. She stripped to her underclothes and slipped the dress over her head, buttoning it with quick fingers. She smoothed down the front of the dress and eyed her reflection in the window. It was not an entirely flattering dress—it hung loosely from her shoulders, as though made for a larger woman—but it had cost little and seemed to cover her appropriately. She took it off and hung it back in the armoire, and put on a fresh shirtwaist and skirt. Then she blew out the lamp, lay down on the bed, closed her eyes, and waited for the day to begin.

9.

It took the Djinni nearly a week to recover from his run through the rain. He spent the time working in the shop as though nothing had happened, but he was paler than usual, and moved more slowly, and stayed close to the heat of the forge. He declared that his adventure had been worth the ordeal. Arbeely, however, was furious.

"You could have been caught!" yelled the tinsmith. "The girl's servants could have found you, or worse, her family! What if they'd trapped you there and called the police?"

"I would've escaped," the Djinni said.

"Yes, I suppose you'd think little of handcuffs, or a prison cell. But think of me, if not yourself. What if the police had chased you here, to my shop? I would have been dragged to prison as well. And I can't melt through iron bars, my friend."

The Djinni frowned. "Why would *you* be arrested?"

"Don't you understand? The police would round up everyone in Little Syria, if the Winstons demanded it." He covered his face with his hands. "My God, Sophia Winston! You'll bring the whole city down upon us." A thought occurred to him. "You aren't thinking of going *back*, are you?"

The Djinni smiled. "Perhaps. I haven't decided." Arbeely only groaned.

But there was no denying that the Djinni's mood was vastly improved. He began to work more quickly, and with enthusiasm. The encounter—and perhaps the danger—had returned something of him to himself. Soon the shelves of the back room were cleared of dented pitchers and scorched pots. With his apprentice handling the repair work, Arbeely was free to take on larger orders for new cookware. The weather turned colder, the nights longer; and one day, while entering

October's orders and expenses on his ledger, Arbeely realized to his great shock that he was no longer poor.

"Here," he said, giving the Djinni a number of bills. "This belongs to you."

The Djinni stared at the handful of paper. "But this goes beyond our agreement."

"Take it. This is your success as well as mine."

"What should I do with it?" the Djinni asked, nonplussed.

"It's long past time you found yourself somewhere to stay. Nothing too ostentatious—no glass palaces, if you please."

The Djinni followed Arbeely's advice and took a room in a nearby tenement. It was larger than Arbeely's—though not by much—and on the top floor, so that at least he could see over the rooftops. He outfitted the room with a number of large cushions, which he scattered about the floor. On the walls he hung a profusion of small mirrors and candle sconces, so that at night the candlelight would reflect from wall to wall, and make the room seem larger than it was. But he could not quite trick himself; even if his eyes were deceived, he felt the closeness of the room like an itch on his skin.

He took to spending more of his nights out on the streets, exploring. When the streets felt too confining he would travel the rooftops, which were like a city unto themselves, populated with groups of men who huddled together around fire-barrels, sharing cigarettes and whiskey. He tended to avoid conversation, only nodding at their greetings; but one evening, curiosity overcame his reserve, and he asked an Irish laborer if he could try his cigarette. The man shrugged and handed it over. The Djinni placed the cigarette in his mouth and drew in a gust of air. The cigarette disappeared into ash. The men around them goggled, then burst out laughing. The Irishman rolled another, and asked the Djinni to show how he had accomplished the trick; but the Djinni only shrugged and then inhaled more gently, and the new cigarette burned as theirs did. All agreed that the first cigarette must have been faulty somehow.

After that, the Djinni was rarely without tobacco and rolling papers. He appreciated the taste of the tobacco, and the warmth of the smoke in his body. But to the puzzlement of all who stopped him on the street to ask, he never carried matches.

One night he returned to the park at Castle Garden, where he had stood at the railing with Arbeely that first afternoon, and discovered the aquarium. It was an otherworldly place, both fascinating and unnerving. After melting the front-door padlock off its hasp, he stood for hours in front of the gigantic water-tanks, staring at the long, dark shapes that glided inside. He'd never seen fish before, and he wandered from tank to tank, enthralled by the variety—this one large and gray and sleek finned, that one flat as a coin and gaily striped. He studied the rippling gills and tried to guess at their purpose. He placed his hands on the smooth glass of the tank and felt the weight of the water behind it. If he heated the glass enough to shatter it, the water would kill him in an instant; and a thrill coursed through him, the same a man might feel if he stood on the edge of a high cliff and half-dared himself to jump. He returned again and again, nearly every night for a week, until the staff posted a guard. Their strange burglar never seemed to steal anything, but they'd grown sick of replacing the locks.

He was becoming a familiar figure among the nocturnal population of southern Manhattan: a tall, handsome man who wore no hat or overcoat, and who surveyed his surroundings with a detached, bemused air, like a visiting dignitary. The policemen found him particularly puzzling. In their experience, a man roaming the streets at night was generally looking for a drink, a fight, or a woman, but he seemed interested in none of these. They might have thought him an uptown gent slumming in costume, which happened sometimes; but when he spoke to them, which was rare, it was in an accented English far from that of the New York swell. Someone suggested he might be a high-class gigolo, but then why would he be trawling the streets like a two-penny whore? Finally, their speculations exhausted, they categorized him as a miscellaneous oddity. One of them took to calling him the Sultan, and the nickname stuck.

On rainy nights, the Djinni stayed in his tenement room and occupied himself by practicing his metalwork. He was now making regular trips to the Bowery storefront where he purchased gold and silver, and fashioned them into small birds of every kind. He made a kestrel, with its wings outspread, building the sculpture from the base upward to distribute the weight evenly. He sculpted a silver peacock and decorated its tail feathers with melted gold, painting it onto the cooled silver with a straw from Arbeely's broom. Soon he had amassed a half-dozen of these sculptures, all in various states of completion.

The month lengthened, and it began to rain nearly every night. Sick of his sculptures, the Djinni took to working all night in the forge, or else merely pacing his room, waiting for sunlight. What, he wondered, was the point of emerging from the flask, if he was only to be caged again?

Finally, on a night in early November, the rain ended and the sky cleared, revealing a few weary stars hanging above the gas lamps. The Djinni walked through the streets with swift relief. He traveled north and east, choosing his turns at random, enjoying the cold air on his face. The restlessness of his pent-up nights had turned him lonely; and now, without quite consciously willing it, he found himself heading for the Winston mansion.

It was early enough that the Elevated was still running. The Djinni purchased his ticket and waited with the crowd; but when the train came, instead of boarding he stepped between two cars, onto the metal platform above the coupling. He braced himself and held on as the train lurched away. It was a wild, giddy ride. The noise was deafening, a rattle and screech that penetrated his entire body. Sparks from the track leapt past, blown by a violent wind. Lamp-lit windows flashed by in bright, elongated squares. At Fifty-ninth Street he jumped out from between the cars, his body still shaking.

It was past midnight now, and the genteel thoroughfare of Fifth Avenue was nearly deserted. He reached the Winston mansion and found that the hole he had created in the fence had been repaired. He wondered what they had made of that, and smiled to think of their consternation.

He removed the same two bars, and stepped through. The garden was dark and silent, the windows on the upper stories unlit. Climbing to Sophia's room was even easier, now that he knew the route. In a matter of minutes he was standing on her balcony, gazing through the beveled glass.

Sophia lay in her bed, asleep. He watched her chest rise and fall beneath the covers, piled deeply against the night's chill. He placed a hand on the door handle. To his surprise the door moved under his hand. She had left it open—only a crack, but open.

The hinges were well oiled, and silent. Slowly he opened the door just wide enough to pass through, and then closed it again. His eyes adjusted to the dark of the room. Sophia's face was turned toward him, her hair tangled across her pillow. He felt an unexpected pang of guilt at the thought of waking her.

After so long spent in his cramped room, the space felt shockingly large and opulent. The walls were upholstered in a fine, dove-gray fabric. An enormous, ornate armoire took up most of one wall. A porcelain washing basin and a pitcher of water rested on a marble-topped table next to the bed. Under his feet was a white rug, made from the hide of something large and furry. A nearby movement startled him—but it was his own reflection, multiplied in a three-paned mirror. The mirror was set on top of a narrow dressing table covered with bottles, gilt-backed brushes, small delicate boxes, and other trinkets—including the bird in its cage, looking a bit lost amid the clutter.

He went to the dressing table and examined the mirror. Its quality was exceptional, with no flaws or distortions. He wondered at the technique; even had he all his powers, he never could have achieved such precision. Then his attention turned from the mirror to his own face reflected in it. He'd seen it before, of course, but never so clearly. A broad forehead. Dark eyes, set below dark eyebrows. A chin that came to a rounded point. A strongly angled nose. Strange, that this was truly he. In his old life, he'd never concerned himself about physical appearance; he'd merely thought *jackal* and become one, giving no thought to the particulars. He had nothing against the face in the mirror; he supposed his features were pleasing enough, and he was certainly aware of the effect they had on others. So why did he feel as though he'd been robbed of some essential choice?

Movement behind him, and a gasp: Sophia was sitting up in bed, staring at him, her face white. "It's only me," he whispered quickly.

"Ahmad." One hand had raised in fright. She sighed now, and let it drop to the covers. "What are you doing here?"

"Your door was open." It came out awkwardly, like an excuse.

She looked to the door, as if puzzled at its betrayal. But then she said, "I started leaving it open. After . . ." She rubbed her eyes, took a deep breath, and started again. "For a week I barely slept. I left the door open every night. And then, I decided you weren't coming back. Some days I tried to convince myself I'd imagined the whole thing." She said the words quietly, without emotion. "But I never could, quite."

"Should I leave?"

"Yes," she said. "No. I don't know." She rubbed her eyes again, but now the gesture spoke of some inner conflict. She stood from the bed and drew a dressing gown about herself, keeping some distance between them. She regarded him. "Why *did* you come back now, after so long?"

"To see you again." It sounded insufficient even to his own ears.

She laughed once, quietly. "To *see* me. I thought it might be for something else."

He frowned. This was growing ridiculous. "If you want me to leave, you only need to say—"

But in one brief moment she crossed the distance between them. Her arms slid around him and her lips covered his, ending his words, and then his thoughts.

This time she allowed him to carry her to the bed.

Afterward they lay together, beneath the tangled covers, and he held her. The sweat of her body pricked at his skin. Slowly his thoughts came back. It was strange: this second tryst had been more satisfying physically—they'd had more time to explore and respond to each other, and let their pleasure build—but he found he preferred their first. Danger and transgression had charged that encounter. Now, lying in this gigantic bed with its drapes and covers, his lover half-asleep in his arms, he felt merely out of place.

"You are so very warm," she murmured. He trailed a hand idly across her hip and said nothing. He could hear small movements in the house—a servant walking downstairs, the creaking of pipes. Out beyond the garden, a horse went by at a slow trot, its hooves ringing distantly against stone. He felt, against his will, his restlessness begin to resurface.

She turned in his arms, nestling into his chest. Her hair tickled his shoulder; he brushed a few strands away. Her hand came up to entwine with his, and found the iron cuff. He stiffened.

"I hadn't noticed this," she said. Her head came up from his chest as she examined it. He felt her tug at the slender chain that held the pin. "It's stuck," she said.

"It doesn't open."

"Then you always wear this?"

"Yes."

"But it's like something a slave might wear."

He didn't answer. He didn't want to discuss it, not in this room; not with her.

She rose to one elbow above him, her expression worried and frankly curious. "Ahmad, were you a slave? Is that what this means?"

"It's none of your concern!"

The words rang sharply between them. She flinched and pulled away.

"I'm sorry," she said, her voice edged with hurt. "I didn't mean to pry."

He sighed inwardly. She was only a child, and it was not her fault. "Come here," he said, and reached for her. After a moment she relented, and drew in close, returning her head to his chest.

He asked, "Have you ever heard of the djinn?"

"You used that word before," she said. "Is that the same as a genie? When I was young I had a picture book, about a genie who was trapped in a bottle. A man released him, and the genie gave the man three wishes."

Trapped. Released. If he winced at the words, she didn't notice. He said, "Yes, the djinn can become trapped. And sometimes they have it in their power to grant wishes, though that is very rare. But every one of them is made of a spark of fire, in the way that men are made of flesh and bone. They can take the shape of any animal. And some of them, the strongest, have the power to enter a man's dreams." He glanced down at her. "Should I go on?"

"Yes," she said, her breath warm on his chest. "Tell me the story."

He said, "Many, many years ago, there was a man, a human king, named Sulayman. He was very powerful, and very canny. He gathered the knowledge of the human wizards and increased it tenfold, and soon he'd learned enough to gain control over all the djinn, from the highest, most powerful to the lowest, meanest *ghul*. He could summon any of them at whim, and give them tasks to do. He made one djinn bring him the most beautiful jewels in all the land, and made another fetch endless basins of water to feed the gardens of his palaces. If he wanted to travel, he would sit on a beautiful woven carpet, and four of the fastest djinn would pick it up and carry it with them as they flew."

"The flying carpet," Sophia murmured. "That was in the story."

He went on, his voice a whisper, his words all but swallowed by the hush of the room. "The humans revered Sulayman, and long after his death they still spoke of him as the greatest of kings. But the djinn resented Sulayman's power over them. When he died, and his knowledge was scattered to the winds, they rejoiced at their freedom. But it was rumored among the oldest of the djinn that one day, the lost knowledge would be found. Mankind, they said, would again be able to bind even the strongest djinni to its will. It was only a matter of time."

He stopped. The story had poured out of him—he could not recall ever speaking so much at once.

Sophia stirred. "And then?" she whispered. "Ahmad, and then what?"

He stared up at the flat white ceiling. *Yes*, he thought, *and then what?* How could he explain how he'd been bested, when he himself didn't know? He'd pictured it often enough: a spectacular battle, the valley shuddering and the walls of his palace cracking as he traded blows with his foe. He imagined—he *hoped*—that it had been a close contest, that perhaps the wizard had even been gravely injured. Could that be why he had no memory of it? Had he won in the end, but too late? The frustration of *not knowing* coiled inside him like a viper. And how would Sophia ever understand? To her it would be a child's tale. A dead legend, from long ago.

"That's all," he said at last. "I don't know how it ends."

Silence. He felt her disappointment in the tension of her body, the changing of her breath. As if it had mattered to her, somehow.

After a moment she pulled away from him, to lie on her back. "I'm sorry, but you can't be here in the morning," she said.

"I know. I'll leave soon."

"I'm engaged," she said suddenly.

"Engaged?"

"To be married."

He took that in. "Is he to your liking?"

"I suppose so. Everyone says it's a good match. We'll be married next year."

He waited to feel jealousy; none came.

They lay together for a few minutes more, their bodies separated, only their hands brushing. Her breathing grew more even; he surmised that she was asleep. Carefully he rose from the bed and began to dress himself. Dawn wouldn't break for hours yet, but he wanted to be gone. The thought of lying motionless next to her for hours was more than he could bear. The button of his shirt cuff caught on the chain at his wrist, and he cursed under his breath.

When he straightened from dressing, he saw that she was watching him. "Will you come again?" she asked.

"Do you want me to?"

"Yes," she said.

"Then I will," he said, turning to leave; and he did not know if either or both of them were lying.

Night fell in the Syrian Desert, a cold spring night. Earlier that day, a lone Bedouin girl and her doting father had both looked down into the valley, and seen a shining palace that could not possibly be there. And now, lying in her family's tent beneath a pile of hides and blankets, Fadwa began to dream an unusual dream.

It started with a mix of images and emotions, at once portentous and meaningless. She glimpsed familiar faces: her mother, her father, her cousins. At one point she seemed to be flying across the desert, in pursuit of someone. Or was she being chased? And then it shifted, and she was in the middle of an enormous caravan, hundreds of men marching through the desert, on foot and on horseback, their eyes dark and stern. She walked among them, jumping up and down and shouting, but they took no notice, and her voice was only a thin echo. She realized that this was the caravan that her father had seen when he was a young boy. It had been there all this time, traveling on its endless path. But now it was herself, not the caravan, that was the phantom.

An unnamed fright filled her. She had to stop the caravan. She stepped directly in front of one of the men, bracing herself, clenching her fists. The impact knocked her off her feet as easily as if she were made of nothing at all.

She spun, and fell. Dizziness took hold of her. Finally she landed with a jarring thump and lay sprawled on the ground, gripping cool, sandy soil between her fingers. She waited for the whirling to stop, and opened her eyes.

A solitary man was standing over her.

She staggered to her feet and took a few steps backward, wiping the dirt from her hands. He was not one of the caravan men. He wore no traveling-clothes, only a spotless white robe. He stood taller even than her father. She searched his features, and did not recognize him. His face was bare, not even a hint of a beard; and to her eyes it gave him a strikingly androgynous appearance, despite his obvious masculinity. Could he see her, unlike the caravan men? He smiled at her, a knowing smile, and then turned and walked away.

It was clear he wanted her to follow him, and so she did, making no effort to muffle her footsteps. A full moon was rising over the valley, though some part of her knew it couldn't be so—in the waking world the moon was waning, close to new.

She followed him to the edge of a small hill, where he paused, waiting for her. She drew to his side, and realized that they were standing on the crest where she'd seen the mirage. And indeed, there in the valley beneath them was the palace, whole and solid and beautiful, its curves and spires glowing in the moonlight.

"This is a dream," she said.

"True," said the man. "But the palace is there regardless. You saw it, this morning. And so did your father."

"But he told me he saw nothing."

The man cocked his head, as if thinking. The world spun again—and then she was down in the valley below, looking back at where she'd just been. It was daylight. Her father was standing on the crest. She knew it was him even from this distance; and she could see, with eyes somehow stronger than her own, the shock and fear on his face. He blinked, and then backed away from the hillside; and Fadwa felt a quick stab of hurt at his lie.

She turned back toward the tall man, and day melted once more into night. In the impossible moonlight she studied him with a frankness she never would have shown when awake. Distant pinpricks of golden red flickered in his dark eyes.

"What are you?" she asked.

"A djinni," he said.

She nodded. It was the only answer that made sense.

"You aren't afraid?" he asked.

"No," she said, though she knew she should be. This was a dream, but not a dream. She looked down and saw her own hands before her, felt the cool earth under her bare feet; but she could also feel her other body, her sleeping body, sheltered in the warmth of blankets and hides. She existed in both places at once, and neither seemed more real than the other.

"What is your name?" he asked.

Her back straightened. "I am Fadwa, daughter of Jalal ibn Karim, of the Hadid."

He bowed, matching her solemnity, though with a hint of a smile.

"What do you want from me?" she asked.

"Only to talk. I mean you no harm. You interest me, you and your kind."

He leaned back on a deep cushion, his eyes still watching her. She looked around, surprised. They were in an enormous glass room. Moonlight shone through the curving walls, bathing the floors a bright silver-blue. Rugs and sheepskins were scattered across the floor. She and the man were facing each other, seated on cushions of a beautiful weave.

"This is your palace," she said, realizing. "It's beautiful."

"Thank you."

"But why bring me here? I thought that the djinn feared humans."

He smiled. "We do, but only because we're taught to."

"We're taught to fear you as well," said Fadwa. "We aren't supposed to whistle after dark, because it might attract you. We pin iron amulets on our clothes, and tie iron beads painted blue around babies' necks, for protection."

"Why blue?" he asked, puzzled.

She thought. "I'm not sure. Are you afraid of blue?"

He laughed. "No. It's a good enough color. Iron, though"—and he bowed to her, a dip of the head—"that I do fear."

She smiled, amused at his double meaning, for the word for iron was *hadid*.

Her host—her guest?—was watching her. "Tell me about yourself," he said. "What is your life like? How do you spend your days?"

The intensity of his gaze flustered her. "You should ask my father, or one of my uncles," she said. "Their lives are much more interesting."

"Perhaps someday I will," he said. "But now, everything is interesting to me. All is new. So, please. Tell me."

He seemed sincere. The soothing glow of moonlight, the delicious warmth of her other, sleeping body, a handsome man's gratifying attention—all conspired to put her at ease. She relaxed onto her cushion and said, "I wake early in the morning, before the sunrise. The men leave to tend the sheep, and my aunts and I milk the goats. With the milk we make cheese, and yogurt. I spend the day weaving, and mending clothing, and baking bread. I fetch water and collect firewood. I watch out for my brothers and my cousins, and bathe and dress them, and make sure they don't get into trouble. I help my mother cook the evening meal, and serve it when the men return."

"So much activity! And how often do you do these things?"

"Every day," she said.

"*Every* day? Then you never simply go about, and see the desert?"

"Of course not!" she said, surprised by his ignorance. "The women must take care of the home, while the men are busy with the sheep and the goats. Although," she said with a hint of pride, "my father does let me tend a few goats, from time to time, when the weather is good. And sometimes we women must do men's work as well as our own. If a tent collapses in the wind, a woman's arms will lift it the same as a man's. And when we move our encampment, then all must work together."

She paused. Far away, that other body, her sleeping self, was stirring. In the distance she heard the sounds of the morning: a child's yawn, footsteps, a baby mewling with hunger. The glass walls of the palace were growing dim and distant.

"It seems I must go," the man said. "But will you speak to me again?"

"Yes," she said, without hesitation. "When?"

"Soon," he said. "Now, wake."

He bent over her, and his lips brushed her forehead. She felt it, somehow, in both waking and sleeping selves; and a thrill ran through her, down to her bones.

Then she was awake, staring up at the familiar walls of her tent, which were billowing in a breeze that felt strangely warm for a spring morning.

The details of the dream soon faded, as all dreams must. But certain things remained clear. Her father's face as he glimpsed the impossible palace. The way the moonlight had picked out the angles and hollows of the man's face. The searing touch of his lips on her skin. And his promise, that he would come again.

If, that day, Fadwa smiled to herself more than usual—the way a girl might if she were thinking on a secret—then her mother did not notice.

IO.

Damp winds blew through the forest outside the city of Konin. In his dilapidated shack, Yehudah Schaalman sat in a half-rotted arm-chair, an old blanket about his shoulders. Dead leaves and scraps of paper skittered across the dirt floor. The fire in the hearth guttered and spat, and Schaalman found himself wondering: what was the weather like in New York? Were Otto Rotfeld and his golem sitting by their own fire, blissfully whiling away the hours? Or had the furniture maker already tired of his clay wife and destroyed her?

He caught himself, and scowled. Why this unending preoccupation with Rotfeld? Usually he spared no second thought for his customers and their illicit acts. He took their money, gave them what they wanted, and slammed the door in their faces. What made this one so different?

Perhaps it was the golem. He'd worked hard on that creature, much harder than he usually did for someone else's benefit. It had been a pleas-ing puzzle, to bring Rotfeld's disparate requests together in one creation, and he'd regretted that he wouldn't see it brought to life. Though likely that was for the best, given the unpredictable nature of golems in gen-eral. Far safer to be on the other side of the ocean, and not with Rotfeld when he reached New York and woke his bride.

Scowling again, he resisted the urge to shake his head like a dog. He had no time for this. Rotfeld's money was nearly gone, and even with all his studies he was still no closer to his quarry, the secret of unending life.

Beneath the straw-stuffed bed in one corner of the shack was a locked chest, and inside that chest was the sheaf of papers he'd taken from a burnt synagogue, long ago. The brittle fragments were now in-terleaved with fresh pages on which Schaalman had written formulas, diagrams, observations, trying to fill in the gaps in his knowledge. It was both a chronicle of his studies and a diary of his travels. After that day in the synagogue, he'd wandered from town to town, shtetl to shtetl, through the Kingdom of Prussia to the Austrian Empire to Russia and back, searching for the missing pieces. In Kraków he had sought out a woman rumored to be a witch, stolen her knowledge, and turned her mute to keep her from cursing him. One spring he'd been chased from a Russian village after every pregnant ewe within three leagues gave birth to a two-headed lamb. Someone had thought to accuse the strange Jew of witchcraft—rightly, as it happened, though in their zeal they'd also chased out a harmless old midwife and the village idiot. In Lvov he'd visited an old rabbi on his deathbed, and taken on the guise of one of the *shedim*, the demon-children of Lilith, escaped from Gehenna to torture him. In this way he forced the terrified rabbi to reveal that he'd once seen a formula for something called the Water of Life. But when Schaalman pressed him for more, the old rabbi's heart had burst. Schaalman watched the rabbi's soul pass beyond his reach, and he'd howled with anger and frustration, looking even more like a demon from Gehenna than before.

After that he'd mostly ceased his wanderings, and settled close to Konin. He was growing too old; the roads were full of dangers, and he couldn't dodge them all. But always, always, every day, he drew closer to the death he was desperate to avoid.

Staring into the fire, he made his decision. He couldn't afford to spend the winter brooding over an ill-mannered furniture maker. Best to scratch the itch, and be done with it.

He stood and put on an ancient overcoat, wincing as his bones creaked. From his workbench he fetched a wide basin and went outside. An unseasonable snow had fallen in the night. Kneeling, he scraped heaping handfuls of snow into the basin. Returning to his shack, Schaalman placed the basin near the hearth and watched as the snow slumped and melted. He wished it hadn't come to this. When the last crystals disappeared, Schaalman pulled the water-filled basin from the hearth. He fetched the broken book from its chest and leafed through the relevant pages, checking that he had remembered the formula correctly. From a leather purse he took one of the coins with which Rotfeld had paid him.

Then he sat cross-legged on the dirt floor, in front of the basin of water. Gripping the coin tightly in his left hand, he muttered a long incantation. With his right hand he carefully picked up the basin. Another incantation, a deep breath—and then he leaned back and tipped the basin over his head.

The shock of frigid water on his face—

And then he was gone, he was elsewhere.

There was an immense weight on his chest. An eternity of water lay above him, pushing down, breaking his body and grinding his bones. He had never been so cold. He felt the nibblings of a thousand tiny teeth. A sucking blackness stretched in every direction.

The corner of his mind that was still Schaalman realized that Rotfeld had never even made it to America. All that toil, and for nothing. Unwoken, the Golem would have fallen apart by now, an unclaimed wooden crate filled with moldering earth and a soiled dress. A pity.

And then, unexpectedly, the scene changed.

The weight above him was gone. He was no longer buried beneath the ocean but flying above it, moving low and fast, faster than any bird. Shifting water disappeared behind him, mile after mile. The wind roared in his ears.

In the distance a city grew.

He rose higher as he approached until he was floating far above it. The city was spread across a hemmed-in island. Towers and church spires pointed up at him like lances.

He stared down at the narrow streets and saw that this city was also a labyrinth. And like all labyrinths, it hid something precious at its heart. What did it hide?

A voiceless voice whispered the answer.

Life unending.

Schaalman surfaced, coughing. The basin lay upside down on the floor. Freezing water dripped from his face and clothes. His left fist burned: the coin had turned colder than ice.

For the rest of the day he lay huddled and shivering on his bed, wrapped in every blanket and rug he owned. His joints ached and his frostbitten palm sent jolts of fire up his arm. But he was calm, and his mind was clear.

The next morning he rose from his bed, ran his fingers through his beard, and went into town to buy a steamship ticket for New York.

On a cold and wet autumn morning, Michael Levy arrived at the Sheltering House to find the stoop plastered with flyers printed in Yiddish from a group calling itself the "Jewish Members of the Republican State Committee." The fliers urged all self-respecting Jews to cast their lot with Colonel Roosevelt for governor. After all, Roosevelt had recently trounced the Spanish at San Juan Hill—and had not the Jews once been robbed and cast out by Spain, and hounded by its Inquisitors? *Vote to express your approval of Spain's defeat!* the flyer cried. Michael peeled them from the rough stone as he passed, and squeezed out the water before tossing them in his office wastebasket. Synagogue advertisements he could abide, but not shameless vote-mongering from Republican elites.

It had been a difficult autumn for Michael. He'd stretched the Sheltering House budget to its breaking point and still did not know how they would make it through the year. The price of coal climbed ever higher; the roof was leaking, and the top-floor ceiling was damp with mold. Worst of all, a young Russian man named Gribov had recently gone to sleep in a second-floor bed and failed to wake up. Michael had called in the Health Department, and the Sheltering House was threatened with two weeks of quarantine. In the end, the inspector, who'd glanced over the immigrant's body with clinical distaste, decided against it—there were no signs of typhus or cholera, and no one could recall the man complaining of anything. But for the next week the House's mood was tense and somber, and Michael barely slept for worry. It seemed to him that the entire enterprise was hanging by a thread.

His friends took in the new hollows under his eyes and told him he was working himself into an early grave. His uncle might have counseled him similarly, but Michael hadn't seen him in some time, not since he'd visited with the woman named Chava. He wondered vaguely if he should be worried. Was his uncle ill? Or was it something else?

Michael's thoughts trailed back to the tall woman and her box of pastries, and the fond and protective way his uncle had looked at her. Could
she . . . ? And he . . . ? But no, it seemed too ridiculous. He shook his head
and resolved to check in on his uncle soon.

But one thing led to another, and the top-floor ceiling threatened
to crumble, and Michael's attention was pulled elsewhere. And then,
one morning, the Sheltering House cook came into Michael's office and
placed a box of almond macaroons on his desk.

"The new girl at the bakery said to give these to you," she said,
plainly amused. "For free, if you can believe. She found out I was from
the Sheltering House and insisted."

The new girl? After a moment he realized, and smiled. The cook's
eyebrow went up.

"A tall woman?" he asked, and the cook nodded. "She's a friend of
my uncle's. I was the one who suggested she go to Radzin for a job. Most
likely she meant these as a thank-you."

"Oh, most likely," she replied airily.

"Dora, I only met her once. And she's a widow. A recent one."

The cook shook her head at his naïveté, and plucked a cookie from
the box as she left.

He lifted a macaroon in his palm. It was thick and slightly domed,
but felt light as air. The top was decorated with almond slivers, arranged
in a circle like flower petals. He popped it in his mouth, and felt happy
for the first time in weeks.

Slowly the Golem grew more accustomed to the bakery and its rhythms.
Her turns at the register were no longer so frightening. She was beginning to learn which customers bought the same thing every day, and
which of them appreciated it when she made up their order in advance.
She smiled at all of them, even when she didn't feel like it. Led by a hundred little prompts, she very carefully tried to give each of them exactly
what they wanted from her. And when she was successful, they would

step away from the register with a lighter heart, glad that at least one thing, this one simple errand, had gone right that day.

There were still problems to solve. She tended to work too quickly, and the customers would grow anxious or irritated, thinking that she was rushing them: and so she trained herself to slow down, and ask after their health and their families, even when the line was long. She even learned to deal with those customers who were perpetually indecisive, who stood at the counter debating the merits of this or that. The breakthrough came when one day, a woman told her to simply choose for her, from what she herself liked best. But the Golem had no particular favorites: she had tried all the pastries, and could distinguish one from another, but for her there was no like or dislike. Each was merely a different experience. She thought of choosing at random—but then, in a moment of inspiration, she did what she rarely allowed herself to do. She focused on the woman, and sifted through the tangle of her conflicting desires. *Something economical would be best, but she also wanted something sweet . . . she had been feeling so low this week, what with the landlord raising the rent and then that awful argument with her Sammy, so didn't she deserve something nice for herself? But then it would be gone, and she would feel no better, only poorer . . .*

"I like the raisin challah on days like this," the Golem said. "It's sweet, but it's filling. And one challah lasts a long time."

At once the woman beamed. "That's it," she said. "That's exactly what I wanted." And she paid for the challah and left, her spirits lifted.

Happy with her success, the Golem tried this technique on other indecisive customers. She was right more often than not, and tried not to take her failures personally. She was coming to realize that some people, for whatever reason, would never be satisfied.

She still made mistakes on occasion, especially at the end of the day when a mental fatigue would set in, and her thoughts would drift. She'd reach for the wrong thing, or call someone by the wrong name, or make some other silly little error. Once in a while a customer would walk out with the wrong order, and then come back to complain. She would apologize profusely, horrified by her poor performance—but it was just as well, for otherwise her employers might have thought her too good to be true. Mr. Radzin was a meticulous accountant, and he had been over the figures repeatedly. There was no question: sales were up, and for no good reason, while on the other side of the ledger his costs were shrinking. Intuition told him it had to do with the new girl. She might make a mistake or two at the register, but she never misread a recipe, or added the salt twice by accident, or left a sheet of cookies too long in the oven. She was never sick, never slow, never late. She was a miracle of productivity.

Though there were also times when she acted as though she was from another world. One morning Mrs. Radzin caught her peering oddly at an egg. "What's wrong with it, Chavaleh? Is it bad?"

Still staring at the egg, the girl had absentmindedly replied, "Nothing—it's only, how do they make them the exact same size and shape, every time?"

Mrs. Radzin frowned. "How do *who*, dear? The chickens?"

At her table, Anna gave a snort of laughter.

The girl carefully put down the egg and said, "Excuse me," and disappeared into the back.

"Don't tease, Anna," scolded Mrs. Radzin.

"But what an odd question!"

"Have some compassion, she's a widow in mourning. It does strange things to the mind."

Ignoring the women, Radzin went into the back for more flour. The door to the water closet was closed. He listened for the sounds of crying—but what he heard instead was her voice, in a whisper: "You must be more careful. *You must be more careful.*" He fetched the flour and left. A few minutes later she emerged from the back as though nothing had happened, and went to her silent work, ignoring Anna's periodic giggles.

"What do you suppose is wrong with her?" Radzin asked his wife that night.

"There's nothing the matter with Chava," she snapped.

"I have eyes, Thea, and so do you. She's different, somehow."

They were in bed together. Next to the wall, Abie and Selma lay curled on their pallets, sunk in the bone-deep sleep of the young.

"I knew a boy, growing up," Thea said. "He couldn't stop counting things. Blades of grass, bricks on a wall. The other boys would gather round and yell numbers at him, because if he lost his place he had to start all over again. He would just stand there counting, with tears rolling down his face. It made me so angry. I asked my father why he couldn't stop, and he told me there was a demon in the boy's mind. He said I should stay away, in case he did something dangerous."

"Did he? Do anything dangerous?"

"Of course not. But he died, the year before we left. A mule kicked him in the head." She paused, and then said, "I always wondered if he provoked it. Deliberately."

Radzin snorted. "Suicide by mule?"

"Everyone knew that animal had a temper."

"There would be a dozen better ways to do it."

His wife rolled away from him. "Oh, I don't know why I talk to you. If I say it's black, it must be white."

"If I see Chava standing behind any mules, I'll be sure to let you know."

"Awful man. Go boil your head like a turnip." They were quiet a moment, and then she said, "I'd like to see a mule try to kick her. She'd braid its legs like a challah."

Radzin laughed once, loud in the small room. Below them, the boy mumbled something. His sister shifted on her pallet. Their parents waited, tensed—but the children grew silent again.

"Go to sleep," Thea whispered. "And leave me some covers, for once."

Radzin lay awake for a long time, listening to the breathing of his children and his wife. The next morning, he took his newest employee aside and told her he was raising her pay by ten cents a day. "You deserve it," he said, gruffly. "But one word to Anna, and you'll be splitting it with her. I don't want her clamoring for money she doesn't deserve." He'd expected her to thank him but instead she only stood, looking chagrined. "Well? I just gave you a raise, girl. Aren't you happy?"

"Yes," she said immediately. "Yes, of course. Thank you. And I won't tell Anna." But she seemed more thoughtful than usual that day; and once or twice he saw her glance at Anna, her face full of a poorly disguised guilt.

"But it isn't fair that they should pay Anna less money than me," the Golem protested to Rabbi Meyer. "She can't work as hard as I can! It's not her fault!"

The Golem was pacing the Rabbi's living room. It was a Friday night and the dishes from the small supper were still on the table. The Golem looked forward to her Sabbath evenings with the Rabbi—it was the only time all week when she could ask questions and talk freely. But on this night, her dilemma eclipsed the rest of her thoughts. The Rabbi, concerned, sat watching her pace.

"It's not as though I *need* the money," she muttered. "I have nothing to spend it on."

"Why not buy something nice for yourself, as a reward for your work? Perhaps a new hat?"

She frowned. "I already have a hat. Is there something wrong with it?"

"Not at all," he said, reflecting that her creator had certainly not given her a young woman's sense of frivolity. "Chava, I understand why you're upset, and it speaks well of you. But from Radzin's perspective, you're worth more than Anna. To pay you both the same would be dishonest. Say I needed to buy a new kettle, and could choose between a large one and a small one. You'd expect the larger kettle to cost more, wouldn't you?"

The Golem said, "But what if the man who made the smaller kettle was poorer, and had a larger family to look after? Wouldn't that figure into your decision?"

The Rabbi sighed. "Yes, I suppose it would. But if these facts were hidden from me, as they so often are, then all I would know is that there are two kettles in front of me, one large and one small. That's all Radzin knows, as well. And please, Chava, stop pacing. You're making me dizzy."

Instantly she stopped, and sat in one of the parlor chairs, watching her hands twist together in her lap. "Perhaps I should give away what I don't need," she said. "Or"—the Golem's face lit with the thought—"I could give it to you!"

Instantly she saw the Rabbi recoil from the idea. "No, Chava. That's your money, not mine."

"But I don't need it!"

"Perhaps not now. But one must always plan for the future. I've lived long enough to know that there will come a time when you'll need it, and probably when you least expect. Money is a tool, and you can do great good with it, for others as well as yourself."

It sounded like good advice, but the Golem was not completely mollified. All the Rabbi's answers had been like this lately, pertaining to the matter at hand but also addressing something larger that was yet to come. It made her uneasy. She felt as though he were trying to teach her as much as he could in as little time as possible. His cough hadn't worsened, but it was no better either, and she'd noticed that his clothing had begun to hang on him, as though he'd shrunk. The Rabbi insisted that all was as it should be. "I'm an old man, Chava," he'd said. "The human body is like a piece of fabric. No matter how well one cares for it, it frays as it ages."

And what about a golem's body? she wanted to ask. *You say I won't age—but will I fray?* But she held her tongue. She'd begun to worry that questions such as these were too large a burden for both of them.

"Besides," the Rabbi went on, "from what you tell me about this Anna, she sounds like a less than serious-minded woman. Perhaps she can learn from your example, even if it doesn't come naturally to her."

"Perhaps," the Golem agreed. "She doesn't seem to wish me ill as much as before. But then, she's been preoccupied with her new suitor. She thinks about him quite a lot, and hopes he will walk her home from the bakery, so they can—" Caught up in her description, she bit back the words just in time.

"Yes, well." The Rabbi had colored slightly. "She's a foolish girl, if she's given herself to him before marriage. Or at the very least, before a promise of one."

"Why so?" the Golem asked.

"Because she has everything to lose. Marriage has many benefits, and one of them is the protection of a child, the likely result of their . . .

current behavior. An unmarried man is free to leave a woman, whatever condition she may be in, without consequence to himself. And what of the woman? She's now burdened, and may not be able to support the child, or even herself. Women in these situations have turned to the ugliest of crimes out of desperation, and then lose whatever virtue they have left. From there, it's a short journey to disease, poverty, and death. It's no exaggeration to say that a night of pleasure can cost a young woman her life. I saw it far too often as a rabbi, even among the best families."

But she seems so happy, the Golem thought.

The Rabbi stood and began to clear the dishes from the table, coughing once or twice. Quickly the Golem went to help him, and they did the dishes together in silence. "Rabbi, may I ask you something?" she said after a while. "It might embarrass you."

The Rabbi smiled. "I'll do my best, but don't expect miracles."

"If the act of love is so dangerous, why do people risk so much for it?"

The Rabbi was quiet for a while. Then he said, "If you had to guess, what would you say?"

The Golem recalled what she knew of such longings, the nocturnal lusts of passersby on the street. "It excites them to be dangerous, and to have a secret from the rest of the world."

"That's one aspect of it, but not the whole," said the Rabbi. "What you're missing is loneliness. All of us are lonely at some point or another, no matter how many people surround us. And then, we meet someone who seems to understand. She smiles, and for a moment the loneliness disappears. Add to that the effects of physical desire—and the excitement you spoke of—and all good sense and judgment fall away." The Rabbi paused, then said, "But love founded only on loneliness and desire will die out before long. A shared history, tradition, and values will link two people more thoroughly than any physical act."

They were silent for a while, and the Golem thought about this. "Then this is what is meant by true love?" she asked. "Tradition, and values?"

The Rabbi chuckled. "Perhaps that's too simplistic. I'm an old man, Chava, and a widower. I left this all behind years ago. But I do remember what it was to be young, and to feel that there was no one else in the world but the beloved. It's only with the benefit of hindsight that I can see what truly lasts between a man and a woman."

He trailed away, lost in memory, staring at the dish towel in his hand. In the light of the kitchen lamp, his skin looked sallow and spotted, and as thin as eggshell. Had he always seemed so fragile? Rotfeld had looked like this, she thought, pale and sweating in the kerosene light. She'd always known that she would outlive the Rabbi, but now the cold truth hit her as if for the first time. A pulse of grief ran through her—and the drinking glass that she'd been drying shattered in her hand.

Both jumped at the noise. Clear shards fell glittering to the floor.

"Oh, no," the Golem said.

"It's all right," said the Rabbi. He bent to gather up the pieces with the dishrag, but the Golem took it from him, saying, "I'm the one who broke it. And you might cut yourself."

The Rabbi watched as she swept up the glass and rinsed the nearby dishes. "Did something upset you?" he asked quietly.

She shook her head. "I was only careless. It was a long day."

He sighed. "It *is* late. Let's finish the dishes, and then I'll take you home."

It was nearing eleven o'clock by the time they reached her boardinghouse. The air had turned crisp, with a cutting wind. The Golem walked headfirst into it as though it were little more than a breeze. The Rabbi walked hunched at her side, coughing occasionally into his muffler.

"Come inside the parlor and get warm, at least," she said at the boardinghouse steps.

He shook his head, smiling. "I must be getting back. Good night, Chava."

"Good night, Rabbi." And she watched him walk away, a small old man on a windy street.

The Rabbi's walk home from the Golem's boardinghouse was torturous. The wind battered his face and cut through his overcoat and thin

trousers. He shook like a half-frozen animal. But at least he had succeeded. Not once during the evening had he thought of the satchel of
books and papers hidden under his bed. What would have happened,
had she caught the edge of a fear, a desire? *I hope she will leave soon, so
that I can go back to my texts, and find a way to control her!* Might she
have attacked him, out of an instinct toward self-preservation? Or
would she have agreed willingly, even encouraged his research? He'd
never asked her whether she would prefer to have a master again, and
now the thought of such a conversation made his throat tighten. In a
sense it would be like asking someone whether they'd like to escape
their present difficulties by killing themselves.

Constantly he had to remind himself that she wasn't human. She
was a golem, and masterless. He forced himself to remember his own
little golem at yeshiva, its indifferent destruction of the spider. They
were not the same creature; but at heart they had the same nature. That
cold remorselessness existed somewhere in her as well.

But did she also have a *soul*?

On its surface, the answer was a simple no. Only the Almighty could
bestow a soul, as He had ensouled Adam with His divine breath. And the
Golem was a creature of man, not God. Any soul she could have would be
at most partial, a fragment. If he turned her to dust, it might be an unwar-
ranted act of destruction; it would not, however, count as murder.

But these scriptural reassurances paled when faced with the Golem
herself: her disappointments and triumphs, her clear concern for his ill
health. She would talk in energetic tones about her work at the bakery,
and her growing confidence with the customers; and he saw not an animated lump of clay but a young woman, learning to live in the world. If
he succeeded, and bound her to a new master, he would be robbing her
of all she'd accomplished. Her free will would disappear, to be replaced by
her master's commands. Was that not murder, of a sort? And if it came
to it, would he have the strength to do it?

By the time he reached his tenement, his footsteps had been reduced
to a shuffle. Inside, the staircase stretched up into the dark. He took the
steps one at a time, his hand clammy on the wood banister. He began
coughing halfway up. By the time he reached his door, he couldn't stop.

The key fumbled in the lock; shaking hands lit the lamp. He went to the kitchen for water, but the cough deepened, gripping his entire body. He bent double, nearly knocking his head on the washbasin. Finally the spasms slowed, then stopped. He lowered himself to the floor and breathed shallowly, the taste of blood in his mouth.

He'd asked his doctor to come see him, not a week ago. *A bit of a cough*, the Rabbi said. *I only wanted to check.* The doctor had spent long minutes with his cold stethoscope on the Rabbi's chest and back, his expression growing more and more unreadable. At last he'd packed the equipment away in a battered leather case, saying nothing. *How long*, the Rabbi asked. *Six months at most*, the doctor said, and then turned away, tears on his cheeks. Yet another fear to keep from the Golem.

He drank a finger of schnapps to steady himself, and put the kettle on for tea. His hands were not shaking so badly now. Good. There was work to be done.

II.

The long stretch of rainy nights had grown nearly unbearable, and so the Djinni broke down and did something he'd vowed he wouldn't: he bought an umbrella.

It was Arbeely who'd first suggested it, more to preserve his own sanity than anything else. After three weeks of damp weather, the Djinni was a terrible workmate, sullen and distracted, and liable to leave smoldering irons lying about. "You look like you're about to crawl out of your skin," Arbeely said. "Why not just buy an umbrella, instead of sitting every night in your room?"

"I thought you didn't like my going about at night," the Djinni said.

"I don't. But it's better than you burning the shop down, or one of us murdering the other. Get an umbrella."

"I don't need one," the Djinni said.

Arbeely laughed. "I think it's clear you *do*."

Still, he was rather shocked a few days later when the Djinni strolled out of the morning drizzle, shaking out a large midnight-silk umbrella more suited to a West Side dandy than a Syrian immigrant.

"Where," Arbeely said, "did you get *that*?"

"A pawnshop in the Bowery," said the Djinni.

Arbeely sighed. "I might have guessed. Did they wash the blood off it?"

The Djinni ignored this and reversed the umbrella, holding it out. "Look," he said. "What do you think?"

The handle was made of a dark, fine-grained hardwood. The last six inches were wrapped with filigreed silver, in a spiraling lattice of leaves and vines.

"It's beautiful," said Arbeely, holding it to the light. "You did this? How long did it take you?"

The Djinni smiled. "Two nights. I saw one like it in a shop window. Simpler than this, but it gave me the idea."

Arbeely shook his head. "It's far too fine. People will think you're taking on airs."

The Djinni stiffened. "Let them," he said. He took the umbrella back from Arbeely, and leaned it in a corner—careful, Arbeely saw, not to muss the silk.

That night, the Djinni went back to the Bowery. It was a fascinating place, both intriguing and repellent: a vast, cacophonous labyrinth that snaked up the south end of the city. He had a feeling he'd tire of it soon; but meanwhile, it was good for a few evenings' entertainment.

He was still getting used to the umbrella. Walking under it, he felt hemmed in, surrounded. The rain pattered against the taut silk, making it buzz like a swarm of flies.

The rain subsided to a light drizzle. Carefully he closed the umbrella—the mechanism tended to stick—and furled it, to protect the silk against stray embers from the Elevated. He had an errand to run.

The shop where he bought his gold and silver was halfway up the Bowery, near Bond Street. To all casual appearances it was an undistinguished storefront tobacconist's, set above a saloon and below a brothel. The distant overhead rhythm of thumping furniture punctuated most of the transactions. It was run by a fence named Conroy, a small, neat Irishman. Conroy's eyes were sharp and intelligent behind his round spectacles, and he carried an air of quiet precision. He seemed to be in charge of a collection of heavily muscled men. Sometimes one of them would appear at Conroy's side, and whisper in his ear. Conroy would think a moment, and either nod or shake his head, always with the same expression of mild regret. Then the tough would disappear, off to run some baleful errand.

Two drunken men were buying tobacco and papers when the Djinni entered the shop. Conroy smiled to see him. The two men left, and Conroy drew the shop door closed, and flipped the sign in the window. Then he reached below the counter and began pulling out an assortment of fine silver objects: cutlery, pendants, necklaces, even a small candlestick.

The Djinni picked up the candlestick, examined it. "Solid silver?"

"All the way through."

There were no nicks or scratches to indicate that Conroy had checked, but the man hadn't been wrong yet. "How much?"

Conroy named a price. The Djinni halved it, and they went back and forth in this way, ending at a number that the Djinni guessed was only slightly extortionate. He paid, and Conroy wrapped the candlestick in paper and tied it with string, like a cut of meat. "If you'd like to go upstairs," he said neutrally, "it'd be at no cost."

"Thank you, but no," said the Djinni. He nodded farewell, and left.

Outside, the candlestick tucked into his coat pocket, the Djinni rolled a cigarette and glanced up at the windows of the brothel. *That*, he'd decided, was one thing he wouldn't pay for. The only pleasure in the encounter would be purely physical, and what would be the point?

His errand over, he decided to walk the Bowery's length. He passed tattoo parlors, mortuaries, shuttered theaters, filthy cafés. A gaming house threw harsh and tinny music onto the street. Rats scurried at the edges of the gutters and darted off below the Elevated, into the murk. Women with overpainted faces scanned the streets for marks and saw him, a solitary, handsome, clean-looking man. They beckoned to him from their doorways, and scowled when he walked past without stopping.

All at once the Djinni's tolerance for the Bowery evaporated. It was as though they'd taken everything good about desire and turned it ugly.

He found a fire escape and climbed it, the umbrella held awkwardly under one arm. The silver handle knocked against a rung, and he nearly dropped it. He cursed the rung, cursed the umbrella, cursed his circumstances that he should be in need of either.

On the roof, he rolled another cigarette and smoked it, looking down on the street. It irritated him that he'd grown tired of the Bowery so quickly. The sun would be coming up soon; he would take himself back to Washington Street.

Footsteps crunched behind him on the tar paper, and for an unexamined moment he was glad of the company.

"That's a nice umbrella, sir."

It was a young woman—barely more than a girl. She wore a shabby, dirt-stained dress that had once been of good quality. She was holding her head at an odd angle, as though it had grown too heavy for her neck.

Her hair was dark and long, and fell in a curtain over her eyes, but from underneath it she was watching him.

She raised one languid hand, to push back the hair from her eyes; and the gesture tugged at something in the Djinni's mind. For a long moment he was certain that he knew her, and that as soon as he saw her face he would remember her.

But she was merely an unremarkable girl, a stranger. She smiled dreamily at him. "Looking for company, sir?" she asked.

"Not really," he said.

"A nice-looking gentleman like you shouldn't be alone." She said the words as if by rote. Her eyes were drifting closed. Was something wrong with her? And why had he thought he'd known her? He peered into her face. She took the attention as encouragement, and pressed herself up against him. Her arms snaked around his waist. He could feel her heart beating against him, a high fast fluttering in her chest. She sighed, as if settling in for the night. He looked down at the top of her head, strangely unsure. Lifting a hand, he watched his own fingers as they ran through her hair.

She whispered, "Twenty cents gets you whatever you want."

No. He pushed her away, and she stumbled. A small bottle fell between them. He reached down and picked it up. It was a stoppered glass, half-full of an oily liquid. TINCTURE OF OPIUM, read the label.

A sudden squawk from the girl. She reached out and snatched the bottle from his hand. "That's mine," she spat. Then she turned and walked unsteadily away.

He watched her go, then climbed down from the roof and headed home. There was no reason for the girl to have rattled him like this. But something in the motion of her hand, as she pushed back the dark veil of her hair, had seemed so very familiar.

In her father's goat pen, Fadwa al-Hadid straightened up from her crouch on the milking stool and pushed her curtain of dark hair back from her eyes. She had tied it at her neck, but it always came loose when she milked the goats. Something to do with the rhythm.

The goat bleated and turned to look at her, barred pupils rolling. She stroked its back and whispered soothing words into its leather-soft ear. The goats had been skittish all morning, refusing to stand still, shifting their weight about and threatening to overturn the pail. Perhaps they sensed the summer coming. It was only midmorning, and already the sun was beating down on them, turning the air thick and the sky brassy. She took a drink from the pail, then undid her hair completely.

From his spot a little ways away, the Djinni watched her retie her hair at the nape of her neck. It was a becoming gesture, unselfconscious and private.

For days now, he'd been watching the girl and her family, trying to learn their ways. They seemed to live in a constant hum of comings and goings, all within a carefully circumscribed world that had the encampment at its center. The men ventured out farther than the women, but they too had their boundaries. They hadn't even journeyed out again within sight of his palace, and he wondered now if that had been a special occasion of some sort.

He watched as Fadwa released the goat and moved on to the next one. Her life truly was as she had described it: an endless repetition of tasks. The caravan men at least had a destination ahead of them, a purpose beyond the horizon. Fadwa's existence, as far as he could tell, was nothing but milking and cleaning and cooking and weaving. He wondered how she could stand it.

The milking finished, Fadwa untied the final goat and checked the water in their trough. Then she carefully lifted the brimming pail of milk and brought it to the fire pit.

"You're spilling," said her mother. She was busy at the grindstone, her arm going around and around. Wheat dust trickled from between the flat stones. Fadwa made no reply, only poured the milk into a beaten bowl and placed it above the embers. Sweat ran into her eyes, and she flicked it away with distant irritation.

"You haven't said three words together all morning," her mother said. "Is your flow coming on?"

"I'm all right, Mama," she said absently. "I didn't sleep well, that's all."

The milk began to bubble, and she removed the bowl from the fire and stirred in a few spoonfuls of yogurt, held back from the morning meal. She covered it with a cloth, and left it to thicken.

"Take the girls to the cave for more water," her mother said. "We'll need it today."

The walk to the cave seemed interminable. The empty water jar sat heavy on her head. Her cousins laughed and dodged ahead of her, playing a game where they tried to step on each other's shadows without dropping their jars. It was true, what she had told her mother: she hadn't been sleeping very well. Her strange visitor had not returned the next night, or the night after; and now, nearly a week later, she was beginning to wonder if she had imagined the whole thing. It had seemed so vivid, so real; but within a few days it had begun to blur around the edges, like an ordinary dream.

Would this be the night he kept his promise, and returned to her? Or was there no *him*, no promise to be kept? How would she know if he truly visited her, or if she were merely dreaming such a thing? It sent her mind in circles. She would fall half-asleep, only to startle awake again with excitement, then chide herself for waking. And when she did manage to sleep, her dreams were only full of ordinary nonsense.

The spring where the Hadid clan fetched their water flowed into a cave that a long-ago people had fashioned into a temple. Its entrance was a flat, square doorway cut into the sloping hillside. To Fadwa, it looked as though a giant had sliced off the edge of the hill with a knife. Words in an unknown, angular alphabet were carved into the flat lintel above the cave's mouth. Sand and wind had worked on them until they were barely visible. Her father had told her that the temple's builders were from the world far beyond the desert. *They pass through in every age*, he'd said. *They try to conquer the desert. They make their marks in it, as though to claim it, but then they disappear. And all the while we Bedu endure, unchanging.*

Inside, the air was cool and damp. A sloping pool was carved into the rock floor; a crack at its bottom connected it to the underground spring. At the height of the rains, the pool had overflowed its edge, spilling out the door and down the path. Now it was barely halfway full. Soon, Fadwa knew, it would be reduced to a trickle, and then run dry completely. They would live on the milk of their animals until the water returned.

Her cousins were at the pool's edge, filling their jars. She waded in and watched the dark water spill over the jar's lip. In a niche above the pool, the face and figure of a woman had been carved into the rock. A water goddess, her father had said, a woman with a hundred names. The ones who'd built the temple had thought that they brought her to the desert, when in fact she'd been there from the very beginning. Her hair flowed about her lightly, in waves. She stared out of the wall with blankly serene eyes, the years having robbed her of any expression.

Do you think she really exists? Fadwa had asked her father. And he had smiled, and said, *When so many others believe in her, who am I to say otherwise?*

Her cousins began to splash each other. Fadwa frowned, and moved her water jar farther away.

Tonight, she told herself. If he did not come to her tonight, then she would try to resign herself to the truth: it had all been in her mind.

Please let him come, she pleaded silently to the stone woman in the niche. *Or I might start to think that I'm going mad.*

The Djinni watched Fadwa leave the temple, the water-jar balanced expertly on her head. To compensate for its weight, she took slower steps, her hips swinging from side to side. One hand rested lightly on the jar, to steady it. All in all, a most appealing picture. The water even added a touch of danger.

He smiled. He hadn't forgotten his promise. Perhaps, he thought, he would visit her that night.

Early on a Friday morning, the Rabbi discovered the formula to bind a golem to a new master.

It had been a long and terrible week. He'd had a growing, unshakable sense that it was time to finish and be done with it, that circumstances and his own health would not stand for much more. And so he'd sent messages to all of his students' families, telling them that he was taking a week-long sabbatical, for prayer and fasting. (He couldn't simply say he was ill; their mothers would come to his door armed with bowls of soup.) As it happened, the lie became truth: the entire divination grew to resemble one long, drawn-out prayer, and around Wednesday he simply forgot to keep eating.

Books and papers covered the parlor floor in a pattern that felt more intuitive than reasoned. He snatched sleep an hour at a time, curled on the couch. His dreams were a twilight of prayers and diagrams and names of God. Among them floated faces known and unknown: his wife, speaking gibberish; an ancient, twisted man; his nephew Michael, frightened of something unseen; and the Golem, smiling, her eyes full of a terrible fire. He would cough himself awake from these dreams and stumble back to work, still half in their grasp.

He suspected he was harming his soul. But he put the thought away. He had started this; he would see it to its end.

That end, when it came, was not a burst of fevered inspiration, but a quiet and thorough adding-up, like a bookkeeper reconciling the year's accounts. He looked at the brief lines he'd written at the bottom of the page, watching the ink soak into the paper. A part of him wished he could take pride in this accomplishment, for its own sake. For despite the formula's brevity, it was an elegant and complex masterwork. Simply to bind a golem to a new master, without destroying it—this alone was an unheard-of accomplishment. But the Rabbi had gone a step further. For the formula to work, the Golem would have to consent freely to the removal of her will. This was his compromise with himself, the deal he'd struck with his conscience. He would not steal her life, like a murderer in an alley. He would leave the final decision to her.

She might refuse, of course. Or the question itself might be too much for her nature to bear. Could he subdue her, if necessary? His fatigued mind recoiled from the thought of coming this far, only to be forced to destroy her.

He glanced around, blinking, and winced: his parlor looked like the grotto of a mad mystic. He stood on weak legs and collected the papers and books from the floor. The books he put in his satchel, to return to their owners after the Sabbath, with his apologies. The papers he ordered in a neat pile, save for the final page, which he put to one side. He needed a wash; he felt filthy. Outside it was a rare cloudless morning. The sky beyond the parlor's soot-streaked windows was turning a rich sapphire.

He lit the stove and put a pot of water on, watching himself as if from a distance, almost amused. He remembered this boneless, floating detachment from his yeshiva days, the all-night study sessions in which he'd seemed to dive into the Talmud itself and become one with it. He watched the bubbles form in the bottom of the pot, his vision blurring with fatigue and, he realized now, insistent hunger. He searched the cupboards but found only fossilized bread-heels and a questionable jar of schmaltz. He'd have to go out, after he washed and prayed, and buy food for Sabbath dinner. And then he'd set the rooms to rights, before the Golem arrived.

Finally the water was heated. He stripped in the cold kitchen and dabbed at himself with a washcloth, shivering and trying not to cough. For the first time, he allowed himself to consider the issue of potential masters. Meltzer? A good rabbi, but too old now, too set in his comfortable life. The same went for Teitelbaum, which was a shame. Kaplan was a possibility: younger, but still a child of the old country, not so likely to scoff at the very idea. But perhaps Kaplan had too much learning, and not enough compassion.

Any one of them would need a careful approach. First he'd have to convince them that old age and solitude hadn't driven him mad. Even then there would be resistance. *Why not just destroy her?* they would ask. *Why ruin your own life, and ask me to ruin mine, and let this danger exist?*

Would he reply that he'd grown exceedingly fond of her? That in her eagerness to learn, her determined forbearance, she'd made him as proud as a father? Was it her future he was arranging, or her funeral?

Tears sprang to his eyes and clotted his throat, making him cough.

He went to the bedroom to look for clean clothes. In the bottom drawer of his dresser, something else caught his eye: a leather drawstring pouch. With shaking hands—he *must* get something to eat—he opened the pouch and removed the small oilskin envelope, labeled COMMANDS FOR THE GOLEM. It belonged with the other papers, he decided. He would give the watch and the billfold to the Golem and apologize for keeping them so long. But this, he would pass on, or else burn. Once he decided what to do.

He was carrying the envelope to the table in the parlor when the attack hit him. He doubled over, coughing; and then his breath left him entirely. It was as though someone had wrapped a steel girder around his chest, and was twisting it tighter and tighter. He gasped for air; a thin wheezing reached his ears. His arm went numb.

The parlor elongated, turned gray at the edges, tilted and spun. He felt the old wool rug under his cheek. He tried to stand, but only rolled onto his back. A distant crackling sensation: the oilskin envelope, still in his hand.

In the last moments left to him, Rabbi Meyer realized he never could have done it. The smaller murder of his new formula, or the utter destruction of the spell in the envelope: either would have been beyond his power while she was still his Chava, still innocent, still the newborn woman he'd first spied holding a sparrow in the palm of her hand.

He tried to hurl the envelope away from himself, below the table. Had he done so? He couldn't tell. She would need to make her way alone, he had done all he could. The feeling was leaving his body, draining away from his limbs toward his center. It occurred to him to say the *viddui*, the prayer before death. He struggled to remember it. *Blessed are You, who has bestowed me with many blessings. May my death atone for all I have done . . . and may I shelter in the shadow of Your wings in the World to Come.*

He stared up into the sky beyond the parlor window. The vivid blueness stretched so high that it seemed to draw him up inside it, pure and wide and all-encompassing.

The Golem went to the Rabbi's that night carrying an apple strudel, carefully wrapped. She walked with long strides, stretching her legs, feeling the cold night air settle into her body. Lamps glowed in the windows as she passed.

There was no answer to her knock at the Rabbi's door.

She knocked again, waited. Likely he had fallen asleep. She imagined him on the other side of the door, dozing in a parlor chair. She smiled. He'd chide himself for falling asleep, and making her wait.

She knocked again, louder. Still nothing. She stood there for a few uneasy minutes, unsure of what to do. She wondered what the Rabbi himself would advise, and the answer came as clearly as if he'd spoken in her ear: *You know I don't lock my door during the day. This is your home as well as mine. Come in!*

She opened the door.

The Rabbi's rooms were dark, the lamps unlit. She peered into the bedroom. The twilight sky threw shadows onto a neatly made bed. She went to the kitchen, set down the strudel, and lit a lamp, her anxiety growing. The fire in the grate had gone out. The air was cold and had a stale smell, like dirty clothes.

She went into the parlor, and there she found him. His legs were twisted to one side. His eyes stared blindly up at the windows behind him.

At first there was no horror, no shock, only a pure, clear disbelief. This was not real. This was a painted picture, an illusion. She would reach out and sweep it away with her fingers.

Trembling, she crouched down and touched his face. It was cold and hard.

Distantly—almost disinterestedly—she sensed something building inside her, and knew that when it reached the surface and broke free it would have the strength to tear down buildings.

His hair had mussed from his fall, and his skullcap had gone askew. He wouldn't like that. She smoothed it all back into place, taking care to use the lightest of touches. One of his arms was bent at an odd angle from his body. An envelope had slipped from his hand, one edge still balanced on his fingertips. She saw there was something written on it. She bent closer, and read:

Commands for the golem

She reached down and lifted the envelope away. The slick material crackled in her grip; in the silence of the room it was as loud as a firework. She tucked it into the pocket of her cloak.

Still he didn't move. But now she could hear something, a ragged high keening sound, thin but growing louder. And then louder. There was a knocking at the door, and she realized the sound was coming from herself, and that she was rocking back and forth, hands over her mouth, crying out, and now there were words. *Rabbi, Rabbi!*

Someone's hands were on her shoulders, someone's voice was in her ear. Other cries, now, not her own.

Footsteps ran out into the hallway and down the stairs. She allowed herself to be pulled from his side and led to a chair. Someone had put a glass of water in her hand. And now neighbor women were walking in and out with quiet purpose, wiping away their tears and talking quietly, nodding and parting again. A man hurried in with a doctor's leather bag; his dinner napkin was still tucked into his belt. He bent over the Rabbi, peeled back one eyelid, put his ear to the Rabbi's chest. Then he shook his head. He sat back on his heels, all sense of urgency gone.

A woman placed a sheet over the Rabbi. It billowed, catching the air, and then settled over his body. With another, she draped the mirror in the parlor.

More murmuring. And now the women were casting glances at the Golem, their curiosity plain. Who was she? What had she been doing in the home of a widowed old rabbi? The Golem knew that soon they would work up the nerve to ask who she was. And she wouldn't be able to lie to them. Not with the Rabbi lying there, underneath the sheet. She had to go. She felt their stares as she passed, imagined the whispers that would follow her. But she didn't care. The dark thing was still rising inside her; she had to get home.

Outside it was pitch-black, and the wind had picked up. It fought at her clothing and threatened to pull the hat from her head. She took it off, and carried it in one hand. Others paused to stare as she went by, a tall, pale woman in a dark dress and cloak who moved as if driven by some terrible force. One inebriated man saw a lone woman out for a nighttime stroll, and decided to ask after her company. The Golem saw him coming, noted the intent in his eyes and his mind, and thought about how easy it would be to knock him to the ground. She wouldn't even have to break stride. But as she came closer, the man got a good look at her face, and stepped back, crossing himself. Later he'd tell his friends he'd seen the Angel of Death on Orchard Street, out collecting souls.

Her room at the boardinghouse seemed even smaller than usual. She sat on the edge of her bed. She looked down, and saw her hands were full of dark shreds of felt and ribbon. What were they? Then she realized: it was her hat. She'd pulled it to pieces without noticing.

She tossed the shreds of her hat on the floor, and took off her cloak. If she went through the motions of a usual night, perhaps it would calm her.

She took her dress from the armoire, pulled her chair next to the window, and began to pick apart the stitches. But the passersby kept distracting her. They were the usual motley assortment of drunkards and giggling girls and workingmen, young couples out for secret strolls, the same fears and desires as ever; but now it struck her as obscene. They walked about as though nothing had happened! Didn't they know that the Rabbi was dead? Had no one told them?

Her hands were moving too quickly, and the scissors slipped. One blade tore the fabric, making a gash as long as her finger.

The Golem cried out, and threw the dress to the floor. Her hands flew to her face. Moaning, she began to rock herself back and forth. The walls seemed to be drawing closer. She couldn't stay there any longer. She needed to get out. She needed to move. Or else she'd lose control.

Without hat or cloak or destination, the Golem fled from the boardinghouse. She walked without aim, paying little attention to her surroundings. The evening was chill now, with frost in the air. A near-full moon shone high above the gas lamps, turning their light yellow and sickly.

She walked from street to street. The neighborhoods dissolved into each other, the languages changing on the storefronts. Oblivious she walked through Chinatown, barely noticing the red banners that flapped in the wind above her. The signs changed again, to yet another language, and still she kept on, walking her grief into submission.

It was a long while before she began to feel calmer, before her thoughts became smoother, less fractured. She slowed, and then stopped, and looked around. A tenement street stretched out before her, with its walls of buildings to either side. The brick facades were dilapidated and filthy, and the air stank. She turned about: there was no familiar land-mark, no river or bridge she could use to orient herself. She was, she realized, utterly lost.

Cautiously she walked on. The following street seemed even less promising and ended in a small park, little more than a stretch of dead grass. She walked to its middle, trying to get her bearings. No fewer than six different streets intersected at the park's edge. Should she go back the way she came? How would she ever get home?

And then, down one of the streets, a strange light appeared, seem-ing to float in midair. She paused, alarmed. The light was coming her way. It grew closer, and she saw that it was not a light, but a face; and the face belonged to a man. He was tall, taller than she, and bareheaded. His dark hair was cropped close to his skull. His face—and his hands as well, she saw now—shone with that warm light, like a lamp shaded with gauze.

She watched him come nearer, unable to take her eyes away. She saw him glance at her, and then look again. Then he too stopped. At that distance she could not feel his curiosity, but his expression made it plain. What, he was thinking, is *she*?

The shock of it rooted her to the spot. Only the Rabbi had ever been able to see her as something different.

She knew she should turn and run. Get away from this man, who by seeing her, truly *seeing* her, already knew too much. But she couldn't. The rest of the world had fallen away. She had to know who he was. *What* he was.

And so, as the man started his cautious approach, the Golem stood her ground, and waited.

Until now, the Djinni's evening had been rather disappointing.

He'd taken advantage of the clear skies and gone out, but without much enthusiasm. Feeling uninspired, he'd planned to visit the aquarium again but found himself instead at City Hall Park, an unremarkable patchwork of lawn, broken to pieces by wide, intersecting concrete paths. From there, he'd made his way to the Park Row terminal shed, a long low building that stood on thick girders. He walked beneath it and looked up at the trains sleeping on their tracks, waiting to ferry the morning's passengers across the Brooklyn Bridge.

He hadn't been to Brooklyn, and he didn't want to go, not yet. He felt he needed to parcel out these new experiences carefully, to keep from running out. He had a fleeting image of himself, ten, twenty, thirty years hence, wandering in ever-widening circles, exhausting every source of distraction. He rubbed at the iron at his wrist, then noticed what he was doing and stopped. He would not, would *not*, succumb to self-pity.

He wandered northeast along Park Row and realized he was nearing the Bowery. He had no wish to go back again so soon, so he took a random turning, and landed on a street lined with squalid-looking tenements. This, he thought, was no better.

The buildings on either side narrowed to wedges ahead of a large intersection, a cracked wasteland of pavement. Beyond lay a narrow, hemmed-in park. There was a woman standing alone at its center.

At first he only saw that she was a respectable-looking woman, out by herself in the dead of the night. Such a thing was odd, if explainable. But she wore no hat or cloak, merely a shirtwaist and skirt. And why was she staring at him, tracking his every move? Was she deranged, or merely lost?

He reached the middle of the intersection, and glanced at her again, unsettled; and saw that she was not human, but a living piece of earth.

He stopped cold. What *was* she?

Now he, too, was staring. Hesitantly he walked forward onto the grass. When he was a few feet from her she stiffened, and made to draw back. Immediately he stopped. The air around her held a breath of mist, and the scent of something dark and rich.

"What are you?" he asked.

She said nothing, gave no indication she'd understood. He tried again: "You're not human. You're made of earth."

At last she spoke. "And you're made of fire," she said.

The shock of it hit him square in the chest, and on its heels an intense fear. He took a step backward. "How," he said, "did you know that?"

"Your face glows. As if lit from within. Can no one else see it?"

"No," he said. "No one else."

"But you can see me as well," she said.

"Yes." He tilted his head, trying to puzzle it out. Looked at in one way, she was merely a woman, tall and dark-haired. And then his vision shifted somehow, and he saw her features carved in clay. He said, "My kind can see all creatures' true natures, it's how we know each other when we meet, in whatever shape we may be wearing. But I've never seen . . ."

He reached out, unthinking, to touch her face. She nearly leapt backward.

"I shouldn't be here," she gasped. She glanced wildly around, as if seeing where she was for the first time.

"Wait! What's your name?" he asked; but she shook her head and began to back away like a frightened animal.

"If you won't tell me your name, then I will tell you mine!" Good: that had stopped her, at least for the moment. "I'm called Ahmad, though that's not my true name. I am a djinni. I was born a thousand years ago, in a desert halfway across the world. I came here by accident, trapped in an oil flask. I live on Washington Street, west of here, near a tinsmith's shop. Until this moment, only one other person in New York knew my true nature."

It was as though he'd opened a floodgate. He had not realized until that moment how much he'd been longing to tell someone, anyone.

Her face was the portrait of a struggle, some inner war. Finally she said, "My name is Chava."

"Chava," he repeated. "Chava, what *are* you?"

"A golem," she whispered. And then her eyes widened, and her hand flew to her mouth, as if she'd told the most dangerous secret in the world. She stumbled backward, turned to run; and he saw in her movements her enormous physical power, knew that she could easily bend one of Arbeely's best plates in half.

"Wait!" But she was running now, not looking back. She darted around a corner, and was gone.

He stood alone on the grass, for a minute or two, waiting. And then he followed after her.

She wasn't very difficult to track. As he'd guessed, she was lost. She hesitated at corners, glancing up at the buildings and street signs. The neighborhood was a warren of slums, and more than once she crossed the street to avoid a man stumbling her way. The Djinni kept a good amount of distance between them but often had to duck quickly around a building when her confused path doubled back on itself.

At last she found her bearings and began to walk with more certainty. She crossed the Bowery, and he followed her into a somewhat cleaner and more respectable-looking neighborhood. From behind a corner he watched her disappear into a thin house crammed between two enormous buildings. A light came on in one of the windows.

Before she could look out and see him, he was walking away west, memorizing the streets as he went, the turnings and landmarks. He felt strangely buoyant, and more cheerful than he'd been in weeks. This woman, this—*golem?*—was a puzzle waiting to be solved, a mystery better than any mere distraction. He would not leave their next meeting to chance.

In his dank cellar room, Mahmoud Saleh tossed and turned. This insomnia was a recent development. In summer, Saleh had been so exhausted at the end of each day that he'd barely had the strength to stagger back home. But now it was late autumn and the children had long since stopped buying ice cream. For weeks after the weather turned he'd churned the ice cream each morning and plodded the rainy streets, regardless of the lack of customers. He'd made no plan for survival, for he had no intention of living through the winter.

But then the universe intervened again, in the form of Maryam Faddoul. She'd stopped him one morning in front of her coffeehouse to say that all the Syrian café and restaurant-owners, Maronite and Orthodox both, had decided to purchase ice cream from Saleh during the winter months, and then sell it to their own patrons.

"It'll be a novelty," she said. "A taste of summer, to remind us it'll come again."

Surely, he thought, *they would rather eat something warm when it's cold?* But he knew logic would be useless, for it was clear that Maryam had organized the entire scheme. Most idealists lived in their own impossible worlds, sealed away from reality; Maryam, it seemed, effortlessly reached out from hers and drew others inside. Her unstudied goodness affected their judgment, even to the point of buying large quantities of ice cream in winter.

Leave me alone, he felt like saying. *Let me die in peace.* But there was nothing he could do. She'd simply decided that an indigent, half-mad peddler would survive a killing winter if she wished it. He wanted to resent her, but all he felt was an irritated bemusement.

Under this new scheme, Saleh spent much less time on his feet. He traveled from restaurant to restaurant, churning ice cream in exchange for handfuls of coins. And there was more charity as well: his neighbors had begun leaving him their own castoff clothing, folded in neat, anonymous stacks on the cellar stairs. He accepted it in the same half-resentful spirit as Maryam's generosity. Some he wore, layer upon layer; others he stitched together haphazardly with a thick needle and twine, creating a sort of many-limbed blanket.

But his body, used to punishing work, rebelled at this new warmth and ease. He would fall asleep at his usual hour and then wake in the dead of night, watching verminous shadows move in the corners. To keep them away from his pallet, he'd surrounded it with concentric circles of mousetraps and lines of powdered carbolic. The tiny room now looked like an infidel altar, with himself as the sacrifice.

He shifted underneath his blanket, trying to find a more comfortable position. It was a particularly bad night. He'd lain there for hours, counting each beat of his stubborn heart. Finally he could stand it no longer. He rose, donned a torn overcoat, wrapped a scarf about his head, and went up to the street.

The evening was crisp and clear, with a touch of frost on the windows. Even to his broken eyes, it was eerily beautiful. He inhaled the bracing air and blew out great clouds of steam. Perhaps he'd walk for a while, until he was tired.

A glowing light appeared in the corner of Saleh's eye. He squinted against it, trying to make it out. A man was walking down the street toward him. His face was made of fire.

Saleh gaped. It was impossible! Why didn't the man burn away? Wasn't he in pain? He certainly didn't look it: he wore a nonchalant look in his glowing eye, a half-smile on his lips.

His *eyes*. His *lips*.

Mahmoud Saleh's knees nearly buckled with the realization that he was staring at the man's face.

The man passed within feet of him, taking him in with a quick distasteful glance. Half a block farther on, the man vaulted the steps of an unremarkable building—a building that Saleh passed every day!—and was gone.

Shaking, Saleh crept back down to his cellar. Sleep wouldn't come again to him that night. He had looked into a man's face, and not suffered for it. A man, tall, with Arab features that glowed as though lit from within. He'd been the only real thing on a street full of shadows, and now the world seemed even more spectral for his absence.

It was nearly dawn by the time the Golem returned to her boarding-house. Her dress still lay on the floor, the torn fabric gaping like a scolding mouth.

How, *how* could she have been so careless? She shouldn't have been alone on the street! She shouldn't have wandered so far from home! And when she saw the glowing man, she should have run away! She *certainly* shouldn't have spoken to him, let alone told him her nature!

It was the Rabbi's death; it had made her weak. The glowing man had found her at the worst possible moment. And the force of his curiosity, his desire to know more about her, had overwhelmed what little self-possession she'd had left.

She'd have to be stronger than that now. She could afford few mistakes. The Rabbi was gone. She had no one left to watch over her.

The force of the loss hit her again. What would she do? She had no one to talk to, nowhere to turn! What did people do when the ones they needed died? She lay curled on her bed, feeling as though part of her chest had been roughly scooped out, left raw and exposed.

Finally she drew herself together and stood. It was time to leave for the bakery. The world hadn't stopped, no matter how much she might wish it, and she couldn't hide in her room. Feeling leaden, she put on her cloak, and heard something crackle in the pocket.

It was the envelope. COMMANDS FOR THE GOLEM. She'd forgotten.

She opened the flap, drew out a square of thick paper, torn roughly at its edges and folded twice. She opened the first fold. There a shaking hand had written:

The first Command brings Life. The second Destroys.

The second fold gaped open slightly, as though it could not wait to divulge its secrets. Through the gap she saw the shadow of Hebrew characters.

Temptation roiled inside her like a fog.

Quickly she folded the paper back up again, and stuffed it in the envelope. Then she put it in the drawer of her tiny desk. She paced for a few minutes, then grabbed it out of the desk, stuffed it between her mattress and the bed frame, and sat on top of it.

Why had the Rabbi given her this? And what was she supposed to *do* with it?

The docks at Danzig were thronged with travelers and their loved ones. The *Baltika* sat at the end of its dock, an immense, towering solidity ready to disappear into the morning haze.

For Yehudah Schaalman, after so long in his hermit's shack, the noise of the docks was unbearable. Gripping his small, battered suitcase, he tried to shoulder his way through the crowd. A warning blast from the ship's horn made Schaalman jump nearly out of his skin. It was the largest thing he'd ever seen; he realized he was gaping at it like an imbecile.

The crowds thinned, and he shuffled up the gangplank with the others. On deck, he watched the land pull away. The relatives waving farewell on the docks dwindled and disappeared. The haze thickened, and the shoreline of Europe became a thin smudge of brown. Soon even the smudge vanished, swallowed by mist and ocean. And Schaalman found he could not account for the tears that ran in rivers down his face.

12.

Early on the morning after Rabbi Meyer died, one of Michael Levy's roommates woke him, gently shaking his shoulder. There was a rabbinical-looking man at the door, asking for him. Michael went to the door and recognized one of his uncle's old associates. He saw the sorrow in the man's face, and the discomfort at his task, and began to cry, without needing to be told.

We aren't sure when it happened, the rabbi said. *A woman found him. We don't know who she was. The neighbors didn't recognize her.* A pause, and a message in the man's silence: his uncle should not have been alone with a strange woman, but this would be kept between them. Michael thought of his uncle's friend Chava but said nothing.

He spent the morning weeping, awash in guilt. He should have visited, like he'd told himself he would. Made an effort, apologized, patched up their differences. *Helped* him. Hadn't he sensed that there was something wrong?

That afternoon he went to his uncle's tenement. Someone had already hung black crepe about the hallway door. In the bedroom, a young man with sidelocks, wearing a dark hat, sat in a chair next to the bed, where his uncle lay. Michael glanced at the unmoving figure, and then away again. His uncle looked stiff, shrunken. Not as Michael wanted to remember him.

The young man nodded distantly at Michael, and then went back to his silent watching: the *shmira*, the vigil over the body. Were it any other day of the week, there would be a flurry of activity, of men praying together, washing his uncle's body, sewing it into the shroud. But it was the Sabbath, the day of rest. Funeral arrangements were forbidden.

He wanted to ask how he could help, but it was out of the question. He was an apostate. He wouldn't be allowed. Perhaps if he were a son, not merely a nephew, his uncle's colleagues would've taken pity on him, allowed him to play some role. As it was, he was surprised he was even allowed inside.

A soft knock at the door. The young man went to answer it. A woman's voice in the hallway: the young man stepped back, shaking his head quickly. Here, at least, was something Michael could do. "Let me," he said, and went out into the hallway. His uncle's friend stood there, a picture of misery.

"Michael," she said. "I'm so glad you're here. I should've known I wouldn't be let in, I should have realized . . ."

"It's all right," he said.

But she was shaking her head, her arms wrapped around herself. "I wish I could see him," she said.

"I know," he said. Beneath Michael's grief, he felt the familiar ire building against the religious restrictions. How well did the man in the bedroom know his uncle, anyhow? What made him more worthy than Michael to sit the vigil? "You're the one who found him," he said, and she nodded. "I'm sorry," he said, hating himself but needing to know, "it's none of my business, but were you and he—"

"No, no, nothing like that," she said quickly. "Only . . . good friends. He was very kind to me. We had dinner together, on Fridays."

"I shouldn't have asked."

"It's all right," she said quietly. "Everyone else thinks it too."

They stood there together in the doorway beneath the crepe, a pair of outcasts.

"I never thanked you," he said. "For the macaroons."

A hint of a smile. "I'm glad you liked them."

"Then you're doing well at the bakery?"

"Yes. Very well."

A silence.

"When is the funeral?" she asked.

"Tomorrow."

"I won't be allowed," she said, as if to confirm it.

"No." He sighed. "No women. I wish it were otherwise."

"Then please say good-bye for me," she murmured, and turned to leave.

"Chava," he said. She paused, one foot on the stair, and Michael realized he was about to ask her if she would have coffee with him. A hot wave of shame washed over him: his uncle lay dead, only a few feet away. They were both in mourning. It would be indecent by any reckoning.

"May God comfort you among the mourners of Zion and Jerusalem," he said, the old formula rising unbidden to his lips.

"And you as well," she said; and then she left him alone with his thoughts in the dark of the hallway.

"I met an interesting woman last night," the Djinni told Arbeely.

"I don't want to know," Arbeely said. Together they were forging a batch of skillets. Arbeely shaped each one, and then the Djinni smoothed it and applied the finishing touches. It was repetitive, bland work, but they were developing a rhythm.

"It wasn't like that," the Djinni said. He paused, and then asked, "What's a golem?"

"A what?"

"A golem. That's what she called herself. She said, 'I am a golem.'"

"I have no idea," Arbeely said. "You're certain she didn't say *German*?"

"No, golem."

"I can't help you there."

They worked in silence for a minute. Then the Djinni said, "She was made of clay."

"I beg your pardon."

"I said, she was made of clay."

"Then I did hear correctly."

"This is strange? You haven't heard of this before?"

Arbeely snorted. "Strange? It's impossible!"

Raising an eyebrow, the Djinni picked up the wrong end of Arbeely's burning-hot iron with his bare hand.

Arbeely sighed, conceding the point. "But you're certain? What did she look like?"

"Light-skinned. Dark hair. About your height, dressed plainly."

"Then she didn't look like a clay woman?"

"No. You wouldn't have noticed anything out of the ordinary."

Arbeely drew breath to challenge this, but the Djinni said, "Enough, Arbeely, she was made of clay. I know it as surely as I know I am fire and you are flesh and bone."

"All right, but such a thing isn't easy to believe. What else did she tell you, this clay woman?"

"She said her name was Chava."

Arbeely frowned. "Well, it's not a Syrian name. Where did you meet her?"

"A slum near the Bowery. Our paths crossed."

"What were you doing—never mind, I don't want to know. She was alone?"

"Yes."

"Then she isn't a very careful woman. Or perhaps she has no reason to be."

"She wasn't a prostitute, if that's your meaning."

"Perhaps you should tell me the whole story."

And so the Djinni related the entirety of his encounter with the strange woman made of clay. Arbeely listened with a rising feeling of unease. "And she recognized you as—well, different?"

"Yes, but she didn't know what a djinni was."

"And you *told* her? Why?"

"To keep her from running away. But she did anyway."

"And when you followed her home, where did she live?"

"East of the Bowery."

"Yes, but what *neighborhood*? What nationality was she?"

"I have no idea. The language on most of the signs looked like this." The Djinni took up a pencil and found a scrap of paper, and drew out a few of the characters he remembered from the awnings and windows.

"Those are Hebrew letters," Arbeely said. "You were in a Jewish neighborhood."

"I suppose."

"I don't like this," muttered Arbeely. He was not a politically minded man, and what prejudices he harbored were mostly mild and abstract; but the thought of the Djinni causing trouble in a Jewish neighborhood made him fearful. Mount Lebanon's Turkish overlords had long made a game of pitting its Christian and Jewish populations against each other, forcing them to compete for Muslim favor. The disagreements had at times turned bloody and edged into riot, fanned by accusations of Christian blood in Jewish bread—a claim that always struck Arbeely as ridiculous on its face, though he knew many were willing to believe it. Of course the Jews of the Lower East Side were European, not Syrian; but here they were by far the larger community, and it seemed more than plausible that they'd bear a grudge on their brethren's behalf.

"You told her too much," Arbeely said.

"And if she repeats it, no one will believe her."

"That doesn't mean that she can't cause trouble. What if she comes here, and starts spreading rumors? Or worse, what if she tells the Jews of the Lower East Side that she's discovered a dangerous and terrible creature that's living with the Syrians on Washington Street?"

"Then we'll laugh at her and say she's mad."

"Will you laugh at an entire mob? Will you laugh when they loot Sam's store, or set fire to the Faddouls' coffeehouse?"

"But why would they—"

"They'd need no reason!" shouted Arbeely. "Why can't you understand? Men need no reason to cause mischief, only an excuse! You live among good, hardworking people, and your carelessness puts them in danger. For God's sake, don't destroy their lives to suit your whims!"

The Djinni was startled by the man's vehemence. He'd never seen Arbeely so angry. "All right," he said. "I apologize. I won't go back there again."

"Good," said Arbeely, in surprise—he'd been expecting a fight. "That's good. Thank you." And together they resumed their work.

A few nights later, the city was hit with the first real snowfall of the season. The Djinni stood at his window and watched the city silently disappear. He'd seen snow before, drifting dry and white across the desert floor, and shining from the high peaks. But this snow softened all it touched, rounding the sharp edges of buildings and rooftops. He watched until it stopped falling, and then he went down to the street.

He walked to the docks through the unbroken white, feeling the flakes crumple beneath his feet. Tethered boats bobbed in the black water, their decks and rigging lined with snow. Somewhere nearby there was a saloon; the men's voices and laughter carried in the still air.

It was a tranquility unlike any he'd experienced in this city, but it felt fragile, a moment he'd managed to steal. In the morning he'd be back to making skillets, playing the Bedouin apprentice. Living in secret. He remembered the rush of gladness he'd felt when he told the woman what he was. As though, for a moment, he'd been freed.

Occasionally a small voice spoke up inside him, saying, *you're a fool for not going home*. But he could barely consider the thought before crushing it beneath a thousand fears and objections. Even if he survived the ocean crossing, he could not return to his glass palace, his earlier life, bound as he was. He'd be forced to seek refuge in the djinn habitations, among his kind but utterly apart, pitied and feared, pointed out as a cautionary example to the wayward young. *Avoid humankind, little one, or this will be your end.*

No, if he must live estranged from his own kind, then let it be in New York. He would find a way to free himself. And if he couldn't? Well, then, he supposed he would die here.

The Golem sat in her window, and watched the snow fall. The cold seeped in around the window frame, and she pulled her cloak tighter against it. She'd discovered that although the chill itself did not bother her, it stiffened the clay of her body, turning her restless and irritated. She'd taken to wearing her cloak even in her room, but it didn't help much. Already her legs ached, and it was only two in the morning.

The snow was beautiful, though. She wished she could go out in it, and feel what it was like while it was still pristine and fresh. She imagined the Rabbi's new grave across the river in Brooklyn, lying beneath a growing white blanket. She would visit him soon, she thought, but first she'd have to figure out how. She had never been to Brooklyn; she'd barely been out of the Lower East Side. And were women permitted in a cemetery? How could she ask anyone, and not reveal her ignorance?

The Rabbi's death had revealed how little she knew of the culture in which she lived. Within moments of her terrible discovery, the neighbors had begun to play their roles, following the script they all knew by heart: the fetching of the doctor, the covering of the mirror. When she'd encountered the young man sitting the vigil the next day, she'd been appalled by the force of his distaste, the wrongness of her presence. She'd appreciated Michael's anger on her behalf; but he at least understood what he trespassed against, while she merely blundered in the dark.

Michael. She suspected that even without her ability, she would have known what it was he wanted to ask her in the hallway. She was thankful that he hadn't. *Judge a man by his actions, not his thoughts.* The Rabbi was right: Michael was a good person, and she was glad to have met him again. Perhaps they would encounter each other occasionally, on the street or in the bakery. They might be acquaintances, friends. She hoped he would accept that.

Meanwhile her life, it seemed, went on. At work, Mrs. Radzin offered her condolences, and mentioned that Mr. Radzin would be paying their respects at shivah at the Rabbi's tenement. (The Golem wondered, did Mrs. Radzin stay home because women weren't allowed, or simply to take care of the children? How was she to *know* these things?) Anna and Mrs. Radzin both offered to take the Golem's shifts at the register, so that she could work quietly in the back. It was a kindness, and she accepted thankfully.

The solitude allowed her to think hard about the events of the previous days, and register that they'd truly happened. The encounter with the glowing man, in particular, seemed like something she might have imagined. He'd left no real mark or trace of his existence, save in her memory.

She winced, thinking of how she'd revealed her secret to him. But it had been almost beyond her control. He'd told her his own so easily that for a moment her caution had seemed excessive, even silly. And then, he'd asked *What are you?*; and the frank, eager curiosity of the question had broken her open.

At least she'd run from him before she could do any more damage. It had been a chance encounter, an aberration. It wouldn't be repeated.

But in unguarded moments, mixing dough or counting stitches, her thoughts came back to him, pondering what he'd said. He was a djinni—but what was that? Why did his face glow the way it did? How had he come here *by accident*?

Sometimes she even imagined searching him out, going to Washington Street and asking him her questions. Then she would catch hold of her thoughts, and turn them to something else. It was too dangerous a fantasy to entertain.

There was one more loose end from that night that still needed her attention. She'd thought long and hard about the envelope she'd taken from the Rabbi's hand, with its small square of folded paper. She hadn't opened it again, hadn't trusted herself not to unfold the paper all the way. She wondered now if the Rabbi had even meant to give it to her. Wouldn't he at least have put her name on the envelope, or disguised its contents somehow? But all this speculation was useless; she would never know for certain. Briefly she considered burning it, but the thought only made her clutch at it more tightly. Whatever the Rabbi's intentions, the envelope had come to her, and she couldn't destroy it.

The question then became where to put it. She couldn't keep it at the boardinghouse: her landlady might find it, or the house might burn down. The bakery was even riskier. It seemed best to keep it with her. And so, taking some of the money from the cookie tin beneath her bed, she went to a jeweler's and bought a large brass locket that hung from a sturdy chain. The locket was plain and oblong, with rounded corners. There was just enough room inside for the square of paper, folded tightly. She closed the clasp, hung the chain about her neck, and tucked the locket inside her shirtwaist. The collar was high enough to hide most of the chain; one would have to look hard to see its glint at the nape of her neck. Now, as she stared out at the snow, the locket rested against her skin, cool and secret. It was an odd sensation, but already she was growing used to it. Soon, she supposed, she would hardly notice.

On the last night of shivah, Michael Levy stood in the corner of his uncle's parlor and listened to the Mourner's Kaddish as it was read yet again. Its sad, swaying rhythm had pulled at him ever since the funeral service. He felt ill. He passed a hand over his forehead; he was sweating, even in the cold air of the room. The men in the parlor were a wall of black coats, their yarmulkes bobbing up and down as they chanted in deep, froggy voices.

At the cemetery in Brooklyn he'd stood next to the open grave and gathered a handful of frozen dirt, then extended his arm and opened his hand. The frozen clumps had struck the plain pine coffin with a flat and hollow sound. The coffin had seemed too small, too far away, like something at the bottom of a well.

May God comfort you among the mourners of Zion and Jerusalem. The prescribed words of mourning, the words that had come to his lips in the hallway with his uncle's friend: he'd heard them dozens of times in those few short days, and they were starting to grate on his nerves. Why "among the mourners of Zion and Jerusalem?" Why not "among the mourners of the world"? So parochial, so small-minded. As though the only loss that mattered was the ancient loss of the Temple, and all other losses merely reflected it. He knew that it was meant to remind the mourner that he was still part of a community, and among the living. But Michael had his community: his friends from school, his colleagues at the Sheltering House, his brothers and sisters in the Socialist Labor Party. He didn't need these pious strangers. He'd seen their sidewise glances at him, taking in the apostate nephew. *Let them judge*, he thought. It was the last night. They'd all be rid of each other soon enough.

The black-hatted men came and went. They stood by the parlor table eating hard-boiled eggs and slices of bread, talking quietly. A few times Michael saw older rabbis, men he vaguely remembered as friends of his uncle's, scanning the bookshelves, looking for something. Each one would come to the end of the shelves and frown, disappointed, and then glance about guiltily and move on. Were they browsing for valuable volumes they might appropriate? Professional covetousness, even at a shivah? He smirked without mirth. So much for the purity of mourning.

Well, they could have it all. He was the designated heir to what little there was, but he planned to donate most of it. He had nowhere to put the furniture, no use for the religious items. After everyone was gone he roamed about the rooms with a box, setting aside the few things he would keep. The silver-plated tea set, of which his aunt had been so proud. Her shawls and jewelry, which he'd discovered in a wardrobe drawer. In the same drawer, a pouch containing a water-stained billfold and a broken watch. The watch had once been fine; he'd never seen his uncle carry it. In the billfold was both American and what looked like German currency. He added both to the box, wondering if they were relics of his uncle's crossing. Personal correspondence, the few family daguerreotypes in frames, including—hidden in a drawer—his own parents' wedding portrait. His mother a round-cheeked girl, peeking out from beneath a lace veil spangled with flowers. His father, tall and thin in a silk hat, staring not at the camera or his new wife but off to one side, as if already planning his escape. The old anger at his father rose briefly before dissolving back into sorrow. Under the bed he found a satchel half-full of dilapidated old books. These he added to their brethren on the bookshelves. He knew of a charity that sent books to new Jewish congregations in the Middle West—no doubt they would be interested.

Under the cloth on the parlor table he found a slim sheaf of papers covered with his uncle's handwriting. In their haste to right the parlor and make it ready for mourners, his uncle's associates hadn't noticed it. One paper was set to the side, as if more important than the others. On it was written two lines in strange, indecipherable Hebrew. It all looked very arcane, and he considered handing the whole stack over to the first rabbi he saw; but his uncle's handwriting exerted a visceral pull on him. He couldn't, not yet. It was all too fresh. Wearily he tossed the papers into the empty leather satchel. He would sort through them later, once he had regained his sense of perspective.

He lugged the box and the satchel back to his own tenement rooms, and shoved them beneath a table. He was still sweating, and nauseated, though he'd eaten barely anything for days. He vomited in the water closet and then collapsed onto his pallet.

In the morning, one of his roommates found him soaked and shaking. A doctor was brought in. Perhaps a mild influenza, the doctor said; and within hours the entire building was quarantined, its doors impassable.

They took Michael to the Swinburne Island hospital, where he lay among the terrified and heartbroken immigrants turned away at Ellis Island, the dying and the misdiagnosed. His fever swelled. He hallucinated a fire on the ceiling, and then a writhing, dripping nest of snakes. He struggled to get away from them, and realized he was tied into his bed. He cried out, and a cool impartial hand came to rest on his forehead. Someone brought a glass of water to his lips. He drank what he could, then descended back into his terrible visions.

Michael's were not the only cries of delirium in the ward. In a nearby bed lay a Prussian man in his forties, who'd been hale and sound when he boarded the *Baltika* at its stop in Hamburg. He'd made it to Ellis Island without incident, and had been at the front of the line for the doctor's examination when he'd felt a tap on his shoulder. The man turned around, and saw behind him a small, wizened old man in a too-large overcoat. The old man beckoned to him, obviously wishing to speak. He bent down closer to hear in the crowded hall, whereupon the old man whispered a string of meaningless, harshly babbling words in his ear.

The man shook his head, trying to get across that he hadn't understood—but then he was shaking his head more violently, because the muttered syllables had taken up residence inside his head. They grew louder, ricocheting from one side of his skull to the other, buzzing like wasps. He put his fingers in his ears. *Please help me*, he tried to say, but he couldn't hear his own voice over the din. The old man's face was all innocent puzzlement. Others in the line were beginning to stare. He clutched his head—the noise was impossible, he was drowning in it—and then he was falling to his knees, shouting incoherently. A froth began to form on his lips. Doctors and men in uniform were grabbing at him now, prying back his eyelids, shoving a leather belt in his mouth. The last thing he saw, before they wrapped him in a straitjacket and took him to Swinburne, was the old man pausing at the unattended desk to stamp his own papers before disappearing into the crowd on the other side.

The Bureau of Immigration officer looked over the papers in his hand, and then scrutinized the man in front of him. He looked older than sixty-four, to be sure, but he had that weathered peasant's look that meant he could be anywhere under a hundred.

"What year were you born?" On the other side of the desk, the Yiddish translator bent and murmured in the old man's ear. *Eighteen hundred and thirty-five*, the answer came back. Well, if he said so. The man's back was straight and his eyes were clear, and the health stamp was still drying on his papers. He'd already shown his wallet, which held twenty American dollars and a few coins. Enough to keep from being a nuisance. There was no reason not to let him in.

That name, though. "Let's call you something more American," he said. "It's for the best." And as the old man watched, confusion gathering in his eyes, the officer struck out *Yehudah Schaalman* and above it wrote *Joseph Schall* in a dark, square hand.

13.

The Christmas season descended on Little Syria, with all its attendant decorations and feasts. Suddenly it seemed to the Djinni that Arbeely was always at church. *For Novena*, the man would say, or *to celebrate the Immaculate Conception*, or *for the Revelation to Saint Joseph*. "But what does any of that *mean*?" the Djinni asked. And so, with a feeling of dread, Arbeely found himself giving the Djinni a potted history of the life of Christ and the founding of His Church. This was followed by a long, convoluted, and at times quite bitter argument.

"Let me see if I understand correctly now," the Djinni said at one point. "You and your relations believe that a ghost living in the sky can grant you wishes."

"That is a gross oversimplification, and you know it."

"And yet, according to men, we djinn are nothing but children's tales?"

"This is different. This is about religion and faith."

"And where exactly is the difference?"

"Are you honestly asking, or being deliberately insulting?"

"I'm honestly asking."

Arbeely sank a finished skillet into a tub of water—by now both of them were heartily sick of skillets—and waited for the steam to clear. "Faith is believing in something even without proof, because you know it in your heart to be true."

"I see. And before you released me from the flask, would you have said that you *knew in your heart* that djinn do not exist?"

Arbeely frowned. "I would have put it at a very low probability."

"And yet, look at me. Here I stand, making skillets. Does that not call your faith into question?"

"Yes! Look at you! You yourself are proof that labeling something as superstition doesn't necessarily make it so!"

"But I've *always* existed. Djinn may not choose to be seen, but that doesn't mean we're imaginary. And we certainly don't ask to be worshiped. In any case," he said with relish—he had been saving this salvo for its proper moment—"you told me yourself that sometimes you aren't certain there is a God."

"I never should have said that," muttered Arbeely. "I was drunk."

On a recent night, buoyed by their growing commercial success, Arbeely had decided to introduce his apprentice to *araq*. The anise-flavored alcohol had no effect on the Djinni, only a pleasant taste and a sudden warmth as it burned away inside him. He'd been fascinated by the *araq*'s transformation as Arbeely added water to the small glass, the liquor going from clear to cloudy white. He'd insisted on trying it over and over, diluting the *araq* drop by drop and watching the hazy, opaque tendrils extend themselves through the glass.

But how does it work? he'd asked Arbeely.

Don't know. The man had grinned, tossing back another of the Djinni's experiments. *It just does.*

"Because you were drunk, does that make it less true?" the Djinni asked.

"Yes. Liquor is an evil influence. And besides, even if I didn't believe, what would that change? You existed without the benefit of my belief. So does God, without yours."

But the truth was that Arbeely's faith rested on uncertain ground. Worse, the argument was forcing him to scrutinize his own shaky beliefs when all he wanted was the comfort of the familiar. At night, alone in his bed, doubt and homesickness weighted his heart and made him feel like weeping.

Nevertheless, on Christmas eve he went to Mass. In the candle-lit hall he took Communion with his neighbors, the wine-soaked bread heavy on his tongue, and strove to feel something of the miracle of the Christ Child's birth. Afterward, at a dinner organized by the ladies of the church, he sat at a long table among the other unmarried men, and ate tabouleh and flatbread and kibbeh that tasted nothing like his mother's. A couple of the men produced an oud and a drum, and they all danced a *dabke*. Arbeely joined in, less from real enthusiasm than because it would hurt too much not to.

He left the dinner and walked back toward his tenement room. It was a bracing, frost-bitten night; the air knifed at his lungs. Perhaps, he thought, he would have a glass of *araq*—just one this time—and retire early. Then he saw that the lamp was still burning in the shop. Strange—usually at this hour the Djinni was out roaming the city, bedding young heiresses and doing whatever else it was he did.

Arbeely entered to find the shop empty. He frowned. Didn't the Djinni know better than to leave the lamp burning? Irritated, he went to extinguish it.

On the worktable, inside the circle of lamplight, sat a small silver owl.

Arbeely picked up the figurine and turned it over in his hands. The owl was perched on the stump of a tree, staring at him with enormous, wide-set eyes. The Djinni had used a tiny blade to carve out a ruff of startled feathers and a thin, pointed beak. In all, he'd contrived to make it the most indignant-looking owl Arbeely had ever seen.

He laughed aloud, delighted. Not a Christmas present, surely! Was it meant for an apology, or merely a whim? A bit of both, perhaps? Smiling, he pocketed the figurine and took himself to bed.

The owl was indeed meant as an apology, but for more than Arbeely knew.

The bickering about religion had taken its toll on the Djinni as well. Never before had humans seemed so foreign to him. Distantly he understood that the subject was difficult for Arbeely to explain, tied as it was to the man's feelings for home and family. But then Arbeely would say something ridiculous, like when he had tried to explain how this God of theirs was somehow three gods and one at the same time. It left the Djinni drowning in a sea of exasperation.

Certainly the man meant well, but the Djinni wanted to talk to someone else, someone who might understand his frustrations, even share them. Someone who, like him, was forced to hide away her strengths.

He had no idea if she would even consent to speak with him. But he needed to know who she was. And so, as Arbeely entered his shop and discovered the waiting figurine, the Djinni was already retracing the route he had memorized, in search of the woman made of clay.

Over the weeks the cold had deepened, and with it the Golem's night-time restlessness. At the end of each workday she'd contrive to spend one or two more minutes in front of the fading ovens, soaking up the last of their heat. The walk home had become an unhappy march to an endless-seeming incarceration. One night she tried getting into her bed, beneath the eiderdown, thinking it might warm her, but her restless limbs wouldn't allow it. She nearly tore the bedclothes apart in her rush to get out again.

On Saturdays, her day off, she fought off the stiffness by walking the bounds of her neighborhood, up and down the overfamiliar streets. *Rivington, Delancey, Broome, Grand, Hester. Forsyth, Allen, Eldridge, Orchard, Ludlow.* Fir wreaths and red velvet bows had appeared in a few of the tenement windows; vaguely she was aware that it was for a holiday, but that it was a gentile affair, and she wasn't supposed to take notice. She passed the innumerable synagogues, from humble storefront congregations to the soaring structures on Eldridge and Rivington. At each one she felt the same outpouring of prayer, like a deep river with powerful currents. Sometimes it was so strong that she had to cross the street, or risk being pulled under. She began to realize why the Rabbi had never taken her to a service. It would be like stepping into a hurricane.

On the western boundary of her walks, she would always pause and look down the block toward the Bowery. To her, the street was a sort of borderland, a gateway to the vast, dangerous expanse of the city. She'd only crossed it once, on the night she'd met the glowing man.

She wondered where he was. Did he feel the cold like she did? Or did he drive it away, by burning more brightly?

Back and forth she'd walk, willing the sun not to set. But the earth insisted on turning, and before long she was home again, steeling herself for the night. Bored with sewing her one dress, she'd begun to take in clothes that needed mending or alterations. Most of her clients were her fellow boarders in the house, the clerks and accountants who'd never learned to thread a needle. They thought her awkward and spinsterish, if they thought of her at all; but even they noticed the precision of her stitches, the almost invisible mends. They recommended her to their friends and colleagues, and soon the Golem had more than enough piece-work to occupy her fingers, if not her mind.

One particularly cold night, she was repairing a rip in a pair of trou-sers when the needle fell from her stiff fingers. She tried to grab it, but fumbled, and the needle vanished. She searched the trousers, her own clothing, the floor, but couldn't find it. At last a glint from the candlelight caught her eye: and there it was, sticking out of her right forearm. It had sunk in nearly half its length.

She peered closer, dumbfounded. How had it happened? She'd driven it in by accident, and not even noticed!

Carefully she plucked the needle from her arm and pulled back her sleeve. There was a tiny dark hole, its edge slightly raised where the needle had pushed the clay aside. She pressed the spot with her thumb, and felt a twinge of discomfort. But already the puncture was sealing itself over, the clay spreading back into place; and when she removed her thumb the mark was nearly gone.

The Golem was fascinated. She'd grown used to thinking of her body as never changing. She didn't bruise when she bumped into the worktable, and never twisted her ankle on the ice, as Mrs. Radzin had done. Her hair didn't even grow. This was something new, and unex-plored.

Her gaze fell on her satin pincushion and its dozens of long, silver pins.

Within minutes she'd stuck them all in her arm to varying depths, a few nearly down to the head. It took a good deal of force. The clay that formed her was strong and thick, and didn't give way easily. After dent-ing her thumb on the pinheads, she took off her boot and used it as a hammer.

Finally she examined her work, touching each pin in turn. She'd laid them out in a neat grid along her left forearm, from the wrist to the elbow. All were held fast. She flexed and opened her hand, feeling the clay gather and pull around the pins near her wrist. There seemed to be no underlying structure, no bone or muscle or nerve: she was clay through and through.

She removed a pin, prising it out with her fingernails. Soon the hole had closed of its own accord. She pulled out another one, and checked the clock: only three minutes until there was nothing left but a dark spot. What if the hole was bigger? She took the pin and inserted it directly next to another one, making the hole twice as wide. The discomfort grew, but she ignored it. Then she removed both pins, and watched. Eight minutes passed before the hole had closed over completely.

How interesting! But what if she stuck three pins together, or four? Or she could use something other than pins, something wider—the embroidery scissors! She snatched them from the sewing basket, closed her fist around the handles, and held them like a dagger above her wrist, ready to strike.

Then, slowly, as though not to startle herself, she put the scissors down. What in the world was she doing? She had no idea how much her body could endure, how far it could be pushed. What if she'd permanently maimed herself? And if the hole had indeed closed, then what next? Would she slice off her own arm out of boredom? No need to worry herself with thoughts of others discovering and destroying her. She would destroy herself soon enough, piece by piece.

She pulled each pin from her arm and replaced them in the pincushion. Soon the only damage was a faint grid of blemishes. She checked the clock. Only two in the morning. There were still hours left to fill. And already her fingers were beginning to twitch.

How long could she keep on like this? Years, months, weeks? Days? *You will go mad before long*, said a voice in her mind, *and put all in danger.*

Her hand came up to touch the locket, and then faltered. She shook her head distractedly. Then she wrapped her cloak tighter about herself, and glanced out at the street below.

The glowing man was strolling up the sidewalk toward her boardinghouse.

She stared, shocked. What was he doing on her street? Had he followed her home that night? No; perhaps it was a coincidence. He might be headed anywhere.

Warily she watched his approach. He wore a dark coat, but no hat, even though it was freezing cold. Near the boardinghouse, he slowed, and then stopped. He glanced about, as if checking for onlookers. And then he raised his head and looked directly at her window.

Their eyes met.

She flew back from the window, nearly stumbling against her bed. She'd been discovered, hunted down! She clutched at the locket, waiting for the pounding on the door, the angry mob.

But the street remained silent. There was no knock at the door, no approaching wave of fearful anger.

She crept back to the window's edge and peered out. He was still there, alone, leaning against the lamppost. As she watched, he rolled himself a cigarette, and then, without benefit of a match, touched his finger to the end and inhaled. All this without glancing at her window. He was, she realized, certain of his audience. And he was *enjoying* himself.

Her panic subsided, was replaced by ire. How dare he follow her home? What right did he have? And yet—how many times had she thought to go to Washington Street and seek him out? And now here he was, under her window, and she had no idea what to do about it.

For almost an hour she watched as he stood there, for all the world as though he had nothing better to do than hold up the lamppost and smoke cigarettes. He nodded at the occasional passersby, who all stared at his uncovered head and thin coat.

Then, as if struck by a sudden impulse, he pulled something from his pocket. It was roughly the size of an apple, though not as round, and it glinted in the thin pool of gaslight. He held it cupped in his hands, and for a few long moments his hands blazed so brightly it almost hurt to look at them. Then from another pocket he withdrew a long, thin stick, pointed at the end like a needle. He held the object up and peered at it, and began to poke at it gently with the stick.

Curious despite her caution, she crept closer to the window and watched as he worked. Every so often he frowned and rubbed a thumb over whatever he had done, as if erasing a mistake. She realized that the light inside him didn't shine beyond his own body; for although his hands were half as bright as the gas lamp, the thing he held remained in shadow.

Finally he slowed his work and then stopped. He held up the object for inspection, turning it this way and that, before bending down and setting it next to the lamppost. Then, without so much as a backward glance, he walked away down the street again, the way he'd come.

The Golem waited ten minutes. Then she waited five more. The day was about to begin. Already the traffic on the sidewalk was increasing. One, two, three people walked past the lamppost. Soon someone would notice whatever it was he'd left there, and claim it for themselves. Or it would be kicked into the gutter, and lost. And then she would never know what it was.

She grabbed her cloak and rushed down the stairs. At the front door, she paused: had he doubled back to lie in wait for her, having baited his trap? She opened the door a crack and poked her head around, but saw no glowing faces, only ordinary men and women. She went to the lamppost and retrieved the object, examining it in the gaslight.

It was a small silver bird, still warm to the touch. He'd formed it as though it were sitting on the ground, its feet tucked up underneath itself. Its round body tapered to a short spray of tail feathers. Small carvings and indentations created the suggestion of plumage. Its head was turned to one side, watching her intently with smooth half-globe eyes.

He had made this with his bare hands, while standing beneath her window.

Thoroughly perplexed, she brought the bird back to her room, placed it on her writing desk, and stared at it until it was time to leave for work.

That morning the Golem burned a pan of cookies for the first time. At the register, she miscounted two customers' change and gave a woman prune Danishes instead of cheese. The mistakes mortified her, though everyone else was amused—she was so celebrated for her exactness that catching her in error seemed a fortuitous event, like a shooting star.

Anna, of course, enjoyed it to the hilt. "What's his name?" she whispered as the Golem passed her worktable.

"What?" Startled, the Golem stared at the girl. "Whose name?"

"Oh, no one's." Anna smiled, satisfied as a cat. "Forget I said any-thing."

After that, the Golem went to the water closet to collect herself. She would not let the glowing man unnerve her. She would be calm and controlled, her best self. She would act the way the Rabbi would want her to act.

She came home that night and positioned herself by the win-dow, waiting. Finally, at nearly two in the morning, he appeared from around the corner. Again, he was alone. He returned to his spot next to the lamppost and again gave every indication of staying there for the night.

Enough of this, she thought. She put on her cloak, then tiptoed down the staircase and quietly opened the front door.

The street was nearly empty, and her shoes on the boardinghouse steps were loud in the cold night air. Surprise flickered across his face; it was replaced by a self-assured nonchalance as she approached. She stopped a few feet away from him. Silently they watched each other.

"Go away," she said.

He smiled. "Why should I? I like it here."

"You're a nuisance."

"How can that be? I do nothing but stand on a sidewalk."

She only stared at him, rigid and severe. Finally he said, "What else was I to do? You refused to stay and talk."

"Yes, because I don't want to talk with you."

"I don't believe that," he said.

She crossed her arms. "You followed me home, and now you call me a liar?"

"You're being cautious. I understand. I live with the same consider-ations."

"Did you tell anyone about me?"

"No one." Then he winced, remembering something. "Ah. One man."

She turned and started back up the sidewalk.

"No, wait!" he called, coming after her. "He's the one I told you about, the tinsmith. He knows my secret, and has told no one. He can keep yours as well."

"Lower your voice!" she hissed. She glanced up at the boarding-house, but there was no light at any of the windows.

He sighed, clearly making an effort to be patient. "Please. You're the only one I've met here who isn't . . . as *they* are. I only wish to talk with you. Nothing more."

Was he telling the truth? She frowned, trying to see. Distantly she could feel his curiosity, but it was eclipsed by something else that lay deep inside him, like a vast, dark shadow.

She reached out to it—and was nearly pulled under by a longing like nothing she'd ever experienced. It was as though a part of his soul had been trapped and held fast in an endless moment. It couldn't move, or speak, or do anything except cry out silently against its bonds.

She shuddered, and backed away. He watched her, puzzled. "What is it?" he asked.

She shook her head. "I can't. I can't talk with you."

"Do you think I mean to harm you? I'd like to meet the man who would try. I can see the strength in you, Chava."

She started—but of course, she'd told him her name that night. Rash, far too rash!

"All right," he said. "Let us say this. One question. Answer me one question honestly, and I will answer one of yours. And then, if you want, I'll leave you alone."

She considered. He already knew too much. But if it would make him go away . . . "All right," she said. "One question. Ask it."

"Did you like the bird?"

This was his question? She looked for a hidden catch or meaning, but it seemed plain enough. "Yes," she said. "It's beautiful." And then, belatedly, "Thank you."

He nodded, pleased. "Not my best work," he said. "The light here is too poor. But you put me in mind of it. It's a desert bird, and quick to startle." He smiled. "Now. Your turn."

There *was* a question, actually, something she'd been wondering all day. "How did you know that I don't sleep?"

Now it was his turn to look startled. "What do you mean?"

"You came here last night and stood beneath my window, and you knew I wouldn't be asleep in bed. How?"

That brought him up short. He laughed in genuine surprise. "I don't know," he said. "I didn't even consider it." He thought for a long moment, and finally said, "That night, when we met, you didn't move like someone who should be home in bed. Perhaps that's how I knew. Everyone else walks differently at night than during the day. Have you noticed?"

"Yes!" she exclaimed. "As though they're fighting off sleep, or running away from it, even if they're wide awake."

"But not you," he said. "You were lost, but you were walking as though the sun was high overhead."

Little else could have weakened her defenses so thoroughly. It was the sort of observation that she couldn't have shared with anyone else, not even the Rabbi. He would have appreciated the insight, but he wouldn't have felt its truth with the same estrangement, the same sense of watching from a distance.

He was searching her face, judging her reaction. "Please," he said. "I only want to talk. No harm will come to you. You have my word."

Caution commanded her to turn her back on him, to return to the boardinghouse. But she felt the cool, bracing air on her face, and the stiff ache in her limbs. She looked up at her own window; and suddenly the thought of spending the rest of the night in her room, silently sewing, seemed unbearable.

"Do you promise," she said, "to never tell anyone else about me, ever again?"

"I promise." He raised an eyebrow. "Will you do the same?"

What could she do? He'd shown no duplicity; she'd have to match him. "Yes. I promise. But we must go somewhere else. Somewhere private, where we can't be overheard."

He smiled, pleased at his success. "All right. Somewhere private." He considered, and then said, "Have you ever been to the aquarium?"

"Amazing," the Golem murmured, half an hour later.

They were standing in the main gallery of the aquarium, in front of a tank of small sharks. The long, elegant shapes moved slowly in the dark water, their wide-open eyes tracking their visitors' every movement.

The Djinni studied her as she wandered from tank to tank. She'd been an alert presence at his side on the walk to Battery Park, and then a disapproving pair of eyes boring into his back as he melted through the padlock on the door. (The guard must have tired of his post, or else the weather had grown too cold, for he was nowhere to be seen.) Her looks were pleasing enough, but not tempting, by any stretch. Had she been human, he would've passed her on the street without a second thought.

"I crossed the ocean once," the Golem said. "I never knew there were creatures like this below me."

"I've never seen the ocean, only the bay," the Djinni replied. "What was it like?"

"Enormous. Cold. It stretched on forever, in every direction. If I hadn't known otherwise, I would've thought that the whole world was ocean."

He shivered at the image. "It sounds terrible."

"No, it was beautiful," she said. "The water was always changing."

They stood together, silent and tense. It was strange, he thought— now that she'd consented to talk with him, he had little idea how to go about it.

"I was brought to life on the ocean," she said. Then she paused, as if listening to the echo of her words, not quite believing she'd said them aloud.

"Brought to life," he said.

"In a ship's hold. By a man. He was my master, for a brief time. A very brief time." Each phrase seemed dragged from deep within her, as though she was fighting herself to say it. "He died, soon afterward."

"Did you kill him?"

"No!" She turned, shocked. "He'd been sick! I would never have done such a thing!"

"I meant no offense," he said. "You called him your *master*. I assumed he forced you to be his servant."

"It wasn't like that," she muttered.

The wary silence fell again. They watched the sharks for a while, and were themselves watched.

"I had a master as well," the Djinni said. "A wizard. I gladly would have killed him." He frowned. "I hope I *did* kill him. But I can't remember." And he laid bare the tale: his life in the desert, the loss of his memory, his capture and incomplete release, the iron cuff that still bound him to human form.

Her face softened somewhat while he talked. "How terrible," she said when he was finished.

"I don't mean to gain your pity," he said, irritated. "I only want to explain myself, so that you don't run from me like a scared child."

"If I'm overcautious, it's for good reason," she retorted. "I must be careful."

"And the night we met? If you must be careful, how did you come to be so lost?"

"I wasn't myself then," she muttered. "That was the night the Rabbi died."

"I see." He had the grace to feel slightly embarrassed. "Who was he?"

"A good man. My guardian. He took me in, after my master died."

"You've had poor luck with masters and guardians."

Stung, she flinched. "My master was sick, and my guardian was old."

"And you're so helpless, that you have need of either?"

"You don't understand," she said, hugging her arms close to her body.

"Tell me, then."

She eyed him. "Not yet," she said. "No, I'm not certain of you."

He was growing impatient. "Then what else should I tell you?"

"Tell me what you do at night while the people are sleeping."

He gestured around himself. "This is what I do. I walk the city. I go where I will."

Longing darkened her eyes. "It sounds wonderful."

"You say that as though something keeps you from doing the same."

"Of course it does! How could I go out alone, after dark? I would be noticed, an unaccompanied woman on the street. The night our paths crossed was the only time I've ever gone out at night on my own."

"You mean you stay in your room, every night? But what do you *do*?"

She shrugged, uncomfortable. "I sew clothing. I watch the people go by."

"But surely you, of all people, would be in no danger!"

"Say someone approaches me, a man looking to attack or rob me. What if I pull away from him, and he notices my strength? Or, worse, what if I injure him? Word will spread—and then what? I'd be hunted until I was found. Innocent people would be hurt."

Her fears echoed the scenario that Arbeely had painted for him— and yet she had submitted so meekly, accepting the very imprisonment he fought against. He pitied her; he wanted to push her away. "But how can you stand it?"

"It's difficult," she said quietly. "Especially now that the nights are so long."

"And this is how you'll live out your life?"

She turned away. "I don't like to think about it," she said. Her fingers were twisting around one another, and she looked about, as if searching for escape.

"But why can't you—"

"I just can't!" she cried. "Whatever you'll suggest, I've considered it! Anything else would endanger myself and others, and how could I be so selfish? But there are nights when all I want to do is run and run! I don't know how much longer—" She stopped suddenly, one hand over her mouth.

"Chava . . ." Pity won out, and he placed a hand on her arm.

She wrenched away from him. "Don't touch me!" she cried; and then turned and ran into the darkness of the next gallery.

He was left somewhat stunned. She'd pulled away from him with astonishing force. In this, at least, she was correct: if others saw her strength, she'd certainly be noticed.

He was beginning to wonder if he'd been wise to pursue her attention. When they'd met, her fear and reticence had piqued his curiosity; now they only seemed debilitating, a sign of deeper troubles. But still he followed her into the next gallery. She stood before one of the largest tanks in the aquarium, full of tiny, colorful fish. He approached, but kept his distance.

"There are almost a hundred fish in this tank," she muttered. "I can't count them properly, they keep moving."

"I only meant to help," he said.

"I know."

"Arbeely—the tinsmith I told you about—he tells me I must be cautious. And I know he is right, to a degree. But if I hide away forever, I'll go mad. And neither of us should have to give every night over to our fears." The idea had been building in his mind as he spoke, and now he said, "Come walking with me instead."

Her eyes widened in surprise—and instantly he wondered what had compelled him. She was so cautious, so afraid! She'd hold him back, surely. Yet the thought of her caged in her room filled him with such horror—as if it were his own fate, and not hers—that he'd spoken without truly considering.

Doubtfully she said, "You're offering yourself as company?"

He resigned himself to his offer. "Let us say, one night a week. It makes sense, doesn't it? A lone woman would draw attention, but this way you wouldn't be alone."

"And where exactly would you take me?"

He began to warm to the task of convincing her. "I could show you many things. Places like this." He gestured to the water and glass around them. "The parks at night, the rivers. We could walk all night long, and only see a fraction of this city. If all you've seen is your own neighborhood, then you have no idea." To his surprise, his enthusiasm was growing genuine.

She turned back to the fish, as if looking to them for her answer, or reassurance. "All right," she said at last. "For now, we'll say one night only. A week from today. But there's something you need to know first. It wouldn't be fair to you otherwise." Visibly she gathered her courage, and said, "When you told me what had happened to you—with the wizard—it answered a question. There's a *need* in you." He gave her a quizzical look, but she went on. "Golems are meant to be ruled by a master. A golem senses its master's thoughts, and responds to them, without thinking. My own master is dead. But that ability didn't go away."

It took him a moment to realize what she was saying. He felt himself start to recoil. "You can read minds?"

Quickly she shook her head. "Nothing as certain as that. Fears, desires. Needs. If I'm not careful, they can overwhelm me. But—you're different."

"Different how?"

"Harder to see clearly." She was searching his face now; he repressed the urge to back away. "I see your face as lit from within, and shaded without. Your mind is the same. It's as though part of you is constantly struggling to be free. It shadows everything else."

This, he thought, was much more than he had bargained for. He now understood her uncanny presence, her sense of listening to something unheard; but the explanation was even more unsettling.

"I only wanted you to know," she said. "I'll understand if you withdraw your offer."

He considered. Well, it was only one night. If she proved too eerie, they would part company.

"My offer still stands," he said. "One night. One week from today." And she smiled.

They left the aquarium and made their way back to her neighborhood. The streets were uncommonly quiet, the dark broken by a lamp-lit window here and there. As they walked, he found himself examining his own thoughts; he found no desires that he was ashamed of her sensing. And his fears? Captivity, boredom, discovery. Each of which she knew as well as he.

Perhaps, he thought, *it will not be so terrible*. They would walk about, they would talk. It would be a novelty, if nothing else.

At her request they stopped in the alley next to the boardinghouse, away from her neighbors' eyes. He asked, "Have I at least convinced you that I mean you no harm?"

She smiled slightly. "For the most part."

"I suppose that will have to do. Until next week." He turned to go.

"Wait." She touched his arm. "Please, remember your promise. I must stay hidden. If not from you, then from everyone else."

"I keep my promises," he said. "As I trust you keep yours."

She nodded. "Of course."

"Then I will see you in seven nights."

"Good-bye," she said, and with no more ceremony disappeared around the corner.

He walked home unsure of what he had just let into his life. It was early yet, perhaps four in the morning. He thought he'd work on one of his figurines—there was an ibis only half completed. He couldn't work the proportions correctly, the bill was all wrong and the legs too thick.

As he climbed the front steps of his building, a figure interposed itself between him and the door. It was a man, old and gaunt, in what looked like layers of rags and a smirched overcoat. A grubby scarf was wound about his head. The man's stance, his dark accusatory stare, made the Djinni think he'd been lying in wait.

"*What are you?*" croaked the man.

The Djinni frowned. "I beg your pardon."

"I can look at you," the man said. "There's no death in your face." His tone was hysterical, his eyes so wide the whites shone. He grabbed at the front of the Djinni's coat and shouted up at him. "I can see you! You're made of fire! *Tell me what you are!*"

The Djinni froze, horrified. A pair of boys, up early and drawn by the shouts, crept around the doorframe to watch the commotion. The old man cried out and turned away from them, letting go of the Djinni. His throat worked for a moment; and then he backed down the stairs, one hand shielding his eyes, and trudged unsteadily down the street.

"You all right, mister?" one of the boys asked.

"Yes, of course." It was a lie. He'd been terrified enough to consider pushing the man down the steps.

"That's Ice Cream Saleh," the other boy said. "He's funny in the head."

"I see," the Djinni said. "A madman. And why is he allowed to live here?"

"He don't break no laws, I guess. And he makes the best ice cream around. But he can't look no one in the face. He gets sick."

"Interesting," said the Djinni. "Thank you." He found a couple of pennies in his coat pocket, and gave one to each of them. Satisfied, they ran off down the stairs.

The Djinni was profoundly disturbed. If this man—whoever he was—could truly see him, should he be worried about his safety? He couldn't tell Arbeely; the man would only panic and demand that the Djinni stay locked in his room with the window covered. Besides, he thought, growing calmer, if the man was considered a lunatic—and he certainly looked the part—then whatever he might say could be dismissed as meaningless. For now, the Djinni decided, he would merely be watchful.

Arbeely was in a good mood that morning—another large order had come through, of soup pots this time—and he greeted the Djinni cheerfully. "Good morning! Did you have an exciting night? Meet with any more clay women? Or women made of anything else?"

For a moment the Djinni considered telling him about the Golem. Arbeely already knew about her, after all; he'd only promised to tell no one else. But he liked the idea of having a secret from Arbeely, something that the man could not scold him about.

"No," the Djinni said. "I saw no one special." And he set out his tools and tied on his apron while Arbeely bustled about the shop, none the wiser.

14.

After three days in the ward at Swinburne Island, Michael Levy's fever finally broke. The doctors kept him there for another two weeks, feeding him broth and mashed vegetables, helping him walk up and down the drafty halls. He was malnourished, they told him, and dangerously anemic. *Get yourself married*, they said. *You need a wife to fatten you up.*

He ate, and slept, and his body healed. A letter came from the Sheltering House board wishing him a quick return, which he took to mean that the House was coming unglued without him. One night the nurses caught him walking around the ward, talking with the patients, encouraging them to petition the Ellis Island officials for reentry. They shooed him back to bed and threatened to tie him down again.

It was almost New Year's when Michael was discharged. He stood at the ferry's rail bundled against an icy wind that turned the water dark and choppy. He'd put on five pounds and felt better than he had in months. He'd begun to think of his illness as a strange parting gift from his uncle, an opportunity to rest and be cared for. Not quite taking the waters at Saratoga, but as close as he'd ever get.

The ferry pushed away from the thin pilings, chugging against the current. Night had fallen. Staten Island and Brooklyn slumbered to either side, their clapboard villages battened down for the winter. The tip of Manhattan appeared at the north end of the bay, and Michael's equanimity wavered. What chaos would be waiting for him at the House? The wind picked up, but he stayed on deck and watched the Statue of Liberty go by, and tried to draw strength from her calm and compassionate gaze.

In the Sheltering House, it was just past lights-out. A hundred and fifty men lay on their cots, covered with thin blankets. Some were awake with fears for their new life; others soon gave in to the exhaustion of the voyage, or a day spent looking for work.

On a cot near the window on the third floor, the man now known as Joseph Schall slept as deeply and peacefully as a child.

It was chance pure and simple that had brought Schaalman to the Sheltering House. After that bureaucrat at Ellis Island had changed his name—any number of revenges had risen to his lips, but he'd pushed them all down again—he'd descended the wide staircase and come face-to-face with the Manhattan skyline, framed in tall windows at the end of the hall. It was a forbidding and majestic view, and it stopped him in his tracks. Ever since his dream of the city he'd known the task before him to be difficult; but now, facing the real thing across the bay, it struck him as flat-out impossible. He spoke no English, was unused to people and crowds, didn't even have a place to sleep. Were there inns in New York? Or stables? Surely at least there were stables?

A hand touched his arm, and he turned, startled. It was a young woman with a round-cheeked face. She asked, "Sir, do you speak Yiddish?"

"Yes," he said warily.

She explained that she was a volunteer with the Hebrew Immigrant Aid Society. Was there anything he needed? Could they offer him any assistance?

Were it any other time or place, he would have searched her for weaknesses to exploit, or simply fuddled her mind and then robbed her. But now, tired, depressed, and defeated, he resorted to his most hated gambit: the truth. "I have nowhere to stay," he muttered.

She told him of a place called the Hebrew Sheltering House and said there was a boat that could take him there. Meekly he followed her out to the dock, clutching his suitcase like a frightened child.

But within a day of arriving at the Sheltering House, he was returned to his old self-confidence. In a way, life at the House was like being incarcerated again. The cots, the dormitories, the foul water closets and the communal meals, the ever-changing roster of faces: here was a place he understood, with overseers to manipulate, and rules to be bent or broken. All in all, the perfect bolt-hole.

There were only two hard and fast rules at the Hebrew Sheltering House: meals had to be eaten in the dining hall at the appointed times, and no man could stay more than five days. Breaking the second rule proved even easier than the first. By luck, the director of the Sheltering House had fallen ill. The cook and the housekeeper had divided his duties between them and spent all day running frantically this way and that, trying to maintain order. On Schaalman's third day, forty newcomers stepped off the ferry and came through the door, to find only eighteen unoccupied cots. The new arrivals milled uneasily on the landing, while the cook and housekeeper searched for the misplaced roster that would have set everything to rights. Failing to find it and both near tears, they went to each dormitory and asked if the men who'd overstayed would please own up to it. They were met with nothing but blank stares. With so many men coming and going, and so much time spent searching for work or a place to live, even the ones who might have reported the rule breakers had little idea where to point.

But Schaalman had been observing them all for days. He looked about, and found a number of men who'd been there when he arrived. He watched their faces as the women pleaded, and saw the telltale signs of guilt and defiance. He took the women aside for a brief conversation. With his help, they recruited two large men from among the new arrivals. Then they went from dormitory to dormitory and tossed out the wrongdoers while Schaalman looked on, a stern yet mild judge.

The cook and the housekeeper couldn't thank him enough. He replied that he was glad to help—of course order had to be kept, everyone must follow the rules—and if they needed him for anything else, he was at their disposal. They kissed his cheek like grateful daughters. Later that night Schaalman retrieved the missing roster from under his cot and replaced it in the office, between the pages of a newspaper.

The next day, he volunteered to help with the new arrivals. While the women checked off names and bustled about, he directed men to their bunks and explained the rules of the house. Afterward, with all settled, the women invited him into the office and gave him a glass of schnapps.

"What Mr. Levy doesn't know won't hurt him," the housekeeper whispered, and struck Joseph Schall from the next day's departure list.

Over the next week Schaalman solidified his position. He took to straightening up the parlor, folding the newspapers, and refilling the tea-pot. At mealtimes he monitored the queue and told the cook how many mouths were left to feed. He seemed to be everywhere at once, helping with one thing or another, even adjudicating the men's paltry quibbles.

When he wasn't insinuating himself into the fabric of the Sheltering House, he was out learning the neighborhood. At first the streets had been overwhelming, a churning porridge of people and wagons and animals; but after a week he could step off the curb and melt seamlessly into the crowd, just another old Jew in a dark overcoat. He'd walk for hours, taking note of the streets and shops, marking in his mind the edges of the neighborhood where the Yiddish faded from the shop windows. As he went he'd make a mental list of the largest Orthodox synagogues, the ones most likely to have decent libraries. And then he'd reverse his steps and go back to the Sheltering House, in time to help settle the newest group of men.

The cook began to set aside a stash of the best food for him, fat pickles and chunks of pastrami. The housekeeper called him an angel sent from heaven, and piled him with extra blankets. And meanwhile, in his battered suitcase beneath his cot, his piecemeal book lay sleeping. If one of his housemates had happened to come across it, the man would have seen nothing special—only a worn and unremarkable prayer book.

The Djinni appeared beneath the Golem's window a few minutes past midnight. She'd been pacing for nearly an hour—she knew the neigh-bors would hear, but she couldn't help it, her entire body ached with cold and apprehension. With each turn she stopped to peer out the window. Would he come as he'd said? Would it be better if he didn't? And what had possessed her to agree to this in the first place?

When finally she saw him she felt both a burst of relief and a fresh wave of misgiving. She was in such a state that she made it halfway down the stairs before realizing she'd forgotten her cloak and gloves, and had to go back for them.

"You came," she said to him when she reached the street.

He raised an eyebrow. "You doubted it?"

"You might have thought better of it."

"And you might not have come down. But since we're both here, I thought we might go to Madison Square Park. Is that agreeable?"

The name meant nothing to her, and in a sense all possible destinations were the same: unknown places, unknown risks. She had two choices. She could say yes, or turn back.

"Yes," she said. "Let's go."

And with no more discussion, they set off along Broome Street. Suddenly she wanted to burst out laughing. She was outside, she was walking! Her legs were so stiff the joints almost creaked, but the movement felt delicious, like the scratching of a long-denied itch. He went quickly, but she easily matched his pace, keeping to his side. He didn't offer to take her arm, as she'd seen other men do, and she was glad: it would have meant walking slowly, and too close together.

At Chrystie he turned north, and she followed. They were at the edge of her neighborhood now, the border of her knowledge. The cacophony of the Bowery echoed from the next block. A few men crossed their path, and she pulled the hood of her cloak lower.

"Don't do that," the Djinni said.

"Why not?"

"You look like you have something to hide."

But didn't she? The euphoria of movement was subsiding; she was growing scared all over again, frightened of the liberties she'd allowed herself to take. They reached Houston Street, and she glanced sidelong at her companion. Was it strange that they weren't talking? The people she saw walking at night usually talked to each other. But then, he usually traveled on his own. And the silence was not uncomfortable.

They came to Great Jones, and then the electric-lit expanse of Broadway. The buildings here stretched higher, wider, and she pushed her hood back, the better to see it all. Brick and limestone gave way to marble and glass. Shop-front windows beckoned with dresses and fabrics, feathered hats, jewels and necklaces and earrings. Mesmerized, she left the Djinni's side to peer at a dress-form bedecked with a sweeping, intricate gown in sapphire silk. How long it must have taken to sew something so beautiful, so complicated! She traced the seams with her eyes, trying to learn its construction; and the Djinni, growing impatient on the sidewalk, came to retrieve her.

At Fourteenth Street they came upon a large park, with an enormous statue of a man sitting on a horse, and the Golem wondered if this was their destination. But the Djinni continued on, skirting the west side of the park until it rejoined Broadway. The streets were now eerily quiet and stretched empty in all directions save for the occasional slow-trotting brougham. They passed a thin triangle of empty land at Twenty-third Street, strewn with snow-rimed newspapers that rattled in the wind. The triangle lay at a wide confluence of avenues; in one street stood a magnificent white arch and colonnade. The arch shone with electric lights that turned the colonnade into tall bars of light and shadow, and cast a faint glow along the lowering sky.

Madison Square Park sat before them, a dark grove of leafless trees. They crossed into it, and meandered along the empty paths. Even the homeless had left to search out warm doorways and stairwells. Only the Golem and the Djinni were there to take in the quiet. The Golem left the Djinni's side to study whatever caught her eye: dark metal monuments of solemn-faced men, the iron curl of a park bench. She stepped across the snow to lay a hand on a tree trunk's rough bark, then looked up to see the naked branches spreading themselves across the sky.

"This is better than sitting in your room all night, is it not?" asked the Djinni as they walked.

"It is," she admitted. "Are all the parks this large?"

He laughed. "They come much larger than this." He glanced at her sidelong. "How is it that you've *never* been to a park?"

"I suppose it's because I haven't been alive for very long," she said.

He frowned, confused. "How old are you?"

She thought. "Six months. And a few days."

The Djinni stopped short. "Six *months*?"

"Yes."

"But—" He gestured at her, the sweep of his hand taking in her adult form and appearance.

"I was created as you see me," she said, feeling uneasy; she wasn't used to talking about herself. "Golems don't age, we simply continue as we are, unless we're destroyed."

"And all golems are like this?"

"I think so. I can't be certain. I've never met another golem."

"What, *none?*"

"I might be the only one," she said.

Clearly astonished, the Djinni said nothing. They continued on together, walking the perimeter of the park.

"And how old are you?" the Golem said, to break the silence.

"A few hundred years," he said. "Unless some mishap ends me, I'll live another five or six hundred."

"Then you're also young for your kind."

"Not as young as some."

She frowned. "You hold my age against me?"

"No, it explains much. Your timidity, for instance."

At that, she bristled. "I make no apologies for being cautious. I have to be. As do you."

"But there's caution, and then there is overcaution. Look at us. Walking at night in a park, far from home. And yet the moon doesn't fall from the heavens, and the ground refuses to tremble."

"Just because nothing has happened doesn't mean that nothing *will* happen."

He smiled. "True. Perhaps I'll be surprised. And then you can declare that you were right all along."

"It would be small comfort."

"Are you always this humorless?"

"Yes. Are you always this exasperating?"

He chuckled. "You really should meet Arbeely. You two would get along wonderfully."

She did smile at that. "You keep mentioning him. Are you very close?"

She'd expected him to launch into an enthusiastic description of his friend; but he only said, "The man means well. And he's helped me, certainly."

"And yet?" she prompted.

The Djinni sighed. "I'm less grateful to him than I should be. He's a good and generous man, but I'm not accustomed to relying on someone else. It makes me feel weak."

"How is relying on others a weakness?"

"How can it be anything else? If for some reason Arbeely died to-morrow, I'd be forced to find another occupation. The event would be outside my control, yet I'd be at its mercy. Is that not weakness?"

"I suppose. But then, going by your standard, everyone is weak. So why call it a weakness, instead of just the way things are?"

"Because I was above this once!" he said with sudden vehemence. "I depended on no one! I went where I would and followed my desires. I needed no money, no employer, no neighbors. None of this interminable *good morning* and *how are you*, whether one feels like it or not."

"But weren't you ever lonely?"

"Oh, sometimes. But then I'd seek out my own kind, and enjoy their company for a while. And then we'd part ways again, as we saw fit."

She tried to imagine it: a life without occupation or neighbors, with-out the bakery and the Radzins and Anna. With no familiar faces, no set pattern to her days. It felt terrifying. She said, "I don't think golems are made for such independence."

"You only say that because you've lived no other way."

She shook her head. "You misunderstand me. Each golem is built to serve a master. When I woke, I was already bound to mine. To his will. I heard his every thought, and I obeyed with no hesitation."

"That's terrible," the Djinni said.

"To you, perhaps. To me it felt like the way things were meant to be. And when he died—when that connection left me—I no longer had a clear purpose. Now I'm bound to *everyone*, if only a little. I have to fight against it, I can't be solving everyone's wishes. But sometimes, at the bakery where I work, I'll give someone a loaf of bread—and it answers a need. For a moment, that person is my master. And in that moment, I'm content. If I were as independent as you wish you were, I'd feel I had no purpose at all."

He frowned. "Were you so happy, to be ruled by another?"

"Happy is not the word," she said. "It felt *right*."

"All right, then let me ask you this. If by some chance or magic you could have your master back again, would you wish it?"

It was an obvious question, but one that she had never quite asked herself. She'd barely known Rotfeld, even to know what sort of a man he was. But then, couldn't she guess? What sort of man would take a golem for a wife, the way a delivery man might purchase a new cart?

But oh, to be returned to that certainty! The memory of it rose up, sharp and beguiling. And she wouldn't feel as though she was being used. One choice, one decision—and then, nothing.

"I don't know," she said at last. "Maybe I would. Though in a way, I think it would be like dying. But perhaps it would be for the best. I make so many mistakes, on my own."

There was a noise from the Djinni, something not quite a laugh. His mouth was a hard line; he stared up beyond the trees, as though he couldn't bear to look at her.

"I said something to offend you," she said.

"Don't do that," he snapped. "Don't *look into* me."

"I didn't need to," she retorted. An unaccustomed defiance was rising in her. She'd given him an honest answer, and apparently it had repelled him. Well, so be it. If he didn't want her company, she could find her own way home. She was no child, whatever he thought.

She'd half decided to turn back toward Broadway; but then he said, "Do you remember what I told you before? That I was captured, but have no memory of it?"

"Yes, of course I remember."

"I have no idea," he said, "how long I was that man's servant. His *slave*. I don't know what he made me do. I might have done terrible things. Perhaps I killed for him. I might have killed my own kind." There was a tight edge in his voice, painful to hear. "But even worse would be if I did it all *gladly*. If he robbed me of my will, and turned me against myself. Given a choice, I'd sooner extinguish myself in the ocean."

"But if all those terrible things did happen, then it was the wizard's fault, not yours," she said.

Again, that not-quite laugh. "Do you have colleagues at this bakery where you work?"

"Of course," she said. "Moe and Thea Radzin, and Anna Blumberg."

He said, "Imagine that your precious master returns to you, and you give yourself to him, as you say you perhaps would. Because you make so many *mistakes*. And he says, 'Please, my dear golem, kill those good people at the bakery, the Radzins and Anna Blumberg. Rip them limb from limb.'"

"But why—"

"Oh, for whatever reason! They insult him, or make threats against him, or he simply develops a whim. *Imagine* it. And then tell me what comfort it gives to think it wasn't your own fault."

This was a possibility she'd never considered. And now she couldn't help but picture it: grabbing Moe Radzin by the wrist and pulling until his arm came free. She had the strength. She could do it. And all the while, that peace and certainty.

No, she thought—but now, having started down this path, her mind refused to stop. What if Rotfeld had made it safely to America with her, and the Rabbi had noticed them on the street one day? In her mind, the Rabbi confronted Rotfeld—and then she was dragging the Rabbi into an alley, and choking the life from him.

It made her want to cry out. She put the heels of her hands to her eyes, to push the images away.

"Now do you understand?" the Djinni asked.

"Leave me alone!"

It rang across the square, echoing from the stone facades. Startled, the Djinni backed away, hands raised—to placate her, or to ward off an attack.

Silence descended again. She stretched her fingers wide, trying to calm herself. The things she'd pictured were imaginary. She hadn't hurt the Radzins or Anna. There was no reason why she would. Rotfeld was dead; his body lay at the bottom of the ocean. She would never have another master.

"All right," she said. "Yes. I see your point."

"It wasn't my intention to upset you," the Djinni said.

"Wasn't it?" she muttered.

A pause. "If it was, then I was in the wrong."

"No. You were right. I hadn't considered it like that." She looked away, feeling guilty and uncomfortable.

They heard the footsteps at the same time. Two policemen were jogging toward them from down the path, their wool greatcoats flapping at their boots. In the sleeping square, with no one else about, their concern for the Golem struck her with almost physical force.

"Evening, miss," one of them said, touching his cap. "Is this man bothering you?"

She shook her head. "No, he isn't. I'm sorry, you needn't have come."

"You yelled awful loud, miss."

"It was my fault," the Djinni said. "I said something I shouldn't have."

The policemen were looking from one of them to the other, trying to read the truth of the situation: a man and a woman, clearly not vagrants, out together at this hour, in the freezing cold . . .

She had put them in this position. Perhaps, if she said the right thing, she could get them out of it again.

"Dearest," the Golem said, placing a hand on the Djinni's arm, "we should be getting home. It *is* rather cold."

Surprise flared in the Djinni's eyes, but he stifled it quickly. "Of course," he said, and tucked her hand into the crook of his elbow. He smiled at the men. "I apologize, officers. My fault entirely. Good night."

And they turned and walked away.

"Good night," one of the officers called halfheartedly after them.

Silently they walked back through the park, the air tense between them. Not until they were at Broadway did the Djinni risk looking back. "We're alone," he said, dropping her hand.

"I know. They didn't follow. They wanted to go back to their precinct-house and get warm again."

"That's a strange gift you have," he said, shaking his head. Then he smirked down at her. "*Dearest?*"

"It's what Mrs. Radzin calls her husband when she's angry at him."

"I see. That was clever."

"It was a risk."

"But it worked. And still the sky hasn't fallen."

So it hadn't, she thought. No lasting harm had been done. For once, she had said the right thing at the right time.

They walked on, retracing their path south. The thin traffic on Broadway was changing: no longer elegant broughams, but delivery wagons hitched to workaday horses, pulling the day's goods to the heart of the city. On a corner a shoeshine boy set up his box, then huddled in on himself, blowing on his naked fingers.

They'd just passed Union Square when the snow began to fall. At first it was only a thin sleet, but then it grew heavier, turning to clumps of flakes that blew into their faces. The Golem pulled her cloak closer about herself, and noticed that the Djinni had quickened his pace. She had to hurry to catch up. She was about to ask him what was the matter; but then she noticed that his face wasn't wet, despite the driving snow. As she watched, the flakes landed on him and instantly disappeared. She recalled what he'd said when they were arguing: *I would sooner extinguish myself in the ocean.*

"Are you all right?" she asked.

"I'm fine," he replied; but his distracted tone clashed with his words. And she would have sworn that the glow of his face had dimmed.

Quietly she asked, "Are you in danger?"

His jaw tightened, in anger or irritation; but then he relaxed, and gave her a rueful smile. "No. Not yet. Did you see it, or did you guess?"

"Both, I think."

"From now on I'll remember that you're far too observant."

"The winter must be dreadful for you."

"I certainly haven't enjoyed it."

They moved to walk under the protection of the awnings; but even so, by the time that they reached Bond Street he was looking pale indeed. The Golem couldn't help casting worried glances in his direction.

He muttered, "You can stop looking at me like that, I'm not about to perish."

"But why don't you wear a hat, or carry an umbrella?"

"Because I can't stand either."

"Are all your kind so stubborn?"

At that he smiled. "Most of us, yes."

Near Hester they stopped beneath the awning of an Italian grocer's; in the window hung enormous red sausages suspended by twine, next to twisted strings of garlic bulbs. A warm and pungent smell came from the open door. "I can go the rest of the way on my own," she said.

"You're certain?"

She nodded. They were only a few blocks from the Bowery, and beyond it her own neighborhood. "I'll be fine," she said.

They stood there together, both uneasy.

"I don't know if we should see each other again," she said.

He frowned. "You're still uncertain of my intentions?"

"No, your tolerance. We angered each other."

"I can stand a little anger," he said. "Can you?"

It was a challenge, but also an invitation. He *had* angered her, and made her feel ashamed; but she'd also talked freely with someone for the first time since the Rabbi's death. She felt something loosening inside her that had nothing to do with her body's stiffness.

"All right," she said. "On one condition."

"Yes?"

"If the weather looks threatening, you must wear a hat. I refuse to be responsible for your ill health."

His eyes rolled heavenward. "If I must," he said, but she caught a hint of a smile. "Next week, at the same time?"

"Yes. Now please, find somewhere dry. Good-bye." She turned and walked away.

"Until next week," he called after her; but she was already around the corner, and he couldn't see her smile.

"I told you I would come again," the Djinni said to the dreaming Fadwa. "Did you doubt me?"

In her dream, they stood together on the ridge near her family's camp, where she had first seen his palace. It was nighttime, and still warm. The ground was soft beneath her feet. She was wearing only a thin shift, but she felt no self-consciousness.

"No," she said. "Only—it's been so long since I saw you last. Weeks and weeks."

"A long time for you, perhaps," he said. "My kind can go years without seeing each other and think little of it."

"I thought perhaps you were displeased with me. Or . . ." She paused, and then burst out, "I'd convinced myself you were just a dream! I started to think I was going mad!"

He smiled. "I'm real enough, I assure you."

"Yes, but how can I be certain?"

"You've already seen my palace once." He pointed down into the valley. "If you were to ride in this direction, and were lucky in your aim, you'd find a clearing swept clean of brush and rocks. That is where my palace is."

"Would I be able to see it again?"

"No—it's invisible unless I choose otherwise."

She sighed. "You must live in a *very* different way, if you think this is a reassurance."

At that, he laughed. Surprising, that a human girl could make him laugh! But she was still frowning, clearly unhappy. Perhaps he'd waited too long, as she said. There was still so much to learn about these brief human lives, their constant sense of urgency.

He reached out, still not quite knowing how he did so. A blur of stars and desert—and then they were in his palace again, among the dark glass walls and embroidered cushions. This time, atop the cushions, a feast: platters of rice and lamb and yogurt, flatbreads and cheese, and pitchers of crystalline water.

Fadwa laughed, delighted.

"It's for you," he said, gesturing. "Please, eat."

And so she ate, and chatted, telling him of small victories, a sick lamb nursed to health, the summer that was proving relatively mild. "There's even still water at the spring," she said. "My father says it's unusual for so late in the season."

"Your father," the Djinni said. "Tell me more about him."

"He's a good man," she said. "He takes care of us all. My uncles look up to him, and all of my tribe respect him. We're among the smallest of the Hadid clans, but when we gather together, others will seek out his advice before bringing important matters before the sheikh. If his father had been the first son of my great-grandfather, and not the third, then my father might be the sheikh himself."

"Would your life have been very different, then?" He was not quite following all this talk of tribes and clans and sheikhs, but the fondness in her voice and her eyes intrigued him.

She smiled. "If my father were sheikh, then I would not exist! He would have been promised to a different woman, from a more important clan than my mother's."

"Promised?"

"Betrothed. My father's father and my mother's father agreed on it, when my mother was born." She saw his confusion, and giggled. "Do djinn not marry? Don't you have parents?"

"Of course we have parents," he said. "We must come from *somewhere*. But betrothal, marriage—no, these things are unknown to us. We are much more free with our affections."

Her eyes widened as she took this in. "You mean . . . with *anyone*?"

He chuckled at her astonished face. "I prefer women, but yes, you have the sense of it."

She colored. "And with . . . *human* women?"

"None as of yet."

She glanced away. "A Bedouin girl who did such things would be shunned."

"A harsh punishment for acting on natural impulses," he said. This, he thought, was growing ever more intriguing—not the human ideas, which were ridiculous, rigid, and unnecessary, but the push and pull of their conversation, the way he could elicit blushes from her with only the barest mention of a plain fact.

"It's our way," she said. "How much harder would our lives be, if we must worry about love affairs and jealousies? It's better this way, I think."

"And you," he said. "Are you also promised? Or will you choose your own mate?"

She hesitated; she was, he sensed, uneasy on this subject. And then—a sharp jolt, as though the ground beneath them had shuddered.

Fadwa clutched at her cushion. "What was that?"

It was the morning. He'd stayed too long. Someone was trying to wake her.

Another shudder. He reached across and took up her hand, pressed it briefly to his lips. "Until next time," he said, and let her go.

Someone was calling her name. She opened her eyes—but hadn't they already been open?—and there was her mother, leaning above her.

"Girl, what is wrong with you! Are you sick? I had to shake you and shake you!"

Fadwa shivered. For a moment, her mother's face had turned sepulchral, the eyes like dark hollows.

A hot breeze billowed the inside of the tent. A sudden noise from outside: the goats braying in their pen. Her mother glanced around, and when she turned back Fadwa saw only her usual face, consternation written in its deep sun-carved lines.

"Now, girl, get up! The goats need milking, just listen to them!"

Fadwa sat up and rubbed her face, half-expecting to wake again in the glass palace, as though that had been reality and this now the dream. All morning, as she worked, she would close her eyes and imagine herself there again, feeling the trail of his lips on her hand, and the glow that had answered it low in her stomach.

15.

The Golem stood on a hillside in a Brooklyn cemetery, next to a plot of recently turned earth. Above the plot sat a headstone with Elsa Meyer's name and dates engraved on one side. The other was still blank, as though it hadn't yet heard the awful news.

Michael Levy had brought her to the cemetery, and he stood behind her now, lost in sadness and guilt. He'd come to see her at the bakery a few days earlier, at closing time, and apologized for not visiting before. "I was at Swinburne," he said. "A case of the flu."

She knew it was the truth, but to the Golem's eye, Michael was healthier than she'd ever seen him. There was a pink tinge to his cheeks, and the dark circles under his eyes had faded. The eyes themselves, though, were still heavy and sad, and too old for his face. His uncle's eyes.

He said, "I just wanted to see if there was anything you needed. I don't know if my uncle was helping you with money, but I know a few people at the Hebrew Immigrant Aid Society . . ."

"Thank you, Michael, but that's quite all right," she said. "I have all I need."

"I suppose your needs are the same as mine," he said with an awkward smile. "A little food, a little sleep, and then back to work."

Her own smile faltered a bit, but he didn't notice and pressed on. "I'm going to visit my uncle's grave tomorrow. I don't know if you keep the Sabbath, but I thought, if you wanted to come . . ."

His nervous hopefulness was making her uncomfortable, but this was something she dearly wanted. "Yes," she said. "I'd be grateful."

They arranged to meet at her boardinghouse at ten in the morning. The bell over the door rattled as he left, jarring in the now-quiet shop.

She found she was relieved that he was gone. If only things could be different between them! It would be good to have a friend to talk to, someone who'd known the Rabbi. But his attraction to her complicated matters, not the least because she saw—perhaps better than he did—how it had grown tangled with guilt and remorse. Instead of a fleeting infatuation, she was becoming a dark fascination. She would have to say something to him. Kindly, if possible.

Anna had been lingering in the back, pretending to fuss with her bootlaces. Now she smiled slyly as the Golem retrieved her cloak.

"Don't look at me like that," the Golem muttered. "He's a friend, nothing more."

"Do you want him to be more?"

"No, I don't!" She paused, forcing her hands to relax; she'd been in danger of ripping the clasp from her cloak. "I don't feel that way. But he does, for me." She turned to Anna, plaintive. "Why can't we just be friendly? Why do there have to be complications?"

"It's the way of the world," Anna said, shrugging.

"It's a nuisance," said the Golem.

"Don't I know it. The boys I've had to turn away! But, Chava, you can't spend the rest of your life alone, either. It just isn't natural!"

"Would it be better to lie to Michael, and say things I don't feel?"

"Of course not. But feelings need time to grow. And I hate to think of you in that boardinghouse with all those dusty bachelors, mending the holes in their drawers."

"I don't mend their *drawers*, Anna!"

The girl burst into giggles. After a moment the Golem smiled as well. She was still uncertain what to make of Anna, with her tempestuous romances and flights of fancy; but the young woman was becoming a surprising source of comfort.

The next morning Michael Levy arrived at the boardinghouse exactly on time. They took a streetcar to Park Row, and then boarded the train to Brooklyn. Nervous among the crush of passengers, she said, "I've never been across the bridge before."

"Don't worry." He smiled. "It's not quite as dangerous as crossing the ocean."

With a series of jolts, the train pulled out of its shed and up the ramp. She watched as they rose, passing delivery wagons and men plodding along on foot. Rooftop chimneys belched soot and steam to either side, and then fell away as they reached the bridge. She'd hoped to see the water, but the train was caged on the inner track behind a stuttering fence of poles and girders. Seen through the fence, the horses and carts on the outer roadway seemed to move with a broken, palsied gait.

The train shuddered to a halt in the Brooklyn shed. With little conversation, Michael led them off the train and onto a succession of streetcars. And then, finally, they were walking up a long drive toward a pair of large, ornate gates.

The world seemed to go quiet as they passed through. The drive narrowed to a curving path, and then opened to a calm vista of snow-topped hills covered with rows of stones.

"It's lovely here," she said, surprised.

They passed tall monuments and ivy-hung mausoleums, and pillared busts of solemn men. At last Michael led her down a row, and there it was: the rectangular mound of white-dusted earth, and the stone with its half-blank face.

She stood at the foot of the grave, wondering what to do. Was Michael expecting her to show her grief? To cry?

Michael cleared his throat. "I'll give you a moment."

"Thank you," she said, grateful. He wandered down the path, out of sight; and she was alone with the Rabbi.

"I miss you," she murmured. She crouched down next to the grave and tried to imagine him there beneath the ground. It seemed impossible, when all her senses told her he had disappeared from the world.

She cast about for what to tell him. "Everyone at the bakery is well," she said. "Anna has a new suitor, and seems happy, though I know you wouldn't approve. I've started taking in mending, to have something to do at night. The nights are still the hardest. But—I went walking this week, at night, with a man. He has to hide himself, like me. I'm seeing him again next week. I'm sorry, Rabbi. I know I shouldn't. But I think it will help, to walk with him."

She trailed a hand along the snow, half-expecting some sort of sign:

a trembling in the ground, a sense of recrimination. But none came. All lay silent.

After a few minutes Michael reappeared on the path and came to stand by her side. "I should give you time," she said, and turned to leave; but he put a hand on her arm. "Please stay," he said. "I don't like being alone in cemeteries." And it was true: a low, formless dread and unease was growing in him.

"Of course," she said, and stood close by his side.

"He was a wonderful man," Michael said; and then he began to cry. "I'm sorry," he said, wiping his face. "I should have done something to prevent this."

"You can't blame yourself," she protested.

"But if I hadn't been so stubborn—if *he* hadn't—"

"Then you would have been different people," the Golem said, hoping that it was the right thing to say. "And he thought very highly of you. He called you a good man."

"He did?"

"Why does that surprise you, when you help so many?"

"I turned my back on religion. How could he not feel I'd turned my back on *him*?"

"I think he understood, in his way," she said hesitantly. She wasn't certain if it was the truth—but Michael seemed comforted, and that, she was sure, was what the Rabbi would have wanted.

Michael sighed, and wiped his face. Together they stared at the headstone. "I'll have to have the engraving done," he said. "Later this year." He glanced at her. "I don't usually pray, but if you'd like—"

"It's all right," the Golem said. "I prayed already, on my own."

Streetcars and trains and more streetcars again, and they were back in the Lower East Side. The sun was low in the sky; a thin snow blew down the alleyways.

"Let me take you to a café," Michael said, and then added, "if you have the time, of course. I don't mean to monopolize your day."

She'd been looking forward to going home; the streetcars had been far too crowded with bodies and their stray desires. But she could come up with no ready excuse, and his hopefulness was tugging at her. "All right," she said. "If you like."

They went to a place he knew, a dark café filled with young men who all seemed to be arguing with each other. He ordered coffee and almond-speckled biscuits, and they sat together, listening to the debates that raged around them.

"I'd forgotten how loud it is here," he said, apologetic.

The voices were in her mind as well, asking for abstract things: *peace, rights, freedom.* "They all sound very angry," she said.

"Oh, absolutely. Each of them has a different theory about what's wrong with the world."

She smiled. "Do you have a theory too?"

"I used to," he said. He sat thinking for a moment, and then said, "I see hundreds of men every week at the Sheltering House. They all need the same things—a place to stay, a job, English lessons. But some will be happy with whatever comes their way, and others won't be satisfied with anything. And there's always a few who are only looking to take advantage. So when my friends talk about how best to fix the world, it all sounds so naïve. As though there could be one solution that would solve every man's problem, turn us into innocents in the Garden of Eden. When in truth we will always have our lesser natures." He looked up at her. "What do *you* think?"

"Me?" she said, startled.

"Do you think we're all good at heart? Or can we only be both good and bad?"

"I don't know," she said, trying not to fidget under his scrutiny. "But I think, sometimes men want what they don't have *because* they don't have it. Even if everyone offered to share, they would only want the share that wasn't theirs."

He nodded. "Exactly. And I can't see that changing. Human nature is the same, no matter the system." Then he chuckled. "I'm sorry, I didn't bring you here to argue politics. Let's talk about something else."

"What should we talk about?"

"Tell me about yourself. I really know very little about you."

Her spirits sank. She'd have to choose her words very carefully.

She'd have to lie, and remember the lies for later. "I was married," she said uncertainly.

"Oh, yes." Michael's face fell. "That I did know. You must miss him."

She could say *Yes, I loved him very much*, and avoid all further inquiry. But didn't Michael deserve some measure of the truth? "I do, sometimes," she said. "But . . . to be honest, we didn't know each other very well."

"Was it an arranged marriage?"

"I suppose, in a sense."

"And your parents gave you no choice?"

"I had no parents," she said flatly. "And he was a wealthy man. He bought what he wanted." That much, at least, was true: she remembered Rotfeld's pride at what his money had paid for, his perfect wife in her wooden box.

"No wonder my uncle wanted to help you," Michael said. "I'm so sorry. I can't even imagine how lonely that must have been."

"It's all right." Already she felt guilty. What stories was he creating in his mind, to fill in the details? Time to turn the conversation back to him, if she could. "And any life must seem lonely compared to yours. You're surrounded by hundreds of men every day."

He laughed. "True enough. Though I don't get to know them very well, since they're only at the House for five days. Although—there's one man who's been with us for a few weeks now, ever since I got sick. He's helping to keep the place together." He smiled. "I couldn't believe my luck. I came back expecting to find the place in ruins and here was this kind old man, running things and keeping order. He's got my staff practically eating out of his hand! I've insisted on paying him a little, though it's nothing close to what he deserves."

"It sounds like you're lucky to have found him," said the Golem.

He nodded. "You should meet him sometime. He reminds me of my uncle, in a way. I think he used to be a rabbi—he just has that air about him. Like he knows more than he's saying."

It was growing late. Men were slowly drifting from the café, leaving each argument in its usual stalemate. Outside, a lamplighter boy walked by, pole slung over his thin shoulder like a bayonet. "I should be going home," the Golem said. She had a sudden dread of the walk back with him.

"Of course," he said. "Let me take you."

"I don't want you to go out of your way."

"No, I insist."

As they approached her boardinghouse, the Golem grew conscious of how much they looked like a couple out strolling in the twilight. Michael, she saw, was beginning to gather courage to ask her if she would see him again, if they could perhaps have dinner sometime—

"I can't," she said and stopped walking, her hand pulling away from his arm. Surprised, he stopped too. "What's wrong?" he asked.

The words tumbled from her mouth. "I'm sorry, Michael. I know you're interested in me."

He paled, then attempted a wry smile. "Was it that obvious?"

"You're a very good person," she said, miserable. "But I can't. I just can't."

"Of course," he said. "Too soon. Of course. I'm sorry. If I gave you any distress—"

"No, no, please don't apologize!" Frustration rose up in her chest. "I want us to be friends, Michael. Can't we simply be friends? Isn't that all right?"

Instantly she was certain it had been the wrong thing to say.

"Of course!" he said. "Yes, of course. That's the important thing, after all. Friendship."

No longer trusting herself to speak, she could do nothing but nod.

"Good!" His voice was hollow. "That's settled, then." He replaced her hand on his arm, as if to show that nothing had changed; and they walked the last block to her home as the most perfectly matched couple on the street, as with each step they both desperately wished to be elsewhere.

It was long past midnight and the full moon was sinking toward the East River, threading between bridge cables and water tanks to shine into the windows of the Sheltering House. It crept across the drab wool of the cot blankets, and into the open eyes of Yehudah Schaalman, who'd been waiting for exactly this. He needed the moonlight to write by.

So far, things were progressing better than Schaalman had dared hope. He'd thought the director's return would be a hurdle, that he'd have to charm the man or addle his mind; but it seemed Levy was even more of a pushover than his staff. Schaalman had protested the offered stipend at first, but then accepted, as he must. No one was *that* altruistic, not even the man he was pretending to be.

He'd solidified his position and gained their trust. It was time to put the next part of his plan into action. His dream had promised him that New York held the secret to *life eternal*, but he needed a way to narrow his search, a dowsing rod to point him in the right direction. And what better way than to turn himself into that very dowsing rod?

He reached under his cot and found the tattered sheaf of burned papers. He sorted through them in the moonlight, setting aside the ones that held some bearing on his purpose. Taking up a fresh sheet of paper and pencil, he began to scribble notes. If he combined this incantation with this name of God . . . He wrote formulas and scratched them out, drew diagrams of branching trees whose leaves were the letters of the alphabet. He worked for hours until finally, near dawn, he experienced a rush of clarity as the diagrams and formulas and incantations all melted into one. His pencil danced ecstatic across the page. Finally his hand stilled, and he looked at what he had written, feeling in his bones that he'd succeeded. The old familiar pang passed through him—what he could have been, given the chance! Oh, what he might have accomplished!

He glanced around once more, but his neighbors all were asleep. Taking a deep breath, he began to quietly read aloud what he had written.

A long, unbroken string of syllables issued from Schaalman's mouth. Some were soft and languid as a lazy stream. Others were harsh and jagged, and Schaalman spat these from between his teeth. If one of the old sages had been listening, one schooled not only in Hebrew and Aramaic but also in centuries of mystical lore, even he would have been hard-pressed to make sense of it. He might have recognized snatches here and there: portions of various prayers, names of God that had been woven together letter by letter. But the rest would have been a terrifying mystery.

He gathered momentum as he reached the apex of the formula, the letter in the very middle: an *aleph*, the silent sound that was the beginning of all Creation. And then, as if that *aleph* were a mirror, the formula reversed itself, and letter by letter Schaalman tumbled down the other side.

He was nearing the end, he was almost upon it. Bracing himself, he spoke the final sound and then—

—*suddenly all of Creation was pouring through him. He was infinite, he was the universe, there was nothing that he did not encompass.*

But then he looked upward and beheld that he was nothing, a mite, an insignificant speck cowering beneath the unblinking gaze of the One.

It lasted forever; it was only a moment. Waking to himself, Schaalman blinked back tears and drew a clammy hand across his brow. It was always this way, when he tried something new and powerful.

The moon sank below the window, leaving only the yellow glow of the gaslights. Schaalman had hoped to test the efficacy of his formula immediately—to see if, indeed, he had turned himself into that dowsing rod—but exhaustion overcame him, and he fell into a dreamless sleep until morning, waking only when the noise of the dormitory grew too loud to ignore. Men were dressing themselves for the day, straightening their mussed blankets with the nervous courtesy of houseguests. Some prayed next to their beds, phylacteries strapped to their foreheads and wound about their arms. A line for the water closet stretched down the hallway, each man blearily clutching his soap and towel. Schaalman dressed and donned his coat. He was ravenously hungry. Downstairs he discovered the cook had left him a few slices of bread and marmalade for breakfast; he devoured them without pause. Resisting the urge to lick the marmalade from his fingers—the habits of a life spent alone were still with him—he walked past the parlor and out the front door of the Sheltering House. It was time to see what he'd accomplished.

Five hours later, he returned to the Sheltering House, dejected and angry. He'd walked the length and breadth of the Lower East Side, past all the rabbis, scholars, synagogues, and storefront yeshivas he could find—and yet there had been no sign from the dowsing spell. No pull down a particular street, no sense that perhaps he should go into *this* doorway, or talk to *that* man over there. But his formula had worked, he was certain of it!

Once again, he counseled himself to be patient. There were still private libraries, the giant yeshiva he'd learned about on the Upper West Side, not to mention the conclave of urbane German Jews to the north—not as schooled in esoteric wonders as their Russian and Polish cousins, but still, he might uncover something. He would not give up.

But he was nervous. He'd passed a funeral procession on Delancey: some distinguished personage, judging by the crowd of mourners and their weighty silence. Most likely a respected and prominent rabbi, dead after a long and peaceful dotage, certain of his place in the World to Come. Schaalman had stood to one side and looked away, repressing a childish urge to hide lest the Angel of Death spy him there, hidden away among the Jews of New York.

Back at the Sheltering House, he paused at the director's door. Levy was sitting at his desk, pen uncharacteristically still. His eyes were vacant. Schaalman frowned. Had someone charmed or altered him? Was there another force at work here? He tapped once on the door. "Michael?"

The man gave a guilty start. "Joseph, hello. Sorry, have you been there long?"

"Not long, no," Schaalman said. "Are you all right? Not sick again, I hope."

"No, no. Well, not exactly." He smiled faintly. "Matters of the heart."

"Ah," said Schaalman, his interest evaporating.

But now the director was looking at him speculatively. "Can I ask you a personal question?"

Schaalman sighed inwardly. "Certainly."

"Were you ever married?"

"No, I never had that blessing."

"Ever been in love?"

"Of course," Schaalman lied. "What man hasn't, by my age?"

"But it didn't work out." It wasn't quite a question.

"It was a long time ago. I was a different man then."

"What happened?"

"She left. She was there, and then she was gone. I never knew why." The words had simply come to him; he'd said them without thinking.

Levy was nodding, in unwanted sympathy. "Did you wonder, afterward, what you might have done differently?"

Every day. Every day of my life since, I wonder.

He shrugged. "Perhaps I was too difficult a man to love."

"Oh, I have a hard time believing that."

Enough, he thought. "Is there anything else you need? Otherwise I'll see how the cook is getting on with dinner."

Levy blinked. "Oh, of course. Thanks, Joseph. For letting me bend your ear."

Schaalman smiled in reply, and removed himself from the doorway.

16.

You wore a hat," the Golem said. "Thank you."

They were walking north, away from her boardinghouse, in a thin sleet fine as frozen mist. It was the third trip they'd taken together since the night in Madison Square Park. Two weeks before, they'd visited the grounds at Battery Park—skipping the aquarium, as she'd insisted he not melt the lock again—and then curved north along West Street to the Barrow Street pier. In summer the pier was a bustling recreation center and promenade, but now it was barren, its guardrails dressed with icicles. Wary of the slick wood, the Djinni had stayed near the boarded-over refreshment windows at the landing and watched as the Golem went out to the end of the pier, her cloak fluttering in the harbor wind. "It's quiet out there," she'd said when she came back. They'd walked a bit farther along West Street, but the views of water and distant lights turned quickly to cargo warehouses and steamship offices. They were about to turn around when he saw a glow in the sky a few piers away and dragged her over to investigate. The crew of a freighter, desperate to make the morning tides, had rigged the deck with electric lights and was working through the night. Stevedores raced about, hauling cargo, their breath blowing in white gusts. The Djinni and the Golem watched until the crew boss yelled at them in Norwegian to clear out, they had no time for rubberneckers. The Golem, not thinking, apologized in the same language, and they hastily retreated before the boss could corner his presumed countrymen and ask what town they hailed from.

The week after that, they'd walked north through the Lower East Side into a melange of Jewish and Bohemian shops, interspersed here and there with faded German signs: the remnants of Kleindeutschland adrift in an Eastern European sea. The Golem had been in a poor mood that week, distracted and unhappy. She'd said little of why, only that she'd gone to a cemetery in Brooklyn with an acquaintance, a man named Michael. The Djinni got the impression that this Michael desired more from their relationship than she did.

"I pity whoever tries to court you," he'd said. "You have them at a serious disadvantage."

"I don't want to be courted," she'd muttered.

"By anyone? Or just him?"

She'd shaken her head, as if to dismiss the question itself.

She was hard to comprehend, this woman. She had a prudish streak that seemed of a piece with her caution and serious-mindedness. She was as curious as he, but hesitated to explore. She smiled occasionally, but rarely laughed. In all, her character was completely opposed to what he usually looked for in a woman of his company. She would make a terrible djinniyeh.

They'd cut north and west, heading deeper into the sleeping neighborhoods. "What's it like?" he'd asked her. "To feel all those desires and fears."

"Like many small hands, grabbing at me."

He'd almost squirmed, imagining it. Perhaps he himself would make a terrible golem.

"I'm getting better at not responding to them," she'd said. "But it's still difficult. Especially when I'm the object of the fear. Or desire."

"Like your friend Michael's?"

She'd said nothing, her face a studied blank. Perhaps she worried that *he* would develop desires for her. But he hadn't, not even mildly, which was surprising. He'd rarely been so long in a woman's company for any other reason.

He liked her well enough, he supposed. It amused him to show her around, to see now-familiar places through her new eyes. She noticed different details than he did: he took in a landscape all at once before devoting his attention to its elements, while she examined each thing in its turn, building to the whole picture. She could walk faster than he, but she was usually the one lagging behind, enthralled by something in a shop window or a gaily painted sign.

And at least she no longer seemed frightened of him. When he'd arrived at her boardinghouse for their fourth journey, he'd had only seconds to wait before she joined him. And she'd stopped trying to hide conspicuously at his side, though she wore her hood up until they were a ways from her home.

They continued on a zigzagging northwest path, in their now customary near-silence. Already he regretted his promise about the hat. The sleet was no danger, barely an irritation; in fact the hat itself was worse than the sleet. He'd bought it from a pushcart without trying it on, a mistake he wouldn't make again. The fabric was cheap and rough, and the brim made him feel like a horse with blinders on.

"Stop *fidgeting*," muttered the Golem.

"I can't stand this thing," he said. "It feels like I've got something on my head."

She snorted, almost a laugh. "Well, you do."

"You're the one who made me wear it. And it *itches*."

Finally she pulled the hat from his head. From her sleeve she took a handkerchief, unfolded it, and placed it inside the hat. She put the hat back on top of his head and tucked the corners of the kerchief beneath the brim. "There," she said. "Is that better?"

"Yes," he said, startled.

"Good," she said grimly. "Now perhaps I can concentrate on where I'm going."

"I thought you couldn't hear my mind."

"I didn't need to. You were fussing enough for the whole street to know it."

They walked on. The temperature had dropped, turning the sleet to snow. The long-choked gutters made each street corner a dark pool. They were forced to step around these, until at one corner the Djinni, after checking that there was no one else on the street, took a running leap, bounding to the other side of the black water. It was a fair distance; few human men could have done it. He grinned, pleased with himself.

The Golem stood on the corner behind him, frowning. He waited, impatient, while she picked her way across.

"What if someone had seen?" she said.

"The risk was worth it."

"To gain what? A few moments' time?"

"A reminder that I'm still alive."

To this she did not reply, only shook her head.

In silence he took them to Washington Square Park. He'd looked forward to showing her the glowing arch, but the weather had forced the city to shut off the lights or risk them shorting. The arch loomed in shadow above them, its lines stark and precise against the clouds.

"It should be lit," he said, disappointed.

"No, I like it this way."

They walked beneath, and he marveled anew at its height, its sheer size. So many larger buildings in this city, and yet it was the arch that fascinated him. In the dark, the enormous marble carvings seemed to change and ripple like waves.

"It serves no purpose," he said, trying to explain his fascination, to himself as much as her. "Buildings and bridges are useful. But why this? A gigantic arch from nowhere to nowhere."

"What does it say, up there?" She was on the other side, peering up at the shadowed inscription.

He quoted from memory: " 'Let us raise a standard to which the wise and the honest can repair. The event is in the hand of God.' Said by someone named Washington."

"I thought Washington was a place," she said, dubious.

"Never mind that, what does it mean?"

She didn't answer, only continued gazing at the letters she couldn't see. Then she asked, "Do you believe in God?"

"No," he said, unhesitating. "God is a human invention. My kind have no such belief. And nothing I've experienced suggests that there's an all-powerful ghost in the sky, answering wishes." He smiled, warming to the subject. "Long ago, during the reign of Sulayman, the most powerful of the djinn could grant wishes. There are stories from that time, of djinn captured by human wizards. A djinni would offer his captor three wishes, in exchange for his release. The wizard would spend his wishes on more wishes, and force the djinni into perpetual slavery. Until finally the wizard would wish for something poorly worded, which would allow his captive to trap him. And then the djinni would be freed." She was still studying the arch; but she was listening. "So perhaps this God of the humans is just a djinni like myself, stuck in the heavens, forced to answer wishes. Or maybe he freed himself long ago, only no one told them."

Silence. "What do *you* think?" he pressed. "Do you believe in their God?"

"I don't know," she said. "The Rabbi did. And he was the wisest person I've ever met. So yes, maybe I do."

"A man tells you to believe, and you believe?"

"It depends on the man. Besides, you believe the stories that *you* were told. Have you met a djinni who could grant wishes?"

"No, but that ability has all but disappeared."

"So, it's just stories now. And perhaps the humans did create their God. But does that make him less real? Take this arch. They created it. Now it exists."

"Yes, but it doesn't grant wishes," he said. "It doesn't do *anything*."

"True," she said. "But I look at it, and I feel a certain way. Maybe that's its purpose."

He wanted to ask, what good was a God that only existed to make you *feel* a certain way? But he left off. Already they were treading the edge of an argument.

They left the arch and walked farther into the park. Sleigh tracks carved long arcs along the ground, around the islands of snow-covered lawn. The oval fountain, shut off for the season, was a shallow bowl of ice. Sleeping men dotted the benches here and there, barely visible under their layers of blankets. The Golem glanced at them and then quickly away, a sorrowful look on her face.

"They need so much," she murmured. "And I just walk by."

"Yes, but what would you do? Feed them all, take them home with you? You aren't responsible for them."

"Easy to say, when you can't hear them."

"It's still true. You're generous to a fault, Chava. I think you'd give your own self away, if only someone wished for it."

She hugged herself, clearly unhappy. The wind had pushed the hood back from her face. Snowflakes clung unmelting to her cheeks and the sides of her nose. She looked like a living statue, her features white and glittering.

He reached out and brushed away the snow from her cheek. The crystals disappeared at once under his hand. She startled, surprised, then realized the problem. Ruefully she wiped a gloved hand across her face.

He said, "If you were to lie down on one of those benches, you'd be buried under snow and pigeons by morning." She laughed at the image. It was gratifying, to hear that rare laugh. He felt as though he'd earned it.

As they neared the far end of the park, they heard a distant jingling behind them. A sleigh carriage was entering from beneath the arch, the hitched pair trotting handsomely. The reins were held not by a coachman but by one of the passengers, a man in evening dress and silk hat. A blond woman in a fashionable cloak sat next to him, laughing as he took the sleigh in a tight figure eight beside the fountain. The sleigh leaned threateningly to the side, and the woman buried her face in her muffler and shrieked, obviously enjoying herself.

The Golem smiled, watching them. The Djinni stepped back onto the grass as the sleigh neared, mindful of the horses. The couple in the sleigh saw them, and the man raised his hand in a jaunty salute. It was clear they were glad for the audience, glad that someone would see them as they wanted to be seen: young and daring, thrilled to be alive and playing at love.

The team, obviously well trained, joggled only once as they passed the Djinni. For a moment the two couples were gazing at each other as though in a mirror; and then the Djinni saw the beginning of something startled, even frightened, in the woman's eyes. The same budding uncertainty rose in the man's face—his hand tightened on the reins—and then they flew by, the horses drawing them away from their own eldritch reflection, the too-handsome man and the strangely glittering woman.

The Golem's smile was gone.

The new century was proving to be a prosperous one for Boutros Arbeely. Since the Djinni's arrival, business had more than doubled. Word of Arbeely's fine and speedy work had spread beyond the Syrian community, and in recent weeks the tinsmith had entertained a number of unusual visitors. The first was an Irish saloon-owner looking to replace his old growlers, which had the tendency to split from their handles—not helped by his patrons' habit of using them as cudgels. An Italian owner of a stable had come as well, looking for horseshoes. Arbeely's limited English would have made communication difficult—and the Djinni could not help, not without the neighbors wondering at his fluency—but all the customers had to do was find the nearest Syrian boy, drop a few pennies in his hand, and ask him to translate.

The strangest visit came late in February from a fellow Syrian, a landlord named Thomas Maloof. The son of wealthy Eastern Orthodox landowners, Maloof had come to America not in steerage but in a furnished cabin, and had brought along a sizeable bankroll and a line of credit. After landing in New York and watching wave after wave of immigrants spill onto the ferry, he'd decided that any man with an ounce of sense would do well to purchase property in Manhattan as soon as possible. Accordingly he had snatched up the deed for a tenement on Park Street. He himself rarely set foot in the building, preferring to live in a suite of rooms at a genteel boardinghouse to the north. When he did speak to his fellow countrymen, it was with a hearty condescension, which he directed at Orthodox as well as Maronite. Relations between the two communities were cool at best, but egalitarian Maloof held himself above both.

Maloof considered himself a connoisseur and a patron of the arts, and after a brief survey of his new building, he decided its most urgent defect was not the poor plumbing nor the dark closeness of the rooms, but the deplorable quality of the pressed-tin ceiling in the entryway. He decided to have a new ceiling installed, to commemorate the change in ownership. He'd traveled to the pressed-tin factories in Brooklyn and the Bronx, but to his disappointment they could only show him workaday flowers and medallions and fleurs-de-lis, all missing that spark of true artistic value. His tenants were good, hardworking people, he told Arbeely, and they deserved a true Work of Art in their downstairs hallway, one that a factory could not provide.

Arbeely listened to this proposal with dubious politeness. Unlike Maloof, he knew why the tinplate panels were only made by factories: they required expensive equipment to produce, and the profit was so small that one had to sell to a neighborhood's worth of tenements to make it worthwhile. Moreover, when Arbeely asked Maloof what sort of Art he had in mind, he discovered that the landlord had no idea whatsoever. "You're the artisan, not I!" Maloof exclaimed. "I ask only that you give me something that sets my mind aflame!" And he left, having sworn to return in a week to view whatever samples Arbeely could produce.

"My God," groaned Arbeely to the Djinni, "the man is insane! We're supposed to make an entryway's worth of tin panels, just you and I, and they must be extraordinary. We can't halt all business for a month while we turn out a ceiling! When he comes back—*if* he comes back— we'll simply explain that it's beyond our capabilities, and that's that."

The weather had turned to a near-constant deluge of sleet and snow, and when the Djinni left that night he reconciled himself to an evening indoors. Returning to his tenement, he paused for a moment in the downstairs hallway, and looked up. Sure enough, the ceiling was pressed tin, and the panels were as unremarkable as Maloof had described: roughly fifteen inches across and embossed with a plain medallion of concentric circles. Dust and soot grimed each square; rust cankered their edges. The longer the Djinni gazed, the more he wished he hadn't bothered.

He shut himself in his room and worked on his figurines, but he was too distracted to make real progress. He glanced up from his work and checked the window. It was still sleeting, worse than before.

He needed something new, something different, more interesting than models of falcons and owls. Something he hadn't attempted before.

He walked down to the lobby again and squinted at the medallions in the dim light. If he allowed his eyes to lose focus, he could almost pretend he was flying above them, looking down onto a series of circular hills, ominously regular . . .

A spark of an idea caught in his mind. What rule said that a pressed-tin ceiling must be constructed from square tiles? Why not simply create one enormous tile that covered the entire ceiling? And perhaps even the walls as well?

As though it had been sitting there all along, waiting for this moment, the image of the finished ceiling came to him in an exhilarating rush. He ran up to his room to fetch his coat, and then dashed across the street to Arbeely's shop. He lit the fire in the forge, and threw himself into his work.

Arbeely did not go straight to the shop the next morning, for he had errands to run: an order to place with a supplier, and then to the tool shop to look at their new catalogs. He made time for a quick pastry and glass of tea at a café. On his way back, he paused before a haberdasher's window to stare with longing at a smart-looking black derby with a feather in its band. He took off his own hat and examined its thin felt, the fraying ribbon and slumping dome. Business *had* been very good. Couldn't he allow himself this one indulgence?

It was past noon when finally he arrived at the shop, cringing at the lateness of the hour. The door was unlocked, but the Djinni didn't seem to be there. Perhaps he was in the back?

Coming around the workbench, he nearly tripped over his unseen apprentice. The Djinni was perched on his hands and knees before what looked, at first glance, to be an enormous carpet made of tin.

The Djinni glanced up. "Arbeely! I was wondering where you were."

Arbeely stared at the strange shining carpet. It was at least eight feet long, and five wide. Much of it was dominated by an undulating wave that broke into smaller waves, swirling around one another as they spread across the tin. There were places where the Djinni had bent and buckled the plate into ragged peaks. Other sections were almost perfectly flat, but stippled here and there to create illusions of shadow.

"It's only half finished," the Djinni said. "Arbeely, did you order more tinplate? We've run out, and I still need to make the panels for the wall. I couldn't remember if Maloof gave you the measurements, so I used my lobby as a model."

Arbeely stared. "This is—you're making this for Maloof?"

"Of course," the Djinni replied, in a tone that suggested Arbeely was being rather slow. "It'll take me at least two days to finish. I have ideas about how to connect the side panels to the ceiling, but they'll need to be tested. I want it to be seamless. A seam would ruin the effect." He peered at Arbeely more closely. "Is that a new hat?"

Arbeely barely heard the Djinni's words; something else he'd said was tugging at him, trying to attract his attention. "You used *all* the tinplate?"

"Well, a ceiling is very large. And I'll need more. This afternoon, if possible."

"All the tinplate," Arbeely said, numb. He found a stool and sat on it.

Finally the Djinni registered the man's distress. "Is there a problem?"

"Do you have any idea," Arbeely said with rising heat, "how much money you've cost me? You used up four months' worth of plate! And we have no guarantee that Maloof will even return! Even if he does, surely he won't want this—he asked for tiles, not one gigantic piece! How could—" Words failed him, and for a moment he simply stared at the tin carpet. "Four months of plate," he mumbled. "This could ruin me."

The Djinni frowned. "But it'll work perfectly. Arbeely, you haven't even *looked* at it properly."

The numb shock was wearing away to despair. "I should have known," Arbeely said. "You don't understand the realities of running a business. I'm sorry, in the end it's my fault. But I'll have to rethink our agreement. I may no longer be able to pay you. The loss of the tin alone."

Now the hurt on the Djinni's face turned to indignant anger. He looked at the tin creation at his feet, and then back at Arbeely. Too furious for words, he grabbed his coat, stepped past Arbeely—who made no move to stop him—and strode from the shop, slamming the door behind him.

In the quiet that followed, Arbeely contemplated his options. He had some money saved; he could borrow more. He could restrict new business to repairs, but he'd have to cancel most of his current orders. His reputation might never recover.

He walked past the tin carpet—something about its waves and folds tugged at him, but he was beyond the reach of distraction—and went to the back room, where he made a quick inventory. It was true: the plate was all gone. Nothing stood on the shelves but scraps and unfinished orders.

He returned to the front room, to look again at the wasted tinplate—perhaps there were sections that were still usable, enough for a few days at least. As he did, the light from the high window filtered through the dusty air and struck the tin carpet, highlighting the peaks and crags, casting the narrow depressions into shadow. All at once it came into focus, and with a dizzy shock Arbeely saw exactly what the Djinni had created: the portrait of a vast desert landscape, as seen from above.

It was not a good day to be selling ice cream.

The wind and sleet had ceased for the moment, but the slush lay frozen on the sidewalks, refracting the feeble daylight into Mahmoud Saleh's dazzled eyes. Carefully he dragged his little cart from restaurant to café, knocking on door after door, scooping his ice cream into whatever container they gave him and pocketing the coins he got in return. He had no doubt his ice cream was headed straight for their garbage pails, for who would want it on a day like this? He could hear the proprietors' ill-concealed sighs and loud silences, the muttered God-be-with-yous that seemed more superstition than courtesy, as though Saleh were an ill-behaved spirit who needed appeasing.

He wrapped his ragged coat about himself more tightly and was almost to Maryam's coffeehouse when the street was lit with a second dawn. Stunned, he shielded his eyes.

It was the man, the glowing man! He was striding from a basement shop, his face a mask of anger. His coat was bunched in one fist. Only a thin shirt and a pair of dungarees separated him from the icy air, but he didn't seem to notice. Those on the sidewalk scurried out of his way. He was headed north, toward the vegetable market.

Saleh had never seen him in daylight before. And if he waited too long, he'd lose him.

He dragged his cart to Maryam's as quickly as he could. She must have seen him coming, as she was outside before he even reached the door.

"Mahmoud! What's the matter?"

"Maryam," he panted, "I must ask you—please watch my cart for me. Will you do that?"

"Of course!"

"Thank you." And with that he headed north, following the glowing man's retreating form.

The Djinni had never been so furious in his life.

He had no destination in mind, no purpose but to get away from his small-minded employer. After everything the Djinni had done for him, spending day after day mending pots until he thought he might expire from boredom—and all the man could do was complain about how much tin he'd used? The business he'd brought in, the money he'd made for the man, and now this flat-out dismissal?

The traffic thickened as he neared the market, forcing him to slow down and consider his direction. His anger was now demanding a purpose, a destination. It had been weeks since he'd even thought of Sophia Winston, but now her face rose before him, her proud and beautiful features. And why not? Perhaps she'd be angry with him for presuming; but then again, maybe her door would be open and waiting as it had been before.

He considered taking the Elevated but couldn't stand the thought of sitting packed among a crowd of strangers, batting their newspapers away from his face. A voice inside whispered that running to Sophia's was no good, that he'd still have to consider what to do with himself afterward—but he ignored it, and picked up his pace.

Half a block behind, Mahmoud Saleh struggled to keep the glowing man in his sights. It was difficult: the man was long-legged, and propelled by anger. To keep pace, Saleh half-ran, bumping into people and pushcarts and walls, muttering apologies to everyone and everything. He waded through mazes of horses and carts and pedestrians, into puddles of half-frozen mud. At each intersection he waited to feel the fatal blow of a cart, the trampling of horses' hooves, but somehow it never happened. At one corner he took a misstep and fell, landing on his shoulder. A spasm of pain ripped through his arm, but he righted himself and went on, holding the arm close to his side.

Slowly he began to realize that he'd never find his way home without help. He couldn't even read the signs. The only words in English he knew besides *sorry* were *hello, thank you,* and *ice cream.*

With something like relief he resigned himself to his fate. Either the glowing man would lead him home or he'd spend his last mortal day on an unknown street, surrounded by strangers. In the morning he'd be merely a frozen beggar, nameless and unmourned. He felt no sadness at this, only wondered what Maryam would do with his churn.

In the end, tracking down Thomas Maloof was a relatively simple task. Arbeely merely went to the landlord's tenement—noting in passing that the ceiling in question was, indeed, rather awful—and began knocking on doors. He begged the pardon of the women who answered, but did they know where Thomas Maloof lived? They replied that they didn't know, as he rarely came to the building, and sent a boy around to collect the rent. After a while Arbeely thought to ask after the boy.

It transpired that the boy was one Matthew Mounsef, who lived on the fourth floor. His mother, a tired-looking woman whose sunken eyes and pale skin hinted at some illness, said that Matthew was at school but would be home at three o'clock. Arbeely passed the intervening time at his shop in a state of nervous frustration. Now that he knew what the tin ceiling was, he couldn't stop looking at it. As the day wore on, the winter sunlight cast it in different moods—now draped in shadows, now illuminated with brilliant white pinpoints as the sun struck a miniature peak.

Finally it was three o'clock, and he returned to the tenement. A boy of seven or eight opened the door. He had his mother's features, though with a healthier cast, below a large and tangled crown of curly black hair. The boy gazed patiently up at Arbeely, his hand twisting back and forth on the knob.

"Hello," Arbeely said hesitantly. "My name's Boutros. Your mother told me that you run errands sometimes for Thomas Maloof."

A nod of assent.

"Do you know where he lives?"

Another nod.

"Can you take me there?" In his palm he held out a dime.

With disconcerting speed the boy plucked the dime from Arbeely's hand and disappeared back inside. There was a murmur of exchanged words and the soft smack of a kiss; and then the boy was slipping past Arbeely down the stairs, a cap jammed atop his curls, his thin arms lost in the sleeves of a large gray coat.

Arbeely followed behind as the boy walked purposefully toward Irish-town. He felt silly, trailing in the wake of this tiny woolen scare-crow, but when he caught up Matthew only went faster. They passed a group of older boys who sat loitering on a stoop, smoking cigarettes. One of them called out in English, his tone derisive. Matthew didn't reply, and the others snickered as he passed.

"What did he say?" asked Arbeely, but the boy didn't answer.

The building Matthew led him to seemed cleaner and brighter than its neighbors. The door opened to a well-appointed hall with a parlor beyond. A round, dough-faced woman stared out at them. The boy whispered a question in English, almost inaudible; the woman nodded once, cast a dark glance at Arbeely, and then closed the door. Arbeely and the boy were left together on the stoop, avoiding each other's eyes.

Maloof emerged a few minutes later. "The tinsmith!" he exclaimed. "And little Matthew! Is something the matter?"

"No, nothing is wrong," said Arbeely—though of course this was not quite the truth. "There's something at the shop I need to show you." Maloof frowned, and Arbeely added quickly, "I wouldn't trouble you if I didn't think it was important. My assistant conceived of an idea for your ceiling, and frankly, it's incredible. But you must see it yourself to understand."

Something of the tinsmith's excitement must have impressed itself upon Maloof, for he fetched his coat and followed them back to the shop. Matthew waited patiently for Arbeely to unlock the door before filing in behind, as though he too held a stake in the proceedings.

The afternoon light was thinner but, Arbeely hoped, still strong enough. He didn't say anything, merely stood back and let Maloof walk warily around the tin sculpture.

"It's certainly large," the landlord said. "But I'm confused. What am I looking at?"

A moment later he stopped walking. He blinked, and perceptibly rocked back on his heels. Arbeely smiled—he'd felt the same way at the change of perspective, as if the floor had dropped away from him. Maloof began to laugh.

"Amazing!" He crouched down and looked at it up close, then stood up and laughed again. He strolled the perimeter of the sculpture, examining it from different angles. "Amazing," he repeated. The boy only sat on his heels, arms wrapped around his knees, and stared at the tin with wide eyes.

Maloof chuckled to himself some more, then saw Arbeely watching him. Instantly his face became a neutral mask of business. "But I have to say, this isn't what I had in mind," he said. "I requested repeating tiles, not one large piece, and I was expecting a more classical style. In fact I'm surprised and, yes, unhappy, that you would go so far without consulting me."

"I must beg your pardon. It wasn't I who made this, but my assistant. And to be honest, I'm as surprised as you. I didn't know about this until a few hours ago."

"The tall man? He made this, by himself? But it's only been a little more than a day!"

"He tells me that he was . . . inspired."

"Unbelievable," said Maloof. "But why isn't he here himself, to tell me this?"

"I'm afraid that's my fault. When I saw what he'd done, I was angry. As you said, this isn't what you asked for. He went too far without your consent, or mine. This is no way to do business. But he's an artist, and the concerns of business sometimes pass him by. I'm afraid that we quarreled, and he left."

Maloof looked alarmed. "Permanently?"

"No, no," Arbeely said quickly. "I think he's nursing his wounded pride, and will return once he decides I've suffered enough." *Please, let it be so*, he thought.

"I see," said Maloof. "Well, he sounds like a difficult man to work with. But that's the way of the artistic temperament, is it not? And we can't have art without artists."

Together the men regarded the sculpture. The detail was such that Arbeely could picture tiny jackals and hyenas emerging from behind the hillsides, or a minuscule boar, stout and barrel-chested, the last of the sun glinting off tin-plated tusks.

"It isn't what I asked for," said Maloof.

"No," Arbeely agreed sadly.

"And if I say no? What happens to it then?"

"Since it's too large to keep in the shop, and there are no other prospective buyers, I'd have to salvage it for scrap and throw away the rest. A shame, but there it is."

Maloof winced, as if pained. He ran a hand through his hair, and then turned to the child near his feet. "Well, Matthew, what do you think? Shall I buy this gigantic piece of tin, and hang it in your building?"

The boy nodded.

"Even though it isn't what I asked for?"

"This is better," said the boy. It was the first time Arbeely had heard him speak.

Maloof laughed once. He stuck his hands in his pockets and turned his back on the tinplate ceiling. "This is preposterous," he said. "If I say yes, I'm buying something I didn't ask for. And if I refuse, I'm like a man who complains that someone stole the eggs from his henhouse and replaced them with rubies." He turned back to Arbeely. "I'll buy it, under one condition. Your assistant must return and explain to me, in detail, the rest of what he means to do. Any more surprises, and I withdraw my offer. Agreed?"

Relief rushed through Arbeely. "Agreed."

The men clasped hands. Maloof took one last melancholy look at his new ceiling, and left.

Matthew was still sitting on the floor next to the tin desert, which now lay almost entirely in shadow. The boy raised a hand and traced the peaks of a nearby mountain range, hovering above the tin's surface, as if afraid to touch—or, Arbeely thought, as though he were imagining his fingers to be hawks or falcons, skimming the mountain crests, traversing the backbone of the world.

"Thank you, Matthew," Arbeely said. "You were a great help to me today."

Matthew gave no reply. An impulse struck Arbeely: he must somehow make this strange, solemn boy smile! He said, "Would you like to meet my assistant Ahmad? The one who made this ceiling?"

That earned him the boy's full attention.

"Then come back tomorrow, after school, if it is all right with your mother. Will you do that?"

A vigorous nod, and then Matthew clambered to his feet and up the stairs. He did not actually smile, but there was a lightness and energy to his small frame that hadn't been there before. Then he was gone; the door slipped shut behind him.

"Well," Arbeely said, alone in the empty shop. "Well, well, well."

Night was falling, and still Saleh followed the glowing man. It seemed inconceivable that they were still in New York. The frigid wind sliced through his clothing. His wrenched arm had gone numb, and his legs trembled with fatigue. A memory rose: a carved wooden lamb attached to a string, with wheels for hooves. His daughter's favorite toy. She would pull it around the courtyard for hours, calling "baaa, baaa," the lamb trailing behind her. He grinned, rictuslike, fixed his broken vision on the glowing man, and kept walking. *Baaa*.

On and on they went, until the buildings to either side of them turned from glass-fronted shops to gigantic brick houses behind tall black fences. Even with his shadowed vision he could see the gleam of marble columns and rows of lighted windows. What business could the man possibly have here?

At perhaps the most magnificent house of all, his quarry slowed, then continued past it and turned a corner. Saleh caught up and poked his head around the corner in time to see the glowing man step through a metal fence. There was a rustling of branches.

He stumbled over to where the man had vanished. Two of the fence's bars were gone. Beyond was nothing but a dense and forbidding wall of shrubbery.

The glowing man had gone through, hadn't he? Then so could Saleh.

He stepped over the bottom rail, nearly tripping into the hedge. There was a narrow space between the hedge and the fence, and he wormed his way along it, crabbing sideways, until he was free. He stood at the edge of an enormous garden that ran the length of the mansion, and was bordered by a high brick wall. Even in the dead of winter, the garden had a stately, formal grace. Dark evergreen borders marked out empty flowerbeds. Along the wall, austere, leafless trees stood pinioned, their branches trained into candelabras. Next to the house sat a patio with a marble fountain, its basin full of rotting leaves.

The glowing man, it seemed, had disappeared—but then Saleh looked up, and saw him climbing the face of the mansion, snaking from drainpipe to railing. Saleh goggled. Even in his youth, he could never have accomplished such a feat. The man reached one of the larger balconies on the top floor, vaulted over, and disappeared from view.

The Djinni stood on Sophia's balcony, the door handle unmoving beneath his hand. Locked. He cupped a hand to the glass and peered inside.

The room was dark and uninhabited. Large white drop cloths shrouded her writing desk and dressing table. The bed had been stripped of its linens. Sophia Winston, it seemed, was no longer at home.

He'd never even considered she might not be there. He'd pictured her as a princess trapped in a brick-and-marble palace, waiting for her release. But of course that wasn't so. She was a wealthy young woman. Likely she could go wherever she wished.

His anger and anticipation began to drain away. Had he been in a better mood he might have laughed at himself. What to do now? Go back to Washington Street, tail between his legs?

As he stood pondering, the door on the other side of Sophia's bedroom opened. A woman in a plain black dress and apron entered, carrying a large feather duster.

She saw the Djinni and froze. The duster fell from her hand.

The maid's piercing scream rattled the windowpanes as the Djinni cursed, vaulted onto the railing, and grabbed for the drainpipe.

Saleh stood, wavering, in the middle of the garden.

Perhaps, he thought, *I should sit down to wait.*

In the next moment his legs crumpled beneath him like straws. The frozen ground cradled him, bleeding his heat away. The windows and darkened balconies stared down at him. His eyes drifted to the roof, where four chimneys stood in a line above the gables. Smoke wafted gray-white from one of them. So many chimneys, for only one house.

His eyes drifted closed, and the noise of the world receded. Waves of fatigue washed over him, almost like the contractions of a woman in labor. As though his musings had come to life, he thought he heard a woman scream. At last a slow, dreamy warmth rose in his core and began to spread throughout his body.

Someone tried to peel back one of his eyelids.

Irritated, he tried to bat the hand away, but his arms could barely move. He cracked open his other eye, then squinted against a glare.

The glowing man was crouching in front of Saleh. "What are *you* doing here?"

Leave me alone, Saleh said, *I'm trying to die.* All that came out was a croak.

There was a shout, and distant sounds of a commotion. The glowing man hissed something unintelligible. "Can you stand? No—you'll be too slow—"

With almost no effort the glowing man bent down and hoisted Saleh over his shoulder. Then he turned and ran.

All hope of a peaceful death fled as Saleh hung over the glowing man's back, his head lolling and banging. The mansion disappeared as the glowing man dragged Saleh through the hole in the fence. Saleh couldn't see the men following them, but he could hear the slaps of their shoes, their angry English shouts.

The glowing man ran faster, ducking down alleys, turning right and then left. Saleh jostled on the man's shoulder and cried out against a wave of agony. For a long moment the world went away. When his eyes opened again, cobbles and pavement had turned to a forest floor. The air smelt of cold water. The trees gave way to open sky, and the pavement of a carriage path sounded under the glowing man's feet—and then they were plunged into forest again.

Time slowed, turned elastic; and then the glowing man was lowering him carefully from his shoulder, leaning him against what felt like a wooden wall.

"Stay here," the glowing man said. "Don't move." And then he was gone, soft footsteps running away.

Saleh hitched himself up on the wall and peered around. There was a dusty window inches from his nose. It looked into a large storeroom, where neat lines of wooden rowboats lay on their sides, their oarlocks threaded with thick chains. He turned his head in the other direction, and decided that his senses had indeed left him—or he'd died after all and simply not noticed—for spread before him was a vista of incredible beauty. He was at the edge of a frozen lake that stretched away to either side, its shore curving sinuously, closely edged with bare-limbed trees. At the far side of the lake—he blinked, and tried to wipe at his eyes, but it was still there—a tall, winged figure floated above the frozen water. It was an angel.

He laughed once, raw in his throat. *At last.*

But the angel did not move. It only hovered, as if waiting. Considering.

Footsteps, and then the glowing man's voice: "They're still looking for us—can you walk?" But he could make no answer, and darkness overtook him.

He woke again when the Djinni set him on his feet. Lake and forest had disappeared; they were on a city street. "You must walk," the glowing man said, impatient. "We'll be too conspicuous if I carry you."

"Where are we?" Saleh croaked.

"West of Central Park."

Saleh took a few steps, leaning on the man's arm. The pain in his legs was unbelievable. He retched once, but nothing came up. He saw the glowing man grimace with distaste.

"I was nearly caught because of you," the man said. "I should have left you there."

"Why didn't you?"

"You might have led them back to me."

Saleh took one more step, and his legs buckled. The glowing man caught him before he hit the pavement.

"This is intolerable," the man muttered.

"Then leave me here."

"No. You accosted me once, and now you've followed me. I want you to tell me why."

Saleh swallowed. "Because I can see you."

"Yes, you said that before. What does it mean?"

"There's something wrong with my eyes," Saleh said. "I can't look at anyone's face. Except for yours." He looked up at the man, into the flickering light behind his features. "You look as though you're on fire, but no one else seems to notice."

The glowing man regarded him in wary silence. Finally he said, "And you look half-dead. I suspect you need food."

"I don't have any money," muttered Saleh.

The glowing man sighed. "I'll pay."

They found a plain, clean-looking cafeteria, full of men coming off their evening shifts. The glowing man bought two bowls of soup. Saleh ate slowly, afraid to overtax his stomach, holding his injured arm carefully at his side. The soup warmed him, an honest heat. The glowing man didn't touch his own bowl, only watched Saleh. Finally he asked, "Have you always been like this?"

"No. It started ten years ago."

"And you can't see faces at all?"

Saleh shook his head. "No, that's not it. I can't see faces . . . as they are. They have holes in them." His throat tightened. "Like skulls. If I look at them, I develop nausea and seizures. And it's not just faces—the whole world is distorted. I suspect it's a type of epilepsy, affecting my sight."

"How did this happen?"

"No," Saleh said. "I've told you enough. Now tell me why I can see you."

"Perhaps I don't know."

Saleh laughed, harshly. "Oh, you know. That much, I can see." He ate another spoonful of soup. "Is it some sort of illness?"

The man's face hardened. "What makes you think I'm *ill*?"

"It seems logical. If healthy people look dead to me, then perhaps a sick man would appear whole and glowing."

The man gave an insulted snort. "What use is logic, when it takes you so far in the wrong direction?"

"Then tell me," said Saleh, growing irritated.

A long pause, while the glowing man regarded him. Then he leaned forward, peering deep into Saleh's eyes, as if searching for something. Saleh froze, feeling giddy as the glowing face filled his vision. He could feel his pupils dilating against the light.

The man nodded, leaned back. "I can see it," he said. "Barely, but it's there. Ten years ago, you were still in Syria, weren't you?"

"Yes. In Homs. *What* can you see?"

"The thing that possessed you."

Saleh froze. "That's absurd. A girl had a fever. I treated her, and I caught it. The fever caused the epilepsy."

The glowing man snorted. "You caught more than a fever."

"Bedouin such as yourself might believe in these superstitions, but it's simply not possible."

The glowing man laughed, as though he had a secret hidden in his pocket, and was waiting for the right moment to bring it out.

"All right, then," Saleh said. "You say that something possessed me. An imp, I suppose, or a djinni."

"Yes. Probably one of the lower *ifrits*."

"Oh, I see. And what evidence do you have?"

"There's a spark deep in your mind. I can see it."

"A *spark*?"

"The smallest ember, left behind. The mark of something passing."

"And I suppose," Saleh said sarcastically, "it wouldn't have been visible to any of the half-dozen doctors who examined me."

"Not likely, no."

"But you can see it." Saleh laughed once. "And who are *you*, that you have this ability?"

The man smiled, as though he'd been waiting for Saleh to ask. He picked up his soup spoon, a twin to Saleh's: thick and ugly metal, built to withstand years of customers. He glanced around, as if to ensure their neighbors weren't watching. Then all at once, he crumpled it like paper into his fist. His hand began to glow more brightly—and then molten metal spilled into the man's untouched bowl. The soup exploded with steam.

Saleh pushed back from the table so quickly his chair overturned. The other diners turned to look as he stumbled to his feet. The glowing man was wiping his hand nonchalantly on a napkin.

The scaffolding of rationality and reason that held Saleh together began to tremble at its base.

He turned and lurched for the door, not daring to look back. Only once he was on the street did he remember how cold it was, and that he had no hope of making it back alone. But none of that mattered. He had to get as far as possible from that *thing*, that monstrosity—whatever it was—that had sat across the table from him, speaking like a man.

His injured shoulder slammed into a pole, and a field of stars broke out over his eyes. Dizziness reached up for him, familiar and awful.

He awoke sprawled across the sidewalk, a froth on his lips. Men were stepping around him; a few were bent over, speaking to him. Quickly he looked away from their faces, stared instead at the sidewalk. A pair of shoes came into view. Their owner crouched down; the glowing man's beautiful, horrible face hovered inches above his.

"For the love of God," Saleh panted, "just let me die."

The Djinni paused, as if truly considering it. "I think not," he said. "Not yet."

Saleh would've fought the man off if he'd had the strength. But once more he was lifted and carried, like a child this time instead of a sack of grain, held tight against his captor's chest. He closed his eyes against the shame of it. Exhaustion pulled him under.

He surfaced once, briefly, on the Elevated. He moaned and tried to stand, but was held down by a pair of glowing hands, and fell back into sleep. His fellow passengers glanced over their newspapers, and wondered what their story was. When he woke again, he was slumped in a doorway within sight of Maryam's coffeehouse. Painfully he stood and hobbled down the steps. Down the street the glowing man's head was like a second moon, dwindling into the distance.

As he deposited Saleh in the Washington Street doorway, the Djinni wondered if he too had gone mad. Why hadn't he done what Saleh had requested, and left him to die? Even worse, why had he revealed his nature?

He passed Arbeely's darkened shop, and only then remembered the cause of his long day's misadventure. Anger blossomed, fresh and painful. By now Arbeely had certainly dismantled the ceiling. He couldn't bear to go in and check; he'd put in too much effort to see it turned to scrap.

So intent was the Djinni on these thoughts that he didn't notice the man lying in front of his hallway door until he nearly tripped over him. It was Arbeely. The tinsmith lay curled in a ball, head pillowed on a folded scarf. Quiet snores drifted from his half-open mouth.

The Djinni stared down at his sleeping visitor for a few moments. Then he kicked the man not very gently in his side.

Arbeely shot upright, blinking, his head knocking against the door-frame. "You're back."

"Yes," the Djinni said, "and I'd like to go inside. Should I guess at the password, or do you mean to ask me a riddle?"

Arbeely scrambled to his feet. "I've been waiting."

"I can see that." He opened the door, and Arbeely followed him in.

The Djinni made no move to turn on the lamp; he could see well enough and had no wish to make the man feel comfortable.

Arbeely peered around in the gloom. "You don't have chairs?"

"No."

Arbeely shrugged, sat down on a cushion, and grinned up at the Djinni. "Maloof bought the ceiling."

He'd so resigned himself to its loss that the Djinni was caught speechless. "It didn't take long to find him," Arbeely continued brightly. "I had to pay a boy named Matthew ten cents. He runs errands for Maloof, the rents and such. You'll meet him tomorrow." He looked around. "Why do you keep it so dark in here?" Without waiting for a reply, he stood and went to the nearest lamp. "Where are your matches?"

The Djinni only stared at him.

Arbeely laughed. "Of course! How silly of me." He gestured at the lamp. "Would you?"

The Djinni removed the glass, turned the valve, and snapped his fingers over the jet. The gas burst into blue flame. "There," he said. "You have light. Now tell me your story straight, beginning to end, or I will summon a hundred demons from all six directions of the earth and make them torment you till the end of your days."

Arbeely stared. "Goodness. You could really do that?"

"Arbeely!"

Eventually the entire tale came out. As the Djinni listened, the day's anger and frustration turned to glowing pride. Vindication, from Arbeely's own mouth!

"I don't think your tale will be complete without an apology," he said when Arbeely was done.

"Oh, really?" Arbeely crossed his arms. "Then, please. I'd love to hear it."

"*I*, apologize? You were the one who wanted to destroy the ceiling! You said Maloof would never purchase it!"

"I said most likely he wouldn't, and he very nearly didn't. That can't happen again. I've worked too hard to see you gamble away my livelihood."

The Djinni's ire rose again. "So, our agreement is still broken? Or are you suffering me to come back, as long as I keep myself to mending pots and skillets?"

Improbably, Arbeely grinned. "No, don't you see? That was my mistake from the beginning! Maloof saw what I didn't—you're no journeyman, but an artist! I've thought it over, and I have the solution. From now on, you'll be a full and fair partner in the business." He paused, waiting for some sign of reaction. "Well? Doesn't it make sense? I can handle the day-to-day finances, the accounting and so forth. We'll budget a certain amount of money for your materials, and you can take on the projects that interest you. The ceiling can be your advertisement, everyone will be talking about it. We'll even put your name on the sign! ARBEELY AND AHMAD!"

Stunned, the Djinni tried to gather his thoughts. "But—what about the orders we already have?"

Arbeely waved a nonchalant hand. "You can help me during the odd moments, when you aren't busy with your own commissions. As you see fit, of course."

For the next hour Arbeely continued to spin plans from thin air—eventually they'd need a larger space, and then of course they'd have to consider advertising—and the Djinni found himself warming to the man's enthusiasm. He began to imagine his own shop filled with jewelry and figurines, fanciful decorations of gold and silver and shining stone. Yet later that evening, after Arbeely had finally left, a slender current of unease darted through his thoughts. Was this really what he wanted? He'd apprenticed himself to Arbeely out of desperation, the need for shelter in a strange place. And now, to have a stake in the business—that implied responsibility, and permanence.

We'll even put your name on the sign, Arbeely had said. But Ahmad was not his name! He'd chosen it on a whim, never guessing that it would come to define him. Was that it, then? Was he Ahmad now, and not his true self, the one who went by a name he could no longer speak? He tried to remember how long it had been since he'd unthinkingly attempted to change form. His reflexes now rested in muscle and sinew and strides across rooftops, in the steel tools of a metalsmith—tools that, once upon a time, he never could have touched.

In his mind he spoke his name to himself, and took some reassurance from its sound. He was still one of the djinn, after all, no matter how long the iron cuff remained on his wrist. He comforted himself with the thought that although he might be forced to live like a human, he'd never truly be one.

17.

On a cloudless night, ink dark, with only a rind of a moon above, the Golem and the Djinni went walking together along the Prince Street rooftops. The Golem had never been on a rooftop before. She'd protested briefly when the Djinni arrived at her boardinghouse and told her their destination. "But is it safe up there?"

"As safe as walking anywhere in this city at this hour."

"That's not very comforting."

"For you and me, it's perfectly safe. Come on."

She could tell, from his posture and his voice, that he was in one of his restless, obstinate moods. Reluctantly she fell in next to him, deciding that if she found it dangerous, she'd make him turn around.

She followed him up a back staircase. Emerging onto the high, tar-papered expanse of a tenement rooftop, she realized he'd gotten the better of her: the scene was far too fascinating to leave. The rooftops were like a hidden thoroughfare, bustling with nighttime traffic. Men, women, and children came and went, running errands, passing information, or simply heading home. Workingmen in greased overalls held parliament around the rims of ash-barrels, their faces red and flickering. Boys idled in corners, eyes alert. The Golem caught the sense of borders being guarded, but the Djinni, it seemed, was a familiar face. Mostly their doubts were directed at herself: a strange woman, tall and clean and primly dressed. Some of the younger boys took her for a social worker, and hid in the shadows.

The Golem began to realize that if she knew which route to take, she could walk the entire Lower East Side without once touching the ground. Many rooftops stretched for an entire block, divided only by the low walls that marked where the tenements met each other. Where one building was taller than another, rope ladders hung between the roofs.

In some places there were even plank bridges spanning the narrow gaps of the alleyways. The Djinni crossed the first of these with indifference, not even glancing at the four-story drop, and then turned around and waited for the Golem to follow. Thankfully, the bridge proved thick and sturdy enough for her to cross without fear. He raised his eyebrows, impressed, and she shook her head at him. She wasn't sure which was more irritating: his thinking the feat might be beyond her, or her own folly at rising to his bait.

They were navigating a crowded passage when a shout turned all heads. A man was tearing toward them across the rooftops, pursued by a uniformed policeman. The policeman was quick, but his quarry was quicker, vaulting ledges and barrels like a horse at a steeplechase. All stepped aside as the man raced past. He jumped the bridge and ran to the stairwell door, wrenched it open, and disappeared.

The policeman huffed to a stop near them, clearly not relishing the thought of following the man down into a darkened tenement. Sourly he glanced about at the spectators, all of whom found their attention drawn elsewhere. Then he noticed the Djinni, and smiled, touching the brim of his cap in jest. "Well, it's the Sultan. Good evening to ya."

"Officer Farrelly," the Djinni replied.

"Ye're getting slow in yer old age, Farrelly," said a grizzled, drunken-looking man who sat slumped against the wall nearby.

"I'm quick enough for the likes of you, Scotty."

"Go on, bring me in then. I could do with a hot meal."

The officer ignored this, nodded to the company, and began to trudge back the way he'd come.

"Hey, Sultan," said the man called Scotty. "Who's yer lady-friend?" His rheumy eyes went to the Golem, and without waiting for a reply, he said, "Now, missy, if yer friend here is the Sultan, I suppose that makes you a sultana!" And he wheezed with laughter as they continued on their way.

They walked until they found what the Djinni was looking for: a particular well-placed rooftop with a tall water tower at its corner. To discourage climbers, the tower's ladder ended about six feet off the ground;

the Djinni jumped, caught the bottom rung easily, and pulled himself up, hand over hand, landing on a broad ledge that ringed the tower at its middle. He leaned over the railing. "Are you coming?"

"If I don't, you'll say I haven't the nerve, and if I do I'm only encouraging you."

He laughed. "Come up anyway. You'll like the view."

Looking around to make sure no one was watching, the Golem jumped and caught the ladder. She felt ridiculous, with her skirt billowing out beneath her, but it was an easy climb, and soon she joined the Djinni on the ledge. He was right, the view was beautiful. The rooftops lapped each other into the distance, like an illuminated spread of playing cards. Beyond them, just visible, the Hudson was a black band dividing the harbor lights from the glow of the farther shore.

She pointed to the river. "That's where I came ashore, I think. Or farther south. I can't tell."

He shook his head. "Walking across the bottom of the river. I can barely think it, much less do it."

"No doubt you would've escaped some other way."

At that, he grinned. "Oh, no doubt."

A cold, steady breeze was whipping her hair about her face, carrying the smells of coal dust and river silt, the smoke of a thousand chimneys. She watched the Djinni roll a cigarette, touch its end, and inhale. "That policeman," she said. "Do you know him?"

"Only by name. The police leave me alone, and I do likewise."

"They call you the Sultan."

"I can't say I encouraged it. But it's no less my true name than Ahmad." A bitter note had crept into his voice; the issue was newly painful, for some reason. "And now you have another name as well. Though I think the man meant it as a joke, and I'm not sure why."

"A sultana is a queen, but also a kind of raisin," she said.

The Djinni snorted. "A raisin?"

"We use them at the bakery."

He laughed, and then leaned back and regarded her. "Can I ask you a question?"

She raised an eyebrow. "Certainly."

"You have such amazing abilities. Doesn't it gall you to spend your days baking loaves of bread?"

"Should it? Is baking bread less worthy than other work?"

"No, but I wouldn't call it suited to your talents."

"I'm very good at it," she said.

"Chava, I've no doubt you're the best baker in the city. But you can do so much more! Why spend all day making bread when you can lift more than a man's weight, and walk along the bottom of a river?"

"And how would I use these abilities without calling attention to myself? Would you have me at a construction pit, hauling blocks of stone? Or should I license myself as a tugboat?"

"All right, you have a point. But what about seeing others' fears and desires? That's a more subtle talent, and might be worth a lot of money."

"Never," she said flatly. "I would never take advantage like that."

"Why not? You'd make an excellent fortune-teller, or even a confidence-woman. I know a dozen shops on the Bowery that would—"

"Absolutely not!" Only then did she see the smile hidden at the corner of his mouth. "You're teasing me," she said.

"Of course I'm teasing. You'd make a terrible confidence-woman. You'd warn off all the marks."

"I'll take that as a compliment. Besides, I like my job. It suits me."

He leaned on the railing, propped his chin in his hand; she wondered if he knew how human he looked. "And if you could do whatever you wanted, without worrying about staying hidden? Would you still work at a bakery?"

"I don't know," she said. "Perhaps, I suppose. But I *can't* do whatever I want, so why dwell on it? It'll only make me angry."

"And you'd rather blinker your own thoughts than be angry?"

"As usual you put it in the worst way possible, but yes."

"Why not be angry? It's a pure, honest reaction!"

She shook her head, trying to decide how best to explain. "Let me tell you a story," she said. "I stole something once, on the day I came to New York." And she laid out the tale: the starving boy, the man with the knish, the shouting crowd. "I didn't know what to do. I only knew that they were furious, they wanted me to pay. I took it all in, and then . . .

I wasn't there anymore." She frowned, remembering. "I was standing outside myself, watching. I was calm. I didn't feel anything. But I knew that something awful was about to happen, and that I would be the one to do it. I was only a few days old, I didn't know how to control myself."

"And what happened?"

"In the end, nothing. The Rabbi rescued me, and paid for the man's knish. I came back to myself. But if he hadn't been there . . . I don't like to think about it."

"But nothing happened," the Djinni said. "And you have more control now, you've said so yourself."

"Yes, but is it enough? All I know is that I must never hurt another person. *Never.* I'll destroy myself first, if I have to."

She hadn't meant to say it. But now that it was out, she was glad. Let him see how strongly she felt, how much this mattered.

"You can't mean that." He seemed horrified. "Chava, you *can't.*"

"I mean it absolutely."

"What, at the first sign of anger? A man bumps into you on the street, and you destroy yourself?"

She shook her head. "No, none of your what-ifs. I won't argue about this."

They stood in tense silence.

"I imagined you to be indestructible," he said.

"I think I am, almost."

His eyes went to her neck—and she realized that she had, without thinking, reached for her locket. Quickly she dropped her hand. Both glanced away in something like embarrassment. It was growing colder; the wind had picked up.

"I forget sometimes," he said, "how different we are. I would never talk of destroying myself. It would feel too much like giving up."

She wanted to ask, *And there's nothing you'd give yourself up for?* But perhaps that was going too far, prying too deep. One of his hands was twisting idly at the cuff at his wrist. She could see its outline, through the fabric of his shirtsleeve. "Does it hurt?" she asked.

He looked down, surprised. "No," he said. "Not physically."

"May I see?"

He paused a moment—was he ashamed to show her? Then he shrugged and rolled up his sleeve. She peered at the cuff in the dim light. The wide metal band fit close to his skin, as though it had been made to measure. It was crafted in two half-circles held together by two hinges. One hinge was thick and solid; the other one was much thinner, and fastened with a slender, almost decorative pin. The pin's head was flat and round, like a coin. She tried to pull it out, but it held tight.

"It doesn't move," he said. "Believe me, I've tried."

"The pin should be the weakest point." She looked up at him. "I can try to break it, if you'd like."

His eyes widened. "By all means."

Carefully she worked her fingers around the edges of the cuff. His skin was shockingly warm. He started at her touch and said, "Are your hands always so cold?"

"Compared to yours, they must be." She gripped the metal with her fingertips. "Tell me if I hurt you."

"You won't," he said, but she could feel him tense.

She began to pull, steadily, and with growing force, up past the point where ordinary metal would've given way. But both pin and cuff held fast, without bending even a fraction of an inch. The Djinni was bracing against her, his free hand around the railing; and she began to realize that the railing or else the Djinni would break long before the cuff did.

She slackened and stopped, looked up into his face, saw the hope there fade away. "I'm sorry," she said.

His dark eyes stared unseeing and unguarded—but then he pulled his hand from hers and turned away. "I doubt any amount of strength would do it," he said. "But thank you, for trying." He busied himself with rolling another cigarette. "It's getting late," he said. "I expect you'll be wanting to go back soon."

"Yes," she murmured.

Together they walked back across the rooftops, past men eating early breakfasts of bread and beer, past young boys curled together under blankets, past Scotty asleep against his wall. Near her boardinghouse they found a fire escape and descended, navigating splintered and missing steps. In the alley they said their usual good-byes. She glanced back as she rounded the corner and was surprised to find him still there, gaz-ing after her, as though deeply perplexed: a tall man with a shining face, the strangest and most familiar of the city's sights.

Arbeely had been right about the interest that the tin ceiling would generate. Word had spread through the neighborhood that Arbeely's Bedouin apprentice was creating a bizarre metal sculpture and meant to hang it in Maloof's new lobby. The little shop grew crowded with visi-tors. The Djinni was less than thrilled with the constant interruptions, and soon abandoned all attempts at politeness. Eventually Arbeely closed the shop to all but their paying customers.

The one person granted an exception was young Matthew Moun-sef. The boy had begun spending his after-school hours in the shop, watching the Djinni as he worked. Against all expectations, the Djinni seemed to genuinely take to Matthew, perhaps helped by the boy's ha-bitual silence. Occasionally the Djinni assigned him minor tasks and errands, which freed him up to use his hands while Matthew wasn't watching. For these services the Djinni paid the boy in pennies, the oc-casional nickel, and, when he was feeling indulgent, small tin animals rendered out of scrap.

In that first frenzy of the ceiling's construction, the Djinni had thought to be done in four days, five at the most, but reality proved far different. Never before had he worked to such demanding specifications. It wasn't enough to measure the ceiling roughly; it must be exact to within a fraction of an inch, or else it simply wouldn't fit. One entire day was spent perched on a ladder in the lobby, measuring and double-checking and shouting numbers to Matthew, who wrote them down carefully in a little notebook. After that, he pulled down the old tiles, a grimy job that coated him in cobwebs and plaster dust. Then the ceiling was replastered and carefully smoothed. It was all painstaking, arduous work. More than once the Djinni thought about abandoning the project entirely, even melting it down, but something always stopped him. The ceiling seemed to belong to everyone now—Maloof, Matthew, Arbeely, the tenants, the well-wishers who stopped him on the street and asked how it was coming. In an odd sense, it was no longer his to destroy.

At last, the preparations were complete. As Arbeely watched, his nerves fraying, the Djinni carved the finished ceiling into large irregular pieces, following the lines of the valleys and steep cliffs, turning it into a gigantic puzzle made of tin. They loaded the pieces into a straw-packed cart, and pulled it to Maloof's building. Matthew was waiting for them, excitement on his face, and Arbeely hadn't the heart to ask if he shouldn't be at school. Soon Maloof arrived as well. The Djinni was surprised to see the landlord roll up his sleeves and prepare to lend a hand.

It took almost the whole day to install the ceiling. The difficult part came in holding the pieces steady enough to nail in place. In the end it required the Djinni, Arbeely, and Maloof each on their own ladders, with much repositioning and arguing and displays of temper. Every time someone wanted to pass through the lobby, two of the ladders would have to come down, leaving the Djinni to hold up the half-attached piece. As the day wore on, more and more people gathered to watch them work. Even Matthew's mother came down, taking the stairs slowly, one hand on the banister. Apparently her health was no better.

At last the Djinni drove the final nail home, to a spontaneous thunder of applause. For half an hour he shook hands with what felt like every Syrian in New York. Afterward they all milled about, gazing up at the ceiling. Many laughed and stretched their hands into the air, as if trying to touch the mountains. A few older residents grumbled of vertigo and went upstairs to supper. The children spun about with upturned faces, and crashed into their parents' legs. Finally, one by one, they all drifted away until Arbeely and the Djinni were left alone.

All at once the Djinni felt drained to his depths. It was over, finished. He looked up at his masterpiece, trying to decide what he'd accomplished.

"Everyone adores it," Arbeely said next to him. "It's only a matter of time before you have your own shop." Then he noticed the expression on the Djinni's face. "What's the matter?"

"My palace," the Djinni said. "It isn't there."

Arbeely glanced around quickly, but they were alone. "You could still put it in," he said quietly. "Call it a stroke of artistic whimsy, or what have you."

"You don't understand," the Djinni said. "I did it deliberately. It's only fitting that you can't see it, that they can't see it. But *I* should see it. It should be there." He gestured to a spot near the center of the ceiling. "Just beyond that ridge. The valley looks empty, without it."

Something came together in Arbeely's mind. "You mean this is a *map*?"

"Of course it's a map. What did you think it was?"

"I don't know—a work of imagination, I suppose." He looked up at it with new appreciation. "And it's accurate?"

"I spent two hundred years traveling every inch of these lands. Yes, it's accurate." He pointed to a mountain in the corner near the stairwell. "I mined a vein of silver on that mountainside once. A group of *ifrits* tried to steal it from me. I fought them off, though it took a day and a night." His finger moved to a narrow plain, deep in shadow. "That's where I met up with a caravan bound for ash-Sham. I followed them invisible until they reached the Ghouta. It's the last thing I can remember, from my life before."

Arbeely listened with chagrin. He'd hoped that the Djinni would've found some solace by now: in his work, the life he'd built for himself, the nighttime excursions that still gave Arbeely palpitations. But how could that replace the life he'd led for centuries? He put a hand on his partner's shoulder. "Come on, my friend," Arbeely said. "Let's go open a bottle of *araq*, and drink to your success."

The Djinni consented to be led outside, into the falling night. And behind them, Matthew crept down the staircase and stared up at the ceiling again, his eyes wide with wonder at what he'd overheard.

Passover approached, and the daily offerings at Radzin's Bakery began to change: from braided breads to flat matzos, rugelach to macaroons. But even with the Passover selections and wholesale orders, business at the bakery turned woefully thin. Since Mr. Radzin didn't like his employees to appear idle, they had to work as slowly as they could, stretching each task to near-absurd lengths. For the Golem, it was like moving through glue. Minor annoyances magnified themselves: the jangling bell over the door, the shuffling and coughing of the customers. Their thoughts rang out in the silence, hopelessly monotonous and self-absorbed.

After days like this, the long nights were a relief and a torture both. She was thrilled to be alone, but her accumulated tension had nowhere to go. She would've tried quiet exercises—once, casting about from boredom, she'd spent an hour lifting her desk above her head like a circus strongman—but she needed all her time for sewing. Anna had let it slip to the customers that the Golem was an expert seamstress, and now the Golem was inundated with repairs. She kept the damaged clothing in a teetering stack in the corner until her landlady complained that it was impossible to clean around—"and besides, Chava dear, this is a respectable boardinghouse, not a sweatshop." She'd apologized and stuffed the clothing in her armoire. She sewed as quickly as possible, irked by the monotony. Why on earth couldn't men keep their trousers whole? Why were they constantly losing their buttons?

One night, in the slow hours before dawn, a stray thought snuck into her mind: the Djinni was right. These occupations weren't enough to hold her interest, not for the long years that her clay body promised. "Go away," she muttered, and forced her thoughts elsewhere. It was all his fault, of course. She'd been content enough before; now she was turning as moody as he.

She was wallowing in these preoccupations at the bakery, and trying to ignore Mrs. Radzin's small talk with a customer, when a burst of pure panic drove all other voices aside. Anna was standing stock-still at her table, her face white as wax. She put down her rolling pin and walked to the back room as casually as she could; but the bakery's low chatter couldn't mask the sound of her vomiting in the water closet. She emerged a few minutes later and went back to work as though nothing had happened; but the Golem knew the truth of it, for the girl's thoughts were a jumbled torment: *Oh God, there's no doubt now. What if the Radzins heard? What will Irving say? What am I going to do?* And all the rest of that day Anna proved that she might've had true success as an actress, for she chatted and smiled as though all was well, with no outward clue to the terrified din in her head.

While the Djinni had been preoccupied with Maloof's tin ceiling, spring had taken root in Manhattan. In the desert he'd seen the seasons change countless times, but this one felt like a magic trick. A day of hard rain washed the garbage from the half-frozen gutters, and then, improbably, the sun emerged. The filthy snowdrifts that had sat on the corners since November began to crater and dissolve. Windows shuttered for months were flung open, clotheslines restrung. Rugs and counterpanes were hauled onto the fire escapes and joyously beaten. The air began to smell of dust and sun-warmed cobblestones.

As the Djinni walked to the Golem's boardinghouse that week, he tried to decide whether to tell her about the tin ceiling. Usually he made a point of saying little about his daytime work, but this she would want to hear about. She'd praise him, tell him how glad she was for his success; and something in him rebelled against it. He didn't want praise from her, not for this. Not when she knew how much more he'd once been capable of. To even mention the ceiling felt dangerously close to giving in, settling, declaring this life to be good enough, in a way that it hadn't with Arbeely.

He reached her boardinghouse and found that, as usual, she'd been watching for him. But instead of her usual caution, she wrenched open the front door and barreled down the steps as though fleeing a terrible argument. She cast no worried glance at her neighbors' windows; she didn't even bother to put up her hood. "Where are we going?" she asked by way of greeting.

"Central Park," he said, taken aback.

"Will it be a long walk?"

"I suppose, but—"

"Good," she said, and set off without waiting. He hurried to catch up with her. Every line of her body spoke of frustration. She walked with her head down, impatiently jumping the maze of puddles, apparently forgetting she'd once scolded him for doing the same. Her hands flexed at her sides. He'd never seen her like this.

They walked for some blocks, and at last he said, "If it's myself you're furious with, please let me know. I'd rather not go on guessing."

Instantly her anger turned to chagrin. "Oh, Ahmad, I'm sorry! I'm poor company, I shouldn't have come. Except I might have torn down the house rather than stay inside another minute." She pressed her hands to her forehead, as though fighting a headache. "It's been a terrible week."

"How so?"

"I can't say much. There's a secret that isn't mine to tell. Someone at the bakery is extremely frightened, and trying to keep it hidden. I'm not even supposed to know."

"I can see how that would distract you."

"I can barely think of anything else. At least a dozen times I've had to stop myself from saying the wrong thing." She hugged herself, scowling. "I've been making so many mistakes. Yesterday I had to throw away an entire batch of dough. And then today I burned all the butter-horns. Mr. Radzin shouted at me, and Mrs. Radzin asked me if everything was all right. Asked *me*! While Anna goes on smiling as though nothing—"

She stopped, hands flying to her mouth. "There, you see? Oh, this is intolerable!"

"If it helps, I'd already guessed it was Anna. You don't have that many colleagues."

"Please don't tell anyone."

"Chava, who would I tell? *What* would I tell? I don't even know the secret!"

"And I'm not going to say it," she muttered.

At length the gates at Fifty-ninth Street appeared, and they entered the park along the darkened path, leaving the streetlights behind. Twigs and branches shivered above them in the sudden hush. The Golem slowed and looked around with fascination, her ill mood visibly fading. "I've never seen so many trees."

"Just wait," he said, smiling.

They rounded a corner, and the full scope of the park came into view, the rolling stretches of lawn and distant groves. She turned around as she walked, trying to see the whole panorama at once. "It's enormous! And so quiet!" She put her hands over her ears and uncovered them again, as though to make sure her hearing hadn't deserted her. "Is it always like this?"

"At night, it is. During the day it's full of people."

"I never would've thought the city could be hiding this. How far does it go?"

"I'm not sure. It would take weeks to explore properly. Months, perhaps."

They walked north toward Sheep Meadow. He'd hoped to take her off the main carriage drive, but the lawn had thawed to a swamp, and the smaller paths were submerged. The sheep were nowhere to be seen; he supposed they'd been stabled somewhere less muddy.

"I feel different here," the Golem said suddenly.

"How so?"

"I don't know." She shivered lightly once, then again.

He frowned. "Are you all right?"

"Yes, I'm fine." But her voice was distracted, as though she were listening for something far away.

They left the carriage drive, and descended the steps to Bethesda Terrace. The fountain had been stilled for the evening. Coins lay scattered at the bottom of the basin, dark and perfect circles. The water was so transparent that it seemed an illusion.

The Golem looked up at the winged statue. "She's beautiful. Who is she?"

"She's called the Angel of the Waters," the Djinni said, recalling that first conversation with Sophia. How long had it been since he'd seen her last? He remembered the locked door, the draped furniture, and felt a vague unease.

The Golem said, "I read about angels, once. In one of the Rabbi's books." She glanced at him. "You don't believe in them, I suppose."

"No, I don't," he said. He thought she might be waiting for him to return the question; but he didn't want to talk about angels, or gods, or whatever else the humans had invented that week. The park was too calm, too hushed, for an argument. He thought again of bringing up the tin ceiling but could see no graceful way to do it. She'd think he was a child, hunting for praise.

For a while they sat against the basin's rim—the Djinni ever mindful of the water behind him—and watched the lake as it lapped against the terrace. The night had grown heavy with fog, and it set his skin prickling. The Golem was a cool and solid presence at his side. Her head was tilted upward; she was looking at the sky. Even this far into the park, the city's lights illuminated the haze of clouds, giving them depth and texture.

"I wish my life could always be like this," the Golem said. "Calm. Peaceful." She closed her eyes, and again it seemed she was listening for something.

"You should come here on one of your Saturdays," he said. "It's different here, during the day."

"I couldn't come alone," she said absently.

He wanted to protest this, but then he recalled how noticeable Sophia had been, a solitary woman by the fountain. The Golem didn't have Sophia's beauty, but she drew the eye nonetheless. Perhaps a chaperone wasn't the worst idea. "What about that friend of yours, Michael? You could bring him."

She opened her eyes, gave him an odd look. "I'd rather not."

"Why, have you quarreled?"

"No, not as such. I haven't seen him since we went to Brooklyn. But he might . . . misconstrue the invitation."

He frowned, not understanding, but then remembered what he'd forgotten: this friend wanted more from her, and it made her uneasy. "It would be an afternoon in a park, not a lifelong mating."

She winced at this. "He's a good man. I wouldn't want to lead him on."

"So you'll avoid him for the rest of his life, to keep him from getting the wrong impression."

"You don't understand," she grumbled. "He has *desires* for me. And they're very loud."

"And you have no romantic feelings for him at all?"

"I don't think so. It's hard to tell."

He snorted. "Maybe you *should* lie with him. It might clarify things."

She jerked as though he'd slapped her. "I would never!"

"*Never?* You mean with him, or with anyone?"

She turned away. "I don't know. It's difficult to think about."

It was a clear signal, but he decided to ignore it. "It should be easy. *They're* the ones who complicate it beyond reason."

"Of course *you* would say so! And I suppose I should follow your example, and take all the pleasures I can!"

"Why not, when there's no harm done?"

"By which you mean that *you* aren't harmed, and that's what matters!" She'd rounded on him, full of ire. "You go here and there leaving God knows what in your wake, and then you think less of them for worrying about the consequences. Meanwhile, I have to hear every *I wish I hadn't* and *what'll I do now*! It's selfish and careless, and inexcusable!"

Her startling anger seemed to have run its course. Frowning, she turned away in stony silence.

After a moment he said, "Chava, have I done something I don't know about? Did I harm someone?"

"Not as far as I know," she muttered. "But your life affects others, and you don't seem to realize it." She looked down to her hands, tangled in her lap. "Perhaps it's unfair to wish otherwise. We're our natures, you and I."

Her words hurt, more than he'd have thought. He wanted to defend himself—but then, maybe she was right, maybe he was selfish and careless. And he was right as well, to think her prudish and overcautious. Both of them had their reasons, as well as their natures. He looked out over the lake, which lay dark and still, somehow unruffled by their argument.

"We can't seem to talk without fighting." Her words were uncomfortably close to the drift of his mind; he wondered, sometimes, if he was as opaque to her as she thought. "It's strange that we can be friends. I hope that you *do* consider me a friend, and not a burden. I don't want these walks to be something you dread." She glanced at him quickly, as if embarrassed. "It feels strange, not knowing. Were you anyone else, I wouldn't have to ask."

It took him a moment to respond, and he had to dare himself to match her honesty. "I look forward to walking with you. I think I even look forward to the arguments. You understand what my life is like, even when we disagree. Arbeely tries, but he can't see it the way you can." He smiled. "So yes, I consider you a friend. And I would miss this, if we stopped."

She returned the smile, a bit sadly. "So would I."

"Enough of this," he said. "Are we seeing the park, or aren't we?"

She chuckled. "Lead on."

They left the terrace and walked up the steps to the Mall. The thickening fog had wiped the world away, leaving only the broad, elm-lined path and a misty horizon. Next to him, the Golem seemed like a manifestation of the landscape. "This place makes me feel strange," she murmured.

"Strange, how?"

"I'm not sure." Her hands came up, as if feeling for the words in the air. "Like I want to run and run, and never stop."

He smiled. "Is that so strange?"

"It is to me. I've never run before."

"What, *never*?"

"Never."

"Then you should give it a try."

She paused, as if considering—and then she leapt from his side. Her legs stretched behind her, her cloak flowed outward like a wing; and for a long moment her body was a dark shape flying away from him at incredible speed.

He stood, stunned, watching; and then he grinned and took off after her, shoes pounding the slate, the trees blurring to either side. Was he gaining on her? He couldn't tell, she'd disappeared; she'd run from him so quickly!

A copse of trees loomed up out of the fog: it was the end of the Mall. He slowed, came to a stop, looked around. Where was she? "Chava?"

"Come see!"

She was in the middle of the copse, crouching low over something.

He stepped across the low fence, and sank up to his ankles in cold mud. Cringing, he picked his way over to her. "Look," she said.

A thick shoot had poked its way through the mud. At its crown was a knot of petals, tightly furled. He looked around, and saw smaller shoots scattered here and there: the first flowers of spring. "You could see this from the path?"

She shook her head. "I knew it was here. The ground is waking." He watched as she pressed her hand into the mud. Her hand vanished, then her wrist. For a wild moment he thought she might sink in entirely. He wanted to pull her away, to keep her from disappearing. But then she sat back, and gazed down at the mess of her skirt and shoes, her mud-spattered cloak. "Oh, look what I've done," she murmured. She stood up, becoming again her brisk and businesslike self. "What time is it?"

Together they made their way back to solid ground. His shoes were ruined; he took them off and thumped them on a tree. Next to him, the Golem tried to brush the mud from her cloak. They glanced at each other, smiled quickly and looked away, like children who'd been caught at something.

They took the carriage road south again, and soon they were through the gates and back in the world of granite and concrete. The farther they got from the park, the more the Golem seemed to lose her strange energy. She frowned at her muddy boots, and muttered that she'd have to wash out her cloak. By the time they reached Broadway, she seemed as likely to run for sheer pleasure as to sprout wings and fly. In fact, it was he who was still held by an unreal daze. The familiar streets seemed full of new details: the scrollwork on the lampposts, the carved ornaments above the doorways. He felt as though something inside him was about to break open, or fall apart.

In what seemed no time at all they were in the alley beside her boardinghouse. "We'll go back again, when it's warmer," he said.

She smiled. "I'd like that. Thank you." She took his hand and squeezed it tightly, her cool fingers around his. And then as always she was gone, and he was left to walk home alone, through streets still hung with morning mist.

18.

Passover stretched on, and the Lower East Side turned into one giant craving: for a pastry, a bagel, anything really, as long as it wasn't matzo. Finally, mercifully, the holiday ended, and the neighborhood streamed to the local bakeries in relief. Knowing that her morning shopping trip would be akin to a mob scene, the Sheltering House cook deputized Joseph Schall to go with her to Shimmel's, their new supplier, and help carry back as much bread as possible. Michael had justified the switch from Radzin's with talk of better labor practices and the need to support younger businesses; but the cook remembered the gift of almond macaroons, noticed Michael's recent glum mood, and didn't ask too many questions.

On this day, though, Shimmel's was a madhouse. The line stretched far out the door; inside, the employees were running around in a panic, searching for ingredients and frantically rolling out dough, or else apologizing to disgruntled customers whose favorites had already disappeared from the cases. The cook stuck her head in, frowned, came back out. "We're going to Radzin's," she told Schall. "Michael won't know the difference."

Yehudah Schaalman could not have cared less which bakery they bought their bread at. The strain of passing himself as kindly old Joseph Schall was taking its toll. He'd been to every synagogue, every yeshiva, every place of Jewish learning he could find, and he felt no closer to his goal, to the secret to life eternal. Never once had he felt a pull from his dowsing spell, even though he knew without doubt that it had worked. Was this why he'd come to New York, to run errands and settle dormitory squabbles? For a month now he'd gritted his teeth and continued, having no other choice. This was his only hand; he'd play it out until he won, or it killed him.

With as much enthusiasm as he could counterfeit he followed the cook back through the sodden, overcrowded streets. The line at Radzin's was no shorter, but at least it moved. Inside, he hovered near the door, distrusting the crowd. The bakery was packed with people, their steamy exhalations fogging the glass and turning the air thick and humid. Schaalman began to sweat in his wool coat. At least the workers were diverting to look at. They moved quick as machines, especially the tall girl at the near table, who was rolling out dough as if she'd been born to it. He found himself fascinated by her hands. They moved without pause, without a single wasted gesture. He looked up at her face—a plain girl, yet familiar-looking—

There was a sharp, insistent *tug* as the dowsing spell came to bear. And in that moment, he recognized her.

The girl looked up, startled. Her eyes confusedly roved the crowd, as though not sure what she was looking for.

But Schaalman had already slipped out the door. He forced himself to keep calm, his mind clear, until he reached the end of the block, and then leaned against a wall, trembling with shock.

His golem! The golem he'd built for Rotfeld! She was here, in New York! He'd imagined her rotting away in some rubbish dump—but did that mean that Rotfeld had brought her to life on the ship, before he died? He must have; he'd been more than fool enough to do it. And now she was roaming masterless in New York, a hunk of clay with teeth and hair, a dangerous creature who looked like a woman. And Schaalman had no idea what it could possibly mean.

It lasted only the briefest of moments: a sense that someone had *seen* her, seen to the heart of her, and been afraid. But in the next instant there were only the customers, their desires for rye bread and rugelach. Still, she stood listening with all her senses until Mrs. Radzin shot her a strange look. "Chava? Are you all right?"

"Yes, I'm fine. I thought I heard someone call my name." She smiled quickly, and then bent back over her work, wondering. Occasionally someone would wander in off the street with an unquiet mind, from drink or illness or misfortune; perhaps it was one of these, someone who'd arrived at the right answer for the wrong reasons. Or else she'd been working too quickly, and had been noticed. In any case, there was nothing she could do about it, not with a line out the door and six sheets of cookies in the oven. For the rest of the day she listened, but heard nothing; and other, more insistent worries rose to eclipse it.

Anna's situation was growing worse. The girl was now retreating at least twice a day into the water closet to vomit, and the Radzins had, inevitably, taken notice. At each of Anna's hurried departures, Mrs. Radzin's mouth would pinch in distaste, and Mr. Radzin's expression would turn sour. It was clear to all that the jig was up, but still, maddeningly, no one said a word. They said plenty to themselves, though; and by midweek the Golem thought she might go deaf from the noise.

At night, over her sewing, she reviewed the silently gleaned details of Anna's situation. The girl was at least two months along. Her young man still didn't know. She'd told two girlfriends, sworn them to secrecy, though who knew how long that would last. She thought about having it taken care of, but she couldn't afford to go uptown, and the places on the Bowery frightened her more than telling Irving. She liked to tease and quarrel with him, liked making up after an argument even more, but who was he at heart? Who would he be, when she told him?

The Golem turned it over and over, trying to decide what Anna should do, but she could find no advice to give. The Rabbi would say that her friend had acted rashly, made poor choices, and this was undoubtedly true. But when placed next to Anna's her own life seemed a pale shadow, without even the opportunity to make Anna's mistakes. She wasn't human. She would never have children. Love itself might be beyond her. How could she say she wouldn't have done the same as Anna, if she'd been born instead of made?

At dawn she was still hunched over these thoughts, irritably stabbing her needle into someone's trouser-leg. Not even a week had passed since her heedless run in Central Park, and the easy joy of it seemed like someone else's memory. Then again, it had been a strange experience.

She remembered the insistent pull of the earth, and the way her senses had stretched out in every direction, taking in the whole of the park. And the Djinni: he'd looked so oddly lost in the alleyway, so unlike his usual confident self, and she couldn't even guess the reason. She'd grabbed his hand out of an impulse to reassure herself that he was still there.

She tied off the thread, snipped it close to the knot. There. Trousers mended. She only wished these men would stop *ripping* them.

She put on her cloak and walked to the bakery, braced for another day of fears and silences. And then Anna came through the back door and ripped the ground from beneath her feet.

"Chava!" She grabbed the Golem's hands, every inch of her radiating happiness. "Congratulate me, I'm getting married!"

"*What?*"

"Irving proposed last night! He proposed and I said *yes!*"

"Oh, my dear!" cried Mrs. Radzin. She swooped down on the girl, all offenses instantly forgiven. "How wonderful! Come here, tell me everything!"

"Well, we're just terribly in love, so we're getting married as soon as we can—"

Mr. Radzin fell to coughing.

"—and then, you'll never guess, we're moving to Boston!"

Mrs. Radzin gasped, as she was meant to, and Anna went on to explain about Irving's friend who'd left New York to help out at his uncle's textile mill. "And now there's a job waiting there for Irving if he wants it. He'll be an assistant manager, with men under him and everything. Imagine me, a boss's wife!"

The two women went on chatting happily while the Golem stood there dazed. A wedding? Boston? Was this possible? She'd seen Anna's dilemma as a harrowing choice from among deeply flawed options. Now, listening to the women debate the merits of a lace wedding dress versus embroidered satin, she realized that she'd never once imagined a happy outcome.

Soon Mr. Radzin began to complain that they were running behind, and that they should plan Anna's trousseau on their own time. All went back to work, and the mood in the bakery returned to something like normal, though little Abie still snuck occasional peeks at Anna, as though expecting her to turn into a fairy princess. At the end of the day, watching Anna retrieve her cloak in the back room, the Golem realized she hadn't even properly congratulated her. She crossed the room and caught Anna in a hug. Startled, the girl gasped a laugh. "Chava, you're squeezing the life from me!"

She let go immediately; Anna's face was red and smiling, there was no real damage done. "I'm sorry, I didn't mean to, I just wanted to say congratulations! But I'll miss you terribly, is Boston very far away? Can you get there by streetcar? Oh, no, I suppose not."

Anna was laughing now. "Chava, you goose! You're a mystery, I swear."

The words were pouring out, all her week's worry relieved in a single torrent. "I'm just so happy for you! What did he say when you told him—" She stopped, clapped a hand over her mouth. Thankfully the Radzins were in the alley outside, waiting to lock up for the night.

Anna stifled a nervous giggle. "Hush, for heaven's sake! I've done a poor job of hiding it, I know, but everything's all right now. He was surprised, of course, who wouldn't be, but then he got so sweet and solemn, it nearly made my heart break. He started talking about Boston, and how this was a sign he should grow up and settle down. And then he just swooped down on his knees and asked me! Of course I burst into tears, I couldn't even say yes properly!"

"Are you two staying the night?" called Mr. Radzin from the alley. "If not, some of us would like to get home."

Anna rolled her eyes, and they went out and said their good-byes to the Radzins. "What a beautiful evening," Anna said to the Golem as they walked, taking no note of the garbage-smelling alleys, the damp and chilling breeze. The Golem smiled, watching her. Tonight she could relax over her sewing, even enjoy it a little. And tomorrow, she could tell the Djinni that everything was better at the bakery. Perhaps, just this once, they wouldn't even argue.

Anna said, "What are you thinking about?"

"Nothing," the Golem said. "A friend. Why?"

"I've never seen you smile like that. Is this friend a man? Oh, don't turn shy, Chava! You can't hide from the world forever, even widows need to live a little! All due respect to your late husband, of course—but would he have wanted you to lie in an empty bed for the rest of your life?"

She tried to imagine Rotfeld's opinion on the matter. Likely he would have wanted exactly that. "I suppose not," she muttered, conscious of the lie.

"Then come out and have fun for once."

She had the sense of the conversation veering out of her control. She laughed, a bit panicked. "Anna, I wouldn't even know how."

"I'll help you," the girl said, with the grand generosity of the newly happy. "We'll start tomorrow night. There's a dance at a casino on Broome Street. I can get you in for free, I know the doorman. I'll introduce you to my friends, they know all the best men."

A dance? In an unfamiliar place, surrounded by strangers? "But I've never been—I don't know how to dance."

"We'll teach you! There's nothing to it. If you can walk, you can dance." She grabbed the Golem's hands. "Oh, *please* come, Chava. It would mean so much to me. You can meet Irving! He promised me he'll be there." She giggled. "I want to dance with him while I can still see my feet!"

Well, perhaps that changed things. Meeting Irving would put to rest any lingering fears about what sort of man he was. As for dancing, perhaps she could plead fatigue, or sore feet. But, wait: what about the Djinni? She'd be meeting him tomorrow! "What time is the dance?"

"Nine o'clock."

So early? That settled it. The Djinni never arrived before eleven. She could go to the dance hall and meet Irving, and perhaps even dance once or twice if it made Anna happy. And then she'd plead her excuses, and meet the Djinni under her window. "All right," she said, smiling. "I'll come."

"Wonderful!" cried Anna. "Meet me at eight-thirty, at my friends Phyllis and Estelle's place—" and she gave the address, a tenement on Rivington. "We'll walk over together, not too early. You never want to be early to a dance, it makes you look too eager. Don't worry about what to wear, just put on your best shirtwaist, that's what most of us do.

Oh, I'm so excited!" Anna clasped her in a fierce hug, which the Golem returned, amused; and then the girl was off down the street, head high, cloak swinging behind her.

The Golem continued home. It was growing dark, and the street-cart vendors were making their final sales. Near her boardinghouse she passed a man pushing a cart piled high with women's clothing. There was a sign nailed to the side of the cart: BEST WOMEN'S FASHIONS, it said, and then below that, in smaller letters, PARDON ME I'M MUTE. The Golem thought about what Anna had said about shirtwaists. She glanced down at her own tired cuffs, frayed past the point of mending. Her other shirt-waist, she knew, was no better.

She walked up to the man and tapped him on the shoulder. He put down the cart and turned, eyebrows raised.

"Hello," she said, nervous. "I'm going to a dance tomorrow. Do you have shirtwaists for dancing in?"

He raised one hand, a gesture that said, *say no more*. From his pocket he pulled a cloth tape measure, and mimed for her to hold out her arms. She did so, amused at the expressive precision of his gestures, which left no room for dissembling. *Perhaps we should all learn to be mute*, she thought.

He took her measurements with quick movements, then rolled the tape measure away and put one hand to his chin, considering. Turning back to the pushcart, he rifled through a stack of shirtwaists. With a flourish he pulled one out and held it up. It was certainly no workaday waist. The cream-colored fabric was closely woven, much finer than her own. Sheer ruffles ran up the length of the bodice and behind the high collar; the cuffs were ringed with them as well. It tapered to a midriff so narrow that the Golem wondered how a woman would breathe in it. The man proffered it—*yes?*

"How much?"

He held up four fingers; in his mind she saw three. She stifled a smile. Perhaps some subterfuges were universal, no matter the language.

It was an extravagance, but one she could afford. She opened her wallet, counted out four dollars, and handed them to the peddler. The man's eyes widened in surprise. He handed her the shirtwaist, and accepted the money with, she saw, some measure of embarrassment. "Thank you," she said, and went on her way.

She hadn't made it more than a few steps before the peddler hurried around in front of her and held up his hands: *wait*. From a coat pocket he withdrew two imitation tortoiseshell combs, their heads cut to resemble roses. He reached up and neatened the part in the Golem's hair, sweeping a few errant strands across the crown of her head. Then he smoothed back the hair to the left of the part and pinned it with a comb, its teeth snug against her scalp. He performed the same maneuver on the right side, giving the hair a half-twist before setting the comb tightly in place. He stepped back, nodded at his work, and walked back to his waiting cart.

"Wait!" the Golem called. "Don't you want me to pay?"

He shook his head, not even turning, and trundled his pushcart back up the street. She stood there for a few moments, perplexed, and then walked the rest of the way home.

In her room, she slipped out of her old shirtwaist and buttoned up the new one. The reflection in her mirror was wholly startling. The ruffles behind the collar framed her face, accenting the hollows of her cheeks, her wide-set eyes. Her hair, shaped by the combs, spilled in waves to her shoulders. The frilled cuffs softened her hands, turning them slim and elegant. She studied herself for long minutes, pleased but uneasy. A mask or costume would've been less unnerving than these small transformations. She'd changed just enough to wonder if she was still herself.

The next day was full of excited whispers and meaningful giggles from Anna, and by the afternoon Mrs. Radzin had caught wind of their plans. On some pretext she maneuvered the Golem into the back room. "You know your own mind, I'm sure," the woman said. "But be careful, Chavaleh. You're fond of Anna, I am too, but there's no need to risk your reputation. And there are other men, better men than you can find at a dance hall. What about the Rabbi's nephew? Wasn't he sweet on you? I know he's poor as a mouse, but money isn't everything."

The Golem had had enough. "Mrs. Radzin, please. I don't intend to 'risk my reputation,' certainly not in the way you mean. I'm going with Anna to meet Irving, and see what sort of man he is. Nothing more."

The woman snorted. "I can tell you what sort of man he is. No better than the rest." But she released the Golem back to her duties, and confined all further protests to dark looks.

Finally the day ended, and the Golem went home and put on her new shirtwaist. The combs were trickier than she'd thought, but before long she'd arranged her hair to her satisfaction. She went to the address Anna had given her, and the door was thrown open at her knock. "You came!" Anna cried in surprise, as though the Golem hadn't promised her half a dozen times. She beckoned the Golem inside. "You look so lovely with your hair like that—oh, and let me see your shirtwaist! Beautiful!"

In the parlor two young women stood in their underclothes, sorting through a pile of garments. Their chatter stopped as Anna burst in, trailing the Golem behind her. "Girls, this is Chava. Be nice to her, she's shy. Chava, this is Phyllis, and that's Estelle."

The Golem froze beneath their curious gazes, fighting down sudden panic. How could she have thought she was ready to do this, to pass as a woman among women? What could possibly have possessed her?

But the women smiled at her, welcoming. "Chava, so nice to meet you! Anna's told us all about you. Come here, help us pick out what to wear," said one of them—Phyllis? "I think this waist fits me better, but I just adore the buttons on this one."

"*I'm* wearing that one," the other girl said.

"It's too tight on you!"

"It certainly is not!"

Tentatively the Golem joined them, unsure of the etiquette. Should she undress as well? No, they seemed to think it was perfectly natural for her to stand there in hat and boots while they tried on various pieces and then flung them off again. At length they noticed her shirtwaist, and gasped and cooed over it, and begged her to tell them where she'd gotten it. The attention unnerved her, but it was so honestly friendly that she began to relax, even to smile.

All at once she noticed that Anna had disappeared. "Where's Anna?"

Phyllis and Estelle grew quiet and leaned their heads toward her, concerned and conspiratorial. "In the water closet. She won't let us see her get dressed," Estelle said. "I think she's embarrassed."

"She's been crying, too," Phyllis said. "He was supposed to come calling last night, and he didn't."

"But he's coming tonight, isn't he?"

The girls glanced at each other; but just then Anna entered in her usual flurry, dressed in a full-skirted suit that fit tightly at the seams. On her head she wore an enormous straw hat, topped by a quivering, somewhat shabby willow-plume.

"Are we ready?" she said brightly. "Then let's be off!"

The Golem wanted to stay on the periphery of the evening, but on the way to the hall it grew clear that Anna and her friends intended to make her its focus. They clustered around her, peppering her with instructions and advice. "Don't be too eager, but then don't be too choosy," they said. "Don't dance all night with the first one who asks. And if you dislike the look of a man, say no. Stand your ground if he comes on too fresh."

"It's all right," said Anna, seeing the Golem's panicked look. "We'll take it in turns to watch out for you, won't we?" The girls nodded, giggled, squeezed her arm; and the Golem resigned herself to the evening.

They neared their destination, and were caught up in a crowd of well-dressed young women and men, all funneling toward a nondescript Broome Street door. The Golem could hear music. She felt herself pushed and jostled, in her mind as well as her body. Fortunately the crowd was in a good mood, cheerful and flirtatious; the women exclaimed over one another's finery while the men joked and sipped from flasks.

A large man sat on a stool next to the door, collecting the admission: fifteen cents for the ladies, a quarter for the men. "That's Mendel," Anna said. She waved, and flashed him a dazzling smile. Mendel grinned back, a bit stupefied, and waved them through. "He's carried a torch for me for years," Anna whispered.

Through the door was a dark hallway, full of bodies, all pressing forward. For a moment the Golem began to panic, thinking she would crush someone by accident. Then the eager crowd surged behind her—and the Golem was propelled into the most amazing room she'd ever seen. Enormous, high-ceilinged, it swallowed the crowds eagerly. Brass chandeliers hung with cut-glass pendants cast a flickering dazzle on the people below. The walls glittered with gas lamps and candelabra, multiplied by mirrored columns. It looked like a twinkling fairyland that stretched on and on.

The Golem stared, enthralled. Any other time, a crowd of this size might have overwhelmed her; but the sheer unanticipated spectacle, and the uniform high spirits of the dance-goers, tempered her anxiety with something that felt very like delight.

"What do you think?" Estelle nearly had to shout into the Golem's ear to be heard. "Do you like it?"

The Golem could only nod.

Anna laughed. "I told you so. Now come on, before all the good tables are taken."

They passed a long wooden bar stocked with bottles and growlers. Beyond were rows of round, cloth-draped tables. Jacketed waiters passed among the tables, to the bar and back again, their trays laden with beer. The rest of the room was an open expanse of wooden parquet, on which men and women were already congregating. The band sat on a raised stage in a corner. A plump man in faded tails stood in front of them, beating the air with a thin baton.

The Golem followed Anna and her friends to a table at the edge of the dance floor. Soon they were inundated with acquaintances, all hugging and laughing and exchanging gossip. Anna, clearly enjoying her role as the Golem's shepherdess, made sure that everyone was introduced to her. The Golem said hello a dozen times, smiled, learned everyone's names. She was a bit slow to make small talk, but that was easily forgiven: it was her first dance, and they all remembered what it was like. Someone whispered that she was a widow, and instantly her quiet manner was transmuted to an air of sad, romantic mystery.

After a short break the band struck up again, and the dancing began in earnest. As the Golem watched, pairs of women took to the floor, clasping each other at shoulder and waist. They danced in small step-hopping circles, skirts and ruffles bouncing, and glanced over each oth-er's shoulders at the men who now ringed the edges of the dance floor.

"Look at them," said Estelle to the Golem, indicating two men on the periphery. "They're gathering their courage." Sure enough, the men walked out onto the dance floor and approached two of the dancing women. Smiling, the women let go of each other, and took up with their new partners.

"You see?" said Estelle. "That's how it's done. Now it's your turn." She took the Golem's hand and made to drag her onto the floor.

"But—"

"Come on!"

It was no use, she dared not resist: if Estelle pulled on the Golem's arm much longer the girl might notice how very immovable she was. So she followed Estelle onto the floor, suddenly mindful of all the eyes.

Estelle faced the Golem and placed a hand on her shoulder. "You're so tall, you'll have to lead!" She laughed. "Here, hold me." She placed the Golem's hand on her own slim waist. "I'm going to teach you the two-step. Now do what I do, except backward."

As it turned out, the Golem made a very good dancing student. At first she moved awkwardly, afraid to tread on Estelle's toes—but within minutes she was easily mirroring her teacher's moves, aided by her feel for what Estelle wanted her to do. Soon she didn't even need to look at her feet. She was a bit stiff perhaps, but all Estelle noticed was the prog-ress. "Chava, you're a natural-born dancer!" she said.

"You think so?"

"I know so. And don't look now, but I think Anna is telling those boys to dance with us."

"What? Who?" Sure enough, Anna was talking to a pair of young men, one tall and one small, in jackets and porkpie hats. Both men were looking their way. The smaller one nudged the taller one, and they strolled around the table toward the dance floor. The Golem threw Anna a look of desperation, but the girl only waved, laughing.

"Don't worry," Estelle said. "I know them, they're nice boys. You take the taller one, Jerry. He's a lummox, but he's sweet. His friend's a little grabby sometimes. Don't worry, I can handle him."

The Golem felt the men approach. The taller one—Jerry?—wanted mainly to make it through the evening without being laughed at. The smaller one nurtured the hope of a romantic interlude in the alley outside. Both men were eager to dance.

There came the tap on her shoulder. Reluctantly she let go of Estelle, who gave her hand a comforting squeeze before turning to face her partner. The taller man gave her a shy grin. "I'm Jerry," he said.

"I'm Chava."

"Nice to meet you, Chava. I hear you're new at this."

"Yes. *Very* new."

"S'all right, I'm no good at it neither."

There was some confusion as each reached for the other's waist, and then the Golem remembered that the man was supposed to lead. She placed a tentative hand on his shoulder, and put her other hand in his.

"Gosh, you got cold fingers," he said, and they were off.

Jerry, it transpired, wasn't being falsely modest. He had trouble keeping time, and was too busy concentrating on his feet to lead her very well. It wasn't long before the other dancers were giving them a wide berth. But he was a gentlemanly partner, and kept his hand clasped at her waist without letting it drift slowly south, as she'd noticed other men doing. She felt him fight down a mild fear of conversation. "So you're a friend of Anna's," he said.

"I work with her at the bakery," said the Golem. "How do you know her?"

"Oh, from around," he said. "Everyone knows Anna. But, not in a bad way," he added hastily. "She's not, y'know, one of *those* girls."

"Of course not," she replied, vaguely sensing what he meant. "I only thought you might be a friend of Irving's. Her fiancé."

Surprise registered on his face. "They're engaged?"

"Yes, very recently. I suppose the news hasn't spread yet."

"Huh. Whaddya know," Jerry said.

"You're surprised?"

"Yeah, a little. Irving don't seem like the marrying kind. But hey," he said, smiling, "we all gotta settle down someday, right?"

She made no answer, only smiled back. Jerry's friend went sailing past, Estelle on his arm; Estelle gave her encouraging glances over her partner's shoulder.

"You're really good at this," Jerry said. "You sure you just learned?"

The song ended, and the dancers all turned and applauded the musicians. The man with the baton announced a short break, and the dancers drifted back toward the tables, where the waiters descended on them with their growlers of beer.

At their table, Anna was beaming. "Chava, you liar! You said you'd never danced before!"

"I hadn't, honestly," the Golem said. "Estelle's a very good teacher."

"No, I told you, you're just a natural-born dancer." Estelle had come back with Jerry's friend and now spoke from a precarious perch on the young man's knee.

"But I still have to look at my feet sometimes," the Golem said.

"Aw hell, I look at my feet and I've been dancing for years," said Jerry, and his friend snorted.

"Chava never misses a chance to cut herself down," said Anna, wiping beer foam from her lips. "Learn to take a compliment, girl!"

Faced with this barrage of support, the Golem had to relent. "All right, I'll admit it. I'm good at dancing."

"I'll drink to that!" said Estelle, lifting her beer. Anna drank too, and smiled across at the Golem. The table conversation dissolved into a mix of gossip, flirtation, and friendly teasing, and the Golem sat in the middle, feeling strangely pleased. It was such an unaccustomed sensation, to be surrounded by people enjoying themselves. There were needs and fears, of course; everyone had hopes for the evening, and many feared going home alone, or dreaded the workday to come. And the Golem noticed that Anna's attention often left the table, to look for Irving's face in the crowd. But even that nagging anticipation was softened by drink and conversation, and the glitter of their surroundings. Mrs. Radzin's warnings now seemed mean-spirited, even laughable.

The band began again, and this time it was Phyllis who grabbed the Golem's hands, and danced with her until two men cut in. Her new partner was a much better dancer than Jerry, and he wanted to show off. He led her in a variety of complicated moves, but she found she was able to mimic them easily, led by his cues. Surprised and pleased by his partner's adaptability, the young man's thoughts turned more amorous; he spun her away, and when they came back together, his hand was on her bottom.

Instantly she wanted to freeze, make an excuse, run from the floor. But after a moment's hesitation she merely did what she'd seen the other girls do: she lifted his hand from where it had wandered and replaced it firmly on her waist. After that he restrained himself. When the dance was over, he thanked her and then left to seek a more pliable partner. She felt oddly elated, as though she'd won some small but necessary battle.

"Good," said Estelle when the Golem told her what had happened. "Don't let men like that ruin your evening. If he doesn't take the hint, just step away and find one of us. We'll give him a cursing out!"

The next hour was a blur. She sat, she danced, she listened to the chatter and smiled at the jokes. The evening was in full swing; the band seemed never to stop playing. Three more men asked her to dance, the last an inebriated boy a foot shorter than her who kept stepping on her feet. She was trying to decide what to do about it when Jerry stepped in and shooed him away.

"Thank you," she said, relieved.

He was grinning. "I woulda cut in earlier, but he looked pretty funny peeking up over your shoulder. Anna nearly busted her gut." Indeed the young woman was still giggling so hard she looked in danger of falling off her chair.

"I hope Irving gets here soon," she said. "I'd like to see Anna dance."

"Yeah," Jerry said. "Hey, Chava, d'you think—"

But then whatever Jerry might have asked her was lost, as their two-step took the Golem within sight of the large, ornate clock hanging on the wall behind him, a clock whose hands were already long past eleven.

"No!" she cried. How had so much time passed without her noticing? She turned from the confused Jerry and hurried back to the table to fetch her cloak. "I'm sorry, Anna, I have to go!"

Anna and her friends immediately protested. What could she possibly be late for? Didn't she want to meet Irving? "You're having too much fun to leave!" said Anna. But the Golem couldn't stand the thought of the Djinni waiting for her, thinking she'd forgotten him.

Maybe, she thought suddenly, she didn't have to choose. She looked at the faces of her newfound friends, and the beauty of the hall around them. Perhaps, this once, it was her turn to show *him* something new.

"Don't worry," she told them. "I'll be right back."

Impossible as it seemed, the Golem wasn't at home.

The Djinni scowled up at her window, caught between irritation and concern. Where else could she be? Not still at work, surely, and as far as the Djinni knew there were only two places in her life, the bakery and the boardinghouse. Even if she'd lost track of the day, she should still be sitting above him, working by candlelight on her interminable repairs. Certainly she wouldn't have gone out on her own, not with her horror of impropriety. And even if she had, she'd have left him a note, a sign, something. Wouldn't she?

To add insult to irritation, he'd finally made up his mind to take her to Washington Street and show her the tin ceiling. Already it was becoming a local attraction. At least one visitor could usually be found gawking up at it. The neighborhood's Arabic broadsheet had even mentioned it, calling it a "proud civic achievement by a local artisan."

Of course, now the entire decision seemed to be moot. He felt absurdly like a pet dog leashed to a fence post. Did she expect him to hold vigil all night?

There was a noise of pounding footsteps. From down the street, a woman came running. It was the Golem, and she was alone. She ran, if not with the inhuman speed she'd shown in the park, then with an excited urgency that bordered on carelessness. She dashed past two startled men; one of them shouted something after her, but she didn't appear even to notice. "I'm late, I'm so sorry!" she called as she neared. And then, with a simple ceasing of motion, she was standing at his side.

He stared at her, astonished. Why did she look so different? He saw the combs in her hair, the ruffles of the new shirtwaist, but there was something else. Then he realized: she was happy. Her eyes were sparkling, her features animated; she was leaning toward him, smiling, full of eager confidence.

"I'm sorry, I was at a dance hall! Will you come back with me?

Please say you will. Anna and her friends are there, and I want you to meet them. And you must see the hall, it's beautiful!"

A dance hall? Who was this woman? "But I don't dance," he said, bemused.

"That's all right, I can teach you."

And so he forgot about the ceiling and consented to follow along beside her, feeling half-caught up in her newfound exuberance. Whatever it was that had done this to her, he supposed it must be worth a look. Apparently he was walking too slowly for her, for she grabbed his hand and began to practically pull him along. "Is the dance hall on fire?" he asked.

"No, but I promised I'd be right back. And Irving must be there by now. He's Anna's—oh, I didn't tell you! Everything's all right at the bakery, they're going to be married!"

What on earth was she talking about? He couldn't help it, he started to laugh. "Oh, stop it!" she said, but she was laughing too. "I'll explain later."

"But will it make sense?"

"If you keep teasing, I'll leave it a mystery. Look, we're here."

She pointed at an unassuming doorway, from which music was spilling in a torrent. A few coins to the man at the door, and then they were inside.

A long, dark hallway—and then in an instant the Djinni was stunned from levity into silence. It wasn't just the sheer expanse of the dance hall, nor the teeming crowd of people that filled it. No, what left him rooted to the spot, his thoughts thrown into bittersweet confusion, was the simple fact that if he'd wished to create, in the middle of New York, an approximation of his faraway and longed-for palace, the result would barely have differed. The walls were made of mirrors, not opaque glass, and the lights in them shone from gas lamps and chandeliers, not the sun or the stars; but it had the same expansiveness, the same sumptuous play of glittering light and soft shadow. It felt more like home than any other place in New York, but in the face of this shocking familiarity, he found that the gulf between his home and himself had only grown. *This is the most you can hope for*, the dance hall was telling him. *This much, and no more.*

"Do you like it?" the Golem asked. She was watching him, concerned, and the evening seemed to rest on his answer.

"It's beautiful," he said.

She smiled. "Good. I thought you'd like it. Look, there are my friends," she said, pointing to a distant table. "Come on, I'll introduce you."

Again he followed behind her as she weaved politely through the crowd. Here they were, among hundreds of people, and she showed no qualms, no hesitation at all. Had this change been building in her, and he simply hadn't noticed? A few months before she'd hidden her face on the street, and now she couldn't wait to introduce him to her friends. That too—she had friends now?

At the table, a woman in a ridiculous plumed hat looked up at the Golem and said, "There you are! Wherever did you—" Then she saw the Djinni following a few steps behind, and the rest of her words were lost in astonishment.

"Oh, Anna, it's not like that," the Golem said at once. "He's a friend of mine. Ahmad, this is Anna from the bakery, and this is Phyllis and Estelle. That's Jerry, who I danced with, and Jerry's friend—I'm sorry, I don't know your name."

"Stanley," said a small man with a squashed-looking face.

"Ahmad, this is Stanley," she finished triumphantly. She was speaking English—of course, for he wouldn't be expected to know Yiddish.

Anna was the first to recover. "Pleased to meet you, Ahmad," she said in accented English, and shook his hand firmly. She was a pretty girl, the most attractive at the table, but he couldn't help feeling her hat was about to attack him. She asked, "How do you know our Chava?"

A touch of worry colored the Golem's eyes. "By sheer accident," he said. "We crossed paths one day at Castle Garden. She said she'd never been to the aquarium, and I insisted on taking her." He glanced over at the Golem, who gave him a look of grateful relief.

"How nice," said Anna.

"How romantic," Phyllis murmured.

The taller man at the table—Jerry?—was scowling at him. "That's a queer accent you got," he said. "Where you from?"

"You'd know it as Syria."

"Huh," Jerry said. "That's over by China, right?"

"Jerry, you dunce, Syria is nowhere near China," Estelle said in Yid-dish, and Stanley cackled. Reddening, Jerry busied himself with his beer.

They might have been the Golem's friends, but the scrutiny of the table was beginning to bore him. "Chava, you promised to teach me to dance," he said, and the group stared after them as they walked away.

She led him to a corner of the dance floor, and turned to face him. "You place your hands here and here," she instructed, amusingly prim. "And I hold you here and here. Then it's just a step, and a hop. We mir-ror each other."

"Wait a moment," he said. "Let me see the others do it first." They stood out of the way and watched the crowd. How they managed to not all crash into each other he could only guess. He wasn't certain he saw the point of spending so much energy only to end up in roughly the same place, but kept the thought to himself.

"Are you ready now?" she asked.

"I think so."

He placed his hands where she'd instructed, and took his first care-ful steps. The pattern wasn't difficult, and he learned it quickly. At first they bumped up against a few of their neighbors, but then he developed a feel for leading, his hand pressing at her waist in the direction he meant her to go. His height was an advantage; he could seek out openings in the crowd, and keep them from getting hemmed in.

The crown of the Golem's head brushed his chin. "You're doing very well," she said.

He laughed. "How can you possibly judge? You just learned your-self."

"Yes, but you aren't stepping on my feet, or knocking me into the others. You're a natural-born dancer," she said with a certain relish.

"I'm afraid I surprised your friends," he said.

"And you had to lie to them," she said, sobering. "That was my fault. I should've realized."

"I'm glad you didn't. You might not have brought me, and I would've missed this."

"So you're enjoying yourself?"

"Very much," he said, and realized it was the truth.

The dancers turned around them; their enthusiasm, and the band's, seemed inexhaustible. "Anna isn't at our table anymore," the Golem said, craning to look over his shoulder. "Maybe she's found Irving."

"Ah, yes, the mysterious Irving."

She smiled. "I'm sorry, I never explained." And she told him the whole story: Anna's pregnancy, the subsequent engagement, the imminent move to Boston. "I doubt I'll ever see her again," she said. "I know so few people, and they all leave eventually. I suppose that's the way of things."

She sounded so wistful that he said, "Well, I don't seem to be going anywhere."

He'd meant to make her laugh, but she was quiet for a moment. "And what if you do leave? What if, someday, you find a way to free yourself of this?" Her cool fingers brushed his cuff, beneath his sleeve. "Promise me something," she said, with sudden urgency. "If that ever happens, I want you to come see me one last time. Don't leave me wondering what happened. Please promise me this."

Bewildered, he said, "I wouldn't leave without saying good-bye, Chava. I promise."

"Good," she said. "Thank you."

They were still dancing, though the jaunty music now clashed with the serious mood that had fallen between them. He tried to imagine it: freed through some miracle, rising above the dirt-clogged streets and suffocating tenements, flying on the wind to her familiar window. He'd bid her farewell—and here something seized inside him. He missed a step, moved to correct it.

"Are you all right?" she asked.

"I'm fine," he said, and tightened his grip on her waist. "I was only imagining it. Being freed." He paused, not knowing what he would say next, only that he must say something. "I wish I could show you—"

The band ended their tune with a flourish, and the crowd's applause startled him from his words. She was waiting for him to go on, concern on her face, but now the crowd around them was chanting at the bandleader: *A spiel! A spiel!* The Djinni gave the Golem a questioning look; she shook her head, apparently as baffled as he.

The bandleader smiled and bowed in acquiescence. A giant cheer went up. More couples rushed to the dance floor, filling it to overflowing. The bandleader mopped his brow with a handkerchief, and took up his baton again—and this time, the tune was faster, more raucous, with a high, crying melody. Each man grabbed his partner around the waist and clasped her close, much closer than before, and then whirled her in a tight circle, moving quickly from one foot to the other. Peals of laughter rose from the women. Those still at the tables clapped in delight.

The music surged through the Djinni. Whatever half-formed thing he'd meant to say had lost its shape, melted back into the larger pool of yearning. He closed his eyes, at once utterly weary and full of a hectic energy.

"I suppose this is a spiel," the Golem said, leaning close to his ear. "I didn't learn it."

"But I already know it." He pulled her close.

She started with surprise. "Ahmad—"

"Hold tight," he said, and stepped off.

Around and around he spun her, one hand in the small of her back, the fingers of the other twined with hers. He kept his eyes closed, kept his balance by feel. At first he feared she would pull away; but then she relaxed into his arms, a gesture of trust that sent a surge of gladness through him. "Close your eyes," he said.

"But we'll fall!"

"We won't."

And indeed they didn't, nor did they collide with their neighbors. For others were noticing them now, this tall and striking couple that spun together in a world of their own. The crowd began to pull away from them, giving them space, the better to watch. Faster and faster they went—with their eyes closed! How did they do it?—and now the Golem's steps were small precise movements that fitted to his exactly, describing a circle with himself at its center. In the midst of all that movement a stillness rose inside him, and for a long and beautiful moment everything else fell away—

Someone touched his shoulder.

He opened his eyes, and nearly crashed into the girl called Phyllis. The Golem stumbled; he caught her up about the waist and held her steady. Phyllis cringed away until she was certain they wouldn't collide with her; then, with an apologetic glance at the Djinni, she said in Yiddish, "Chava, I'm sorry, but it's Anna. She found Irving with another girl, and now they're fighting. He's drunk, and saying terrible things. I'm scared something will happen. Could Ahmad step in? I hate to ask, but Jerry and Stanley left already."

The Djinni listened, pretending not to understand. An irritating turn of events; but he'd do it, if only to restore peace to their evening. The Golem, though, had gone still. "He's fighting with Anna?" she said—and the tone in her voice made Phyllis pull back in alarm. "Where are they?"

"Outside."

She clamped her hand around his and pulled him nearly off his feet, cutting like an arrow through the crowd. "Chava, wait," he said, but she was past hearing. He could feel the tension in her frame, her rising anxiety on her friend's behalf.

They were through the hallway, and out the door. On Broome a few loiterers stood smoking cigarettes, but there was no sign of Anna or this Irving. Then he heard a man's distant shouts, answered by a woman's. The Golem's head swiveled. "The alley," she said.

They turned the corner, the Djinni still following in her wake. At the end of the alley, her friend Anna was struggling with a man. She was holding on to him, trying to pull herself up, sobbing. The man said something and slapped her across the face, then grabbed her hands away from his jacket and threw her to the ground. Her head hit the cobbles; she cried out.

"Anna!" the Golem cried.

The man stood unsteadily, clearly inebriated. He peered at them as they approached. "Who the hell are you?"

"Leave her alone!" She was advancing on him, almost running; the Djinni struggled to keep up. He wanted to put a hand on the Golem's arm, to slow her down, but she was just out of reach.

Irving stepped forward so that Anna lay behind him. He fixed a bleary eye on the Golem, and then the Djinni. "Your lady needs to mind her own business."

This had gone far enough. "Walk away," he told the man. "Now."

The man smirked and pulled back a fist, his aim weaving.

The Djinni felt the change that came over the Golem as much as saw it. Her movements became even quicker, more liquid as she reached for Irving; she seemed almost to grow—and then, she was upon him. A blur of motion, and Irving lay sprawled across the cobbles, blood pouring from his mouth. With terrible speed the Golem seized him, lifted him up and drove him into the wall. The man's feet dangled above the refuse, kicking feebly.

"Chava!" The Djinni grabbed her shoulders, tried to pull her away. She hurled Irving aside—he hit the ground moaning—and shoved the Djinni backward. Her face was drained of all expression, her eyes flat and dead. It was as though she'd disappeared from her own body.

The Djinni grabbed her waist and pulled her off her feet. They tumbled to the ground, and he felt his head ring against stone. She was on top of him, already struggling to break free. She twisted away and launched herself at Irving. The Djinni jumped up and ran straight at her, ramming her off her course. She fell against the wall and he pinned her there, hands on her shoulders, feet bracing against the ruts in the cobbles. "Chava!" he shouted.

She tried to push away from the wall, grimacing with the effort, her lips stretching back from her teeth like a jackal's. Her strength was incredible. He had the advantage of height, but already his feet were slipping. If she got away from him, she'd tear the man to shreds. He had to do something.

He concentrated—and her shirtwaist began to smolder beneath his hands. There was the smell of burning cotton, and then scorched earth. Her eyes clouded, confused; and then she screamed, a shriek so high it was all but inaudible.

He slapped her hard across the face—once, twice—and knocked her to the ground, pinning her. Even if he'd only enraged her, at least she'd be fighting him now, and not Irving.

But she wasn't struggling. She was blinking up at him, bewildered, like a human waking. "Ahmad? What's happened?"

Was it a ruse? Slowly he released her. She sat up and put a hand to her face, and then to her chest. Her shirtwaist and underclothes hung in charred scraps. Above her breasts were long, dark marks: the outlines of his fingers. She touched them, then looked around, as if for some clue to her condition. Quickly he moved to block her view of Irving. She tried to stand—and then convulsed once, and fell. He caught her just before she hit the ground. Her eyes were half-lidded, unseeing.

A movement in the corner: it was Anna, rising shakily to her feet. He cursed quietly; he'd forgotten all about her. How much had she seen? An ugly bruise was forming on the side of her face, and one eye was swelling shut. Dull with shock, she looked from Irving to the Golem, and then to the Djinni.

In Yiddish he said, "Anna. Listen to me. A strange man attacked your lover and then ran away. You were hit on your head, and you didn't see him clearly. If anyone else says otherwise, they're drunk and mistaken. Now fetch a doctor."

The girl only stared at him. "Anna!" he said; and she jumped, startled. "Do you understand me?"

A nod. She took a last look at Irving's broken form and then picked her way unsteadily back down the alley. Did she believe him? Probably not—but it was no use, there was no time. Someone was already shouting for the police. He dragged the Golem into his arms and rose to his feet, staggering for a moment. And then, he ran.

"We were speaking of you taking a mate," the Djinni said.

Fadwa opened her eyes. No—they were closed, weren't they? She'd just closed them. She was asleep in her tent—no, of course not, she was awake, in the Djinni's glass palace. She'd only been dreaming she was asleep.

A lingering unease pricked at her, but she pushed it aside. She was with the Djinni again; what else did she need to know? She was reclin-ing on a cushion, facing him across the low table that once again bore a week's bounty of food. She nibbled on a date, drank cold clear water. He smiled, watching her. They hadn't seen each other in—days? Weeks? She wasn't certain. Lately she couldn't keep track of time. One morning she'd gone to milk the goats, only to find that their bags were empty. She ran to tell her mother, who told her she must have gone mad, that she'd milked them already, hours earlier. There were other odd happenings too. Shadows moved in the corners of her eyes, even in full daylight. Faces changed when she wasn't looking. One afternoon she was at the pool fetching the last of the water, and the carving of the goddess began telling her stories, of the ridiculous men who'd tried to conquer the des-ert. They'd laughed together, like sisters, until someone called her name. It was one of her uncles. Her mother, concerned at the girl's lateness, had sent him to find her. Fadwa turned back to the goddess, to say good-bye, but she'd gone silent again. Later Fadwa overheard her uncle whispering to her mother that he'd found her sitting in the shallow water, giggling to herself. *Tell none of this to her father*, her mother had said. *Not a word.*

But of course none of that mattered now: she was with the Djinni, safe inside his glass walls, bathing in the starlight. Her eyes were clear, the shadows lay still at her feet. Nothing could hurt her here.

"A mate," she said. "You mean, a husband." She sighed, wishing they'd talk about something else, but it would be rude to change the subject. "My father will find a husband for me, someday soon. There are men in our tribe looking for wives, and my father will choose from among them."

"How will he choose?"

"He'll pick the one with the most to offer. Not just the bride price, but the size of his clan, their grazing, their standing in the tribe. And, of course, whether others think him a good man."

"And attraction, desire—that figures nowhere in his decision?"

She laughed. "Women in stories have that luxury, perhaps. Besides, my aunts tell me that desire comes later."

"Yet you're frightened."

She blushed; had it been so obvious? "Well, of course," she said, trying to sound adult and unconcerned. "I'll be leaving my family and my home, to live in a stranger's tent, and be a servant to his mother. I know that my father spoils me, and I'm not so thankless as to think he will force me to marry someone horrible. But yes, I'm frightened. Who wouldn't be?"

"Then why marry at all?"

Again his ignorance surprised her. "Only ill or feeble girls take no husbands. A girl must marry if she can, or she becomes a burden. Our clan is too small to support an unmarried daughter, not when there are growing children to feed, and wives to find for my brothers and my cousins. No, I must marry, and soon."

He was watching her with pity now. "A hard life, with so few choices."

Pride rose in her breast. "But a good life, too. There's always something to celebrate, a wedding or a birth, or a good calving in spring. I know no other way to be. Besides," she said, "we can't *all* live in glass palaces."

He raised an eyebrow, smiling. "Would you wish to, if you could?"

Was he toying with her? His face gave no hint. She returned the smile. "Sir, your home is very beautiful. But I wouldn't know what to do with myself in a place like this."

"Perhaps you wouldn't have to do anything."

She laughed then, and it was a full laugh, a woman's laugh. "That, I think, would frighten me more than any husband."

The Djinni laughed too, and bowed his head to her, a gesture of defeat. "I hope that you'll allow me to visit you, after you're married."

"Of course," she said, surprised and touched. "And you could come to the wedding, if you'd like." How funny, she thought: a djinni emissary at her wedding, as though she were a queen in a story!

"Your family wouldn't object?"

"We won't tell them," she said, and giggled. It didn't seem immodest, with him.

He laughed too, then leaned back, gave her an appraising look. "A wedding. Indeed, I'd like to see that. Fadwa, would you show me what a wedding is like?"

"Show you?" Had he meant *tell*? She frowned, unsure. But he reached out a hand—he was sitting next to her now; when had he moved?—and smoothed the creases from her brow. Again, the unexpected warmth of his skin; again that strange blossoming in her stomach. *Show me*, he whispered. She was so tired, all of a sudden. Certainly he wouldn't mind if she curled up and went to sleep (and a part of her whispered *silly girl, you're already asleep*, but that was a dream and she ignored it), and his hand on her brow felt so wonderful that she didn't even resist, but gave herself to the fatigue as it pulled her under.

Fadwa opened her eyes.

She was in a tent, a man's tent. She was alone. She looked down. Her hands and feet were painted with henna. She was dressed in her wedding gown.

She remembered her mother and aunts dressing her in the women's tent, painting her hands. The negotiation of the bride price, the display of her possessions. Singing, dancing, a feast. Then the procession, with herself at its head. And now she waited, alone, in a stranger's tent. From outside she could hear laughter, drumbeats, wedding songs. Before her was a bed, heaped with skins and blankets.

A man was standing behind her.

She turned to face him. He was dressed as a Bedouin now, in black wedding garments, slim and elegant. He held out his hands, cupped together, and in them was a necklace, the most amazing necklace she'd ever seen: an intricate chain of gold and silver links, and disks of flawless blue-white glass, all woven through with filigree. It was as though he'd taken his palace and turned it into a bauble to be worn around her neck. She reached out and touched it. The glass disks shifted and chimed against her fingers.

Is this for me? she whispered.

If you would have it.

His eyes danced in the lamplight. She saw desire in them, and it didn't frighten her. *Yes*, she said.

He clasped the necklace around her throat, his arms almost embracing her. He smelled warm, like a stone baking in the sun. His fingers released the clasp, to trail down her shoulders, her arms. She wasn't scared, she wasn't shaking. His mouth lowered to hers, and she was kissing him as though she'd been waiting for years. His fingers buried themselves in her hair. Her dress was gone now, an embroidered heap at her feet, and his hands were on her breasts and she felt no fear. He lifted her effortlessly, and then she was on the bed and he was there too, and he was inside of her, and it didn't hurt, not at all, not like her aunts had warned her. They moved together slowly, they had all the time in the world, and soon it was as if she had always known how. She kissed his mouth and twined herself around him and bit her lip in joy, and held on as the whirlwind that was her lover carried her far, far away—

Wake up!

Something was wrong.

Fadwa! Wake up!

The ground shook beneath them, a tremor first, then harder and harder. The tent began to collapse. He was trying to pull away, but she clung to him, she was terrified, she didn't want to let go—

Fadwa!

She held on with all her strength, but he ripped himself away and was gone. The tent, the world, everything went dark.

Above the Bedouin encampment, the Djinni reeled on the winds. He'd never before been in such pain. He was torn, shredded, near dissolution. Dimly he realized he'd let himself go too deep, drawn in by her dreaming fantasies. It had taken everything he had to escape. A lesser djinni would've been destroyed.

He hung there for a while, recuperating as much as he could before the journey home—weak as he was, he'd be easy prey, and vulnerable until he reached his palace. And if the wind carried to him a commotion of terrified human voices, the wails of women and a father's cries, then the Djinni tried not to hear them.

19.

The Djinni ran, the Golem in his arms.

He was taking her to the Bowery, thinking to hide her among the crowd, or in the warrens where the police didn't dare to go. He found a fire escape and climbed, and began to run rooftop to rooftop, eyes tracking him from the shadows. She was a heavy weight, still in the fugue that had fallen over her. Had he injured her too deeply? If she needed help, where could he possibly find it? Perhaps he could hide her at Conroy's . . .

She twitched once in his arms, and then again, making him stumble as he ran. Slowing, he found a dark and deserted corner behind a chimney. He lowered himself to the tar paper, cradling her, wincing at the sight of her ruined shirtwaist and underclothes. Her hair lay tangled across her face, the rose-carved combs having fallen out somewhere along the way. With her cool skin, and neither pulse nor breath, anyone would think he was holding a corpse. The burns above her breasts had already faded, the outlines of his fingers smoothing away as he watched. Was that why she'd collapsed, so her body could heal?

He moved to gather her up again, and something sparkled from beneath the scraps of cotton: a golden chain, a necklace. At its end was a large, square locket with a simple latch. A memory rose to his mind, of standing with her on a water-tower platform, and the words that had so disturbed him: *I must never hurt another. Never. I'll destroy myself first, if I have to.* She had raised one hand toward her throat, and then dropped it, embarrassed. As though he'd seen too much.

He touched the latch, and the locket sprang open. A square of paper, thick and folded, fell into his hand. As though it had been the key to waking her, the Golem began to stir. Quickly he closed the locket and slipped the paper into a pocket.

Her eyes blinked open, and she struggled to look around, her movements stuttering and birdlike. "Ahmad," she said. "Where are we?" Her words were oddly slurred. "What happened, why can't I remember?"

Had she truly lost all memory? If Anna had been unconscious, and any other witnesses were too far away to see clearly . . . "There was an accident," he said, improvising desperately. "A fire. You were burned, and you collapsed. I brought you away, you've been healing."

"Oh God! Is anyone hurt?" She tried to stand, wobbling on her feet. "We have to go back!"

"It's not safe yet." His mind raced ahead, trying to smooth away any objections. "But everyone is accounted for. No one else was injured."

"Is Anna—"

But then she paused. And he could see, in the focusing of her eyes, the return of her memory, the images of Irving's pummeling at her own hands.

From her mouth came a wordless wail. She sank to her knees, her hands rising to clutch at her hair. Instantly he regretted the story he'd told. Grimacing, he tried to put his arms around her, to help her stand again.

"Let go of me!" She ripped herself from his reach, got to her feet, and backed away. With her knotted hair and torn clothing, she looked like a wraith-woman he might once have encountered, one he'd have tried hard to avoid. "Do you see now?" she cried. "Do you *see*? I killed a man!"

"He was alive when we left. They'll find a doctor, he'll recover, I'm sure of it." He tried to evince a confidence he didn't feel.

"I wasn't careful enough, I let myself forget—Oh God, what have I done? And you—why did you carry me away, why did you lie?"

"It was to protect you! They were calling for the police, they would have arrested you."

"They should have! I should be punished!"

"Chava, listen to what you're saying. You'd go to jail, and explain to the police what you've done?" She hesitated, imagining it, and he pressed the advantage. "No one needs to know," he said. "No one saw, not even Anna."

She was staring at him, aghast. "This is your advice? You'd have me pretend it never happened?"

Of course she never would; it would be beyond her. But he'd backed himself into a corner. "If it were me, and I had attacked a man by accident, with no witnesses, and if there were no way to confess without revealing my nature—then yes, perhaps I would. The harm has been done, why compound it?"

She shook her head. "No. This is what comes of listening to you. Tonight I forgot my caution, and this is the result."

"You blame *me*?"

"I blame no one but myself, I should have had better judgment."

"But it was my evil influence that led you down this path." His concern for her was turning to resentment. "Will you also blame Anna, for tempting you to the dance hall?"

"Anna doesn't know what I am! She acted in innocence!"

"Whereas I tricked you knowingly, I suppose."

"No, but you confuse me! You make me forget that some things aren't possible for me!"

But tonight you were happy, he thought; and heard himself say, "If this is how you feel, you needn't ever see me again."

She reeled back, shocked and hurt—and for the second time that night he wanted to undo his words. "Yes," she said, voice shaking. "I think that would be best. Good-bye, Ahmad."

She turned and walked away. Unbelieving, he watched her go. Halfway across the rooftop she paused: and he pictured her glancing back, the barest hint of regret in her eyes. He'd call after her then, apologize, plead with her not to go.

Instead she bent down and picked up a discarded blanket, wrapped it about her shoulders, and kept walking. He watched her figure dwindle until he could no longer distinguish it from the others that moved about the rooftops, and not once did she look back.

A little while later, the Golem came down from the rooftops and looked for a quiet alley where she could destroy herself.

It was a simple decision, quickly made. She couldn't be allowed to hurt anyone again. And in this, at least, the Djinni was right: no one would be any safer if she sat in prison. Even if she managed to stay hidden, how long before captivity overwhelmed her and she went mad? Which would be worse, waiting endlessly for the breaking point, or the horror when it finally happened?

She clutched more tightly at the stinking blanket; it scratched at the remnants of the burns on her chest. She had never felt pain of her own before. Until the Djinni injured her she'd been somewhere far away, watching calmly through her own eyes as she grabbed Irving and shattered his bones. She'd felt no anger, no rage. Her body had simply taken over, as though she'd been built for no other purpose. The Djinni had appeared, horror in his face, and she'd only thought, *why, there's Ahmad.* His hands on her then, and the pain—and then waking on the rooftop, in the Djinni's arms.

She found an unoccupied dead-end alley free of open windows and prying eyes. She listened with all her senses but heard only the usual sleeping thoughts, safe behind the alley's walls. If the police were looking for her, they weren't yet close enough to interfere. She felt no hesitation, no regret. She was only left astonished at how quickly it had all come to pieces.

She drew out the heavy golden locket, let it rest in her palm a moment. She wondered: would she fall over, unmoving? Or dissolve into a heap of dust? Would she sense it happening, or simply cease to be? She felt at once calm and giddy, as though she'd jumped from a great height and was now watching the ground rise up to meet her.

She placed her thumb against the catch of the locket, and pressed. It sprang open, revealing an empty golden hollow. The paper was gone. It had simply vanished.

She stared at the spot where the paper should have been. Had she lost it long ago and never noticed? Had it somehow been stolen away? In the unreal daze of the evening, it seemed entirely possible it had never existed at all, that she'd invented the whole thing: the Rabbi, his death, the envelope lying next to his hand.

She forced herself to think. She'd have to come up with another solution, but what? Clearly she couldn't be trusted on her own anymore. She'd made terrible decisions, given in to too many temptations. Perhaps she could find someone to watch over her, as the Rabbi once had. Someone decent and responsible. They needn't even know her nature—they could lead her by example, protect her without knowing the good they did.

The answer, when it came, carried the weight of inevitability. Maybe, she thought, this was what she'd been heading toward, all along.

Michael Levy left for the Sheltering House earlier than usual that morning. He'd slept poorly, dogged by sinister dreams, of which he remembered only fragments. In one, his uncle took him by the shoulders to tell him something he *must not* forget, but his words were drowned by the wind. In another, he was walking toward a filthy, falling-down shack, and from the window a man's malevolent eyes peered out like something from a folktale. There was no sleeping again after that one, so he rolled away his pallet, got dressed, and left for work.

He was exhausted, down to his bones. Somehow he'd kept the Sheltering House from collapsing, but on mornings like this he wondered if he was only prolonging the agony. Worse, other Jewish charities were starting to send him their overflow cases, as though he were a magician who could conjure up cots and bread from thin air. He turned away as many as he could stomach, but even so, they were stretched far beyond their limits. Morale among House staff was suffering; even the indefatigable Joseph Schall seemed morose and distracted. And could anyone blame him? Something would have to change, and soon. They all needed a reason to hope.

He turned the corner and saw a dark figure sitting on the Sheltering House steps. For a moment he groaned at the thought of another referral, but then the figure saw him and stood: a woman, tall and straight. He realized who it was, and his heart leapt.

"Hello, Chava," he said. He didn't want to ask why she was there. No doubt it was for some mundane errand and she'd be gone far too quickly.

She said, "Michael, I'd like to be your wife. Will you marry me?"

Could this possibly be real? It must be; his dreams were never so generous. He reached out and touched the side of her cheek, daring to believe. She did not draw away. She did not move toward him. She only gazed back, and he saw himself reflected, hand outstretched, in her dark and steady eyes.

It was nearly three in the morning, and the Bowery was still crowded with men and women, shouting with drunken laughter. Music poured from the gambling parlors and bordello doorways, but the debauchery felt increasingly desperate. Con men in the alleys searched the crowd for their last marks of the evening; prostitutes leaned out of windows, posing idly, their eyes eager and shrewd.

Through this fraying bacchanal the Djinni came walking, down from the rooftops where the Golem had left him. He saw none of it, neither the crowd nor the hunters who noted the wounded anger in his eyes and looked for better prospects elsewhere. He only could see the Golem standing before him, her clothing burned and her hair wild. His mind echoed with the words she'd spoken, the things she'd blamed him for. The finality of her good-bye.

Well then, so be it. She could offer herself up to the police, become the tragic martyr she so longed to be. Or she could return to her boardinghouse cage, to bake and sew for all eternity. He cared not. He was done with her.

As he moved south the crowd thinned and disappeared, leaving only the slums. He kept walking, avoiding the western turn toward Little Syria. Nothing waited for him there but the shop or else his rented room, and he couldn't stand the thought of either.

At length he neared the shadow of the Brooklyn Bridge. He'd always admired the bridge, its elegant curving band, the incredible effort and artistry that had gone into its making. He found the entrance to the pedestrian walkway and walked out until he stood above the very edge of the land. Boats bobbed in the harbor below him, their hulls rasping against the pilings. If he wanted, he could simply walk across to Brooklyn and keep walking. The more he thought about it, the more appealing the idea became. Nothing was keeping him in Manhattan. He could cast off all pretensions to a human existence and go ever onward, never tiring, never stopping! The earth would glide away beneath him as it had once before!

He stood above the water, body tensed, waiting for himself to take the first step. The bridge cast itself out before him, a hanging net of cold steel and glowing gaslight, gathering to a distant pinprick.

All at once the tension drained from him, leaving a deep weariness. It was no use. What was there for him on the other side of that bridge? Endless people and buildings, built on land that was itself another island. He would walk until he reached its end, and then what? Cast himself into the ocean? He might as well jump from where he stood.

He could feel Washington Street pulling at him, as though he were a bird in a snare. Inch by inch it drew him back. There was nothing there he wanted, but there was nowhere else to go.

Arbeely was stoking the forge when the Djinni came in. "Good morning," the man said. "Would you mind watching the shop? I have errands to run, and then I'm going to see Matthew's mother. I'm not sure she knows how much time he's spending here." When the Djinni didn't respond, Arbeely looked up at him, and blanched. "Are you all right?"

A pause. "Why do you ask?"

Arbeely wanted to say that the Djinni looked sick at heart, as though he'd lost something of immense value and spent all night searching for it. But he only said, "You look ill."

"I don't fall ill."

"I know."

The Djinni sat down at his bench. "Arbeely," he said, "would you say you're satisfied with your life?"

Oh God, thought Arbeely, *something's happened*. Nervously he considered his response. "It's difficult to say. But yes, I think I'm satisfied. Business is good. I eat well, and I send money to my mother. I work hard, but I like my work. There are many who can't say as much."

"But you live far from your home. You have no lover that I'm aware of. You do the same thing every single day, with only myself for company. How can this possibly satisfy you?"

Arbeely winced. "It's not as bad as that," he said. "Of course I miss my family, but I'm more successful here than I ever could have been in Zahleh. Someday I'll go back to Syria, and find a wife and start a family. But for now, what more do I need? I've never wished for riches, or adventure. I just want to make a good living, and have a comfortable life. But then, I'm not exactly a complicated man."

The Djinni let out a hollow laugh. Then he leaned forward and put his head in his hands. It was a startlingly human gesture, full of weakness. Chagrined, Arbeely busied himself at the forge. Were the Djinni anyone else, Arbeely would have steered him toward a comforting talk with Maryam. But of course the Djinni couldn't do this, not without leaving out everything that mattered. Was he himself the Djinni's only confidant? The thought made him want to pray for them both.

Perhaps he could offer a distraction, at least. "I've been thinking," Arbeely said. "Would you be interested in making women's jewelry? Sam Hosseini gets a lot of business from wealthy women outside the neighborhood, looking for exotic things to wear. If we approach him with a sample, he might set aside a display for us." He paused. "What do you say? A necklace, perhaps. Not as exciting as a ceiling, but more interesting than pots and pans."

There was a long silence. Then the Djinni said, "I suppose I could make a necklace."

"Good! That's good. I'll call on Sam after I speak with Matthew's mother." He left the shop with a concerned backward glance, hoping that whatever was bothering his partner would resolve itself soon.

The Djinni sat alone in the shop and watched the fire burn in the forge. At the mention of a necklace, an image had come to mind: an intricate chain of gold and silver, with hanging disks of blue-white glass, all woven with filigree. He'd never seen such a necklace before; it had simply appeared before him, like the tin ceiling. He was grateful, he supposed. It gave him something to do.

He got up to gather supplies and felt something shift in his pocket. The Golem's square of paper. He'd forgotten all about it.

He took it out and held it warily, half-daring himself to open it. Her most secret possession, and he'd stolen it from her. The thought was satisfying, in a small and petty way, but as he held it, he felt a growing dread. It crossed his mind to destroy it, but at that he faltered too. He'd taken it almost without thinking, and now it was a weight he didn't want.

What to do with it, then? The shop was unsafe; his own tenement room was little better. After a moment's deliberation, he pulled back his shirtsleeve and maneuvered the paper beneath his iron cuff, fitting it between the warm metal and his skin, as though sliding a note through a crack under a door. There was just enough room. He flexed his wrist, trying to dislodge it, but the paper stayed where it was. He could almost forget it was there.

When Matthew opened the shop door a few minutes later, he spied the Djinni sitting with his back to him, bent over his work. With his noiseless footsteps he came to the edge of the workbench, just beyond the Djinni's sight.

In one hand the Djinni held a short silver wire, clamped in a pair of round jeweler's pliers. With the other hand he was slowly, carefully stroking the wire. Matthew watched as the wire began to take on the shimmer of heat. Then, in a smooth quick movement, the Djinni grasped the free end of the wire and bent it around the pliers so that it formed a perfect circle. He released the wire from the pliers and pinched the two ends together, fusing them. Now Matthew saw that a chain of these links dangled from the one just formed. The Djinni turned to pick up another small piece of wire, and saw Matthew.

Boy and djinni stared at each other for a few long moments. Then the Djinni said, "You already knew?"

The boy nodded.

"How?"

The boy whispered, "The ceiling. I heard you and Mr. Arbeely. You used to live there."

The Djinni recalled the private conversation in the lobby. "Did anyone else hear?" The boy shook his head, no. "Did you tell anyone?" No. "Not even your mother?" No.

The Djinni sighed inwardly. It was bad, but it could have been much worse. "Don't tell Arbeely you know. He'd be angry with me if he found out. Will you promise?"

A firm, wide-eyed nod. Then the boy reached over and lifted one of the Djinni's hands. He began a careful examination, poking at the palm with his fingertips, as though expecting it to burst into flame. The Djinni watched for a while, amused, and then sent a small pulse of heat into his hand. The boy gasped and let go, sticking his fingers in his mouth.

"Are you hurt?"

Matthew shook his head. The Djinni took the boy's hands and examined them: no red spots or rising blisters. He'd only been startled.

"There's a price for knowing my secret," the Djinni said. "You must help me make this necklace." The boy, who'd started to look alarmed, broke into a wide smile. "I need many short pieces of silver wire, about the length of your thumbnail." He cut a piece from the roll to demonstrate, then handed the boy the wire-snips. "Can you do this?"

In answer, the boy began to measure wire and cut it with great care. "Good," the Djinni said. "Be careful not to bend them." He'd have to tell Arbeely that the boy knew; it couldn't be kept a secret for long. Arbeely would be furious. First Saleh, then Matthew: who'd be next? Perhaps his luck would hold, and he'd only be unmasked by half-insane men and silent children.

He rubbed absently at his cuff, wondering if she'd noticed yet that the paper was gone. Then he wrenched his thoughts away. He had work to do.

A few days later, a delivery boy pedaled his way to Washington Street and found the sign that read Arbeely & Ahmad—Tin, Iron, Silver, All Metals. Arbeely answered the knock at the door to see the boy standing there, holding a small parcel. "Afternoon," the boy said in English, touching his hat.

"Ah, hello," Arbeely said in his uncertain English.

"I was told to give this to a smith named Ahmad," the boy said. "That you?"

"I'm Ahmad," the Djinni said, rising from the workbench. "He's Arbeely."

The boy shrugged and handed him the parcel. The Djinni gave him a coin and closed the door.

"Were you expecting something?" asked Arbeely.

"No." There was no return address, no marking of any kind. He undid the twine and unwrapped the paper, revealing a hinged wooden box. Inside, sitting in a nest of excelsior, was a small silver bird. Its round body tapered to a spray of feathers at the tail, and it held its head demurely turned to one side.

Ignoring Arbeely's protestations, the Djinni cast the bird into the fire, and watched as it slumped to one side, then melted into a grayish puddle that ran among the coals. He was through with her, then. Forever. He rubbed at his cuff, and the hidden paper whispered the word back to him: *forever*.

20.

DANCE HALL ATTACK MYSTERY

Victim of Unknown Assailant Near to Death While Police Wrestle with Perplexing and Contradictory Testimonies

Authorities are puzzled over the strange case of Irving Wasserman, 21, a Jew who resides on Allen Street. Three nights ago, Wasserman was the victim of blows delivered by an unknown person or persons behind the Grand Casino on Broome Street, a dance hall popular with the Hebrew youth of the area. Witnesses who came upon the injured man called for help, but the assailant or assailants fled the scene and disappeared. Wasserman now lingers close to death at Beth Israel Hospital.

Police say that descriptions given by the witnesses, mostly youth loitering outside the dance hall, were less helpful than they wished. The assailant was described variously as a man, a woman, or, even more strangely, a man dressed in women's clothing. Still others said that two assailants, not one, fled the scene. After performing an examination of the victim at Beth Israel, physician Philip White declared his belief that the blows were too many and too severe to have been dealt by only one man, and impossible for a woman. "If I didn't know the circumstances," the doctor said, "I'd think he'd been trampled by a horse."

The case was put before Sergeant George Kilpatrick,

who soon discovered that Wasserman was known in the neighborhood for his many love affairs, and that he had been seen that evening arguing with one of his sweethearts. The sergeant speculated that Wasserman had been set upon by the girl's friends or relations—though the girl in question strongly denied this—and suggested that those who'd reported a female assailant were trying to confound the police. For now, the case remains under investigation.

Spring edged its way toward summer. In Central Park, men in straw hats pulled at the oars of their rented rowboats, their sweethearts in the prows searching the banks for friends and rivals. At Coney Island, young parents ate ten-cent frankfurters while their screaming children raced down the beach. In the new subway tunnel beneath the bay, sweating men laid down lengths of track and ignored the killing weight of water above their heads.

Everyone, it seemed, had been rejuvenated by the changing of the seasons, save for one man. It had been weeks since Yehudah Schaalman had first spied the Golem at Radzin's bakery and felt the twinge from his dowsing spell; and in that time he'd fallen into a dark depression. He spent nights awake on his thin cot, endlessly ruminating. Had *she* been the aim of his search? Impossible! She was only a golem! An intelligent one, and apparently blessed with abilities he hadn't intended— but still a golem, made for drudgery and protection. If he wished, he could create a dozen of her. And yet at the sight of her, the dowsing spell had finally awakened. His dream had whispered that *life eternal* could be found somewhere in New York: and could not a golem, nearly invulnerable and free of the confines of a lifespan, be said to enjoy eternal life?

He tossed and turned, the sheets twisting around his bony frame, and wondered if the Almighty was playing games with him. What could he do? He couldn't even follow her, not without alerting her to his thoughts. And all the while the Angel of Death was edging closer.

Enough, he thought. He would gain nothing from self-pity. So the dowsing spell had pointed to his golem; what of it? The spell was one of his own untested creations, and these were imprecise at best. Perhaps it was simply responding to her origins, the deathless knowledge of Jewish mystics from centuries past.

It was a thin hope, perhaps, but he couldn't give up looking. Otherwise he might as well end his own life, and concede the Almighty His victory.

And so, fueled by dogged willpower and little else, Schaalman resumed his search. He retraced his steps, going back to the oldest Orthodox synagogues, the ones with the most learned rabbis, the largest libraries. At each, he begged an audience with the head rabbi, saying that he was a former yeshiva teacher, recently arrived in America. He was interested in volunteering his time, in whatever capacity they needed. What could the rabbi tell him about the congregation? Did it keep to the old ways, the traditional teachings?

Each rabbi, thrilled at this unlooked-for gift—*volunteering, did you say?*—ushered Schaalman into his office and described the virtues of the congregation, how they fought against encroaching secularism and unhealthy modern influences. Some congregations had even begun to allow the taking of snuff during the sermon, could he imagine? Schaalman would nod sadly, commiserating, and then reach over and pat the rabbi's hand in a very particular way.

The rabbi would grow silent and still, a dreamy look on his face.

Your most precious book, Schaalman would say. *The dangerous one, that you hide from your colleagues. Where do you keep it?*

The first few rabbis said, *I have no such book*; and Schaalman released each one, watched them blink away their confusion, made his apologies, and went on his way. And then, one rabbi said:

I no longer have it.

Interesting, thought Schaalman. *What happened to it?*

Avram Meyer took it. God rest his soul.

Why did he take it?

He wouldn't say.

Where is it now?

I wish I knew.

He let the man go, not daring to question him any longer—the charm caused permanent damage in longer doses, and he had no wish to leave a trail of fuddled rabbis in his wake. He wondered who Avram Meyer was, and what had happened to him.

The next day another rabbi told him the exact same thing. And then, a third.

By the end of the week, five rabbis had reported their most secret volumes stolen by this Avram Meyer, now deceased. He began to think of Meyer as an adversary from beyond the grave, a meddling spirit who floated through the city a few steps ahead of him, sniffing out books and snatching them up.

With the last rabbi, Schaalman dared to stretch the interview to one more question. Did this Meyer have any family?

A nephew, the charmed rabbi said. *Apostate. Michael Levy, his sister's son.*

Schaalman left the synagogue, his mind spinning. The name was laughably common; there must be over a hundred Michael Levys in the Lower East Side alone.

And yet, he knew.

At the Sheltering House, the man in question was in his office as usual, shuffling through papers. There was a new energy in his frame that Schaalman hadn't noticed before. But then, he hadn't been paying attention to Levy at all.

"Someone told me," Schaalman said, "that you had an uncle named Avram Meyer."

Michael looked up, surprised. "Yes," he said. "He died, last year. Who was it who told you?"

"A rabbi I happened to meet," Schaalman said. "I mentioned that I worked at the Sheltering House, and your name came up."

Michael gave a wry smile. "With little enthusiasm, I'm sure," he said. "My uncle and his friends wanted me to enter the rabbinate. Things turned out quite differently."

"He said that your uncle had a wonderful private library." It was a guess, but an intuitive one. "I only mention it because there's a book I'm looking for."

"I wish I could help you," Michael said. "I gave all his books to a charity. They've been sent to congregations out west. Scattered to the winds, I suppose."

"I see," Schaalman said, keeping his voice light. "A pity."

"What was the book?"

"Oh, just something from my school days. I'm possessed by these sentimental whims, as I get older."

Michael smiled. "You know, it's strange that you mention my uncle. I've been thinking about him lately, and it's partly to do with you."

That startled him. "How so?"

"You remind me of him, somehow. I keep wishing he could've met you before he died."

"Yes," said Schaalman. "I would've liked that."

"And then there's the wedding, of course. It'll be strange, not having him there." At Schaalman's blank look, Michael laughed, incredulous. "Joseph, haven't I told you? Good lord, where is my mind? I'm getting married!"

Schaalman put on a broad smile. "Congratulations! And who is the fortunate bride?"

"Her name's Chava. She works at Radzin's Bakery. Actually, my uncle introduced us. She came to America as a new widow, and he became her guardian, of a sort." And then: "Joseph? Are you all right?"

"Yes. Yes, I'm fine." His own voice sounded thin and far away. "Too much time on my feet, perhaps. I should rest, before dinner."

"Of course, of course! Don't neglect your health, Joseph. If I'm working you too hard, just say so."

Schaalman smiled at his employer, and then walked unsteadily out the door.

He went out to the street and walked with no purpose, a piece of flotsam led by the swirling crowd. It was early evening, a Friday, and the sun was setting. *Come the Sabbath bride*, Schaalman thought, and coughed out something like a laugh. All hope that the dowsing spell had been mis-taken was now fled. Creation itself was dangling his own golem before him, like a toy for a kitten to swipe at. Silly old Schaalman, the dancing fool: he once tried to outsmart the Almighty.

The evening attractions of the Lower East Side were waking for business. Patrons in their weekend best crowded outside the dance halls and theaters. Casinos and saloons spilled thin yellow light onto the street. He barely noticed any of it. Someone stumbled into him; a knife slashed at his left trouser-pocket. He watched the thief run away, made no move to follow. His billfold was safe on the other side, but even if he'd been robbed he wouldn't have protested. This place was a reflection of Hell, of Sheol, the Pit of Abaddon. Merely a taste of what was to come.

The crowd lifted him up and deposited him in the doorway of a saloon. He went in and sat at a table. A man in a filthy apron placed a drink in front of him, a watered beer that tasted of dregs and turpentine. He downed it, and then another, and then a whiskey. A young woman in a curled yellow wig and little else sat down next to him. She asked him something teasingly in English and put a hand on his thigh. He shook his head, then buried his face in her neck and began to sob.

Eventually she led him up the back stairs to a squalid bedroom, where she laid him down on the sprung mattress and stripped him of his trousers. He watched uncaring as she found the billfold, frowned at its contents, and removed all but one of the bills. Then she climbed on top of him. A dumb show began, a grotesquerie of the act of love; but he was unresponsive, and she soon abandoned the attempt. Shrugging, she reached behind the mattress and lifted up a tray of chipped black lacquer. Resting atop it were a thin pipe, a squat oil lamp, a metal needle, and many small lumps of what looked like tar. The girl lit the lamp, speared one of the lumps with the needle, and held it over the flame. When it began to smoke, she dropped it into the pipe, put it to her lips, and in-haled deeply. Her eyes fluttered closed in what looked like pleasure, then opened to see Schaalman watching her. Grinning, she prepared a fresh pipe and offered it to him.

The smoke was harsh and acrid, and sent his head swimming. For a long moment he thought he might vomit. Then his body relaxed, and a slow, delicious lassitude crept through his limbs. Within minutes his despair had been wholly smothered by an overpowering sense of calm and well-being. His eyelids drooped; he began to smile.

The girl giggled, watching, and then her own eyes began to close. Soon she was asleep. Looking at her, he noticed she was not so young as he'd thought: the blush on her cheek was mostly paint, the skin beneath it sallow and lined. But it did not matter. He saw now that the material world was only an illusion, thin as a cobweb. He gazed about in calm wonder. Then he found his trousers, retrieved his money, and left the bedroom.

He went through the dim hall to the back fire escape, and was about to go down to the street when he heard voices and footsteps from above. Idle curiosity made him climb the rusting stairs to the rooftop. To his surprise he found it heavily populated. A dozen young men were smoking cigarettes while girls in rags whispered to one another. Nearby, a group of children threw dice by lantern-light.

Looking over the roof, he felt for the second time the bone-deep pull of his dowsing spell. Even in his altered state, it was impossible to mistake. Every man, woman, and child, even the roof itself—all of it seemed unbearably *interesting*, a fascination that grabbed at his soul.

Joy suffused him, so strong he thought he might weep again. He drifted across the roof, looking at each of their faces, trying to guess at the meaning of it. One man, unsettled by Schaalman's stares, raised a fist in warning, but Schaalman only smiled dreamily and moved on.

The roof's edge abutted the next building, and that roof too was populated by men and women who seemed fascinating for no reason he could name. He climbed over the low ledge between the buildings, ignoring the creaking protest of his bones. The euphoria of the opium was fading, but a new sense of purpose was taking hold. What had he left but to follow the trail, and see where it led?

Soon he was crossing from rooftop to rooftop, judging his direction by feel. He was deep into the Bowery now, far from the Jewish neighborhoods. What business had his golem here? Or—and now, beneath his calm, he felt the first twinges of excitement—did the trail not lead to her at all? Was there something else at work here, in which she only played a part?

At last he found himself on a roof with no outlet except its darkened stairwell. He descended to the street and looked about. A nearby sign practically jumped out at him from above a storefront. CONROY'S, it said. From the window it seemed to be only a small, narrow tobacconist's shop. But on the sign, in each corner, was set a pair of symbols: a blazing sun, overlapped by a crescent moon. For centuries they had been the alchemical marks for gold and silver. He doubted they were there by accident.

A tinny bell rang over the door as he entered. The man behind the counter—Conroy, presumably—was small and narrow shouldered, and wore a thin pair of spectacles perched on his nose. He raised his eyes, examining his new customer. Schaalman saw in his hard gaze and small movements the wariness of the convict and knew that the man could see the same in him. They watched each other for a few moments, neither speaking. Conroy asked a question, and Schaalman shook his head, pointed a finger to his own lips. "No English," he said. The man waited, uncertain and suspicious.

Schaalman thought for a moment. Then he said, "Michael Levy?"

Conroy frowned and shook his head.

"Avram Meyer? Chava?" The same response. Schaalman paused, then said, "Golem?"

Conroy turned his palms upward, clearly baffled.

Sighing, Schaalman nodded his thanks and left. He would have liked to see inside the man's mind, but Conroy was no trusting rabbi to be charmed with a touch on the wrist. Something was at work here, a strange and tangled mystery, waiting to be solved. He walked back through the Bowery crowds, toward the House and his cot, his heart lighter than it had been in weeks.

Far to the north, in Fifth Avenue's loftiest reaches, the Winston mansion was caught in a frenzy of activity. For weeks the household had been preparing for the summer move to Rhode Island, to the family's seaside estate. The china had been wrapped and packed, the trunks filled with clothing. They only waited for the return of Mrs. Winston and Miss

Sophia from their long voyage to Europe, a gift from Francis Winston to his daughter on the event of her engagement.

Then came a startling piece of news: the Winstons would not be summering in Rhode Island after all. The household, it seemed, would remain in New York.

And so the servants, exchanging dark and disappointed looks, un-packed the trunks and restocked the pantry. No reason for the change was offered, but rumors drifted down to the lower quarters, saying that Miss Sophia had become ill in Paris. Still it seemed odd: wouldn't the breezes off the Narragansett be better for a convalescent than Manhattan's nox-ious summer vapors? But the order had been given, and there was nothing they could do. So they uncovered the furniture in Sophia's bedroom, swept away the dust, and polished the items scattered atop her dresser: the boxes and bottles and trinkets, and the little golden bird in its cage.

Meanwhile, the young woman in question lay shivering on a deck chair on the RMS *Oceanic*, wrapped deeply in blankets, a cup of hot broth clutched between her hands. It was morning, and her mother still slept in their cabin. Sophia had woken in the early hours, and stared up at the ceiling until the beginnings of seasickness drove her above-decks. Her persistent chill was worse in the open air, but at least she could see the horizon. And it was a relief to be away from her mother, who'd barely left her side for months—not since the moment she'd found Sophia ly-ing unconscious on the floor of their rented flat on the Seine, her body racked with fever, blood staining her skirts and darkening the rug.

Her illness had started weeks earlier, even before they sailed for Eu-rope. At first there was only an odd, uncomfortable pinprick of heat in her stomach. For a while she'd thought it merely the stress of the wedding plans. Her mother now talked of nothing else, only guest lists and trous-seaus and honeymoon itineraries from sunup to sundown, until the very word *wedding* grew hateful to Sophia's ears. But then the pinprick began to grow, and it occurred to her to wonder if something was wrong.

By the time they reached rain-sodden France it was the size of a coal, a tiny furnace burning inside her. Sophia was beset with a strange nervous energy and wandered from room to room, hemmed in by the terrible weather. She took to opening the shutters in her bedroom and letting the mist off the Seine blow in to soak her through. But not until her mother made a remark about finding a nursemaid for Sophia's eventual lying-in—*it's never too early to think about these things*—did Sophia realize she couldn't remember the last time she'd menstruated.

Thankfully, Mrs. Winston mistook Sophia's look of terror for a fear of her impending wifely duties. She took her daughter aside and, in an uncharacteristic display of tenderness, told her of her own long-ago fears, how they'd proven for the most part unfounded, and how quickly she'd come to take joy in the intimacies of marriage. It was the closest, the most vulnerable that Mrs. Winston had ever made herself to her daughter, and Sophia heard not a word. The girl excused herself and rushed to her room, where she paced, one hand over the fire inside her, counting the weeks since the last time the man named Ahmad had come to visit her. It had been over three months.

Oh God, could it be? But then, what *was* this? For she felt none of the supposed signs of pregnancy, no nausea or fatigue. Far from it: she felt like she could fly. Yet her menses still refused to arrive.

She had to do something, but what? She could say nothing to her mother. In New York there were friends who could help, but in Paris she knew no one. She barely spoke enough French to ask for cream in her tea. Blazing with heat and sick with worry, she stood in the middle of her bedroom, held a fist over her stomach, and closed her eyes. *Go away*, she thought. *You're killing me.*

Amid the dark haze of heat and desperation, she felt something shift inside her. A tendril of fire shot up her spine—and then her mind was filled with a small frightened fluttering, a noise like a candle flame whipped by a breeze. At once she knew that there was something trapped inside her, tiny and half-formed, and that it was drowning in her body, even as it burned her. There was nothing that either of them could do.

Oh, she thought, *you poor little thing.*

Helpless, she felt it gutter and go out—

The next time Sophia opened her eyes, she was in a hospital bed, her mother asleep in a chair next to her. She felt weak and hollowed out, a dried husk shaking in an autumn wind. She began to shiver.

The doctor, his English excellent, said it had been nothing more than an unusual thickening of the womb's lining, which her body had taken care of on its own. No lasting damage had been done, and there was no reason why Sophia's mother shouldn't be a *grandmère* someday. As Mrs. Winston sobbed with relief, the doctor leaned over and murmured to Sophia, "Be more careful next time, *non?*" before smiling and taking his leave.

But Sophia couldn't stop shivering.

Only a lingering anemia, the doctors said; it would end soon enough. But days passed, and then weeks, and still she shivered, sometimes so violently she could barely stand. It was as though her body had grown accustomed to the heat and now refused to readjust.

At a loss, they sent her to Germany, to the spa at Baden, where a large hired nurse dunked her in steaming pools of water and fed her restorative tonics. And she did feel better, for a time—the hot spring water felt pleasantly lukewarm, and if left on her own she would've stayed in the dry-heat rooms till she was mummified. But as soon as she emerged, the chill would return. Finally the German doctors, like the French, washed their hands of her. When Mrs. Winston demanded an explanation, they implied that any remaining ill health rested not in her daughter's body, but her mind.

Even worse, Sophia half believed them. Lying in bed, immobile under her blankets, she would wonder if indeed her wits had left her in that bedroom in Paris. And yet, deep down, she knew the truth of what she'd felt.

Mrs. Winston refused to tolerate any suggestion that her daughter's mind was unsound. If the European doctors would not help, then they would be quit of Europe. As for Sophia's engagement, there was no hint that it might be altered or postponed; her malady, it seemed, belonged in the category of things best left unmentioned, much like the uncle who'd died in a sanatorium and the cousin who'd married a Catholic.

In her one act of rebellion, Sophia announced that she'd only leave Europe if she could return to New York, where she might at least be warm, and not to that drafty, hateful mansion in Rhode Island. Her mother fought her, calling the idea ridiculous, but a cable from her father declared the battle in Sophia's favor. Only then did Sophia think of her father, sitting in his study for months, waiting for secondhand news of his daughter's illness; and her heart went out to him.

To Charles Townsend, her fiancé, Sophia wrote that she'd been ill briefly in France, and had gone to Baden to take the waters. For his amusement she described the more exasperating Teutonic habits of the spa attendants. Charles replied with all the proper sentiments, wishing her a speedy recovery, and ended with a few wry remarks about the dull summer ahead. He was a perfectly nice young man, and handsome, to be sure. But the truth was they were little more than strangers.

Sophia looked out over the ocean and tried to relax. She sighed, and sipped at the cooling broth, and wondered distantly what Charles would think when he saw her trembling. She knew she should be more concerned about these things, but found it difficult to muster the interest. Occasionally her thoughts drifted back to the moments before her collapse, and a raw, unfocused grief would rise inside her. She felt like a sad old woman, cosseted in blankets. And not yet even twenty.

She wished she could blame the man who'd come to her balcony, but she couldn't, not in fairness. He hadn't forced her, had never so much as pressured her. He'd only presented himself as an opportunity, and his confidence had made it seem the most natural thing in the world. Another woman might have tracked him down and told him what he'd done, but she shuddered at the thought. No, she had not lost her pride, merely her health.

From the corner of her eye she saw her mother emerge onto the deck. She closed her eyes, pretending to be asleep. Only a few more days at sea, and then she would be home, where she could shut herself away in her bedroom and sit in front of the fire for as long as she wished. And this time, she would make certain the balcony door was good and locked.

Dressed in a white wedding gown, her gloved hands folded in her lap, the Golem sat on her bed and listened for the step on the stair that meant someone was coming to bring her to her groom.

She'd made the gown herself. The high-necked bodice was adorned with lace and embroidery, the waistline shaped by dozens of tiny pintucks. In the mirror it seemed almost too delicate for her sturdy frame.

Michael, she knew, considered such dresses an impractical extravagance. But she'd sewn it for herself, not him; and she'd worked on it diligently, investing each stitch with her determination to make this arrangement work, to adhere to the path she'd laid for herself. She refused to wear a veil, though. She would go to her wedding with her eyes uncovered.

Noises sounded from the parlor below: men's voices, laughing together. It was nearly time.

She pressed one hand to her chest, feeling the solid shape of the locket beneath her bodice. Inside it, in place of the lost scrap of paper, there was a folded piece of newsprint. DANCE HALL ATTACK MYSTERY, the headline said. She carried it as a reminder of the mistakes she had made, and the path she was leaving behind.

She'd scoured the papers, but there were no further reports of Irving's condition. She had no idea if he was still alive, or if they were still looking for his attacker. Even now, nearly a month later, whenever she went out on the street she half-expected to be arrested.

Anna hadn't come back to work again, after that night. The Radzins sent little Abie around to her tenement, where the landlady reported that the girl had packed up and left, without a word. Mrs. Radzin declared herself worried sick, but Mr. Radzin said he had a business to run, and soon a girl named Ruby was standing behind Anna's table. Ruby was bland and cow-eyed, and would guffaw nervously if anyone so much as looked at her; but she was obedient and spoke little, and for that Mr. Radzin tolerated her.

They were downstairs in the parlor now, the Radzins and Ruby, with her landlady and Michael and his small group of friends. "There's no one else you'd like to invite?" Michael had asked. She'd smiled at his concern and shaken her head. For who else was there? No one at all, except for the one man who knew her best.

She frowned and smoothed her skirt, as though brushing something away. She had to be vigilant now; she could not ruin her chance at a fresh start. She would lock all thoughts of the Djinni away, and would not, would not, speculate on what he would say about this marriage, if only he knew.

The door opened, startling her. A thin, elderly man in a dark suit stood in the doorway.

"You must be Mr. Schall," she said. "Michael has told me so much about you."

The old man smiled kindly. "Please," he said, "call me Joseph."

She stood and placed a hand on his offered arm. She was taller than him by almost a foot, but even so she felt small and unsure. Would her nerves fail her, after all? No: she held herself straighter, firmed her grip, and willed herself to go forward.

Together they stepped from her bedroom.

Yehudah Schaalman led the Golem down to the parlor, careful to maintain his composure. It was difficult; he kept wanting to burst into giggles. When Michael Levy had asked him to stand in for the father of the bride, it had taken all of his considerable will to keep a straight face. "If she agrees, then yes, I think that would be appropriate," he'd managed to say. A week earlier, he'd have felt himself the butt of another cosmic joke, but now it was his turn to laugh. The blushing bride, and he'd built her himself!

He deposited her next to her betrothed, who stood before the black-robed justice of the peace. The temperature in the parlor was rising, and the younger men, no slaves to decorum, had taken off their jackets. Schaalman would've liked to do the same, but he couldn't risk it. His left arm was hampered by a thick bandage below his elbow, and without the jacket it would be far more noticeable, especially if the bandage had started seeping blood again. But his discomfort was a small price to pay. For look at her! Deaf as a post to his thoughts and desires, with no inkling of who he was or what he wanted. His preparations had worked, as thoroughly as he'd hoped.

Once again he'd found the answer in his treasured sheaf of papers. After three nights of intense study, he'd arrived at the solution: a particular diagram, the sort of thing meant to be inscribed on an amulet and hung about one's neck. But with no amulet at hand and no way of making one, he'd resorted to carving the diagram on the inside of his arm. He hadn't expected it to be a pleasant experience, but still the pain had been shocking in its intensity, as though the knife was reaching beyond his body to slice into his soul. He'd spent the next day sick in bed, arm throbbing, racked with waves of nausea. But it had been so very worth it! Now he could follow her without detection, and he need not worry if Levy should bring his new wife around to the Sheltering House unexpectedly.

I will destroy you someday, he thought at the Golem, as loudly as he could—but she merely stood there, listening to the sweating justice as he droned on in English. Occasionally Levy gave his bride a nervous smile; she, on the other hand, looked solemn as an undertaker. Schaalman tried to imagine what people said of her. *A sober woman,* he supposed. *Quiet. Not one for jokes or frivolousness.* As though these were traits of her character, like anyone else's, and not the outward signs of her nature, her limitations. It was remarkable that she'd made it this far without being discovered. More fool Levy, for falling in love with her.

The justice raised his voice in a pronouncement—Schaalman recognized the words *man and wife*—and there was a burst of applause and laughter as Levy took the white-clad creature in his arms and kissed her. The justice gave a tight smile and turned away, his job done.

Schaalman laughed along with everyone else, happy in his secret knowledge. It would take another day or so to regain his strength. And then, the next phase of his search would begin. Whatever it was that linked the Golem and the Bowery, whatever Levy's uncle had conspired to hide from him, he would uncover it. He could feel the secret out there in the city, waiting patiently to be found.

21.

M aryam," said Arbeely, "do you know Nadia Mounsef? Matthew's mother?"

He was sitting at the Faddouls' coffeehouse, drinking cups of scalding coffee despite the heat. Knowing that Arbeely only came when he wished to talk about something, Maryam had kept close to him, polishing the already pristine tables while Sayeed attended to the other customers. Now she paused, cloth in hand. "Nadia? We've spoken a few times, but not lately. Why do you ask?"

Arbeely hesitated. He didn't want to say the truth, which was that the woman's face had been haunting him. "I went to see her a few weeks ago, about Matthew," he said. "She was ill. I mean, she looked ill before, but . . . this was different." He went on to describe the woman who'd answered the door: even thinner than he remembered, her eyes dull and sunken. A strange dark blush, almost a rash, was spread across her cheeks and the bridge of her nose. The crucifix at her throat—three barred, the sigil of the Eastern Orthodox—had fluttered visibly in time with her too-quick heartbeat. She'd blinked at the feeble light in the hallway as Arbeely haltingly explained his concerns. It wasn't that Matthew was a nuisance, far from it: he was a helpful boy, and they enjoyed having him at the shop. But the child was spending mornings there, when he should certainly be in a classroom. And if a truancy officer happened to come by . . . "I don't mean to get Matthew in trouble with anyone," he said. "Including his mother."

She'd given him the barest hint of a polite smile. "Of course, Mr. Arbeely. I'll speak with Matthew. Thank you, for being patient with him." And before Arbeely could protest that patience had nothing to do with it—the boy had real talent, and would make a promising apprentice—she went back inside and closed the door, leaving Arbeely to wonder how he could've handled it better.

"You did what you needed to," Maryam told him. "You can't be re-sponsible for her son's welfare." She sighed. "Poor Nadia. She's all alone, you know."

"I was wondering," Arbeely admitted. "What happened?"

"Her husband was peddling in Ohio. For a while there were letters, and then, nothing."

"He disappeared?"

"Dead, ill, or run away—no one knows."

Arbeely shook his head. It was a common story, but still hard for him to credit. "And she has no one here?"

"No family, at least. And she refuses all attempts to help her. I've invited her to dinner, but she never comes." Maryam looked troubled, and no wonder: it wasn't often that someone succeeded in refusing her generosity. "I think most of her neighbors have given up trying. Her illness is so strange, it comes and goes—it's terrible to say, but many decided she was making it up, to avoid them."

"Or perhaps she just doesn't want to be stared at, and gossiped about."

Maryam nodded sadly. "You're right, of course. And who can blame her? I'll visit her soon, and try again. Perhaps there's some way I can help."

"Thank you, Maryam." He sighed. "At least Matthew stopped com-ing in the mornings. Although, mind you, some days I'd rather he did." At Maryam's quizzical look he said, "It's Ahmad. At this point I think he likes the boy more than me. He's been . . . moody, lately. A failed love affair, I suspect. He tells me little."

Maryam nodded with her usual sympathy, but at the Djinni's name the warmth had faded from her eyes. How was it that Maryam, with her gift for seeing the good in everyone, had taken such a dislike to him? Arbeely would have liked to ask her; but that, of course, would mean venturing into dangerous territory. Instead he thanked her and left, feel-ing more morose than ever.

Back at the shop, the Djinni and Matthew were at the Djinni's workbench, their heads bent together like conspirators. The Djinni in-sisted that Matthew's discovery of his secret had been a complete accident, but still Arbeely felt the Djinni had been far too cavalier about the whole thing. It had sparked their worst argument since the tin ceiling.

How didn't you hear him come in?

Half the time you don't hear him either. Besides, I told you, he knew already.

And you didn't even try to convince him otherwise?

Arbeely, he saw me soldering chain links with my bare hands. What could I have said?

You could've tried, at least. Made up some lie or other.

The Djinni's face had darkened. *I'm sick of lying.* And when Arbeely tried to press the matter, the Djinni had left the shop.

Since then, they'd spent most of their mornings in tense silence. But whenever Matthew arrived and took his silent spot on the bench, the Djinni would treat him with uncharacteristic patience. Sometimes they even laughed together, at a joke or a mistake, and Arbeely would tamp down his jealousy, feeling like a stranger in his own shop.

He tried to keep things in perspective. Business was more profitable than ever, and the necklaces they were making for Sam Hosseini were beautiful—no doubt Sam would fetch a small fortune for each one. He thought back to the morning the Djinni had come in looking like he'd been dealt a mortal blow. It had been only a month, after all. Hopefully soon his partner would be distracted by something—or, God help them all, someone—new and intriguing.

The sun dipped behind the broad backs of the tenements, and the light in the shop's high window faded. Women's voices drifted down from the upper stories, calling their children in for supper. Matthew slipped off the bench and was gone, the shop door barely whispering as he passed. Yet again the Djinni wondered if the spirit world had meddled in the boy's bloodline—it seemed impossible for a human to be that uncanny without help.

Matthew's visits had become the sole bright spot in the Djinni's days. Whenever the boy left and the door slipped shut, something would close in himself as well, something barely acknowledged. Arbeely would turn up the lamp, and they would work in their separate silences until Arbeely, succumbing to hunger or fatigue, would heave a sigh and begin to heap sand on the fire. At that, the Djinni would put down his tools and leave, as wordlessly as Matthew.

His life was no different than before: the shop during the day, the city at night. But the hours now felt interminable, ruled by a numbing sameness. At night he walked quickly, as though driven to it, barely seeing his surroundings. He tried returning to his old favorites—Madison Square Park, Washington Square, the Battery Park aquarium—but these places were haunted now, pinned to memories of particular evenings and conversations, things said and unsaid. He could hardly walk within sight of Central Park before a weary anger turned him elsewhere.

So he went farther north instead, tracing aimless paths into unexplored territory. He walked up Riverside to Harlem's southern border, then cut through the university's new grounds, past the columned library with its gigantic granite dome. He forged up Amsterdam, crossing streets numbered well into the hundreds. Gradually the well-kept brownstones gave way to Dutch clapboard houses, their trellises heavy with roses.

One night he discovered the Harlem River Speedway and walked its length, the river glittering to his right. It was well past midnight, but a few of society's more reckless specimens were still out in their racing carriages, chasing each other up and down the course. Their horses strained white-eyed at their bits, kicking up dust from the macadam. At dawn he found himself at the amusement park at Fort George, its shuttered fairway eerie and silent. The wooden rides seemed skeletal, like the remains of huge abandoned beasts. The Third Avenue Trolley had its terminus at the park's entrance, and he watched as the day's first car disgorged its passengers: carnival barkers and ride operators, yawning beer-garden girls in faded skirts, an organ-grinder whose monkey slept curled around his neck. No one seemed happy to be there. He boarded the car and rode south, watching as the trolley filled and emptied, delivering workers to the factories and printing presses, the sweatshops and the docklands. The more he rode the trolleys and trains of New York, the more they seemed to form a giant, malevolent bellows, inhaling defenseless passengers from platforms and street corners and blowing them out again elsewhere.

Back on Washington Street, he trudged to Arbeely's shop, feeling as though he were caught inside a single day that stretched like molten glass. There was nothing to anticipate, except Matthew. He enjoyed the boy's wide-eyed attention, enjoyed giving him tasks and watching him perform them with silent absorption. He supposed that eventually Matthew would grow older and lose interest, and take his place with the feral young men who slouched on the neighborhood stoops. Or—even worse—he'd become just another streetcar rider, dull-eyed and unprotesting.

He sat down at his bench without a word of greeting. Behind him, Arbeely puttered around the shop, making irritating humming noises. The man was deep into a large order of kitchen graters and had spent an entire week punching diamond-shaped holes into sheets of tin. Just watching him made the Djinni want to go mad. But Arbeely gave no sign that he minded the repetition, and the Djinni was beginning to detest him for that.

You judge him far too harshly, he could hear the Golem say.

He scowled. It was clear they would never speak again, and yet he was hearing her voice more and more often. He rubbed at his cuff, felt the square of paper shift beneath it. Enough: the necklaces were due to Sam Hosseini. He took up his tools and tried to lose himself in the creation of something beautiful.

Michael Levy slowly woke to the thin glow of morning. The other half of the bed was an empty sea of sheets and counterpane. He closed his eyes, listened for his wife. There: in the kitchen, bustling about. It was a comforting sound, a childhood sound. The air even smelled of fresh-baked bread.

He padded out into the tiny kitchen. She was standing next to the stove in her new housedress, leafing through her American cookbook. He snuck his arms around her waist and kissed her. "Couldn't sleep again?"

"Yes, but it's all right."

Apparently it was an insomnia she'd had all her life. She said she was used to it; and indeed, she looked more awake than he felt. If it were him, he'd be dead on his feet. An amazing woman.

He still couldn't believe they were married. At night he'd lie next to her, tracing his fingers around her stomach, up to her breasts, her arms, amazed at how thoroughly his life had changed. He loved the feel of her skin—always *cool* somehow, though the days had been sweltering. "I suppose it's because of the ovens at the bakery," he'd said once. "Your body's used to the heat." She'd smiled as though embarrassed, and said, "I think you must be right."

She was often shy, his wife. Many of their meals together were silent, or nearly so: they were still tentative with each other, unsure of how to act. He'd look across the table and wonder, had they married too quickly? Would they always be strangers to each other? But then, even before the thought had passed from his mind, she would ask about his day, or tell him a story from hers, or else simply reach across and squeeze his hand. He would realize it was exactly what he'd needed, and wonder how she'd known.

Then there was the matter of the bedroom. Their wedding night had begun tentatively. He was well aware that as a previously married woman, she would be much more experienced than he. But what did she like? What *pleased* her? He had no idea how to ask, and not nearly enough nerve. What if she suggested something outlandish, even terrifying? His friends, when they'd had a few drinks, boasted of their exotic nights with "emancipated" girls, but his own fantasies had never ventured far from the prosaic. Perhaps it was a failing; perhaps she'd be disappointed.

If she was, she didn't say so. Seeming to understand his distress—and there, again, was that *knowing*—she had led him into the act with her usual calm and steady demeanor. If their lovemaking was a little too workmanlike—if, afterward, he'd been unsure of her own pleasure—still he was relieved that it had been accomplished at all.

And then there'd been the night a week or so later, when she'd started as though surprised, and placed a hand between their bodies, pressing at a particular spot. To Michael's utter regret he'd frozen, chagrined, as his Orthodox upbringing rushed clamoring to the fore, insisting that this was *immodest*, unbecoming in a wife—and slowly she'd removed her hand, and replaced it on his back, and resumed their rhythm.

He couldn't talk to her about it, later. He just couldn't. He tried, once, to repeat what she herself had done; but she took his hand and moved it away, and that had been that.

Already there were things unsaid between them. But he loved her; he was certain of it. And he liked to think she loved him in return. He imagined them in thirty years, with children grown, holding hands in bed and laughing at how unsure they'd been, how delicately they'd tiptoed around each other. *But you always knew just what to say*, he'd tell her; and she would smile, and nestle her head in his shoulder, both of them completely at home.

He'd ask her about these things someday. He'd find out what had prompted her to propose to him, just when he'd given up hope. Or what she'd been thinking as she stood next to him before the justice of the peace, looking so composed and serene. He only hoped it wouldn't take him thirty years to ask.

The Golem placed a glass of tea and a plate of bread before her husband, and watched as he ate quickly, in big bites. She smiled in real fondness. He was so earnest, in everything he did.

She turned back to the sink to clean the few remaining dishes. They lived now in three tiny rooms crammed at the end of a first-floor hallway. The thin light that filtered down the air shaft illuminated a pile of garbage that climbed halfway up the bedroom window. Sometimes she'd watch as a cigarette butt fluttered down from above. The kitchen was more like a closet, with a stove barely big enough to roast a chicken. At night she did her sewing in the parlor, which hardly merited the name; it was perhaps a third the size of her old room at the boardinghouse. The rooms' main advantage was that they sat at the back of the tenement, which had been dug into a slight rise, so that the earth kept them cool while the rest of the building sweltered. "It'll be warmer in winter too," Michael had said. She hoped this meant she wouldn't feel so stiff and creaky, so driven to walk in the evenings. But deep down she knew that her proximity to Michael's restless mind would hound her to distraction as surely as the weather once had.

Within days of their marriage she'd realized how much she'd underestimated the difficulty ahead. Unlike the Rabbi, who'd been so circumspect, so careful in his thoughts, Michael's mind was a constant churn of wants and fears and second-guesses, most of them directed at herself. The noise wore down her composure and tested her self-control. She found herself serving him second helpings when he was hungry, talking when he wanted conversation, taking his hand when he needed reassurance. She'd begun to wonder whether she still had a will of her own.

Also there were the endless practical dilemmas. The long stretches of lying next to him in bed, remembering to breathe in and out. The excuses for her sleeplessness, her cool skin. Would he notice that her hair never grew? Or, God forbid, that she had no heartbeat? And what would happen when she failed to bear children? She'd hoped to keep marital relations to a minimum, to put some protective distance between them—she was afraid, above all, of hurting him accidentally—but then his desire would grow too strong to ignore, and she would feel driven to respond, or else lie there frustrated by reflected lust. There'd been that one night, when she'd felt her own warm tingle of desire, and tried eagerly to encourage it; but it had been doused by Michael's awkward, guilty horror. It wasn't his fault: she could feel his chagrin at his reaction, and he'd later tried to remedy the situation, but with such tortured ambivalence that she'd put an end to the attempt. Was it the pleasure itself, she wondered, that was somehow shameful? Or only what she'd done to increase it?

Unbidden she heard the Djinni say: *It should be easy. They're the ones who complicate it beyond reason.*

No. She couldn't afford to listen to that voice. It was wrong, ludicrous even, to resent Michael for her decision. She'd bound herself to him; she would see through what she'd begun. And perhaps, one day, she would tell him the truth.

At last the necklaces for Sam Hosseini were finished. Arbeely delivered them to Sam's shop himself, not trusting the Djinni to strike a good bargain. But he needn't have worried, for Sam was so pleased with them that he barely remembered to haggle. Besides the Djinni's original necklace, with its disks of blue-green glass, there were versions with garnet-colored teardrops, brilliant white crystals, and lozenges of a deep emerald green. The Djinni had flattened the links and added the faintest edge of tarnish to the metal, which gave them a timeless beauty, while also looking like nothing Sam had ever seen.

Arbeely had expected Sam to display the necklaces in his largest glass case, but Sam had a better plan. Lately it had become fashionable for Manhattan's society women to pose for portraits while dressed in a fanciful "Oriental" style, such as they imagined a Near Eastern princess or courtesan might have worn. Sam's shop was a popular destination for these ladies, who often sent their maids or even came themselves to buy props and costume pieces. Most of them viewed bargaining as gauche, which meant that Sam was turning a tidy profit in curl-toed slippers, billowing silk trousers, and faux Egyptian armbands. The new necklaces would certainly appeal to them; and Sam knew they would like them even better if they came with a story.

It was only a few days before the first likely customer arrived. A sleek, expensive brougham pulled up in front of Sam's shop—causing a good deal of gawking from the passersby—and a dark-haired young woman emerged. The afternoon heat was baking the sidewalks, but the young woman wore a heavy, dark dress and a thick shawl. She looked about with polite curiosity until an older woman, dressed just as finely in black, stepped from the carriage. The older woman eyed their surroundings with distaste, then took hold of her companion's elbow and led her swiftly into Sam's shop.

They were, indeed, there for a portrait. "My fiancé's idea," the young woman said. "He commissioned it, as a wedding present." Sam ushered them to his best chairs, poured them tea, and spent the next hour bringing them bolts of fabric, beaded scarves, veils hung with coins, and whatever other bric-a-brac he thought they might fancy. Surprisingly, the young woman had a good eye for authenticity and avoided the gaudiest offerings. Soon she'd put together an outfit that truly resembled what an Ottoman woman of means might once have worn.

The sun slanted through the shop's large windows, and the old woman dabbed at her brow with her handkerchief. But the young woman made no move to unwrap her shawl, and Sam noticed that her teacup shook slightly in her hand. Some sort of illness or palsy, perhaps. A shame, in one so young and lovely.

Eventually, as Sam had predicted, they arrived at the subject of a proper necklace. He went into the storeroom and emerged with an old leather box, battered and worn, and blew imaginary dust from its top. "This," he said, "I rarely show."

He opened the box, and the young woman gasped as he took out necklace after necklace. "How gorgeous! Are they antiques?"

"Yes, very old. They belong to my *jaddah*—excuse me, how do you say, mother of mother?"

"Grandmother."

"Thank you, yes, my grandmother. She was Bedouin. You know this? A traveler in the desert."

"Yes, I've heard of the Bedouin," said the young woman.

"My grandfather gives them to her, at their wedding. As part of her . . . hmm. Price?"

"Her dowry?"

"Yes, dowry. When she dies, she leaves me the necklaces, to sell. For a beautiful necklace must have a beautiful woman to wear, or else it is worth nothing at all."

"You wouldn't rather keep them for your own wife, or your children?"

"For them," and he gestured to the shop around them, "I make a business. Much more valuable, in America."

She chuckled. "You're a wise man, Mr. Hosseini." Next to her the old woman sniffed, as though to express her opinion of Mr. Hosseini's wisdom, or perhaps the entire conversation.

"May I see this one?" And the young woman pointed to the necklace with the discs of blue-green glass.

He fetched a hand mirror and held it up while her older companion fastened the clasp. She gazed at herself, and Sam smiled: the necklace fit as though made for her throat. "Beautiful," he said. "Like a queen of the desert."

With her shaking fingers she reached up and touched the necklace. The glass disks shifted, chiming softly against each other. "A queen of the desert," she echoed. And then, a deep and startling sadness crept over her face. Tears began to spill from her eyes; she covered them with a hand and drew her breath in a hitching sob.

"My dear, what's the matter?" cried the old woman. But her young companion just shook her head, trying to smile, obviously embarrassed at herself. Sam fetched her a handkerchief, which she took gratefully and dabbed at her eyes. Chagrined, he could not refrain from blurting out, "You don't like it?"

"Oh, no! I like it very much! I'm so sorry, Mr. Hosseini, I'm just not myself at the moment."

"It's the wedding," said the older woman consolingly. "Your mother makes such a fuss of everything, I wonder how you can bear it."

Sam nodded at this, thinking of his own quiet Lulu, her lingering homesickness. "A wedding is a strange time," he said. "Much happiness, but many changes also."

"There certainly are." The young woman took a deep breath, and then smiled at her reflection. "It's beautiful. What will you take for it?"

Sam named a number he thought slightly less than ludicrous, and she readily agreed. The old woman's eyes widened with alarm, and she looked as though she would've given her charge a stern chiding if they'd been alone. Sensing that the shopping was now concluded, Sam poured them more tea and brought out small cakes dusted with crushed pistachios—"My wife makes these," he announced proudly—and busied himself with wrapping their parcels and carrying them to the waiting carriage. The footman gave him an address on Fifth Avenue where he could send the bill.

When the women finally rose to leave, Sam placed his hand on his heart and bowed to both of them. "Your visit honors me," he said. "If you need anything else, please come again."

"I will," the young woman said warmly, and clasped his hand; he felt the odd tremor in her fingers. She glanced at her companion, who was already making her way toward the door, and lowered her voice. "Mr. Hosseini, do you know many of your Syrian neighbors?"

"Yes," he said, surprised. "I am here a long time, I know everyone."

"Then could you tell me—do you know a man—" But then she looked again to the woman waiting nearby at the door, and whatever question she meant to ask died on her lips. She smiled again, a bit sadly, and said, "It's no matter. Thank you, Mr. Hosseini. For everything." The bells on the door jangled as she passed.

The footman helped Sophia into the carriage. She settled herself next to her aunt, and pulled her shawl a bit tighter. The trip had been a success; she only wished she had not cried like that, and made a spectacle of herself. She supposed she ought to thank her aunt for providing an excuse for her tears, when their true cause had been far different. *A queen of the desert*: that was what she'd imagined herself, in her bed, in his arms. Suffice to say, the irony of her engagement portrait had not been lost on her.

Her perspiring aunt fanned herself with her gloves. She turned to Sophia, as though to say something—*this terrible heat*—but then caught herself, and only gave her a strained smile. Sophia's illness had this benefit, at least: her acquaintances' newfound awkwardness meant a reprieve from all sorts of chitchat.

The footman nudged the brougham away from the curb, and threaded slowly through the morass of carts. "Shall we go to Central Park?" her aunt said. "I'm sure your mother wouldn't mind."

"That's all right, Auntie. I'd rather just go home." She smiled, to soften the refusal. Her aunt was worried about her; they all were. Sophia had never been an energetic girl, but at least she had gone for walks, and visited friends, and done the things a wealthy young woman was supposed to do. Now she merely sat by the fire for hours at a stretch. She knew they all pitied her, but she'd found a real comfort in her protracted convalescence. Her mother had excused her from all social functions—which were few in any case, as the Winstons were the only family of note who still lingered in the city. Her father, indulgent in his concern, had opened his library to her, and at last she could read to her heart's content. In all, these last few weeks had been some of the most peaceable of her life. She had the sense of existing inside a fragile pause, a moment of grace.

But that would soon be over. Her mother was determined to forge ahead with the wedding plans. She'd even told her fiancé's parents that Sophia's tremor was improving, which was certainly not the case. Sophia had merely learned to disguise it more effectively. As for Charles himself, so far he'd taken care to appear undeterred by the sight of his shivering fiancée. At each meeting he asked once after her health—always she struggled to find an answer that was neither a falsehood nor a complaint—and then embarked on a rapid stream of pleasantries. It was exactly the sort of conversation she'd hoped never to have with her husband, and she doubted he relished it either. She feared their married life would be like some dreadful novel: the dissatisfied young husband, the sickly heiress.

She watched the men and women going about their business outside the hansom window, and wondered what it would be like to lose herself among them, the warm press of people carrying her somewhere else, somewhere far away.

And then, she saw him.

The tinsmiths' shop had felt especially stifling that morning. Each thud of Arbeely's hammer, each dull ring of metal on metal, seemed pitched and calculated to be as annoying as possible. So when Arbeely grumbled that the hammer's rawhide was wearing thin, the Djinni declared he would go to the tack and harness shop on Clarkson, and buy him a piece. It was a long walk for a minor errand, but Arbeely had given him no argument. Apparently both of them wanted him gone.

They'd fought again, bitterly, over Matthew this time. Arbeely had learned that the boy had no father to speak of, and seemed to think the Djinni should be concerned about the boy's welfare. The ensuing argument had included phrases such as *moral guidance* and *appropriate father figure*, and other impenetrables that the Djinni suspected were tinged with insult. What business was it of Arbeely's if Matthew chose to spend the afternoons with him? The truth, the Djinni sensed, was that Arbeely was jealous. Matthew paid him hardly any attention, though he obeyed without protest whenever Arbeely pointed out the lateness of the hour, saying, *Your mother will be worried.* But it was on the Djinni's bench that the boy silently materialized every afternoon. And no wonder. Who'd want to spend their afternoons with Arbeely, if they could avoid it? With each day, the tinsmith became more of a misery, his brow furrowing with worry and disapproval, his eyes sunken from lack of sleep. *You look terrible*, the Djinni told him one morning, and in return the man shot him a look of surprising hostility.

He left the shop, his thoughts in their now-usual stew, and crossed the street, navigating with irritation the carts and horses. Many of them had been held up behind a hansom that was trying to pull away from the curb. The hansom inched forward, and the Djinni glanced into the window as he passed.

It was, unmistakably, Sophia—and yet he had to look again. Pallid, black-wrapped, she had clearly undergone some terrible change. Again he remembered her dark and shrouded room. What had happened to her? Was the girl ill?

She looked up, and saw him. Surprise, dismay, anger all passed across her features—but she did not flush or glance away, as once she would have. Instead she held his gaze, and gave him a look of such naked, vulnerable sadness that it was he who glanced away first.

In the next moment the cab passed. Confused, shaken, the Djinni continued on his way. He told himself she was a girl of means, and that her problem, whatever it was, was not his to solve. But he could not let go of the feeling that, in that moment, she had been calling him to account for something.

Abu Yusuf sat on the floor of the sick-tent, holding his daughter's hand. Three days had passed since Fadwa had taken ill, and in that time he had barely moved from her side. He watched Fadwa's dreaming fingers grasp at air, listened to her moan and mutter nonsense. At first they'd coaxed her to open her eyes, but the girl had taken one look at Abu Yusuf, screamed in terror, and begun to choke. After that, they'd blind-folded her tightly with a dark rag.

The word *possessed* hung in the close air of the sick-tent, was ex-changed in every glance, but not a tongue uttered it.

Abu Yusuf's brothers shouldered his duties without a word. Fatim stuck to her work, muttering that *someone* had to keep them fed, it would do Fadwa no good if they all starved. Every few hours she took a bowl of thinned yogurt into the sick-tent and spooned as much of it as she could into her daughter's mouth. Her eyes were red-rimmed as she worked, and she said little, only glanced at her husband as he sat there, silently blaming him-self. He should have raised an alarm, he'd decided, when he'd glimpsed that impossible palace. He should've taken his daughter and ridden far, far away.

By the end of the second day, Fatim's glances had a touch of accu-sation about them. *How long,* she seemed to be saying, *will you sit here, doing nothing? Why do you let her suffer, when you know the remedy?* And an unspoken name rose to float between them: *Wahab ibn Malik.*

He wanted to argue with her, to tell her that prudence dictated he wait and see if Fadwa improved before he traveled that path. That he had no idea if ibn Malik was even still alive. But on the morning of the third day he had to admit that she was right. Fadwa was not improving, and his prudence was beginning to seem like cowardice.

"Enough," he said, standing. "Tell my brothers to ready a horse and a pony. And bring me one of the ewes." She nodded, grimly satisfied, and left the tent.

He packed a week's worth of provisions, then placed Fadwa on the pony, bound her hands, and tied her into the saddle. Her blindfolded head dipped and jerked, like a man falling asleep on watch. He tethered the ewe to Fadwa's pony, giving it plenty of lead. Then he mounted his horse and took the pony's reins, and led them out of the encampment: a pitiful, half-blind procession. No one gathered to see them off. Instead the clan peered out from tent corners and door flaps, and mouthed silent prayers for their safe return, and for protection against the very man they sought. Only Fatim stood in the open, watching until her husband and daughter disappeared.

Ibn Malik's cave lay in the western hills, on a rocky, wind-buffeted slope. Few of the clan ever ventured that way, for there was no grazing, no place for an encampment. Already when Abu Yusuf was a boy—and not yet called Abu Yusuf, only Jalal ibn Karim—to *travel west* had become a euphemism among the clan for seeking out Wahab ibn Malik. Parents traveled west with children who were gravely ill, or in need of exorcisms; barren wives traveled west with their husbands and soon quickened with child. But always ibn Malik took something in return, either from the healed or from the ones who'd brought them—not just a sheep or two, but something intangible and necessary. The father of the exorcised child never spoke again. The pregnant woman was struck blind during the birth. No one exclaimed at the losses, for these were debts paid to ibn Malik, and everyone knew it.

Abu Yusuf's own cousin Aziz had once paid such a debt. Aziz was nine years older than young Jalal, and tall and strong and handsome. All the men of the clan could sit a horse as though born in the saddle, but Aziz rode like a god, and Jalal worshiped him for it. Jalal had been out tending his father's sheep when Aziz's horse stumbled in a hole and threw his rider, breaking the young man's back and neck. Aziz lingered between life and death for a day before his father decided to travel west. There was no way to drag a litter up the rocky hillsides, so he made the trip alone, and returned carrying a sack of poultices. At their touch Aziz's bones healed, and his fever disappeared. Within a week he was up and walking. But from then on, every horse he approached shied at the sight of him. The few he managed to touch would scream in terror and foam at the mouth. Aziz al-Hadid, master of horses, never rode again. He became a shadow of his former self—but still, at least he had lived.

Slowly they made their way west. Every few hours Abu Yusuf would tilt a waterskin to Fadwa's lips or feed her a few mouthfuls of yogurt. Sometimes she spat it out; sometimes she gulped it down as though starving. Soon the flat terrain of the steppes gave way to angled hills and low, jagged peaks. It was hard going, and the ewe started to struggle. When it became clear she couldn't go on much farther, Abu Yusuf dismounted, kneeled on the struggling animal's side, and bashed her skull in with a rock. She'd have to be drained soon, or her blood would turn to poison; but if he did it there, he'd bring down every jackal in the hills. He lashed the carcass to his horse's back, and they continued on.

It was almost evening when ibn Malik's cave came into sight. Squinting against the last of the sun, Abu Yusuf spied a small, thin fig-ure sitting cross-legged on the flat apron of rock just outside its entrance. He was alive. And he'd known they were coming. Of course he'd known.

Wahab ibn Malik had been already in his thirties when Abu Yu-suf's cousin was injured; but even so, as they drew closer, Abu Yusuf found himself shocked at the state of the man who waited for them. He seemed no more than a leathered, yellow-eyed skeleton. He stood as they approached, a spiderlike unfolding, and Abu Yusuf saw he was naked save for a torn loincloth. He glanced back at Fadwa; but of course the girl was blindfolded, and could see nothing.

He dismounted and untied the dead ewe from Fadwa's horse. Cra-dling it in his arms, he approached ibn Malik and laid it at his feet. The man grinned at Abu Yusuf, revealing dark, broken teeth, and looked over at Fadwa, still tied to her pony.

"You want an exorcism," ibn Malik said. His voice was startling: deep and full, it seemed to come from somewhere other than his body.

"Yes," said Abu Yusuf, uneasily. "If you think there's hope."

Ibn Malik laughed. "There is never *hope*, Jalal ibn Karim," he said. "There's only what can be done, and what cannot." He nodded at Fadwa. "Bring her down from there, and follow me. And then, we will see what can be done." With that, he bent and lifted two of the dead ewe's legs, and dragged her into the mouth of the cave.

What Abu Yusuf had taken to be a small cave was only the first of a series of linked, torch-lit recesses that stretched deep into the cliff. As he followed ibn Malik, Fadwa muttered and twisted in his arms, trying to get away from something only she could see. The guttering torches smelled of animal fat, and spat out a greasy black smoke that filled the passageways.

In one of the smaller caves ibn Malik gestured for him to place Fadwa on a rude pallet. Abu Yusuf did so, trying to ignore the general filth of the place, and watched helplessly as ibn Malik started his examination. Fadwa struggled against the man until he poured something in her mouth that made her relax and go still. Then he began to strip her clothing away. His demeanor was entirely dispassionate; still Abu Yusuf wanted to drag him from her side and bash in his head, as he'd done to the ewe.

"Only her mind was violated, not her body," ibn Malik said at length. "You'll be pleased to hear she's still a virgin."

A wash of red passed over Abu Yusuf's eyes. "Get on with it," he muttered.

Ibn Malik removed the blindfold and opened one of her eyes, and then another. Abu Yusuf cringed, waiting for her to cry out or vomit, but she lay silent and still. "Interesting," ibn Malik said, almost in a purr.

"What is it?"

The skeletal man made a shushing gesture so absurdly like Fatim's that Abu Yusuf wanted to laugh. The impulse died as ibn Malik suddenly moved to straddle Fadwa. With both hands he peeled her eyelids back; his dirty forehead came down to touch hers. For long minutes they stared deep into each other's eyes. Neither of them blinked, nor seemed even to breathe. Abu Yusuf turned around, not wanting to see ibn Malik squatting over his daughter's chest like a grotesque insect. The torch-smoke filled his nose and clotted his lungs, making him dizzy. He leaned against the rough wall and closed his eyes.

After some time—he didn't know how long—he heard movement, and turned to see ibn Malik rising from his daughter's side. The ancient man was smiling, his eyes lit like a boy's with excitement.

"I've been waiting for this," ibn Malik said. "All my life."

"Can you heal her?" Abu Yusuf asked dully.

"Yes, yes, it's easy," the man said with impatience. "But"—as Abu Yusuf sagged at the knees, tears springing to his eyes—"not yet. No, not yet. There's something larger here. I must consider carefully. We need a plan, a strategy."

"A strategy for *what*?"

Ibn Malik flashed his broken grin. "For capturing the djinni that did this to your daughter."

22.

Two hours after lights-out, the man known as Joseph Schall woke in the darkness of the Sheltering House dormitory. All day he'd been a model of industry, distributing blankets and cots and bars of soap, and washing dishes in the kitchen. At the evening roll call he'd struck names from the list and settled the inevitable disputes, before taking to his cot and sinking into a deep and grateful sleep. But now, as he dressed quietly and found his shoes, the role of Joseph Schall fell from him like a skin. It was near midnight, and Yehudah Schaalman's day was just beginning.

Ever since the night of his opium-fueled revelations, Schaalman's search had taken on a new energy. He realized now that he'd made the mistake of imagining his quarry as something hidden away, like a jewel at the center of a maze. But his eyes had been opened. Whatever it was, it *traveled*. It was something that could be carried, even passed on, knowingly or unknowingly.

At first he'd returned to the Bowery, hoping to pick up the trail again. For a week of nights he walked across the rooftops, one more anonymous soul among the masses. But the traces that once had felt so fresh had begun to fade. Even Conroy, the trader in stolen goods, had lost his undeniable pull; now he seemed only mildly interesting.

Schaalman refused to be deterred. He'd found the trail once before, completely by accident. Surely he could do so again.

And so he struck out once more, traveling at random, into unfamiliar neighborhoods where the Yiddish faded from the signs. These streets were much less trafficked at night, and with no crowd to hide in, Schaalman felt wary and exposed. But the risk came with reward: soon the dowsing spell was pulling him north past long blocks of columned buildings to a large and open park where stood an enormous illuminated arch, its alabaster-white surface fairly glowing with interest. His quarry had been here, and recently.

He studied the arch for nearly an hour, trying to understand its significance. Had it been part of a building, or the gate of a now-fallen city? An unreadable quotation in English was carved into one side, but somehow Schaalman doubted it would provide answers. He risked muttering a few basic formulae to reveal the unseen, but found nothing. The arch merely hung above him, an incalculable weight of marble. A carved eagle rested on a pediment at the apex of the arch, and stared down at Schaalman with one cold eye. Unsettled, Schaalman left the park and walked back to the House, falling into his cot just before dawn.

He went back to Washington Square Park a few nights later but, like the Bowery, its fascination was already ebbing. So he continued north, wandering the side streets along Fifth Avenue, catching hints of interest here and there. He had to concentrate, for the surroundings themselves were a constant distraction: the monumental granite buildings, the expanses of perfect plate glass. How could a street continue straight as a rod for miles and miles, without bending even once? It felt unnatural; it made his flesh creep.

Eventually the spell pulled him to another park, this one tree lined and studded with bronze figures in antique dress. Derelict men lay asleep here and there on the grass, but none drew his interest. So back to the Sheltering House he went, sunk deep in melancholy, feeling as though he were chasing Levy's uncle all over again.

And that, of course, was the other thread in this tangled knot: the unknown connection between his quarry and the new Mrs. Levy. It hadn't escaped his notice that the dowsing spell showed no interest in her husband. She was counterfeiting the life of an ordinary newlywed; was she counterfeiting a second life as well? It would certainly answer the question of how she spent her nights.

And so he followed her home from the bakery one afternoon, immediately noting with frustration that she too was losing the attention of the dowsing spell. Could it be that her presence in New York was pure coincidence? No, she was too intertwined with his search, with Levy and his dead uncle. There was more here, he only needed to find it.

Even as tall as she was, she was a hard woman to follow. She walked quickly through the crowd, giving peddlers and pushcart-men little chance to approach her. She only stopped once, at a general store, for flour and tea, thread and needles. She shared no womanly chatter with the shopkeeper, wasted no words other than *please* and *thank you*. Carrying her unremarkable packages, she went straight home and vanished into her building.

Well, perhaps an evening's observation would bear more fruit. He went back later that night, tailing Levy after lights-out. The man made no detours on his way home, but that was unsurprising. So far he had proved as interesting as a brick.

Schaalman took up position in a doorway opposite, fortified himself with wakefulness charms, and settled in for a long night's watch. But neither of the Levys appeared until after dawn the next day, when Michael emerged yawning from the front door. His wife followed a few minutes later, striding briskly toward the bakery. Schaalman hadn't put much trust in his theory; still, he felt obscurely disappointed in his creation. What did she *do* with herself all night? Listen to her husband snore while washing his socks by candlelight? He felt like scolding her. The most remarkable golem in existence, and she was content to play house! But then, perhaps it was part of her nature: the urge to replace her lost master, to find someone to obey.

He dragged himself back to the Sheltering House. His feet ached; his head pounded with fatigue and the aftereffects of the charms he'd used. He had to remind himself that he was making progress, slow though it might be. But it was maddening. He collapsed onto his cot, not even bothering to remove his shoes. An hour later he woke again as harmless old Joseph Schall, ready for his daily duties.

And already the day was proving a challenge for the Sheltering House staff. Down in the kitchen, the cook was near apoplexy. No one had put the sign in the window for the iceman, and now she had to serve up three days' worth of herring for breakfast, or else watch it all spoil. What's more, the delivery from Shimmel's Bakery had come up short; there wouldn't be nearly enough rolls for supper.

"I can fetch the rolls, at least," said Joseph Schall. "But perhaps I'll buy them at Radzin's." He smiled. "I'd like to give my regards to Mrs. Levy."

That morning, Radzin's Bakery was faring even worse than the Sheltering House. Ruby, the new girl, had taken the wrong trays from the ovens, and now all the challahs were raw and the pastries burnt. The customers waited at the register, muttering to one another, while everyone rushed about repairing the damage. Feeling their impatience, the Golem rolled and sliced and braided as fast as she dared. She found herself growing more and more irritated. Why should she shoulder the burden of Ruby's mistake? If she slowed herself to a reasonable pace, and let the customers complain, the girl might be more careful next time.

She glanced across at the girl in question, who was frantically mixing a bowl of batter, her thoughts a torment of self-recrimination. The Golem sighed, disappointed in herself. When had she turned so bitter, so uncharitable?

The previous night had been difficult as well. Worried about her insomnia, Michael had urged her to see a doctor. She'd tried to reassure him that she felt perfectly fine; but it became clear that the only way to appease him was to feign sleep. And so she'd spent the entire night lying next to him, eyes closed, diligently breathing in and out. After a few hours it was all she could do to hold still. Her limbs trembled with cramp, and her mind ran riot. She imagined shaking him awake, shouting the truth into his face. How had he not seen it yet? How could a man be so *blind*?

And then at dawn he'd woken, and given her a drowsy smile. "You slept," he murmured; and she cringed with guilt at his gladness.

At last the bakery recovered from the morning's mishap and the customers began to relax. The Golem went into the storeroom to fetch her unnecessary midday meal. From the water closet came the sound of hitching sobs and a torrent of despairing thoughts. She knocked softly on the water closet door. "Ruby?" Silence. "Ruby, please come out. It's all right."

The door cracked open; the girl's face emerged, red and swollen. "No it isn't. He's going to sack me, I know it."

"Of course he won't." It was the truth; Mr. Radzin had been deeply tempted but was too exhausted to contemplate another new hire. "He knows you're new to this. And we all make mistakes, especially at the beginning."

"*You* don't." Ruby's voice was sullen. "You *never* do."

Guilt twisted at her again. "Ruby, I have made more mistakes than I can count. But when something goes wrong, it does no good to hide and cry. You have to take what you've learned, and keep going."

The girl gave a doubtful-sounding sniff, but then wiped away the tear tracks on her face. "All right," she said quietly, and left to face Mr. Radzin's scowls.

The Golem ate her bread and butter with even less enthusiasm than usual. Meanwhile young Selma ran in and out, fetching eggs from the icebox, rolls of twine. A year ago she'd been a round-bellied girl in pigtails; now, long limbed and strong, she hoisted a bag of sugar to her shoulder, then dashed away again. The Golem watched her go, wondered what it would be like to have a daughter. She knew that Mrs. Radzin felt a constant stream of worries and anxieties for Selma, and wished occasionally that she could halt time, to keep the girl innocent of the world and its disappointments. Selma, meanwhile, could not wait to grow up, to at last understand the frustrating adults around her, their whispered arguments and sudden silences.

And where, thought the Golem, did she herself fit in? Somewhere between mother and daughter, she supposed: no longer innocent, not yet understanding.

Distantly she wondered how Michael was faring at the Sheltering House. Working too hard, no doubt. One of these days she would beg an hour for herself for lunch, and take him a plate of macaroons. It would be a wifely thing to do. A gesture of affection.

"Chava?"

She looked up, startled. Selma stood in the doorway. "Papa says it's your turn at the register."

"Of course." She pushed her troubled thoughts to a distant corner of her mind and stepped up to the register, relieving the harried Mrs. Radzin. The woman gave her a grateful pat on the arm, and retreated. The Golem placed a smile on her face and began filling orders.

"Good afternoon, Mrs. Levy."

A small old man was standing before the counter, his eyes twinkling. "Mr. Schall!" she said, surprised. "I haven't seen you since the wedding! How have you been?"

"Oh, well enough, well enough. And yourself? Does married life agree with you?"

Her smile threatened to waver; she steadied it. "Yes, though I'm afraid you see my husband much more than I do."

He chuckled. "A pity. You must wish you didn't have to work, or sleep." Her pause lasted only an instant, before she smiled and agreed.

The line behind him was shuffling impatiently. She asked, "What can I get for you, Mr. Schall?" and focused in on him, ready to fetch whatever he wanted.

But there was nothing there.

She saw his mouth move, heard him say, "Can you spare three dozen dinner rolls? We're having a hard day at the Sheltering House, I'm afraid." But beyond them lay no desire at all. There was only a void, a vast expanse of nothingness.

"Of course," she said weakly. Then, with more conviction: "Yes, of course. We can spare more, if you'd like."

"No, three dozen should be enough."

Quickly she boxed the rolls, wrapped the boxes with twine. To the last one she added a handful of macaroons. "For Michael, if you would," she said. "And one for yourself."

He smiled and thanked her, then paused, seeming to regard her. "You're an exemplary woman, Chava. I never doubted you would make an admirable wife." And then, he was gone.

She turned to the next customer, only half-hearing the order. *Never doubted?* What an odd choice of words! Hadn't he only met her once? Unless perhaps he'd heard Michael speak of their engagement. But—she shuddered to think of that bizarre void, that utter lack of fears or desires. It was quite different from what she'd felt from the Djinni: the Djinni's were still there, only muted, hidden from her sight. With Joseph Schall, it felt as though they'd been deliberately excised. She thought of the surgeon on the *Baltika* cutting out Rotfeld's appendix, lifting it free of his body.

She spent the rest of the afternoon greeting customers and fetching their orders, her habitual smile covering her unease. But all the while, she could not shake her growing conviction that there was something very wrong with Joseph Schall.

"A success!" Sam Hosseini told the Djinni. "An immense success!"

The necklaces, it seemed, had all been sold, and at a handsome profit. "Could you perhaps make another dozen?" Sam had asked. "And this time, with bracelets to match?" So once again the Djinni took up his tools. But the novelty of the necklaces had worn off; soon, he predicted, he'd be as bored with them as he'd been with the skillets.

Meanwhile, Arbeely's hours at the forge were growing ever longer. Swamped with orders, he'd even broached the subject of bringing on another assistant, an apprentice perhaps. The Djinni was less than pleased with this idea. Other than his barely tolerable room, the shop was the one place where he could be fully himself—but no doubt Arbeely would insist he hide his more unorthodox methods from a newcomer.

Despite the silence and the tension—or perhaps because of it—their work progressed steadily; and late one afternoon the Djinni realized that he and Matthew had completed half of Sam Hosseini's order, and were even ahead of schedule. The Djinni smiled as he watched Matthew disappear out the door. Perhaps, he thought, he would open his own shop, without Arbeely, and take Matthew as an apprentice. AHMAD AND MOUNSEF, METALSMITHING. Arbeely was out on one of his occasional errands, negotiating a better price from a supplier, and it felt good to be alone, without the man's grumpy silences. He bent to his work again, feeling a sliver of something that might be contentment.

The door flew open.

It was Matthew, pale with panic. He ran to the Djinni and grabbed his arm, his entire body a plea; and the Djinni found himself pulled onto his feet, and out the door.

The boy dragged him through the street at a run. From the corner of his eye, the Djinni saw Maryam Faddoul look up startled from a conversation at a sidewalk table, watching them dart past carts and pedestrians. They went up the steps of Matthew's building, through the lobby—the tin ceiling flashed above them—and up and up, to the fourth floor. One of the hallway doors hung open, and Matthew ran through it. The room beyond was dim and close, the curtains heavily shaded. The Djinni braced himself and followed Matthew.

A woman lay crumpled on the floor, her face to the bare wooden boards. Matthew ran to her side, shook her arm—there was no response—and looked up at the Djinni, silently begging him.

Carefully the Djinni lifted the woman from the floor and turned her over. She weighed barely more than a child. Even he could see that she was extremely ill. Her eyes were closed, her skin sallow, except for a livid raised blush that spread across her cheeks and nose. Surely that wasn't normal? Beneath it, her face had the same delicate features as Matthew's.

"This is your mother?" A nod, impatient: *yes, of course! Please help her!*

What could he do? Why had Matthew come to *him*? At a complete loss, he laid the woman on the couch and bent an ear to her chest. There was a heartbeat, but far too faint. Sweat ran down her forehead; her skin was nearly as warm as his own. He felt her take a struggling breath, and then another. His own body tensed in response, as though trying to help—but no, that was useless, what was he supposed to *do*?

Footsteps on the stair; and then Maryam ran in, quickly taking in the tableau. Until that moment he'd felt nothing for Maryam Faddoul but wary dislike, but now he felt a wash of relief. "I think she's dying," he told her, the statement somehow a plea.

Maryam only hesitated a moment. "Stay here with Matthew," she said. "I'll fetch a doctor." And she was gone again.

The woman's neck was bent at an awkward angle. He placed a pillow under her head, hoping that might help. Matthew ran from the room, and the Djinni wondered if the boy was too frightened to watch; but then he reappeared, carrying a small paper packet and a glass of water. The Djinni stared while Matthew measured out a spoonful of white powder from the packet and poured it into the water. This was . . . medicine? The boy stirred for a few moments, then held the glass up to the dim lamplight, squinting at it with a critical eye. The gesture spoke of endless repetition. Matthew struggled to lift his mother's head from the sofa and the Djinni quickly maneuvered her into a sitting position. He took the glass from Matthew and tilted it to her lips. She sipped at it weakly, then began to cough and splutter. He wiped the water away, and looked to Matthew; urgently the boy gestured, *more*. He tried to coax her to drink again, but she had sunk back into unconsciousness.

More footsteps on the stair—and then a silver-haired man was in the parlor, carrying a leather satchel. "Move aside, please," he said, and the Djinni retreated into a corner. Wordlessly the man—a doctor, the Djinni surmised—examined the rash on her face, then listened to her breathing. Grasping her wrist in one hand, he removed his pocket watch and timed her pulse. After a few long moments he put the watch away. "Is this woman in your care?" he asked the Djinni.

"No," the Djinni said at once. "I'm—I don't know her."

Instantly the doctor's attention turned to Matthew. "You're her son?" A nod. "What were you giving her just now?" Matthew handed him the packet; the doctor examined it, dipped a finger in the powder and tasted it. Then he frowned. "Acetanilide," he said. "Headache powder. This the only medicine she takes? Nothing else?" Another nod.

Maryam ran in carrying a bucket. "I brought ice," she said.

"Good," said the doctor. "We'll need it." To Matthew he asked, "Was she seeing a physician?" Matthew whispered a name, and the man's mouth tightened in distaste. He pulled his wallet from his pocket, removed a bill. "Fetch him," he said. "If he doesn't want to come, give him this. But don't tell him I'm here." And then Matthew was gone again, running out the door.

The Djinni stood frozen in the corner. He didn't know Matthew's mother. He didn't even know her name. He wanted desperately to leave but couldn't bring himself to move. He watched as Maryam placed a cold cloth on the woman's forehead and murmured quiet words. The woman's eyes moved beneath her lids. From his satchel the doctor extracted a vial of clear liquid, and a cylinder with a needle at one end. He performed some maneuver between vial and cylinder—again that sense of an action endlessly practiced—and positioned the needle's tip at the inside of her elbow. Maryam winced and turned away.

The Djinni watched as the needle disappeared into the woman's arm. "What is that?"

"Quinine," said the doctor. He pulled the needle out again, leaving only the barest drop of blood. It seemed an illusion, a conjurer's trick.

"What about the powder?"

"If she took enough of it," the doctor muttered, "it might relieve her headache."

They sat in tense silence, listening to the sick woman's shallow breaths. The Djinni looked around, seeing the place for the first time. The room was so small it sent his skin crawling. The furnishings were worn and dilapidated. Dusty paper flowers stood in a vase on the mantelpiece, beneath a faded watercolor of a hillside village. Heavy curtains were tacked to the window frames, as though to block out every last ounce of sunlight.

This was where Matthew lived. It wasn't what the Djinni had pictured. He'd pictured—what? Nothing. He'd never thought to picture anything at all.

"Thank you for coming, Dr. Joubran," Maryam said.

The man nodded, then looked up at the Djinni, his sharp eyes curious. "You're Boutros Arbeely's partner, aren't you? The Bedouin."

"Ahmad," the Djinni muttered.

"You're the one who found her?"

"Matthew found her. He brought me here. I've never met her before."

At last Matthew returned, trailing a shabbily dressed man who carried his own leather satchel. The man cringed at the sight of Dr. Joubran. It looked like he might flee, but Maryam quickly rose and blocked his path.

"You've been treating this woman, is that correct?" said Dr. Joubran. "What, if I might ask, was your diagnosis?"

The man shuffled nervously. "She complained of headaches, aching joints, and fevers. I suspected nervous hypochondria, but prescribed acetanilide."

"I suppose you've never seen a case of *lupus erythematosus* before?"

The man blinked. "Lupus?"

"One look at her face should have been enough!"

The man leaned forward and peered in confusion.

"Get out of here," the doctor said. "Go and pray for her." And the man slunk away down the stairs.

"Useless charlatan." Dr. Joubran reached for the needle and vial again. Seeing this, Maryam said, "Come with me, Matthew, let's fetch your mother more ice," and led the boy from the room.

The Djinni watched the needle disappear again, this time into the skin of her stomach. It made him strangely dizzy. He lowered himself into a chair. "And that will make her better?" he asked.

"It's possible," the doctor said. "But not likely. She's too far advanced. Her organs are failing." He picked up the woman's hand and pressed a finger to the back of her palm; for a few moments, her skin kept an impression of the fingerprint. "You see? Her body is filling with fluid, and it's pressing against her lungs. Soon it will reach her heart." He took out his watch again, held her wrist, and then said, "I'll ask Maryam to send for a priest."

The commotion had not gone unnoticed by the neighbors. Timidly a woman poked her head inside. She and Maryam whispered together, and the woman withdrew. Door knocks sounded up and down the hall. Slowly and silently, the room began to fill with women. They brought plates and bowls of food, bread and rice and glasses of milk. They brought chairs and sewing baskets. Solemnly they settled in, unspeaking.

Maryam's husband, Sayeed, appeared as well, and the Djinni watched the two share quiet words. How, he wondered, was their regard for each other so very evident, when they did not embrace, didn't even so much as touch? Sayeed left again, clearly on some errand; and the Djinni felt freshly superfluous, an obstruction in the room.

A weight fell against his leg. It was Matthew. The boy was sitting at his feet and had fallen asleep. Maryam woke him gently. "Matthew? Perhaps you should go to bed." But the boy shook his head, then reached up and gripped the Djinni's hand, as though for protection. She seemed startled for a moment, even wounded; but then she sighed and moved away.

Sayeed Faddoul returned, accompanied by a young priest dressed in long black robes, his face plump above a squarely cut beard. One by one the women stood and bowed to him, and he made a sign above their heads. After a moment's hesitation, he made the sign above the Djinni's as well. He began to speak quiet words, a prayer of some sort. The women bowed their heads; the doctor took Nadia's hand.

The Djinni wondered, if he were on the verge of death, who would come to help him? Arbeely? Maryam? Would they call a priest? Would his neighbors, with whom he'd never exchanged a word, come to his tiny room and keep watch? And how would anyone know to tell the Golem?

It was almost midnight when Nadia Mounsef took her last breath and let it out in a long, thin sigh. The doctor looked at his watch and made a note. Many of the women started to cry. The priest began to pray again. The Djinni stared at the woman's face. He could point to no difference, yet she was entirely changed.

The priest finished his prayer. A pause, a silence; and then the room began to stir. Maryam and the other women gathered near the door, murmuring together. The Djinni heard the word *Matthew* once, twice. A few of them glanced across at him, at the small sleeping form at his side, still clutching his hand. He realized Matthew had slept through his own mother's death. Someone would have to wake him. Would have to tell him.

Carefully the Djinni gathered Matthew in his arms and stood. The knot of women fell silent as he approached. He handed the sleeping boy to Maryam—she took him with a look of surprise—and walked out the door.

On the street, he walked not caring where he went. Every fiber of his being yearned to turn east, to go to the window on Broome, to stand underneath it until she came down to meet him. He would wait there a day, a week, a month. The longing for her, as stark as any he'd ever felt, brought a confused anger; with an effort he turned his steps to the shop. He had left the fire going in the forge. Arbeely would be furious if he knew.

An envelope jutted from the doorframe of the shop, where it had been wedged into a crack. Carefully he removed it. *Ahmad* was written on the front, in Hebrew characters, in a woman's hand.

He tore it open and drew out the letter inside. But within moments his brief hope turned to confusion, then irritation, and finally a swift, incredulous anger.

> Mr. Ahmad:
>
> My name is Anna. We met at the Grand Casino. I remembered that you speak Yiddish, so I hope that you can read it as well. I doubt that you've forgotten what happened that night in the alley. I haven't forgotten it either.
>
> My life hasn't been easy since then. My baby is coming soon and I have no one to turn to. I can't go home to my parents. I have no money and no one will hire me. I am asking you for one hundred dollars. Please bring the money to the corner of Hester and Chrystie Streets at noon tomorrow. The building on the southwest corner has a flowerpot at the top of the stoop. Put the envelope underneath the pot and then leave. I will be watching you.
>
> If you don't bring the money, I will go to the police and tell them the truth. I will say it was Chava who attacked Irving, and tell them where they can find her. I'm not a bad person, but I am desperate, and I must take care of myself and my baby.
> Sincerely,
>
> Anna Blumberg

"Joseph Schall came by the bakery today," the Golem said.

"Did he?" Michael helped himself to more noodle pudding. "Oh, the macaroons! I nearly forgot." He smiled at his wife. "Thank you, they were delicious."

"Mr. Schall's an interesting man," she said. "Can you tell me more about him?"

"Joseph?" His brow furrowed in puzzlement. "What do you want to know?"

"Anything, I suppose. Where he's from, or what he used to do for a living. Does he have any family here?"

She'd meant to feign only a nonchalant interest, but already Michael was beginning to smile. "Chava, you sound like the board at Ellis Island!"

"It's just that I know so little about him, except that he reminds you of your uncle. And you think very highly of him."

"I do indeed. Sometimes I think he's the only thing holding the House together." He chewed for a moment, thinking. "He's Polish. From somewhere near Danzig, I think." Then he laughed. "You know, now that you ask, I know almost nothing about him. He must have been a scholar at one point, if not a rabbi. At least, he talks like one. He never married, and he has no family in America."

"I wonder why he came here, then."

"Times are hard in Europe, you know that as well as anyone."

"Yes, but the elderly are usually set in their ways. To come to a strange country all alone, and agree to live in the Sheltering House, and work so hard, for so little—"

"I *do* pay him, you know," said Michael.

"I only meant that coming to New York must have filled some great desire in him. Or perhaps there was a reason he couldn't stay in Europe."

He gave her a concerned look. "Are you implying that he was running away from something?"

"No, of course not! He's a puzzle, that's all."

"Not as much as others I could name."

She laughed at this, as he'd meant her to, and began clearing the dishes. She hadn't been careful enough; he still wondered at her motive. Well, maybe that was for the best. Perhaps he'd keep a closer eye on Schall, and tell her if he did anything strange.

Michael had a faraway look in his eye. "He asked me about Uncle Avram once," he said.

The Golem paused, a dish in her hand. "He did?"

"About his library, actually. He was looking for a particular book. One from his school days, he said."

"Did he say which book?"

"No, I told him I'd given them all away. He seemed rather disappointed. Do you know, it's the one time I've regretted doing it." He smiled. "But can you imagine, living here with all those books? What would we *do* with them?"

"We'd have to get rid of the bed," she said, and he laughed.

That night she lay next to him, once again feigning sleep, and thought about Joseph Schall. Was there something sinister in his asking about the Rabbi's books? Or was she now creating suspicions from thin air? There were any number of private Jewish libraries on the Lower East Side; perhaps she could volunteer to help find what he was looking for. No, that would seem too strange an offer. She'd have to rely on Michael. Besides, Joseph Schall was likely just a peculiar old man. She was merely inventing distractions for herself.

She turned over, trying to find a more comfortable position. It was barely one in the morning, and already her legs were beginning to ache. The worst of the summer's heat had passed, and most of the building's residents were enjoying a pleasant night's sleep. Only a few remained awake to trouble her with their thoughts. Outside, a man was strolling down the street, enjoying the night air, at ease with himself and his life. He wanted no more than to walk until the sun rose. Beneath a lamppost he stopped to roll a cigarette.

A tentative hope rose inside her.

The man's thoughts turned to frustration as he searched his pockets for his matches. At last he found them, lit his cigarette, and moved on.

She scolded herself for her foolishness. Of course it wasn't him. If it *had* been, she wouldn't have felt him at all. He didn't know where she lived now, had no idea she was married. She would never see him again.

"Chava!"

Oh, no. Michael had woken, terrified. She was too still. She'd forgotten to breathe.

She turned, feigned grogginess: "What is it? What's wrong?"

His eyes were wide with panic. "I thought—for a moment I thought—" Then he sighed. "I'm sorry. It was nothing. A nightmare."

"It's all right. Shhh, go back to sleep."

He wrapped his arms around her, his chest to her back. She twined her fingers in his, pulling them away from where her heart would be. Together they lay until dawn, the Golem caught inside Michael's arms, counting the minutes as they passed.

The remnants of Michael's nightmare still dogged him the next morning, coloring his thoughts. He'd woken—or thought he'd woken—to find his wife lifeless beside him, still as marble. But then she was herself again, alive and breathing. Strange, how dream and reality could merge so seamlessly. He wondered where the dream had come from. There must have been a folktale along those lines, something his mother or his aunt had once told him: a corpse-woman or sinister wooden changeling.

He watched his wife move about the kitchen. "Were you able to sleep at all?"

She gave him a distracted smile. "A bit, I suppose."

"Shall I pick up anything for supper? Some liver from the butcher's?"

"It's not too expensive?"

"Oh, I think we can afford it once in a while." He smiled, reached for her, and kissed her. "Besides, we need to keep you strong."

In case we should start a family, he nearly added, but held back at the last moment. He'd never asked her if she wanted children. It was one of the many conversations they'd passed over on their way to the altar. They would have to discuss it, and soon. Not just yet, though—already he was late to work. He kissed her once more, and left.

He was halfway to the Sheltering House when he recalled Chava's questions about Joseph Schall. It was of a piece, somehow, with his nightmare—folktales, childhood stories . . . Yes, of course: Joseph was looking for a book from when he was a schoolboy. And he'd hoped Michael's uncle might have owned it. He remembered, on that last night of shivah, finding his uncle's satchel of old books and placing them in the bookcase. If he'd known, he might have kept them—perhaps one of them had been the book that Joseph wanted. . . .

He frowned. Hadn't he found a stack of his uncle's papers as well, tossed them into that satchel and brought them home? The memory had the dreamlike quality of illness—it was right before he'd been sent to Swinburne—but yes, he was certain that this had actually happened. What had he done with the satchel? It wasn't at home, surely—they had so few things, he would have seen it. Could it still be at his old building?

He was already late to work, but the memory of the satchel and the papers had seized hold of his thoughts. And his former tenement was only a few streets away. Quickly he changed course.

At the old building, one of his erstwhile roommates opened the door, blinking owlishly, still half in slumber. *A leather satchel? Full of papers? Let me see—maybe there's something like that around . . .* And there it was, hidden in a pile of laundry beneath an occasional table. Exactly where Michael had left it, months before. He took it to the Sheltering House, not wanting to open it until he could be alone. He'd kept so few of his uncle's things that even though the papers would be of no practical use, they seemed nonetheless precious.

At the House, he checked with the staff to make certain that the morning's chaos was still at a manageable level. Satisfied, he closed his office door and opened the satchel.

Instantly his excitement faded. The papers seemed to be notes on some mystical project. He flipped through diagrams, concentric circles and spirals and sunbursts, all scattered about with Hebrew letters. Here and there the esoteric scribbles were interspersed with comments in Yiddish, reporting on his progress. He flipped through the pages, feeling little interest, only fresh sorrow. He'd thought his uncle to be more sensible than to go in for this sort of thing.

Then a sentence caught him, and stopped him cold.

I have named her Chava.

He stared at the words, at the familiar handwriting. He took in the date at the top of the page, not more than a year past. Slowly he turned back to the beginning.

Who am I to destroy her? She's no less innocent than any other newborn . . .

The incident with the knish: she hears others' desires and fears, and they overwhelm her. How to counteract? Training, discipline. Must apply to my own mind as well, or risk causing havoc.

How did her creator instill her mental qualities, her personality? A complicated task . . . Just the power of speech alone requires some degree of free will. Perhaps only within certain boundaries, a middle ground between autonomy and enslavement? Yes, true of all of us, but not nearly so precarious a balance, or so dangerous to miscalculate.

Have resisted testing her physical strength, afraid of where it might lead. But today she picked up a corner of the brass bed-frame to sweep beneath it, as easily as I would lift a tea-kettle.

An experiment today: a walk alone, for five blocks. She performed admirably.

Nights are hardest for her. What would I do, if I didn't need sleep, and was disinterested in reading? My own sleep has been poor lately—always the fears for her future, for the safety of others. She must know, of course, but we do not speak of it.

Her mental discipline is improving. Another walk on her own, to the store and back, without incident. Observation: of all the desires she must condition herself to ignore, none are sexual in nature. Too consistent to be coincidence, unless she's simply not telling me, to protect my modesty. Did her creator, knowing he was building a man's wife, make her resistant to others' advances? Would ensure fidelity—and of course she'd have to respond to her master, by force of their binding. A terrible, sickening thought. Cannot bring myself to broach the subject aloud.

Living arrangement growing uncomfortable. Must find her an occupation. Seamstress? Laundress? Certainly she needs physical activity. If only women could be bricklayers, stevedores . . .

Will she ever be capable of real love, of happiness? Beginning to hope so, against my own better judgment.

Took her to meet Michael today, at the Sheltering House. She did well, though perhaps a bit stiff, and had difficulty ignoring the men's thoughts. Still, I believe she is ready for some measure of independence. Michael, clever as always, suggested Radzin's.

I have named her Chava. Signifying life. A reminder to myself.

Michael put down the paper with a shaking hand. His uncle had gone insane. That was the only explanation. She was a woman, a living woman. She was his *wife*. She was quiet, kind, considerate. An exemplary woman, an excellent cook and housekeeper.

She rarely slept. She always seemed to know what he was thinking.

A torrent of small details began to fill his mind, as though his uncle's words had broken a secret dam. The coolness of her skin. The way she listened with her entire body, as though hearing something beyond sound. Her uncanny habit of anticipating his every need. The rarity of her laugh. The distance in her eyes.

No. He struggled against the flood, ordering himself to be sensible. His uncle was suggesting—what? That she was a creature of some kind? That his nightmare was real?

There were only a few sheets of paper left. He didn't want to read any more—he was beginning to feel sick—but his hand, mutinous, turned the pages. His uncle had begun to simply scribble furiously, like a student cramming for an exam. Ideas were circled, crossed out, rewritten. *Check against fragment from Alphabet of Akiba ben Joseph, then compare with theory of Abba ben Joseph bar Hama. Incompatible? Is there precedence?* As he turned the pages, the handwriting grew more slapdash, the words scattered across the page in haste or fatigue.

On the last page, only two lines were written. One was a long, unbroken stream of letters. And above it, underlined, his uncle's hand shaking with effort:

To Bind a Golem to a New Master

Night was falling in the desert. It woke the serpents and the voles and brought them out from their hiding places, giving fresh meat to the falcons. It flattened the hills and stones, so that from its mouth, ibn Malik's cave seemed an endless abscess in the earth. As the far horizon dimmed, Abu Yusuf built a fire just outside the cave, wrapped himself in sheep hides against the coming cold, and tried not to imagine what might be happening in the darkness behind him.

Ibn Malik, it seemed, had not been exaggerating when he said he'd been waiting for this all his life. "Most djinn are inferior things," he'd told Abu Yusuf as they went deeper and deeper into the warren of caves, pausing only to light the greasy torches set into the passage walls. "*Ifrits, ghuls*, even the minor and middling djinn themselves—I could capture a hundred of them if I wished, but why take the trouble? Dull and stupid, easily distracted, what use is such a servant? But a powerful djinni—oh, that is something very different."

Abu Yusuf was only half listening, concentrating instead on carrying the still-unconscious Fadwa through the narrow, twisting corridor. Some of the passages were barely wide enough for a man, and Abu Yusuf, who'd lived his whole life under the open sky, felt a creeping horror, an urge to turn and run.

"I assume you're familiar with the stories of King Sulayman," said ibn Malik, and Abu Yusuf chose not to dignify this with a reply: only a wild orphan might be ignorant of the tales. "They have all been embellished, of course, but at their heart they're mainly true. The magic granted to Sulayman allowed him to control even the strongest of the djinn, and use them to his kingdom's benefit. When Sulayman died, the magic disappeared with him. Or, rather, most of it disappeared." Ibn Malik glanced back at Abu Yusuf. "I have spent the last thirty years combing the desert for the remnants of that magic. And now, you have brought me the key."

Abu Yusuf looked down at the silent girl in his arms.

"Not your daughter—what's *inside* her. The spark that the Djinni left behind. If we harness it properly, we can use it to find him, and control him."

"And that's why you say she can't be healed yet."

"Of course," ibn Malik said, the words floating over his shoulder. "If we lose the spark, we lose the key."

Abu Yusuf stopped walking. After a moment ibn Malik realized he was no longer being followed, and turned around. With his torch held above his head, he looked like a glowing skeleton, an image that his calm smile did little to alter. "I understand," he said. "Why should you help ibn Malik, that insane old wizard? What do you care whether he finds this djinni or not? You have no taste for revenge, and rightly so— revenge for its own sake is worse than useless. You want nothing more than to heal your daughter, pay the price, and ride back to your tent, to your own bed and your sleeping wife." The torchlight shone in his eyes, like a djinni-spark of his own. "Did you know that next summer will bring the worst drought the Bedu have seen in generations? It will last years, and turn every grazing field between here and the Ghouta to dust. This is no divination, no prophecy. The signs are there for anyone to read, in the movements of the moon and sun, the patterns of snakes, the formations of birds. All point to disaster. Unless, of course, you are prepared."

Abu Yusuf tightened his grip on his daughter. The words might be a lie, to coerce him or throw him off his guard—but his stomach told him they were the truth. Perhaps he was not as skilled at reading the signs as ibn Malik, but he realized now that he had known, in a way beyond knowing. Maybe that was why he had kept Fadwa at home instead of sending her away to a new husband, a new clan, where she would be a stranger in their eyes, the newest mouth to feed. Where she might give birth only to watch her child wither and die.

Keeping his voice steady, he said, "And what has this to do with the Djinni?"

"Use your imagination, Abu Yusuf. Think of what a bound djinni could do for your clan. Why risk life and limb scouting for water, when he could do it for you? Why huddle against the wind in a ragged tent, when you might sleep in a djinni-built palace?"

"Oh, so you plan to bind this Djinni to *my* will? Or do you think he will consent to two masters?"

Ibn Malik smiled. "You're right, of course. It would act under my own command, not yours. And now you will wonder why I would trouble myself to protect your family, what incentive I might have. I might tell you, and truthfully, that I care more for the well-being of my fellow Hadid than you think—"

Abu Yusuf snorted.

"—But I sense you would be a hard man to convince, so think on this instead. By all accounts, the djinn under Sulayman's rule loved their master and accepted his yoke joyfully. At least, by all *human* accounts. The djinn tell their own tales, and in them Sulayman is an enslaver, cunning and cruel. It is not clear which of these is the truth. Perhaps they honestly loved Sulayman, or perhaps he bent their minds as well as their wills, and took their love through force. But this I can tell you: the djinni we seek will not love me. He will loathe me with every measure of his being. He will try to escape my service at every opportunity, through magic or trickery. And yet, whatever I command, he must in fact do."

"You wish to keep him occupied," Abu Yusuf said.

"Exactly. A djinni who must carry your sheep back and forth to the Ghouta will have little time for plotting."

Abu Yusuf considered. If he consented to this, then he would be complicit in enslaving another being. A djinni, yes, but a slave nonetheless. And if not . . .

Ibn Malik was watching him carefully. "Would you value a djinni's freedom over your family's lives?" he said quietly. "The Djinni that destroyed your daughter's mind, no less?"

"You said that revenge is worse than useless."

"Revenge for its own sake, yes. But if it can be gained along the way . . ." Again the jackal's grin.

Abu Yusuf wondered, did he truly have a choice? Already Fadwa's life was in the wizard's hands. If he refused, and went back home with his raving daughter, what would he say to Fatim? Would he subject everyone he loved to ruin, just to preserve his own sense of honor? He asked, "Why take the time to convince me? If I disagree you could simply kill me, take Fadwa, and do whatever you like."

Ibn Malik raised an eyebrow. "True. But I prefer reason and agreement. Allies are much more useful than bodies."

The last of the linked caverns in the hillside was also one of the largest. Its corners were littered with scavenged items of every kind: singed hides and sheep bones, heaps of old metal ornaments, pitted sword-blades, clay jars and dried herbs. In a large cavity at the center of the cavern, ibn Malik had built a fire pit surrounded by a high ring of rough stones. Nearby stood an enormous, tablelike boulder. Presumably the wizard had maneuvered it into the cavern, though Abu Yusuf had no idea how. It was scarred and cracked in places, and covered with dark sooty streaks. Was it an anvil?

He watched ibn Malik as he scuttled here and there, fetching pots and powders and pieces of metal. From some recess he drew out a leather roll, and unwound it to reveal a collection of metal tools: hide-wrapped tongs, curved black hooks, blunt hammers, needle-thin awls. Abu Yusuf paled to see them, and ibn Malik chuckled. "They're for metalwork, not your daughter," the wizard said. With them, he explained, he would forge the instruments they would use to capture the Djinni: a flask to contain him, and a cuff to bind and keep him in human form. "For the flask, copper, I think," said ibn Malik, sorting through his stores. "And iron for the cuff."

"But the djinn can't abide the touch of iron."

"All the better to control him."

The forging, ibn Malik said, would take a day, possibly more. "Take your daughter, and wait outside the caves," he said. "When night falls, build a fire, and don't travel outside its light until sunrise. There are things in the desert I've angered over the years. It would be a shame if they attacked you by mistake."

Abu Yusuf unloaded his supplies from his horse's panniers and set up camp at the mouth of the cave. He created a makeshift pallet for Fadwa and covered her with hides and blankets, hoping their weight would keep her still. The sedative ibn Malik had given her seemed to be wearing off—she stirred occasionally, and muttered to herself. He gathered enough brush and kindling to last until dawn, built a considerable blaze, and settled in, wondering if he should believe ibn Malik's warning about the fire. More likely the wizard wanted to keep him from sneaking away before dawn. But as the sky deepened to blues and purples and the first stars emerged, Abu Yusuf listened to the wind curling along the cliffs and the soft scufflings of unseen creatures, and set more kindling on the flames.

He spent the night tending the fire, watching his daughter, and listening to the desert. Occasionally he caught the edge of some noise in the cave behind him: a high ringing echo of metal on metal, and once a faraway voice that spoke in gibberish. As morning grew closer he slept a few minutes at a time, drifting between dreams. Dawn arrived, and finally Abu Yusuf allowed himself to fall truly asleep.

He startled awake a little while later, disoriented and groggy, his body aching. No sound came from the cave behind him. Fadwa was still trapped beneath the pile of blankets but had freed her arms, and was reaching out into the sky, groping with her fingers. She was, he realized, trying to grab the sun. Quickly he wrapped a cloth around her eyes, hoping she hadn't blinded herself. He fed her as much yogurt as she would eat—it would spoil soon, no use in holding any back—and chewed on a few strips of dried meat. He thought of Fatim, waiting for him at home.

Footsteps sounded behind him. He got to his feet just as ibn Malik emerged from the cave.

At the sight of him Abu Yusuf took an involuntary step back, nearly into the fire's ashes. Ibn Malik's eyes were glittering like jewels in their sockets. The air around him seemed to vibrate with heat. In his hands he carried two objects: a copper flask, and an iron cuff.

"It is finished," the wizard said. "And now, we find him."

23.

It was not yet eight in the morning, and already the sidewalk in front of the Faddouls' establishment was crowded with customers. The pleasant weather had turned humid. The men at the coffeehouse tables mopped their brows with their handkerchiefs, and unstuck their shirt collars from their necks.

Mahmoud Saleh mixed eggs and sugar and milk in his churn, then added ice and salt. He affixed the lid and turned the crank until it felt right. Already an impatient line of school-bound children stood before him, trading taunts and pulling pigtails. Saleh scooped ice cream into tin dishes, kept his eyes on the churn until a whisper of skirts caught his ear.

"Good morning, Mahmoud," Maryam said.

He grunted his hello.

"It's going to be hot today," she said. "And it might rain. Come inside if you need anything."

Her words were familiar; what was new and surprising was her tone. She sounded exhausted, even defeated. He made no comment, only scooped more ice cream, trading it for coins warmed by small fingers.

More footsteps: another child joined the line. And now the giggling and teasing turned to silence. A girl whispered to her neighbor; someone else whispered back. Saleh heard the word *mother* and the word *dead*. The one who'd caused the silence came to the front of the line, and Saleh saw a boy's short pants and pale knees. Saleh gave him his ice cream, received the barest whisper of a *thank you* in return.

Maryam said, "One moment, Matthew." And then in a lower voice: "Are you certain you want to go to school? I could come with you and speak to your teacher . . ." A quiet answer, and then Maryam's sigh. "Well then, don't stay out too long afterward. Supper will be at five.

We'll talk more then." A movement—perhaps a tentative attempt at a hug?—but the boy was already gone, soft footsteps lost in the noise of the street.

Curious despite himself, Saleh went on with his labors. There were only a few more stragglers; those who'd played truant would approach him when Maryam had gone. The line dwindled, ended—but Maryam was still at his side. Likely this meant that she wanted to talk.

At length she said, "That boy worries me so."

As he'd thought. "Who is he?"

"Matthew Mounsef. Nadia Mounsef's son. She died, last night. Sayeed and I are caring for him until we can contact his mother's family."

He nodded. Were she anyone else, the idea of a Maronite woman taking in an Eastern Orthodox child would have made for scandal, even outrage. But not Maryam. One day, he would work out how she managed it.

"He was asleep when Nadia died. I had to be the one to tell him." A pause, and then, hesitant: "Do you think he hates me now?"

Saleh thought back to the mothers he'd seen die, and the children who'd blamed him for not saving them. "No," Saleh said. "Not you."

"I'm no replacement for Nadia, I know. I thought he should stay home from school, but there's only so much I can presume. And I have little experience at caring for children." This last, with a self-conscious offhandedness. After a minute Maryam said, "Have I ever told about how I nearly died, when I was a baby?"

Saleh shook his head.

"I caught a terrible fever, and the doctor told my mother I had little chance. He told her to take me to the Shrine of Saint George, in Jounieh."

Saleh frowned at the thought of a doctor offering this advice. "I know," Maryam said, "but she was desperate. Do you know this shrine?" He shook his head. "It's a pool, in a cave above Jounieh Bay. Where Saint George washed his spear, after slaying the dragon. She took me to the cave, and she lit a candle and dipped me in the water. It was spring then, and the water was freezing cold. The moment I touched the water, I started to howl. And she cried, because it was the first real noise I'd made in days. She knew then that I'd be all right. She told me this story over and over—that Saint George had answered her prayers, and saved my life."

Saleh could think of any number of explanations for the miraculous recovery. The doctor had made a poor diagnosis; or else the cold water had broken the fever. But he said nothing.

"Childless women go to the shrine too," Maryam said. "Sometimes I think . . . But I don't want to ask for his help twice. I feel it would be greedy of me."

"No it wouldn't," Saleh said.

"No? Why not?"

"It's his duty. A good healer can't pick and choose. If he can help, then he must."

A pause. "I hadn't thought of it like that," she said, musing. "A good healer. How I wish Nadia's doctor had been a healer. She might have stood a chance."

"What did she die of?"

"I can't remember the name. It was long, and in Latin. But she had pains that came and went, and fevers, and a rash on her face. Dr. Joubran saw it, and he knew right away."

"*Lupus erythmatosus.*"

He hadn't meant to say it. The words had appeared in his mind, and then their echo was hanging in the thick morning air. He'd give all the coins in his pocket, and the churn as well, to take them back again.

He could feel her looking at him, considering him anew. "Yes," she said slowly. "That was it."

He tried to ignore the feeling of her scrutiny. "The boy," he said, staving off the questions. "No father?"

"Not to speak of. He disappeared, peddling out west."

"His mother's family will take him in?"

"I imagine so. They haven't seen him since he was a baby. It seems cruel to make him leave the only home he's known. But how can he stay here, with no family?" The sigh again. "Maybe he'll do well in a village, a quieter place than this. At least he'll be away from the tinsmith's shop."

"The tinsmith's shop?"

"Oh, I don't mean Boutros! He's a wonderful man, I only wish he would come out of there and *talk* to people. No, it's his partner. The Bedouin." He felt her sudden tension. "Mahmoud, may I tell you something? I've never liked that man. Never. I feel like he's fooling us all somehow, laughing when our backs are turned. And I could not for the life of me tell you why." Her voice had a hardness he'd never heard before. "But Matthew adores him, he'd spend all day in that shop if Boutros let him."

"Don't."

"I'm sorry?"

"Don't let the boy spend time in the shop. With the Bedouin."

"Why not?" She was closer now, leaning toward him; he turned his head away, looking at the gray pavement, the dim shadow of his cart. "Mahmoud, do you know something about him? Is he dangerous?"

"I don't know anything." He picked up the cart's handle. "But I don't like him either. Good day, Maryam."

"Good day," she said faintly. And he trudged away, up the street, the ice cream in the churn long since melted.

Anna Blumberg stood on a baking-hot roof at the corner of Hester and Chrystie, and peered from behind a chimney at the building across the street. She'd chosen the corner carefully: it was well traveled and convenient, and she could see the stoop clearly. But now, drenched in sweat and wreathed in fumes of tar paper, she was beginning to regret her decision. She blotted her face with her sleeve and willed herself not to gag. If all went as planned—if he actually came with the money—then the misery would be worth it.

But what if he didn't? What would she do *then*?

She swallowed against bile and panic, and felt the baby shift below her ribs. Wasn't it past noon already? Her pocket watch was long since pawned, but she'd checked the clock at the pharmacist's—

There. A tall man, walking confidently against the crowd. Even at this distance, she knew him instantly. She watched, heart pounding in her throat, as he reached the bottom of the stoop. He looked around, scanning the traffic and the pushcarts, the men chatting on the sidewalk. She resisted the urge to duck behind the chimney. Even if he thought to look up, the sun would be in his eyes, making her near impossible to see. But then, hadn't she seen him do the impossible already?

From a pocket he took an envelope, thumbed through whatever was inside. She leaned forward, straining to see; but he turned and strolled up the stoop, past the boys that loitered on its bottom steps. At the top he slid the envelope beneath the flowerpot, so graceful and quick that even some-one standing next to him might not have noticed. Without another glance he returned to the sidewalk and disappeared around the corner.

Was that it? Could it possibly be that easy?

She hurried down to the sidewalk, then checked up and down the street. Had he doubled back to catch her? No, he was too tall, too no-ticeable, she would've spotted him instantly. Trying to walk calmly, she crossed the street and climbed the steps, ignoring the boys who snig-gered at her swollen middle. She crouched next to the flowerpot—not nearly so quick as he, not in her condition—and retrieved the envelope with shaking hands. Inside was a stack of five-dollar bills. She counted: twenty of them. It was all there.

Her own building lay farther down the street, and she cried a bit as she walked there, from exhaustion and relief. For weeks now she'd slept on a dirty pallet in a tiny, windowless room with five other women, three Jewish and two Italian. The pallet was so thin and lumpy that she could barely sleep, and the others all hated her because she got up so often to use the water closet. For this luxury she paid the landlady fifteen cents a day. When she woke that morning, she'd had two dollars to her name.

But for now, at least, her newfound luck was holding: none of her roommates were at home. She could take her time and decide where best to hide the money. And after that, she would go to the fancy cafeteria down the street, and treat herself to a plateful of chicken and a baked potato. She lit the candle they kept in a teacup next to the door and began to search for a likely hiding spot: a gap in a floorboard, or a loose bit of plaster.

"I wouldn't," said a voice behind her. "Too easy to discover. Better keep it with you, since you've worked so hard to earn it."

He was standing in the doorway, filling it. In two steps he was inside. He closed the door, slid the bolt home.

Terrified, she scrambled back and struck the wall with her shoulder. The candle fell from its cup and rolled, still lit, across the floor. He bent with that same grace and picked it up, regarding her in its light.

"Sit down, Anna," he said.

She slid down the wall and sat, her arms shielding her stomach. "Please don't hurt me," she whispered.

He gave her a scornful look but said nothing, only glanced about the dark and tiny space. For a moment he seemed uncomfortable, even haunted. "I have no wish to stay here any longer than necessary," he said. "So, let us talk."

He sat down and placed the candle upright between them. Even cross-legged on the floor, he towered over her like a magistrate. She began to cry. "Stop it," he said flatly. "If you have the nerve to blackmail and threaten me, then you can face me without whimpering."

With an effort she calmed herself and wiped her face. She was still clutching the envelope. If she apologized and gave it back, he might forgive her, and go.

Her fingers tightened, rebelling. The money was her future. He'd have to take it from her.

But he seemed uninterested in force, at least for the moment. He said, "How did you find me?"

"Your shop," she said in a thin voice. "I went to Little Syria and walked until I saw your name on the sign. Then I watched until you left, to make sure it was you."

"And you told no one else? You have no accomplices?"

She gave a quavering laugh. "Who would believe me?"

He seemed to accept this, but went on. "Have you blackmailed Chava as well? You might recall *she's* the one who injured your lover. I merely saved his life."

"I remember everything," she said, ire growing despite her terror. "Although *you* might recall that I was being beaten half to death at the time."

"Then answer my question."

She hesitated—and her unguarded face answered for her. "I see," he said. "You're afraid of her. More than of me, it seems."

She swallowed against a dry throat. "What is she?"

"That's her secret. Not mine."

A faint laugh. "And what are *you*?"

"What I am is not your business. You need only know that, like her, I'm dangerous when angered."

"Is that so?" She sat up straighter. "Well, so am I. I meant what I said. I *will* tell the police, if I have to."

"A strange threat, when the money is there in your hand. Or do you mean to repeat your blackmail, when this first payment is spent? Will you rob me little by little, relying on my discretion and goodwill? Because both have reached their limit."

"I'm not a thief," she shot back. "I don't mean to do anything like this ever again. I only need something to live on until the baby is born and I can find work."

"And what will you do with the baby? Keep it here?" He glanced around with distaste.

She shrugged. "Give it away, I suppose. There's plenty of women who want one. Some'll even pay." She affected a carelessness she didn't feel in the least.

"And your lover? He knows of this plan?"

"Don't call him that," she snapped. "He isn't anything to me, or to the baby. Why should I care what he thinks? He told me to get rid of it, that night. Called me a scheming whore and said I couldn't prove it was his. It would be over between us even if Chava hadn't—" Her throat tightened. "But that doesn't make it right, what she did. I heard he can't even walk now. The doctors say he'll be in pain for the rest of his life."

She saw him wince. "Does Chava know this?"

"How should *I* know? I haven't even set foot in the bakery since then. I only heard about her marriage from the papers."

At that, the Djinni went absolutely still. "What marriage?"

"You didn't know?" She stifled a smile, sensing the upper hand at last. "She married again, *very* soon after that night. To a man named Michael Levy." The naked shock on his face emboldened her, made her rash.

"He's a social worker, so of course he's poor as dirt. But she married him anyway, so there must be something between them, don't you think?"

"Be quiet," he whispered.

"And you two seemed so *friendly*, dancing together—"

"*Be quiet!*"

He was staring fixedly at the wall. He wore a look she remembered from her father, whenever he heard bad news: as though he was trying to undo the truth by sheer willpower. In that, then, he was no more than just a man. For a moment, she nearly pitied him.

"The money in your hand," he said, his voice strained. "Consider it a loan. It will be repaid, someday soon. And if any more threats are made against myself—or Chava, or anyone else—they will be answered. My patience with you has reached its end."

With that, he reached out and put a finger to the candle's burning wick. The flame erupted, turning to a white-hot jet of fire. She cried out and turned away, covering her eyes. Almost immediately the candle dimmed to its usual glow; and by the time she could see again, he had disappeared.

Around the corner from the Sheltering House lay a nondescript basement tavern called the Spotted Dog. A popular haunt for dockworkers and day laborers, it was nevertheless a quiet place at midafternoon, while the day shift waited for the whistle and the night shift slept off the morning's excesses. Only two souls were in evidence: the barkeep, who was using the lull to sweep up the old sawdust and spread a new layer; and Michael Levy, who sat at a small table hidden in the shadows.

Michael hadn't gone out drinking in the afternoon since his school years. Back then, his cohorts' ideas had never seemed so right-minded, so *noble*, as when shared over a glass of schnapps. Now, though, he was merely drinking to get drunk. Before him were his uncle's notes, a not-too-clean tumbler, and a bottle of something that called itself whiskey. It had a slippery taste, like rotting apples. The bottle was now a third gone.

He downed another swallow, no longer wincing at the taste. He'd come here to decide what to do with the papers. Written and dated in his uncle's hand, they were a liability and an embarrassment. They said things that could not possibly be true. And yet Michael was beginning to believe them.

He'd told the Sheltering House staff that he felt ill, that he was going home for the day. They'd made sympathetic noises, assuring him that they could manage without him until morning. Joseph Schall in particular had insisted he only return when he felt better. A decent fellow, Joseph. He remembered his wife's probing questions and winced. She'd made it seem as though she suspected him of something; but what if it was the other way around? Had *he* noticed something strange about *her*?

Good God, he would go mad if he continued like this.

He sat up straighter, ignoring the swimming sensations in his brain. Perhaps it would be best to treat the whole thing like a mental exercise. He would assume, purely for the moment, that his uncle had not been in the throes of senility, that the papers weren't merely the fantastic ramblings of a superstitious mind. His own wife was a clay golem with the strength of a dozen men. She knew all his fears and desires. The dead husband—the man she never spoke of—was in fact her master, the man for whom she'd been built.

Suppose all this were true: what, then, would he do about it? Divorce her? Alert the local rabbinate? Go on as though nothing had changed?

He flipped back through his uncle's notes, searching for the line that had had seized him like a fist:

Will she ever be capable of real love, of happiness? Beginning to hope so, against my own better judgment.

Was that not the crux of the matter? Could he stay married to any woman—flesh *or* clay—who wasn't able to love him back?

He took another swig and thought of their first meetings, all those shy smiles and companionable silences. He'd loved her for those silences, as much as for what she said. Before her, he'd met women who thought the way to an intellectual's heart was through an overflow of conversation. But not his wife. He recalled the silent trip to his uncle's graveside. She'd said just enough—she'd seemed to *understand* him, just enough—that he'd hung on every syllable, treated her words like rare jewels. The fact that she was saying exactly what he wanted to hear had only made her remarks seem all the more precious. And when she'd refrained from speaking, he'd taken her silences and filled them with an alluring profundity.

A dull headache was gathering at the front of his skull. He felt the urge to laugh, stifled it with another swig of the liquor. Really, did it matter whether she was woman or golem? Either way, the plain truth remained: he had no idea who his wife really was.

The Djinni stood on the roof of his building, rolling and smoking cigarette after cigarette. The walk back from his meeting with Anna had not even begun to calm him down. He recalled the night he'd stared out Arbeely's window, impatient to begin his exploration of the city. He should have stayed hidden in the shop, blissfully ignorant. He should have stayed in the flask.

She'd married. Well, what of it? Already she'd removed herself from his life. It changed nothing. So why did it still seem to matter?

For weeks now he'd tried to relegate her to some remote corner of his mind, only to have her reemerge when least wanted. Perhaps he was going about it the wrong way; he'd never tried to forget anyone before. But then, he'd never needed to. Relationships between djinn were altogether different. A tryst could be calm or volatile, could last a day or an hour or years on end—and often overlapped with one another in a way that the residents of Little Syria would find completely amoral—but always they were impermanent. Whether begun out of lust, whim, or boredom, each pairing eventually ran its course, and over the years they all had softened equally in his recollection. Why was it not the same with her, when they'd spent so little time together? A few conversations and arguments, nothing more than that—she'd never even been his lover! And yet the memories refused to lie still, to grow weathered and distant, the way he desperately wanted them to.

Married. To Michael Levy. She hadn't even *liked* the man.

He rolled another cigarette, touched the end, inhaled. The iron cuff peeked out from beneath his shirtsleeve, winking at him in the dull afternoon light. He considered it a moment; then carefully, from beneath it, he drew out the square of paper he'd taken from her locket. He opened one fold, so that only a single crease hid the writing from him. The paper was thick and heavy, but still he could see the shadows of the letters on the other side. He could open it and read it. He could drop it into the gutter. He could burn it in his fingers, and scatter the ashes to the wind.

A small hand pulled at his shirt.

He jumped, startled. It was Matthew, manifested from thin air. How did the boy do it? Quickly the Djinni folded the paper again and slipped it back under the cuff.

"I suppose Arbeely sent you," he muttered. He was having a hard time looking at the boy. The morning's events had pushed the previous night from his mind, but now it all came rushing back—the tiny parlor room, Matthew's mother on the couch struggling for breath—and with it an obscure, uncomfortable shame.

The boy shook his head vehemently, then pulled on the Djinni's shirt again. Puzzled, the Djinni leaned down, heard the small, urgent whisper:

"Bring her back!"

Astonished, the Djinni stared at him. Bring her *back*? The woman was dead!

"Who told you I could do this?" he said. But the boy spoke no more, only let his expression of stubborn hope say it all for him.

Slowly the realization dawned on the Djinni. *This* was why Matthew had stayed by his side for these months? Not friendship, or admiration, or a desire to learn? The boy had run to him, instead of Maryam, or Dr. Joubran—someone, *anyone* else, who could've truly helped—and all because he'd thought the Djinni could heal his dying mother, as easily as patching a hole in a teapot!

The day's angers and disappointments roiled inside him. He crouched down, took the boy by his thin shoulders.

"Let me tell you," he said, "about the souls that go on after death, or are brought back against their will. And this is the truth, not some story told to children. Have you ever seen a shadow that flies across the ground, like that of a cloud? Except that when you look up in the sky, there are no clouds to speak of?"

Hesitantly Matthew nodded.

"That is a shade," the Djinni said. "A lost soul. In the desert there are shades of every type of creature. They fly from here to there in perpetual anguish, searching and searching. Can you guess what they are searching for?"

Matthew had gone pale and still. He shook his head.

"They're searching for their bodies. And when they find them—*if* they find them, if their bones haven't long turned to dust—they crouch over them, and weep, and make the most horrible noises. Would you like to know what they do then?"

The boy's frightened eyes were filling with tears. The Djinni felt the first twinge of remorse, but pressed on. "They find the nearest of their kin, and plead with them, asking to help them find rest. But all their kin can hear is a kind of wailing, like a high wind. And all they feel is the cold chill of death." The Djinni gripped the boy's shoulders harder. "Is this what you want, for your own mother? To see her soul go howling down Washington Street, and hear her shrieking like a windstorm? Looking for her bones that lie rotting in the ground? Looking for *you*?"

The boy gave a hiccupping gasp, tore from him, and ran.

The Djinni watched Matthew disappear across the roof, heard his feet clattering down the fire escape. He turned away from the ledge. The boy would go to someone else now: Maryam or Arbeely, or the priest, or one of the sewing women. They would comfort him, dry his tears. And the next time he was in need, he would go to them, and not to him.

Alone, he smoked down the last of his cigarette, letting it crumble to ash between his lips.

Inside the tinsmith's shop, the mood was grim. Maryam had stopped by briefly while the Djinni was away, to give Arbeely the sad news of Nadia's death—a death that apparently the Djinni had witnessed.

"He was here earlier," Arbeely said, confused. "He said nothing of this."

"Boutros, I have no business telling you who to associate with . . . but isn't there something *strange* about him?"

More than you could say, Arbeely thought. "I know he can be difficult—and he's been in a terrible mood, lately—"

"No, it's not that." She hesitated, as if weighing words. "At Nadia's—it was as though he'd never seen someone ill before. He had no idea what to do. He was holding her, and he looked up at me, and for a moment—Boutros, he didn't even seem human." Her eyes turned pleading. "Does that sound awful? Am I making any sense?"

"I think I know what you mean," he said.

Then Maryam had left, and the Djinni had returned from whatever errand he'd run—but still he'd said nothing about Nadia. Watching him now from across the cramped shop, Arbeely wondered what had happened to their feelings of friendship. Perhaps it was simply too unnatural an arrangement to succeed. Wasn't that the moral of the stories he'd been told by his mother, his aunts? That the djinn and their kind were meant to be left alone, far removed from flesh and blood? He'd been blinded by the Djinni's mask of humanity, and had neglected to remind himself that beneath it lay a different creature altogether.

Without warning, the door burst open. It was Maryam again, but she was utterly changed. After a lifetime of empathy and understanding for every soul that had crossed her path, the woman finally looked angry enough to kill.

"You!" She pointed at the Djinni. "Explain yourself!"

The Djinni had risen from his bench; his look of surprise was now replaced by a cold and wary stare. "And what must I explain?"

"Why Matthew Mounsef is now hiding in my storeroom, sobbing and shaking, frightened half to death!"

Arbeely's heart squeezed at the image. He thought he saw the Djinni cringe as well; but then the Djinni said, "Why should I be the cause? Didn't the boy's mother just die? I believe you were there when it happened."

Maryam inhaled sharply, as though slapped. "I don't know who you are," she said, her voice like splintered ice. "You're not who you say you are, that's certain. You've taken in Boutros, because he's too trusting for his own good, and you've taken in this entire street. But you haven't fooled Mahmoud Saleh, and you haven't fooled me. You are dangerous. You have no place here. I knew all this and said nothing, but I won't stay silent any longer. Any man who would tell a seven-year-old boy that his dead mother's soul will come looking for her body, and chase him up and down the street—anyone who would do something so cruel deserves neither compassion nor understanding."

"Oh my God," Arbeely said. "Is that true? Did you really say that to Matthew?"

The Djinni threw him a glance of wounded exasperation, and Arbeely thought he would explain himself. But then he turned back to Maryam and said, "Yes, that is what happened. I did it for my own reasons. Why should I care whether you comprehend them—especially when, as you say, you've disliked me from the start? I never asked for your compassion or understanding, not that you were ever inclined to give them. Neither you, nor Mahmoud Saleh, nor *you* for that matter," he said, looking at Arbeely, "may dictate my actions. My life is my own, and I'll do what I wish."

A held breath of silence. Like two titanic forces of nature, Maryam and the Djinni stared each other down.

"Enough," Arbeely said. "We're through here. Take what's yours and leave."

At first the Djinni seemed not to understand. Then he frowned. "I beg your pardon."

"You heard me. Get out. I dissolve our partnership. You'll do what you wish, but not here. Not anymore."

A hesitation, perplexed. "But—the order for Sam Hosseini isn't finished yet."

"I'll explain to Sam," Arbeely said. "Consider yourself absolved of all responsibility. For you, that shouldn't be difficult."

The Djinni looked from Arbeely's angry glare to the righteous triumph in Maryam's eyes. "You're right," he said. "I'm done here." He put away his tools, then carefully rolled the unfinished necklaces in flannel and placed them atop the worktable. And then, without so much as a backward glance, he was out the door and gone.

Chava,

A number of unavoidable difficulties have arisen at work, and I'm afraid I have to stay for the night. Don't worry about supper, I'll eat at the House. Will see you tomorrow.

Your husband,

Michael

She gave the errand boy a penny and closed the door, then read the note again. Michael had told her once that he'd always fought against staying overnight at the House, afraid that it would become expected of him. She wondered what could have happened, to make him break his rule.

She had only just set the table; now she cleared away the dishes and cups, the bread and schmaltz, the frying pan that sat in anticipation of the liver he'd promised. She paused, her hand on the icebox door. He would expect her to have eaten, of course. Would he notice that there was still as much food as before?

A frustrated anger rose in her—would she always be trying to anticipate his responses? She slammed the icebox shut, harder than she'd meant. If he asked, she would tell him she hadn't been hungry.

She retreated to the parlor, took up her sewing. At least, for one night, she would not have to try to ignore his fears and desires, or lie awake remembering to breathe. She felt her body relaxing at the thought; in the next moment she was seized with guilt. Her husband was working through the night, and all she could think of was her own comfort. Perhaps she should take him supper after all, to show that she was thinking of him.

She put down her needle and thread, then frowned in rebellion and picked them up again. She would stay home. For just one night, she would return to her old life: sewing alone, with a window between herself and the world.

The Djinni was in his room, trying to decide what to take with him.

He was leaving Little Syria. There was nothing left for him there—and what, really, had there ever been? An occupation for his daylight hours, a place to shelter from rain and snow. No more than that. Still, it surprised him, surveying the tiny room, how little he'd accumulated. A few shirts and trousers, two pairs of shoes, a coat. The awful woolen hat that the Golem had insisted on. The cushions on the floor, bought cheaply and with little enthusiasm. A few hand tools that he'd liberated from the shop, intending to bring them back at some point. The jar that held all his money. The necklaces he'd bought from Conroy. The umbrella with the silver handle. And, in a cupboard, his figurines.

He took them out and lined them up on the writing desk. There were birds and mice, tiny insects built from tinplate, a rearing silver cobra with a diamond-patterned hood. The ibis, stubbornly unfinished, its bill still not quite the right shape.

He pocketed the money and the necklaces, and then, after a moment's hesitation, the figurines. Immediately he took the figurines out again, and placed them back on the desk. Let the next tenants make of them what they would. What did he need, besides a roof over his head when it rained? Nothing. Nothing at all.

On the street again, he felt energetic, untethered—as though he were back in the desert, free to go wherever he wished. Why had he partnered with Arbeely in the first place? The old rationales seemed flimsy, cowardly even, compared to this freedom. Where would he go? He glanced up: the sky was turning cloudy. Perhaps he would need somewhere to stay for the night. The Bowery? He hadn't been there in weeks, save to buy necklaces from Conroy.

He passed Matthew's building, and paused. Perhaps, before he left, he would see his ceiling, one last time.

The lobby was dark and cool, the gas jets not yet lit for the evening. Overhead the tinplate desert shone in early twilight. On the wall nearby, someone had hung a framed copy of the newspaper article about the ceiling. *One hopes*, the article declared, *that the ceiling is only the first of many new civic improvements by this distinguished Syrian talent.*

The inverted peaks cast their shadows on the valley floor. His palace, as always, was missing; and he found himself unable to tear his eyes from the spot where it should have been.

All at once his hectic energy drained away. He'd never be completely free of Little Syria, not as long as the ceiling stood. He could rip it down, he supposed, or melt it to a puddle; but the very thought made him cringe. All right, then—they could keep the ceiling. Arbeely would see it, and perhaps remember what the Djinni had done for him and his livelihood. And Matthew—he would see it too.

He returned to the street. Overhead, the clouds were thickening. No more sightseeing; it was time to leave.

On the edge of the neighborhood he passed Saleh, trudging back home with his empty churn. The old man stopped when he saw him, nearly backed himself against the wall.

"Saleh," the Djinni said. "What did you tell Maryam Faddoul?"

There was fear in the old man's eyes, but he said, "Nothing she didn't know already."

The Djinni snorted. Then he dug in his pocket and came up with the key to his room. He tossed it to Saleh, who caught it, surprised. "A farewell present," the Djinni said, and told him the address. "It's paid through the end of the month. I'll be in the Bowery," he added as he walked away, "if anyone should find that they need me."

In his darkened dormitory, Yehudah Schaalman readied himself for another night of hunting. He dressed quietly, padded down the creaking staircase, and crept out the front door.

He'd thought to go north again, back to the park where the dowsing spell had last led him. It seemed less than promising, but what else could he do? He had so little to go on, with these trails appearing and fading at random, like the marks of a restless spirit . . .

The realization exploded through him, and he nearly stopped in his tracks. His quarry, the thing he was looking for: *it was a person.* The Bowery rooftops, the parks—someone was wandering the city, and Schaalman was following him like a bloodhound. It explained why the trails left off the way they did: having reached his destination, the wanderer would then retrace his steps to his home. Which meant that all Schaalman had to do was find a path and follow it back to its source, and there his quarry would be waiting.

He had no sooner reached this conclusion when, as if by reward, a path appeared beneath his feet. He halted, amazed. He was at the corner of Hester and Chrystie, still in the Jewish neighborhood. He'd walked these streets dozens of times—yet now the street corner glowed in his mind, every concrete inch a fascination. His wandering quarry had passed this way so recently it might have been that very day.

He could have danced in the street, but he forced himself to remain calm. He turned in a slow circle. There: the building on the southwest corner, that was the one he wanted. The front stoop was lit with interest—and so, strangely, was the ill-tended flowerpot next to the door. But there the trail ended. The door itself was merely ordinary. So: his quarry had climbed these steps, perhaps for a conversation, or to see if someone was at home, and then set off again. But where?

He wandered down the stoop again, letting his feet direct him. Halfway up the block was another building, shabbier than the first—and at this one, the trail did not stop at the door. Cautiously he entered the lobby, his shoes slipping on filthy tile. The trail drew him up a dark and treacherous staircase that led to a cabbage-smelling hallway, and at last to a particular door. He pressed his ear to the wood, but heard no voices, only what might have been breathing.

As he stood debating whether to knock, someone emerged from the water closet in the stairwell. He retreated down the hallway and watched as a pregnant woman in a white nightgown navigated sleepily toward the very door that had grabbed his interest. The aura that surrounded her was so strong it drew his gaze like a compass-hand. "Excuse me," he said.

He'd spoken quietly, but she jumped nonetheless. "Good God," she panted, one hand to her swollen belly.

"I wonder if you can help me, I'm looking for a friend." He paused to think, plucked a name from the dark. "Chava Levy?"

The woman seemed to shrink from the name. "I haven't seen her in months," she said, fear and suspicion weighing her voice. "Why are you looking here?"

"I was told she might have come this way. By a mutual friend."

"Ahmad? Did *he* send you?"

He took the lead she'd offered. "Yes, Ahmad sent me."

She scowled. "You might have said so. Tell him he won't get his money any more quickly by hounding me. And *you*, old man, you ought to be ashamed of yourself! Frightening a pregnant woman in the dark!"

Her harangue was growing louder. Soon someone would hear, and investigate. The time for subtlety was over. He gripped her wrist, as he had with each of the rabbis. For a moment she tried to pull away; then she went still.

He asked, *Who is Ahmad?*

And before she could open her mouth to reply, a vision shot through his mind: a searing light, an immense singular flame, burning with the strength of an inferno.

He dropped her wrist and stumbled back, trying to rub the light from his eyes. When he could see again, she was watching him with wary suspicion, oblivious to what had happened. "Are you all right?" she asked.

He pushed past her to the staircase, and fled in the darkness.

On the street again, he paused, breathing deeply in the damp air. What *was* that, in her mind? A flame that burned like the fires of Gehenna, a flame that was somehow alive—but she had called it Ahmad, talked about it as though it were a man! How did this make sense? Was there another force at work here, something beyond his own considerable understanding?

Ahmad. He wasn't even sure what sort of name it was.

At the Spotted Dog, the nighttime crowd was turning raucous and un-ruly. Already three patrons had been tossed out for fighting. But Michael, at his table in the corner, was roundly ignored. He wondered what he looked like to the regulars, the muscled factory workers and dockmen. A cowardly, henpecked bureaucrat, afraid to face the long walk home? Not far from the truth, he supposed.

He sifted through his uncle's notes again, his eyes skittering over the formulae and diagrams. He had sent the message to his wife at seven-thirty; it was now passing eleven o'clock. He'd dispensed with the tumbler and was now drinking the dubious whiskey directly from the bottle. Rea-son still insisted that the notes were full of delusions, the products of old age and superstition—but the battlements of his reason were crumbling.

He took one last pull from the bottle, then picked up the papers, stumbled out to the alley, and vomited. It made him feel no better. He wove through the alley and back to the Sheltering House. All was dark and quiet; he'd missed lights-out. In his office, he opened an overflow-ing desk drawer and stuffed his uncle's notes inside. *To Bind a Golem to a New Master*, screamed the one on top. He grimaced and slammed the drawer shut.

The room was spinning. He had nowhere else to go, no destina-tions in his life besides the Sheltering House and his now dubious home. And what about friends? He'd neglected them all, drifted away in a fog of work and exhaustion. There was no one left on whom he could impose, for conversation or a couch to sleep on. He needed someone willing to listen without judging, who could observe with a clear and sympathetic eye.

Joseph. He could talk to Joseph, couldn't he? The man was as close to a friend as he had these days. Even through the alcohol, Michael knew that to wake an employee for a heartfelt outpouring in the middle of the night was beyond the bounds of acceptable behavior. Still, he forged up the stairs to Joseph's dormitory.

Joseph's cot was empty.

He stood in the restless dark, feeling obscurely betrayed. What business could Joseph have elsewhere at this hour? He sat down on the cot. Perhaps Joseph had gone for a walk to escape the dormitory heat. Nevertheless, a prickle of suspicion gathered like an itch. He thought of his wife asking after Joseph, and the measly bits of information he'd been able to tell her. Why had she been so interested in him?

He had never before invaded the privacy of any of his guests. There were men all around him who might wake and watch. But now, with one eye on the hallway door, he rummaged beneath Joseph's cot. His hand encountered the handle of an old-fashioned carpetbag. He drew it from beneath the bed, wincing as it scraped the floor. It smelled old and musty, as though it had been stored beneath innumerable cots for generations. The latch creaked open at his touch. Inside were a few articles of clothing, neatly folded, and an old prayer book. That was all. No photos of relatives, no mementos or trinkets of home. Was this all Joseph owned in the world? Even for the Sheltering House, this was a meager collection. Michael might have felt a surge of pity, except that Joseph's strange absence made the lack of belongings seem sinister—as though the man didn't truly exist.

He knew he should put the carpetbag back and leave, but the liquor and his mood made him feel disinclined to move. He took the prayer book from the bag and began to leaf through it, as though it might tell him what to do. The moonlight caught its edge; and the ordinary prayer book transformed, became ragged and burnt. What he'd thought were prayers were now formulae, spells, incantations.

He turned the pages with growing disbelief. He had come to Joseph for reassurance, and found this instead? His uncle, his wife, and now this: it was as though they were conspiring against him, making him doubt everything he knew to be true.

On one page, smeared with what looked like dried mud, he read, in a slapdash handwriting he recognized as Joseph's:

Rotfeld's desires in a wife: Obedience. Curiosity. Intelligence. Virtuous and modest behavior.

Obedience innate. Intelligence the most difficult. Curiosity the most dangerous—but that is Rotfeld's problem, not mine.

And then, farther on:

She is complete. A fine creation. Rotfeld sails tomorrow for New York.
She will make him an admirable wife, if she doesn't destroy him first.

24.

In the lobby of an otherwise nondescript tenement near the Hudson River docklands, Yehudah Schaalman craned back his grizzled head and stared, perplexed, at an undulating metal ceiling.

He was perhaps half a mile from Hester Street as the crow flies, but it had taken him nearly an hour to come this far. The path had twisted and turned, through back alleyways and up fire escapes to well-traveled rooftops, across plank bridges and down again. At last he'd reached Washington Street, where he faced a baffling profusion of choices. The paths overlaid one another so that every storefront, every alley hummed with interest. He'd walked up and down the street, getting his bearings, until finally the strongest path had pulled him into the tenement with the well-lit lobby. Inside, the spell and the lights had conspired to lift his eyes upward.

He could not have said how long he stood beneath the shining waves and peaks, one hand stretching to the wall for balance. At first he thought it some sort of interesting defect of the building—perhaps the ceiling tiles had melted and begun to drip—before he realized it was a deliberate piece of art.

All at once, as it had for so many other viewers, the ceiling snapped into focus. The world spun—

It was dusk, and he stood on a scorched plain, ringed by distant peaks. The western sun stretched his shadow narrow as a spear, turned his arms to long gnarled branches, his fingers to twigs. Before him lay the late-summer valley, its animal inhabitants beginning to wake. He blinked—and there in the empty valley appeared a beautiful palace made all of glass, its spires and ramparts shining in the last golden rays of the evening.

Something hard and flat struck Schaalman across the face. It was the lobby floor.

He lay there, trying to regain his composure, the tile cool beneath his stinging cheek. Carefully he levered himself up to his hands and knees; the room, thankfully, stayed put. He stood and, shielding his eyes from the ceiling, walked out of the lobby and sat on the front steps, one hand to his throbbing face. The fear he'd felt earlier, in the hallway with the pregnant woman, returned and grew. Yet another phenomenon he could not explain.

He fought down his alarm, and the urge to retreat to the Sheltering House. He felt vulnerable, exposed. Who was his quarry? Was it this mysterious Ahmad? Or the Angel of Death, playing with him?

The pain in his swollen cheek began to dim. He made himself rise from the stoop and continue down the street. The paths danced and wove before him, pulling him toward whatever encounter awaited him next.

Shortly after one in the morning, the Golem abandoned her attempts at sewing. Distraction had made her clumsy, and the shirtwaist she'd been mending now sported a new rip in the bodice. The few waking souls who passed beyond her window were all drunk or had to use the water closet; they only added to her restlessness and anxiety.

Michael's note lay on the table, the paper deeply wrinkled from when she'd crumpled it in frustration. The wording was so unlike him, too formal by half. His usual endearments were conspicuous in their absence. Was there something he wasn't telling her? She thought of their conversation about Joseph Schall. Had Michael run afoul of him some-how? Oh, how she hated bare words on paper! How was she supposed to know the truth, without him there in front of her?

There was no way to calm herself; she'd have to go to the Sheltering House. He might scold her for being out alone so late at night, but she'd explain she was too concerned about him to sleep. She fastened her cloak and left, walking quickly through streets dotted with anonymous, solitary pedestrians, all in search of various forms of release.

The House, from the outside, was dark and quiet. She stood on the sidewalk for a moment, listening. A few of the men were only half-asleep. The rest were sunk in an ocean of dreams, distorted reflections of their longings and fears. She inched the front door open, lifting it on its heavy hinges to keep it from creaking.

The lamp was lit in Michael's office. She crept down the hallway and peered inside the half-gaping door. He had fallen asleep at his desk, slumped forward in his chair. His head lay in the crook of his arm, an open prayer book next to his elbow. He might have been dead, save for the rise and fall of his shoulders. She came closer and crouched down next to him. Why did he smell so strongly of alcohol? "Michael," she murmured. "Michael, wake up."

One hand convulsed, grasping at air. He moaned and pulled himself up. "Chava," he groaned, still half-asleep.

And then he stiffened. His eyes flew open, found her, and focused.

His terror, like that of a cornered animal, hit her square in the chest.

He leapt up from the desk, scattering books and papers, and staggered backward. In his mind she saw a grotesque image: a gigantic woman with a lumbering body and a dark, rough face, her eyes cold in their sockets. Herself, seen in the mirror of his fear.

Oh God—what had happened? She reached for him and he jolted backward again, nearly losing his footing. "Stay away from me," he hissed.

"Michael," she said, but couldn't go on. So many times she'd imagined this scenario, her secret's discovery; and now she found that none of her careful explanations, her sincere apologies, were near to hand. There was only horror and sadness.

"Tell me I'm imagining it!" he yelled. "Tell me I've gone insane!"

No, she realized. She couldn't. She owed him that much. But neither could she bring herself to say the truth out loud. She strained to find words that might suffice. "I never meant to hurt you," she said. "Never."

A bloom of anger pushed Michael's fears aside. She saw his face harden, his hands turn to fists.

She was in no true danger, of course; he was inebriated and had no skill at violence. But her senses reacted nevertheless. Reality began to bleed away into that awful calm. There was time only for one word, forced between clenched teeth.

"*Run*," she told him.

A fresh terror surged through him—and then he did as she'd ordered, his footsteps echoing down the hallway. The heavy front door slammed shut.

She stood alone in Michael's office, trembling, as little by little her control returned. She'd always wondered if she'd be relieved when the truth finally came out; but she would have lived with the strain forever, rather than see Michael run from her. She supposed she should worry about whether he meant to tell anyone, but at the moment she cared little. Let the mob destroy her, if it wanted. At least it would spare her further agony.

She looked around at the chaos she'd created: chair knocked askew, papers spread across on the floor. Numbly she pushed his chair back in place and straightened the mess. She picked up the prayer book she'd glimpsed at his elbow, and it turned into a cascade of loose, half-burnt pages that spilled onto the desk.

In calling forth a demon, one must be certain to know its lineage . . .

The letter chet is one of the alphabet's most powerful, and often misapplied . . .

She frowned. Whose book was this?

She began to turn the damaged pages, skimming the meticulous directions and many-limbed diagrams. It was, she supposed, a type of cookbook, offering lists of ingredients, precise instructions, warnings against mishaps, suggestions for alterations. Except that instead of baking a chicken or a spice cake, the reader could bring about the impossible, could alter Creation itself. Whatever had Michael been doing with this? Had the Rabbi given it to him?

One page, she noticed, was stained at the edges with mud. She read it over—and then again, and again. Stunned, trembling, she turned the page, and read what was written on the reverse.

Obedience. Curiosity. Intelligence. Virtuous and modest behavior.
*   She will make him an admirable wife, if she doesn't destroy him first.*

And in her memory Joseph Schall rose before her, clutching a box of dinner rolls and smiling his secretive smile. *I never doubted you would make an admirable wife.*

Mahmoud Saleh could not sleep, but not for the usual reasons.

He'd waited long past dark to sneak into the Djinni's tenement, the key warm in his sweating hand. The Djinni had given him the key freely—he felt no guilt on that front—but neither did he wish to be labeled a squatter or a thief. He found the door, fumbled the key into the lock. Even in the near pitch-dark, the room had an abandoned, empty feeling. The only light shone from the naked window, a lurid orange glow that illuminated nothing. He walked with outstretched arms, waiting to bump into a chair, a table; but soon his hands touched the far wall. A few candles sat on the sill, and he felt in his overcoat's many pockets for his matches. The light revealed the room as devoid of all furniture, save a writing desk, a wardrobe, and a number of cushions scattered across the floor.

He gathered the cushions together, forming a sort of mattress. When finally he laid himself down, he nearly cried at the comfort. In the morning he would bring up a bucket of water, and wash properly. For now he would merely sleep.

Or so he thought. Hours later, he had to admit that the room had defeated him. It was too quiet, too empty. But then what had he expected, a harem full of houris and a magic lamp for sleeping in? The truth was that in this neat and ordinary room he felt an interloper, a piece of refuse blown in through the window. Resentfully he turned over, sank farther into the cushions. Damn the Djinni, he would *sleep*.

A knock came at the door.

Saleh froze in the darkness. A visitor, this late? What sort of life did that creature lead? He held his breath, willing the room to utter silence. But the knock came again, and with it quiet words in a man's voice, first in a language he didn't understand, and then an inexpert English: "Hello? Please?" A pause. "Ahmad?"

Saleh cursed. He fetched a candle and opened the door. "No Ahmad," he said, staring down at the man's dim and faraway shoes.

A question, in that other language, something that sounded near to German. He shook his head, said *no* again, and decided he'd done enough. Let the man work out his dilemma for himself, whatever it was. He started to close the door again.

One of the man's shoes shot forward, blocking the doorframe.

Saleh jumped back in alarm. The man was pushing his way into the room. Saleh shut his eyes tight and pushed back, opened his mouth to shout for help—but a cool and papery hand grabbed at his wrist, and suddenly he could make no noise at all.

Schaalman peered at the unkempt vagrant who stood rigid in front of him, candle tilted in his frozen grip. *Curious*, he thought. The man had brought a light to the door but would not look at him; his first act of defense had been to close his eyes. Was he blind? Addled in some way?

Schaalman asked, *Who are you?*

The man opened his mouth, moved his lips to speak: but whatever he meant to say was obscured by a thin, high, otherworldly screaming, just on the edge of perception.

Schaalman ground his teeth in frustration. He knew what this meant. He'd seen cases of possession before, half a lifetime ago, in remote Prussian villages and the backwoods of Bavaria. This must be a minor instance, if the man could still speak and function; but even the most paltry demonic fragment would be an unbearable nuisance. The being would take every opportunity to get Schaalman's attention, to beg freedom from its imprisonment. Schaalman had even seen spirits choke their hosts with their tongues, just to gain release. Unless the offender was dealt with, he'd learn nothing but nonsense.

Schaalman weighed his options. It would be quickest to exorcise the thing and be done with it, but the process was not a gentle one. The man would certainly remember it. Any chance of an unobtrusive questioning would be lost.

But he was so close, so very close! And this was no venerated rabbi, but an unwashed vagrant, likely half-mad from his possession. Who would believe the truth, if he tried to tell it? And how could Schaalman afford not to take the risk?

He placed a hand to either side of the man's face, and braced himself.

Mahmoud Saleh only knew that someone, somewhere, was screaming.

A hand was pushing itself into his mind, searching by feel, its fingers sliding between layers of sense and memory. Saleh could only stand rigid and dumb as it burrowed deeper, inch by inch. It paused, and then closed itself about something small and unseen, grasping it in an iron-tight fist; and then slowly, patiently, ripped it out shrieking like a mandrake from the soil.

Saleh tried to collapse, but the paper-skinned hands held him upright. The grip shifted. Long, dry fingers opened his unresisting eyes.

Mahmoud Saleh looked into the man's face.

He was old and thin, his pale skin mottled with age, but his deep-pouched eyes burned with intelligence. A large bruise was blossoming across one cheek. He was frowning in concentration and distaste, like a surgeon elbow deep inside a man's guts. Saleh trembled in his grip.

Who are you? asked the man.

Doctor Mahmoud, part of Saleh replied; another part said, *Ice Cream Saleh.*

Then where is Ahmad?

And before Saleh could think to reply, a memory burst out of him: the Djinni passing him on the sidewalk, tossing him the key. *I'll be in the Bowery, if anyone finds that they need me.*

Abruptly the man let go of Saleh, and he crumpled boneless to the floor. He heard the door close as the man left. The candle rolled from his hand, its wick guttering; and the last thing Saleh thought, before the flame went out and he fell unconscious, was that it had been years since he'd seen a candle burn so brightly.

The Djinni stood on a Bowery rooftop, watching the tattered crowd below. The skies had refused to deliver on their promise of rain; the thick clouds hung low and unmoving over the city like the pale underbelly of some gigantic worm. The rooftop was a patchwork of dirty mattresses, the prostitutes having moved business outdoors, hoping for a breeze.

In the back of his mind sat the nagging sense that he should develop a plan that extended beyond the next quarter-hour. Irritated, he pushed it away. Plans, timetables, contracts—these were all human conceits. He would do what he wished, when he wished. Was that not what he'd told Arbeely? He'd passed Conroy's earlier, had considered going inside. Perhaps he could barter his services, perform odd jobs for silver. No; was that not still servitude of a sort? Besides, why barter at all? In the desert, the silver had simply been there for the taking.

And just like that, the idea took form. He smiled, watching it grow. Why not? It would be a challenging and worthy diversion; it would require all his skill, far more than his siege of Sophia's balcony. And if there was little honor in thieving from a thief, he imagined he would feel little shame in it, either.

Reckless, the Golem said inside him. *Immoral, inexcusable.*

This is how I lived before you, he said. *It's how I'll live again.*

I suppose it will entertain you sufficiently, and that's what matters?

Exactly. Now go and haunt someone else.

The blind and unsettled energy he'd felt earlier in the day was returning. Gladly he gave himself over to it. If he waited, and let himself examine the idea, he might find some reason to hold off. Better, far better, to hurl himself into it headlong.

Saleh came to his senses on the floor of the Djinni's room. His head felt as though someone had scraped it out and used it for a mixing-bowl. He lay there for a moment, trying to remember what had happened. Had he succumbed to one of his fits? No, this felt different, more akin to waking from a nightmare that had already faded, leaving him with only the body's memory of fear. Wait, no: there'd been a knock at the door—he'd answered it—

In the space of a breath, the entire encounter with the stranger came crashing back. He clambered to his feet, then grabbed at the doorknob as his balance wavered. *He could see again!* The room was dimly lit by candles; but oh, still! When had mere shadows ever appeared so rich and full of color? The burning flames were saturated in bright oranges and yellows and thin flickering blues, far too bright to look at for long. The cushions he'd slept on, covered with cheap slubbed cotton, were now masterpieces of shape and texture. He stretched out one hand, touched it with the other: it was exactly where he thought it to be. His face was warm and wet: had he injured himself in the fall? No, he was only crying.

And what of his own face, could he see it now? A mirror, he had to find a mirror! He grabbed the largest of the candles and dashed about the room. In the wardrobe he found only a few articles of clothing, a woolen hat, and, bizarrely, a rich man's silken umbrella, its handle chased in slender silver vines. He admired it for a moment before tossing it back into the wardrobe and resuming his search. What, the creature owned no mirror at all? Didn't he need to shave?

Something sparkled at him from the writing desk.

He brought the candle closer. Arranged on the corner of the desk was a collection of small metal figurines, perhaps a dozen all told. Before, his vision had been too poor to notice them; but now he saw birds, insects, even a tiny cobra, coiled and rearing. Next to the figurines lay a leather-wrapped set of instruments, thin awls and delicate, curved needles, such as a surgeon or dentist might use. Or, he realized, a metalsmith.

He fetched the rest of the candles and set them around the figurines. Some were finished, and polished to a high sheen; others seemed to be works in progress. The snake was wonderfully done, the patterned scales a miracle of steady patience. He marveled at the intricate tin-scrap insects, which suggested rather than described their likenesses: the long limbs and proboscis of a mantis, a beetle's round and glossy carapace. An ibis, on the other hand, looked awkward and off balance—something about the beak, perhaps? He picked it up and examined it. One entire side had been smoothed over, like a mistake erased in frustration.

Tears pricked his eyes again. The figurines were beautiful, would've been so even if they'd not been among the first images to grace his restored sight. They were works of longing, of lonely diligence. They were nothing he'd thought their arrogant, sarcastic, terrifying maker capable of.

And the old man? What business had he with the figurines' maker? Saleh had been so taken with his restored senses that he'd nearly forgotten about him, but now he recalled the crushing pain, the man's obvious distaste at his task. He'd cured Saleh somehow—but not out of kindness or compassion, or even the barest sense of a healer's duty. Saleh had been little more than a tool to him, the flaw in his mind merely an impediment to his goal. And that goal, apparently, was to find the Djinni. Saleh doubted that the man meant the encounter to be a peaceful one.

He held up the unfinished ibis and watched it glint in the candlelight. A day before, an hour even, he would have gladly told the old man where to find his prey, and wished him godspeed.

He put on his coat, slipped the figurine into his pocket, and blew out the candles. He would take a stroll to the Bowery, he decided, and see the world anew. And if he happened to find the Djinni along the way, then perhaps he might find it in his heart to warn him.

Led by Saleh's memory, Yehudah Schaalman walked east along the path of the dowsing spell. Now there were no turnings, no rooftop ascents or time-wasting detours: his quarry, it seemed, had set out for the Bowery with an arrow's unswerving aim.

And what a quarry! A man called Ahmad, with a face that shone bright as a gas lamp. What was he? Some sort of demon? A victim of the same possession that had afflicted Saleh—or perhaps its perpetrator?

Fatigue was warring with Schaalman's excitement, reminding him that on any other night he would be back at the Sheltering House by now, claiming his much-needed hours of rest. But how could he stop now, and let the trail go cold? Ignoring his tired and burning feet, he quickened his pace.

He turned onto the Bowery proper and found it cluttered with men, despite the late hour. The path was so strong now it seemed to be coming from everywhere at once. He scanned the crowd, feeling a sudden panic: what if they should pass each other, without Schaalman noticing?

A familiar sign peered down at him from the storefronts. He read the name CONROY, saw the repeated motif of sun and moon. He paused in the doorway, peered inside. No, his quarry hadn't been here; there were only a few men buying tobacco, and the prim, bespectacled dealer in stolen goods.

He turned from the doorway, to continue his search before Conroy could notice him, and nearly ran straight into a tall, handsome man with a brightly glowing face.

"I beg your pardon," the Djinni said, stepping around the slack-mouthed old man who stood rooted to the pavement. He opened Conroy's door, ringing the small bell above the doorway. Behind the register, Conroy gave him a bland smile and looked meaningfully at the other customers before returning to his well-thumbed newspaper. The Djinni busied himself pretending to scan the shelves of tobacco. It would be no challenge, he'd decided, to wait until Conroy locked up, and then break the lock; far more of an accomplishment to rob the man from under his very nose. He planned to purchase some small piece of silver, and then accept the fence's customary offer of a room upstairs. He'd seen enough of the shop's comings and goings to know that there were numerous passageways from the bordello to the storefront to the alley where Conroy's men liked to congregate. He would linger in the upstairs room—and if he must take advantage of his company in the meantime, well then, he would bear it—and wait until Conroy had retired for the night. If he was careful, the toughs would be easy enough to evade. Perhaps he could create some sort of disturbance. . . .

The bell rang again above the door. It was the old man from the street, the one who'd nearly collided with him. The man was staring at him fixedly, with an almost unhinged intensity.

The Djinni frowned at him. "Yes?"

"Ahmad?" the man asked.

The Djinni cursed silently. The other customers had paid and were leaving the tiny shop; since this man, whoever he was, somehow knew his name, the Djinni would have to wait for him to leave as well. "Do I know you?" he asked in English, but the man shook his head—less an answer than an injunction against speaking, as though the Djinni would ruin the moment.

Conroy traded a glance with the Djinni, folded his paper away. "Can I help you?" Conroy asked.

The old man waved Conroy away, as one would an irritating fly. Then he smiled at the Djinni; and it was a smile both sly and triumphant, the smile of an imp with a secret to tell. He raised a hand, and with two fingers beckoned him closer.

Growing intrigued despite himself, the Djinni took a step toward the man. It was then that he began to feel it: a stirring along the backs of his arms and the nape of his neck. A strange buzzing began inside his mind. One of his hands began to shake. It was the cuff. It was *vibrating*.

He paused. Something here was very, very wrong.

With a clawlike hand, the old man reached out and grabbed the Djinni around the wrist.

What William Conroy saw, in the moment before every pane of glass in the shop shattered, including his own spectacles, was something that he would never tell anyone—not the police, nor the men in his employ, nor even the priest to whom he made his confession every Thursday. In that bare instant, he saw the two figures transformed. Where the thin old man had been, there stood another, naked, with a sun-blasted face beneath filthy wisps of hair. And where the man he knew as Ahmad had been, there stood something that was no man, nor earthly creature at all, but a kind of shimmering vision—like the air above the pavement on a scorching summer day, or a candle flame whipped by the wind.

25.

*A*t the instant of contact, a hidden lake of memory burst its banks. It flooded their minds and overwhelmed them both, drowning them in images, sensations, impressions.

Where before there had been a gap in the Djinni's memory—describing the bare moment between the sight of a hawk wheeling about in a bloodred sunset, and coming to on Arbeely's dusty workshop floor—now there lay weeks, months full of time. He watched a young Bedouin girl as she glimpsed his palace shining in the valley; and then he watched himself enter her dreams. He saw himself visit the girl again and again, noticed his own growing fascination with her. He saw, as he never could have before, how the days between their visits passed so quickly for himself, and so slowly for her; saw the signs that the girl's perceptions of dream and reality were sliding perilously into each other.

He watched, unable to look away, as he entered her mind one last time. He felt her draw him eagerly down (and how little he'd protested!) into her imagined wedding, felt the lust that blinded him to the danger; and then the panic of her waking, and the jagged, terrifying pain as he ripped himself from her mind.

He saw himself hovering near obliteration. He watched as he turned away from the cries of her family, and ran to the safe haven of his own glass palace.

And then he saw what followed.

The day was fading little by little, reaching toward sunset. Above the parapets of his glass palace, the Djinni noted the changing angle of the sun with irritation.

It was nearly a week since his last, catastrophic visit to the Bedouin girl, and still he was not healed. He'd spent his daytime hours since then hanging motionless in the sunlight, allowing the heat to knit him back together. But at night, he retreated back inside, where the glass would protect him. The nights irked him now: his tattered wounds *itched*, turned him impatient and bad-tempered. A few more days of healing and he would be strong enough for his long-delayed trip to his fellow djinn, and the habitations of his birth. Why, *why* had he not gone earlier? He'd grown far too fascinated with humans, allowing himself to be lured into complacency and danger. He couldn't think of Fadwa now without cringing at his own innocence.

Not that he blamed the girl for what had happened! No, the fault lay entirely with himself. He'd been far too taken with her, too impressed by the tenacity with which she and her people clung to the desert, fighting for every stalk of grain and drop of milk. He'd mistaken fortitude for wisdom and failed to see that she lacked a certain maturity of intellect. Well, his lesson had been learned. Possibly he'd allow himself to observe an occasional caravan from afar; but as for the rest of it, he was finished. No more dallying with humans. The djinn elders had been right: the two peoples were not meant to interact. No matter how fascinating, how sensual, the cost of these encounters was too high for comfort.

From the safety of his palace, the Djinni watched as the fading light bred shadows across the walls. Perhaps, he thought, he would wait a few extra days before setting out on his journey. He wanted no wounds or scars to remain of his misadventure. No one would know how close he'd come to his own destruction.

Help!

He turned, startled. A voice, from far away, drifted through the glass wall. . . .

Djinni, help! We are at battle with a band of ifrits, and are injured—we need shelter!

Up he flew to the highest tower, and looked out over the valley. Sure enough, three djinn were approaching from the west, riding the wind. At this distance he couldn't recognize them, but they were unmistakably his own kind. There was no sight of their pursuers, but that was unsurprising; many *ifrits* liked to travel beneath the desert's surface, outdistancing their enemies and then bursting forth in front of them. One of the djinn, he saw, seemed to be carrying another, who indeed looked less than whole.

You are welcome here, he called to them. *Enter quickly, and take your shelter.* He felt a pang that they would see him in this weakened state— but then, they themselves were no better. Perhaps they could all keep each other's secrets.

The gateway to the palace was shielded by a door of thick glass that hung on silver hinges. To open or close it, the Djinni had to be in human form; it had been a conceit of his to pretend he was a human ruler of old, coming home to his seat of power. As he removed the bar that locked the door and swung it open, he reflected that perhaps it was time to modify the gateway. What had once seemed an amusing fancy now felt, in the presence of his own kind, faintly embarrassing.

A hot wind caressed him at the gateway; and the three djinn flew past him and into the palace, one of them—a female, he saw now, a Djin-niyeh of some beauty—supported by another of her fellows. He smiled to himself. The evening had just grown slightly more promising. He closed the door, and then hefted the bar back into place.

A clawlike human hand clamped a metal cuff over his wrist.

Shocked, he tried to pull away—but his arm had turned to frozen fire. The pain was blinding. Desperately he tried to change shape, to get away from the freezing iron, but to no effect. He could feel the cuff hold-ing his body in place, blocking every attempt to transform.

The pain moved past his shoulder to envelop his entire being. He collapsed to his knees, looked up with his dimmed human eyes at the djinni that had done this to him. But all three djinn had vanished. Stand-ing before him was a Bedouin tribesman carrying a young girl in his arms. The girl was Fadwa, bound and blindfolded. Next to them stood something that he first took for an animated corpse—but then he saw it was a grotesque old man in a filthy, tattered cloak.

The old man was grinning hideously, showing dark and broken teeth. "It is accomplished!" he said. "Captured, and in human form! The first since the days of Sulayman!"

"Then he's bound to you?" asked the Bedouin.

"No, not quite yet. For that, I'll need your assistance."

The tribesman hesitated for a moment, and then lowered his cloak-covered burden to the floor. The Djinni, unable to move or even to speak against the freezing agony, watched as Fadwa twitched and whispered. The Bedouin noticed his gaze. "Yes, look!" he shouted. "Look at what you've done to my daughter! This is your payment, creature. However terrible your suffering, know that you yourself have caused it, and it is *nothing* compared to hers!"

"Yes, well put," said the ancient man dryly. "Now come and help me, before the pain unhinges him. I want him fully aware of what's happening."

Cautiously the Bedouin approached. "Hold him steady," the old man said. Fadwa's father grabbed the Djinni roughly. The Djinni tried to cry out, but nothing came. "Hold still," the Bedouin hissed, gripping the back of the Djinni's neck.

The old man had closed his eyes; he was muttering under his breath, as though rehearsing or preparing himself, making ready. Then he knelt down and put one rough and dusty palm on the Djinni's forehead.

The rasping syllables the old man chanted made no sense—but even through the iron's torment he could sense the net of glowing lines that spun out from the man's hand and around his own pain-racked body. He strained against the cuff, panicking, trying desperately to change form as the lines twisted to form a cage. Foolish, careless! Baited and captured like the basest of *ghuls*! Everything, *everything* had been stolen from him!

"I am Wahab ibn Malik," the man growled, "and I bind you to my service!"

And the cage of glowing lines sank inside him, flame joining to flame.

The old man staggered; for a moment it seemed he might faint. Then he righted himself, and smiled in triumph.

"Then it's done?" asked the Bedouin. "You can heal her now?"

"One last thing. The binding must be sealed." The wizard smiled sadly. "My deepest apologies, Abu Yusuf, but here our agreement ends."

A knife appeared in the wizard's other hand. In a swift and powerful motion, he plunged it into Abu Yusuf's ribs. There was a horrible gasping noise; and then, as the wizard withdrew the knife, a hot spray of blood, and the choking smell of iron. Abu Yusuf collapsed, his hand slipping from the Djinni's neck.

The wizard took a deep breath. Again he seemed exhausted. His skeletal frame sagged with fatigue, but his eyes were full of a quiet triumph.

"Now," he said. "Let us talk. Ah, but first . . ." He grabbed the Djinni's wrist again, and muttered something over the iron cuff. In an instant, the pain vanished. Freed from his paralysis, the Djinni fell, sprawling across the bloodstained glass.

"I'll give you a moment," said the old man. He turned his back to check on the girl, who lay bundled on the floor, oblivious to her father's murder.

The Djinni gathered himself, rose shaking to his feet, and launched himself at the wizard.

"Stop," ibn Malik said.

And just like that, the Djinni jerked to a halt, a tamed animal at the end of its leash. There was no way to fight it; he might as well stop the sunrise. The wizard whispered a few words, and the iron's freezing torture roared back to life.

The wizard said, "Do you know that no one, not even the wisest of the seers, has discovered why the touch of iron is so terrible to the djinn?" He paused, as though awaiting a response, but the Djinni was near insensible, curled around his arm. The wizard went on. "Nothing else produces such an effect. But here lies a conundrum, for if I can control you with iron, then so can another. It's no use to send one's most powerful slave to kill an enemy, only to see him driven away by an ordinary sword. I pondered this problem long and hard, and this is my solution."

He muttered the words again; once more the cuff's torment ceased.

"I will be a stern master," the wizard said as the Djinni lay boneless on the floor, "but not a cruel one. You will only feel the iron if you deserve its touch. If, however, your attitude merits reward, I'll allow you to resume your true form from time to time. But don't think you can escape—your actions are mine to control. You are bound to me, fire to flesh, soul to soul, and sealed in blood for as long as you shall live." He smiled down at the Djinni. "Oh, my proud slave. We'll outdo all the stories of old, you and I. Our names shall be sung for generations."

"I'll destroy myself," said the Djinni in a hoarse voice.

The wizard raised an eyebrow. "I see the truth of your position has yet to set in," he said. "Very well. I'll make it clear to you."

The Djinni braced weakly against the expected pain of the iron, but it didn't come. Instead ibn Malik went to Fadwa and crouched over her. The girl had thrashed free of her cloak. A dribble of saliva ran down one side of her face, and her hands jerked and clawed against their bonds.

"You left a piece of yourself inside this girl," the wizard said. "I promised her father I would remove it."

He placed his hands on the girl's face, slipping his fingers beneath the blindfold. Closing his eyes, the man began to mutter. After a moment, Fadwa went still—and then she screamed, a sound that went on and on, as though her soul was being drawn from her body. The Djinni shuddered, tried to cover his ears, but found he couldn't move.

At last the screaming ceased and the girl lay motionless. Ibn Malik smiled, though he looked even more tired than before. He slipped off the blindfold, untied the rag that bound her wrists, and backed away.

"Go to her," ibn Malik told the Djinni. "Wake her."

He had no strength left, but nevertheless his legs carried him of their own accord to Fadwa's side. The binding moved his limbs, made him kneel down and gently shake her shoulder. "Fadwa," he said, struggling against it. *Don't wake*, he thought. *Don't see.*

The girl stirred, brought one hand up to rub at her eyes, then winced at the ache in her wrists. The last of the twilight was shining through the palace walls, casting a blue aura about her wan and drawn features, turning her hair a deep blue-black. Her eyes opened; she saw the Djinni. "It's you," she murmured. "I'm dreaming . . . no, I *was* dreaming. . . ."

She frowned, confused. Slowly she sat up, and looked around.

"*Father!*" the girl shrieked.

And then the binding was moving him again, making him crouch above her as ibn Malik had. His hands went around her throat. He felt the delicate bones as they bent and cracked under his fingers, felt her hands as they scratched and slapped at his face. He could not look away from her eyes as they stared back at him, protesting in disbelief before they bulged with panic, and then, finally, dimmed.

At last the Djinni sat back. His hands still moved with the binding's command, convulsing against air. He watched them until they stopped.

"Now you understand," said ibn Malik.

And it was true. He understood. He stared at the cold glass walls and tried to feel nothing.

The wizard put a hand on his shoulder. "Enough for today, I think," he said. "Rest and regain your strength. Tomorrow your true work begins." He paused to look about at the cavernous hall. "You must prepare yourself for one more disappointment, I fear. Your new quarters are not nearly so elegant."

From his tattered cloak he extracted a long-necked copper flask, etched with intricate loops and whorls. He tipped the flask toward the Djinni, and muttered another series of harsh and meaningless words.

A bright flash seared the Djinni's eyes, lighting the chamber to translucence. There was a horrible sense of *diminishment* as the wizard's spell gathered and compressed his being, banking his essence to the merest spark. Slowly the flask drew him in—and time slowed to an elongated instant, full of the taste of metal and a wild, searing anguish.

Here the Djinni's own memories ended.

But these were not the only memories that he regained in that moment, for the lines of the binding stretched both ways. The Djinni saw himself, remembered what he had done—but he also saw the memories of the wizard ibn Malik, felt his triumph as he enslaved the Djinni with Abu Yusuf's blood and compelled him to kill Fadwa. Like two patterns overlaid, their recollections ran together and diverged, overlapped and intertwined. He was inside the flask, trapped in that endless moment; and he was standing alone in the glass palace, holding a copper flask that was warm to the touch.

Ibn Malik replaced the flask inside the pocket of his cloak. Then he staggered to the nearest wall and sank to the floor, breathing in shallow gasps.

The day's exertions had drained him more deeply than expected. He hadn't meant to put the Djinni in the flask so quickly, but it would have done little for his authority to allow the Djinni to see him panting with fatigue. And still, what a day, what an unparalleled accomplishment! He only regretted the death of the girl. It seemed wasteful to kill one so young and beautiful when she might have served as a menial in his future palace, or a tempting motivation for the Djinni's good behavior. He should have anticipated that, like any powerful animal, his new acquisition would require a certain amount of breaking.

His breathing began to even and slow. He would, he decided, take a small, well-deserved rest, and then return home. The Bedouins' mounts were hobbled safely outside the palace, and it was a clear, warm night with no windstorms. The mounts could wait a little longer. Or perhaps he would leave them behind and command the Djinni to carry him across the valley. He smiled at the thought, and sank into a deep and grateful sleep.

Ibn Malik did not usually dream, but within moments his slumbering mind brought him visions of a city on an island, an impossible city that reached far into the sky. Perhaps it was the city that he would build, he and the Djinni? Yes: a monumental undertaking, but was it not within his reach? For now that he had captured one djinni, who was to say that he could not capture another, and another? He would bind the entire race, and make them build him a kingdom to rival Sulayman's. . . .

The city blurred, coalesced, and became a man, a wrinkled old man with skin pale as milk, carrying a stack of singed parchments. Ibn Malik had never encountered such a man before, and yet he felt he knew him, felt both kinship and a dreadful fear. He wanted to warn the man—but of what? And now the man was reaching out toward ibn Malik, his face full of warning as well—

Pain, sudden and horrible, cut through the dream. The pale man's face disintegrated as ibn Malik woke with his own knife in his stomach, and Abu Yusuf's hand on the hilt.

Either Abu Yusuf had been biding his time, or he'd been revived by his daughter's screams. In either case, he wasn't nearly as dead as he'd appeared. A wide trail of blood showed his slow progress to ibn Malik's side; now he lay next to the wizard, twisting the knife with the last of his strength. Ibn Malik roared and backhanded the man, but it was too late, the damage was done: Abu Yusuf had pulled the knife away with him.

Ibn Malik's vision blurred. Blood filled his mouth. He spat it out and hauled himself to standing. Abu Yusuf lay at his feet, weakly smiling. The wizard pressed a foot to his neck until there could be no question the man was dead.

Beneath the taste of blood ibn Malik could smell the meaty stink of his own intestines. Grimacing, he ripped a length of cloth from his cloak and stuffed it into the hole in his belly. Stomach wounds corrupted quickly—he would need herbs and fire, needle and thread. . . . He thought of the Djinni, and cursed. Weakened and wounded like this, he had no strength to conjure his servant from the flask. The effort alone might kill him.

The horse. He had to get to Abu Yusuf's horse.

He staggered to the palace gate and struggled to lift the bar away, ignoring the feel of his insides shifting. At last the gate was open. He found the stallion and untied it, leaving the pony behind. He hauled himself onto the horse's back, smearing its side with his blood. He tried to kick it into a gallop; the horse, feeling only a gentle nudge, began a slow and jarring trot. *Go, you stinking bag of bones*, thought ibn Malik, but it was all he could do to lace his fingers into the mane and hang weakly on.

He'd made it halfway across the valley when the jackals descended. Frenzied by the smell of blood, they ignored the horse's kicks and pulled ibn Malik screaming from its side. With the last dregs of his energy he fought a few of them off; the rest, sensing his exhaustion, vaulted the charred bodies of their pack mates and tore out his throat.

For all the wizard's strength and power, the jackals found he made rather a small meal.

The desert is a vast and empty place, and travelers are few and far between.

The gnawed bones of Wahab ibn Malik bleached and cracked in the sun. His cloak dissolved into scattered shreds. The copper flask lay tipped on its side. It gathered a light covering of dust, but it did not tarnish. Animals sniffed at it, then left it alone.

In faraway cities, caliphs rose and were overthrown. Waves of invading armies fell upon the deserts, made their brief mark, and were conquered in their turn.

One day, long after the last traces of ibn Malik had vanished from the desert, a caravan outrider stopped by a sheltering rock to relieve himself. The caravan was twenty days out from Ramadi, and bound for ash-Sham. The outrider was tasked with ensuring there would be no surprises along the way, no raiders or mercenaries demanding payment for safe passage. He took a drink from his waterskin and was about to mount his horse again when a glint of metal caught his eye.

In a small depression in the ground lay a copper flask, half-buried in dust and scrub.

He picked up the flask and brushed the dirt away. It was well made and handsome, with an interesting pattern of scrollwork around its base. Perhaps it had been lost from an earlier caravan. He thought it was the sort of thing his mother might like. He placed the flask in his saddlebag, and rode on.

Over the years the flask passed from hand to hand, from son to mother to niece to daughter to daughter-in-law. It was used to hold oil, or frankincense, or simply for decoration. It accumulated a few small dents but was never seriously damaged, even when it should have been. Once in a while its owner would notice that it always seemed warm to the touch; but then the thought would pass, as such idle thoughts always do. Down the generations the flask went until at last it was placed in the luggage of a young woman bound from Beirut to New York—a gift from her mother, to remember her by.

And as for ibn Malik?

You are bound to me, fire to flesh, soul to soul, and sealed in blood for as long as you shall live.

The wizard had been canny and devious in life, but in death he'd outsmarted even himself. Soul to soul they were bound, as long as the Djinni should live: and there the Djinni sat, trapped in his flask, living out a millennium in one eternal moment.

Which meant that death was not the end for Wahab ibn Malik al-Hadid.

The morning after the jackals devoured the wizard's carcass down to the bones, a child was born in a faraway eastern land, in a city called Chang'an. His parents named him Gao. From the beginning Gao was a clever boy. As he grew, he soon outpaced his tutors, who began fretting that perhaps the boy was too clever: by thirteen he had written several treatises on inconsistencies in the most beloved Confucian teachings, declaring them bankrupt and meaningless. By twenty Gao had become a brilliant, embittered outcast. He apprenticed himself to an herbalist and grew obsessed with developing a medicinal formula for immortality. He died at thirty-eight, by accident, from one of his self-administered experiments.

The day after his death, a baby was born to joyful parents in the floating Byzantine city of Venexia. Tommaso, as he was called, proved so interested in the Holy Church and its mysteries that he was quickly set on the path to priesthood. He took orders at a young age and soon immersed himself in politics, rising to spiritual adviser to the Doge. It was clear to all that Tommaso would be satisfied with nothing less than the papal robes—until he was observed one evening in one of the city's catacombs, conducting what appeared to be dark and pagan rites. Tommaso was excommunicated, tried for sorcery, and burned at the stake.

Tommaso's ashes were still glowing in Venexia when, in Varanasi, a boy named Jayatun was born within sight of the River Ganga. Jayatun loved the stories and legends that he learned as a child, particularly that of the Cintamani, a fabulous jewel that would grant its owner any wish—and could even hold back death. When he grew older, what had been a youthful fascination became an obsession, and he set about collecting every mention he could find of the Cintamani, be the source Buddhist or Hindu or mere storyteller's fancy. The search devoured all else, and he'd long since become a friendless pauper when one day, under the influence of a high fever, he waded into the Ganga and drowned, convinced that the river goddess had left the Cintamani there for him to find.

And so it went. As the Djinni's flask was passed from hand to hand, so too did ibn Malik's soul pass from body to body, in one part of the world and then another. He was a Crusader at the Siege of Jerusalem, looking for holy relics to steal. He was a student of Paracelsus, devoted to finding the Philosopher's Stone. He was a Shinto monk, a Maori shaman, an infamous courtier in the House of Orléans. He never married, never fathered children, never so much as fell in love. Presented with a religious tradition, he was drawn to its darkest, most mystical corners; in politics, he displayed an unwavering taste for power.

His lives were usually unhappy, and rarely ended well. But in each and every one he grew consumed with finding the secret to eternal life—not knowing that it was the one thing he already possessed.

Centuries went by in this way, with ibn Malik's soul unable to pass to the next world, not so long as the Djinni still lived. Until at last, in a Prussian shtetl, a squalling infant named Yehudah was placed in his mother's arms.

The Djinni saw all of this.

He saw himself, trapped in the flask, howling in anguish.

He saw ibn Malik born again and again.

He saw Yehudah Schaalman, the last of ibn Malik's incarnations and the most powerful. He watched as the boy grew from student to convict to master of forbidden magic. And he watched as a lonely furniture maker came to Schaalman's door one day, in search of a golem to make him a wife.

And Schaalman saw all of it as well.

He saw his own lives laid before him, misshapen pearls on an endless string, starting with ibn Malik and ending with himself.

He saw the Djinni's memories, experienced his capture and defeat. He saw him emerge from the flask in a tinsmith's shop, a hole in his memory where the Bedouin girl had been. He saw the Djinni learn his way about the city and grow accustomed to his bonds. And he watched as one night the Djinni crossed paths with a strange and astonishing woman, a woman made of clay.

26.

Someone was slapping the Djinni's face. He opened his eyes and saw Conroy standing over him, blood trickling from his scalp.

So it was real. The truth of it hit him full on, the remorseless knowledge of what he'd done. He turned onto his side and curled around the pain, as he'd done on the bloodstained floor of his palace, a thousand years before.

He heard women screaming. There were shouts for a policeman, a fire engine. "Ahmad," Conroy was saying urgently. "Come on, boyo. Get up." Someone else groaned from close nearby. The wizard.

The Djinni lurched to his feet, swaying against Conroy. Fragments of glass slid tinkling from his clothing, joining the shards that carpeted the tiny shop. The old man lay slumped next to a display case, his body dusted with glass and tobacco. The Djinni grabbed him, dragged him up off the floor.

"Release me!" he shouted.

The old man's head lolled on his neck. It would be so very easy to kill him, only a quick motion, one hand to his bare throat—a fitting end, after what he'd done to Fadwa!

But the binding between them would still remain; and tomorrow, in some distant land, another child would be born. . . .

With a cry of anguish and frustration, the Djinni dropped Schaalman to the ground. The old man crumpled to the floorboards, his head knocking the side of the tobacco display.

Conroy's hand was on his arm. "The police will be here any moment," he said. If he felt any alarm at the Djinni's ill treatment of a small and elderly man, he didn't show it.

The Djinni glanced about at the shattered windows and the crowd that had gathered outside. The prostitutes from upstairs had all run panicked into the street, in various states of undress. Conroy's men were forming a cordon in front of the door, holding everyone back as they tried to surge forward. "The police," he said. "Your shop." Distantly he recalled that he'd gone there intending to rob the man.

"Don't worry about me," Conroy said. "The constables and I have a long history together. But what about our friend here? What's to be done with him?"

The Djinni looked down at the old man sprawled on the floor. *Fire to flesh*, he thought, *soul to soul, for as long as you shall live. . . .*

He knew what it was he had to do.

"This man is dangerous, and a murderer," he said to Conroy. "He killed a girl I once knew. She was only fifteen years old." He wavered, braced himself against a countertop. "I can't let the police find me here. There's something I need to do. To set things right."

Conroy eyed the Djinni for a moment, considering. Then he leaned down and punched the unconscious Schaalman across the face.

"The constables will deal with him," said the fence. "And as far as I'm concerned you were never here. Go, now. Out the back."

Until the moment of the blast, Saleh had been roaming the Bowery side-walks, wondering how long he could pretend to himself that he was not in fact looking for the Djinni. He gazed into a thousand faces, grinning with delight at each and receiving a few suspicious looks in return; still, none had that familiar glow, like a shaded lamp. But would Saleh still recognize the glowing man, now that his vision was restored?

He was looking about with growing agitation when the explosion rang through the street. He felt it a moment later: a wave of pressure against his back, knocking him forward. All gasped and turned, then cried out at the falling glass.

He ran forward with the surging crowd. It was a tobacconist's shop, nondescript, and he could see no one inside—but still, could he not guess? After the day's events, it could hardly be a coincidence. He strained to see over the heads of the hard-looking men who'd formed a protective chain, pushing them back. The crowd was calling out for the authorities, buzzing excitedly about bombs and anarchists. A half-naked woman fell against him; he put out a hand to steady her, and she slapped it away.

There: at the alley entrance. It was the Djinni—who, Saleh saw with surprise, still glowed, if only barely. Some part of his illness still remained, then; or perhaps it was a permanent remnant, like a pox mark.

The Djinni was covered with what looked like powdered glass, which added its own eerie shimmer to his appearance. Saleh watched as he cut through the crowd and headed south, away from the fracas. Instead of his usual arrogant bearing, he seemed unsteady, even haunted.

What else could Saleh do but follow?

For the most part, the Chrystie Street tenements were still asleep as the Djinni passed them by, the gray facades stony in their silence. As he walked his new memories rose up and threatened to crush him. It seemed impossible: if a passerby had whispered the name *Fadwa al-Hadid* in his ear only an hour earlier, he'd have had no inkling of its significance.

There was little time. He knew that neither Conroy nor the police could hold Schaalman for long. Even this small errand was a luxury he probably couldn't afford. But he had made a promise once, in a glittering gas-lit ballroom, and he meant to keep it.

He found the tenement, walked down the noxious hallway to the windowless, claustrophobic room, and knocked on the door. "Anna, please," he told the half-awake girl who answered it.

A minute later Anna slipped out into the hallway, scowling, arms folded above her burgeoning stomach; but when she saw his expression, her own turned apprehensive. "What is it? What's happened?"

"I apologize for waking you," he said to her. "But I need you to deliver a message."

He left Anna's tenement and walked into the slowly brightening day. Overhead, the morning's first trains creaked uptown, shedding the evening's soot onto the streets below. He would have preferred to walk, but the Second Avenue Elevated would be faster.

He was almost at the Grand Street platform when he realized he'd been hearing the same pair of footsteps behind him for blocks. He whipped around, and a familiar figure busied itself at a nearby milliner's window, as though admiring the summer fashions. The Djinni waited, half-amused, until the man at last gave up the pretense.

"I was better at following you when I couldn't see," Saleh said. "Now everything is a distraction."

The Djinni looked him over. The man's clothes were as awful as ever, but there was a new straightness and energy to his figure, as though he no longer gazed at the world slantwise. "What's happened to you?" the Djinni asked.

Saleh shrugged. "Perhaps I simply recovered from my illness."

"I told you, that was no illness."

"Then call it an injury."

"Saleh, why are you following me?"

"There's a man looking for you," the man said. "I don't think he means you well."

"I know," the Djinni said. "He already found me."

"At the tobacconist's?"

"You were there?"

"I was in the mood for a walk."

The Djinni snorted. "And will you go home again, now that you've delivered your belated news? Or would you prefer to shadow me throughout the city?"

"That depends. Are you going somewhere interesting?"

The Djinni had meant to make the trip alone. But now he thought that perhaps this man's company would not be so onerous.

"Do you remember when I took you on the Elevated?" he asked.

"Not well. I wasn't at my best that night."

"Then you should ride it again."

The creaking train drew to a halt and Saleh stepped into the near-empty car, gazing around with nervous excitement. The Djinni couldn't help but smile, watching him. No doubt the wizard had something to do with the man's recovery, the removal of the spark from his mind; but the Djinni didn't intend to press him for details. It hardly mattered, as long as the man didn't try to stop him.

They sat near the back. Saleh jumped as the train took off with its customary jolt. The Djinni watched the familiar terrain as it rushed by, catching glimpses of the city's morning tableau: children dashing across the rooftops, couples drinking tea at their windows. His face spasmed once in sorrow; he closed his eyes, leaned back his head.

"May I ask where we're going?" Saleh said.

"Central Park," replied the Djinni. "I'm meeting a woman there."

Radzin's Bakery was an eerie place at four in the morning. The Golem let herself in with the key Mrs. Radzin had given her for emergencies and bolted the door behind her. She knew every pace of the floor, could have made the morning's breads with her eyes closed; yet in the darkness the bakery felt ominous. The familiar worktables stood aloof and tomblike. Streetlight shone through the empty display case, illuminating ghostly handprints.

There'd been nowhere else for her to go. Her home was no longer hers—and she couldn't risk meeting Michael again, not in his current state. Perhaps she'd never see him again. The Rabbi, the Djinni, Anna, and now Michael, all gone from her life.

From her cloak she took the burnt sheaf of pages she'd stolen from Michael's desk. She placed it on her worktable and stared at it. She wanted to run, as far away from it as she could. She wanted to thrust it into the oven and forget she'd ever found it.

Joseph Schall was her creator. Again she saw the sleek, almost preening smile, felt the sinister void in his mind.

Even if she burned the pages to cinders, she wouldn't soon forget the grocery list of Rotfeld's desires in a wife. It was edifying, in a sense, to see her own origins, but at the same time she felt humiliated, reduced to nothing more than words. The request for modest behavior, for example: it rankled her to think of her arguments with the Djinni on the subject, how fervently she'd defended an opinion she'd had no choice but to believe. And if she was meant to be curious, did that mean she could take no credit for her own discoveries, her accomplishments? Had she nothing of her own, only what Joseph Schall decreed she should have? And yet, if Rotfeld had lived, she would have been more than content!

She will make him an admirable wife, if she doesn't destroy him first. So he'd known the danger, and built her anyway. All else she might be able to understand someday, but this? What sort of man created a murderous creature, and called it fine? The Rabbi had said it himself, the day they met: *Whoever made you was brilliant, and reckless, and quite amoral.*

He'd hidden himself in the Sheltering House, in plain sight. He'd walked her down her boardinghouse staircase, led her like a parent to her groom. Had he known Rotfeld was dead, and followed her to America simply to toy with her, to lurk sadistic and grinning at the edges of her life? Why else would Michael have Schall's spells, if Schall had not given him them, so that Michael might discover the truth?

And now the spells were hers. She wondered what form Joseph Schall's anger would take when he found them missing. But then, perhaps she could wield his own weapon against him. The spells were Schall's, yes, and he had done terrible things with them—but they could not be evil on their own, no more than, say, a knife that might be used to slice bread as well as injure a man. All must depend on the wielder, and the intent.

Hesitantly she began to turn the pages. She found a diagram Schall had drawn, describing how to hide one's thoughts: so that question, at least, was answered. Another formula described a process for erasing oneself from another's memory, and this one raised possibilities. With it, she could make Schall forget she existed. She imagined him wandering the city bewildered, wondering what had possessed him to leave Europe. As a solution, it held a certain elegance; it even avoided violence. Likely it was more than he deserved.

A thought struck her, and she hesitated over the formula, considering. Could she remove herself from Michael's mind as well? Maybe it would be a kindness to make him forget he'd ever had a wife, to soothe away his fearful vision of her, the dark and hulking monster. Without her, Michael could go back to being the man she'd once met, weary but optimistic, bent on improving his small corner of the world. What better use for Joseph Schall's knowledge than to undo the damage that his creation had caused?

A bud of hope, so long absent, began to grow inside her, fed by the prospect of correcting her mistakes. On the next page, she found a charm for healing the injured, with nothing but an herb and a touch. She could find Irving Wasserman, repair the harm she'd done to him. The thought made her feel almost physically lighter. She could find Anna as well, and remove her memory of that night. But then, might Anna reunite with Irving, without the memory to warn her away? Already she could see the risk of unintended consequences. On another page she found instructions labeled *To Influence Another's Thoughts*. Well, here was the solution! She would convince Anna that the man was not right for her—certainly this was the truth!—and perhaps steer her toward more sensible conduct in the future.

She turned more pages. *To Erase Love's Infatuation*, she read, and thought of all those dejected souls who'd passed under her window, trapped in unrequited longings. *To Create Abundant Sustenance*: no need to steal knishes, when she could feed the hungry from thin air! *To Locate a Person's Whereabouts*, *To Attract Good Fortune*—the list went on, deluging her in possibilities. She marveled at how much pain she could remove from the world. And Joseph Schall had thought only to create golems!

What of the Djinni? Could she remove his pain as well? She flipped the pages, searching. Perhaps she could unlock the cuff on his wrist, and release him from his bonds. But then, if he were freed, would he be content to stay? No, of course not: she would regain him for only the briefest of moments, and then he would leave her, abandoning the city and returning home. The thought wrenched her. She imagined him wandering the desert, searching always for the next distraction. Even released from his bonds, he would be no more at peace. He would carry his longings and dissatisfactions with him; in this he was no different from anyone else.

But now she could change him! She could make him content to stay in New York, content even with the life of a human. Would it not be a kindness, an act of love, to remove the haunted look from his eye, the bitterness from his voice? She would give him happiness, true happiness—such as she herself had once felt—

No.

With an effort she flung the stack of papers away. They fluttered apart and scattered to the floor, stirring up tiny whirlwinds of flour.

The tide of her exhilaration drained from her, leaving her exhausted and heartsick. She would have bound the entire city, made them all into her golems, to satisfy her own need to be useful. She would've robbed the Djinni of himself, more thoroughly than the cuff on his wrist—he, who valued his freedom above all else.

She swept the pages into a pile, then rummaged in the back room for a flour sack to hide them in. Their contents were far too dangerous to contemplate using. If she must confront Joseph Schall, she would need to find another way.

There was a tap at the front door. She ignored it—customers often tried to get in early—and considered what to do next. She wanted to burn the sack and its contents to cinders, but did she have the right to destroy such knowledge, regardless of where it came from?

The tap came again, more urgent now. Irritated, she went to the door and lifted the shade—and saw a familiar woman, deeply pregnant, in a cheap and garish cloak.

"Anna?" the Golem said, astonished.

By the time Saleh and the Djinni disembarked at Fifty-seventh Street, the New York morning had well and truly begun. Each avenue was an obstacle course of grocers' wagons and ice trucks, out on the day's first deliveries. The oppressive heat had cleared somewhat; the horses pranced with energy, and the men at the reins whistled in piercing notes.

"I remember this neighborhood," Saleh said as they crossed Fifth Avenue. "At least, I think I do." He was doing his best to keep up with the Djinni, who had begun to walk with increased urgency. He'd spoken no more of his appointment, and Saleh had decided not to ask, for the morning splendor had rendered all else irrelevant. Had the sky in Homs ever been this deep, this rich a blue? It was as though the city were giving him its finest dawn, to make up for all the years of skies as gray as a chipped nickel. He remembered his patients telling him they appreciated the world anew once they were healed, a sentiment that had struck him as unbearably mawkish. But now a young girl passed by with a basket of flowers for sale, and the delicate beauty of her figure nearly made him break into tears.

They turned into the park, along the carriage drive. Already Saleh could hear the trees whispering, feel the cool breath of water in the air. It had been a day since he'd truly slept or eaten, but for the moment his fatigue was a minor matter, easy to ignore. The odd carriage passed them once or twice, but it was too early for the usual park-goers: the working classes were readying for the day, and the more genteel pedestrians were still abed. For the most part, it seemed, they had the place to themselves.

The Djinni glanced across at his companion as they walked. "You've said little," he remarked.

"I've been appreciating the morning."

The Djinni glanced upward, as though noticing the fine weather for the first time. He did not smile, but seemed pleased nonetheless.

Saleh gazed at the buildings that rimmed the park, rising above the trees. "I like this view better than last time," he said.

The Djinni smiled thinly. "As you said, you weren't at your best."

Saleh thought of the mansion on Fifth Avenue, the frost-rimed garden. "I believe you were visiting a woman that night, as well."

"A different woman," the Djinni said. Something seemed to occur to him, then. He paused, shook his head as though ashamed, and then said, "Should you ever find yourself there again, I'd appreciate it if you called on Sophia Winston and conveyed my apologies. For my behavior."

"Me?" The image of himself knocking at the mansion's gigantic front door made him want to laugh. Did the Djinni realize he didn't even speak English? "Is there anyone else to whom I should make your apologies?"

"Oh, many others. But I'll burden you only with Sophia."

From the carriage drive, they turned onto a broad path overarched by rows of gigantic, sheltering trees. They passed statuary of serious-faced men—poets or philosophers, judging by the books and quills they held, their plaintive eyes cast heavenward. Their sculpted faces jogged Saleh's memory, and he pulled the small silver figurine from his pocket. "I found this in your room," he said. "It intrigued me." He held it out, but the Djinni said, "Keep it. The silver has value, at least."

"You'd have me melt it down?"

"It's a failure," the Djinni said. "There's no likeness."

"There's some," Saleh said. "And why must there be a likeness? Perhaps it's a portrait of an entirely new animal."

The Djinni snorted at this.

The rows of trees seemed to be ending; before them the path dipped to a set of stairs that ran below a bridge. And beyond the bridge, Saleh could now see a figure rising, coming clearer with each step: a statue of a woman, her head bowed in shadow between an outstretched pair of wings.

"I saw her that night," he said, more to himself than his companion. "I thought she was the Angel of Death, coming for me."

He felt the Djinni flinch beside him. He turned, a question forming on his lips—and glimpsed the Djinni's rising fist, and beyond it his faintly glowing face, his eyes full of a grim apology.

Anna was breathing hard, as though she'd been hurrying. She looked angry, stubborn, and terrified all at once. "I told myself I'd never go near you again," she said. A pause. "Are you going to let me in?"

The Golem ushered her in and closed the door, trying to keep her distance; Anna's fear of her was palpable.

The girl was watching her carefully. "I didn't expect you to be here already," she said. "I was going to wait."

"Anna," the Golem said, "I am so very sorry. I know it changes nothing, but—"

"Not now," said Anna, impatient. "There's something wrong with Ahmad."

The Golem gaped at her. "You've seen him?"

"He was just at my building, with a message for you."

"But—he came to *you*? How did he know where—"

"That's not important," Anna said quickly. She fished in her pocket and drew out a piece of paper. "I wrote down what he told me, as close as I could remember." She held it out.

Tell Chava that she is in danger, from a man who calls himself Joseph Schall. He is her creator, and my master. It will sound impossible, but it's true. She must get as far away from him as she can. Leave the city, if possible.

Tell her she was right. There were consequences to my actions, and I never saw them. I stole something from her once, because I wanted no harm to come to her, but I had no right to do so. Please give it back, and tell her I said good-bye.

"Here," the girl said, and handed her another square of folded paper, one whose dimensions the Golem knew by heart. He'd stolen it from her? And he'd crossed paths with Joseph Schall, as well? She had the disorienting sense of important events happening elsewhere while her back was turned.

She replaced the square of folded paper in her locket, and then read the Djinni's message again, trying to make sense of it. This time she saw what she'd missed in her confusion: the underlying notes of desperation and resolve. He was not simply leaving town. "Oh God," she said, aghast. "Anna, did he say what he was planning?"

"He wouldn't tell me. But, Chava, he looked *terrible*. Like he was going to do something awful."

To himself? she wanted to ask, but didn't need to; Anna's mind had provided the answer, in fearful visions of ropes and guns and bottles of laudanum. No, she couldn't believe he would do such a thing—but was that why he'd returned the paper, because he'd chosen an action he'd once denied her? A breath of panic touched her. The Djinni's veiled mind would've told her no more than the note—but could she not guess? It would not be poison, or a rope or a gun. It would be water.

"Which direction did he go? Was it east, toward the river?" But Anna just shook her head, baffled. It might already be too late—

The burnt pages were calling to her from inside their flour sack.

Hadn't there been a formula titled *To Locate a Person's Whereabouts?* Surely she could risk using Schall's magic, just this once! She grabbed the flour sack, was about to spill its contents onto the floor—and then stopped. *Wait,* she told herself. *Think.* The Djinni would never choose the East River docks, or the oil-stained waters of the bay, or anywhere else so inelegant. She didn't need forbidden diagrams or formulae to tell her his destination. She knew; she knew *him.*

But what about the pages? She couldn't leave them at the bakery; she needed to hide them from Schall, somewhere he'd never go. Pressing the sack into Anna's arms, she said, "Take this, and hide it somewhere no one would think to look. A place only you know about. No, don't tell me where, don't even think it."

"What? Chava, do you know how hard it is *not* to think about something—"

"Just don't! Don't look at it, and don't tell a soul, do you understand?"

"I don't understand *any* of this," the girl said, plaintive.

"Promise me!"

"All right, I promise, if it's that important."

"It is," the Golem said, relieved. "Thank you, Anna." And then she ran: out the back door and up the fire escape to the roof, chasing after the Djinni as fast as she could.

The Djinni caught Saleh as he fell and carried him to a nearby bench: merely another vagrant, sleeping away the morning. He made certain the man was still breathing and then walked on, descending the stairway to the arched and columned darkness of the arcade. His steps echoed off the tiled walls, and then he was out in the sunlight again, crossing the terrace's broad expanse of red brick, coming to the fountain's rim.

The Angel of the Waters gazed down at him, patient, waiting.

The terrace was all but deserted; only a few men could be seen hurrying home after their dubious nighttime activities, using the Park as a shortcut. Hat brims low over their faces, they walked with that hunched defiance against sleep that the Golem had once remarked on. They would not pose a problem.

The fountain stood quiet, its dancing jets silenced. There was little noise at all save for the lapping of the water. He had the strange impulse to take off his shoes, and so he did, lining them up next to the fountain's edge. For a moment he thought to run back to Saleh and wake him, to tell him that yes, there were many people who deserved apologies—Arbeely for one, and young Matthew, and Sam Hosseini for not finishing his necklaces. But time was passing, and it would be one indulgence too many. Besides, he'd taken care of the most important apology when he'd knocked on Anna's door.

He looked up at the Angel again, at her face full of compassionate concern. There was a resemblance, he decided: the plain yet pleasing features, the set of her lips, the wave of her hair. It gave some comfort, at least.

He stepped over the rim's edge into the low pool, shivering at the water's touch, at the numb languor that crept up his legs. Then, without further thought or gesture, he bent and slipped himself beneath the surface, to lie in the shallows of the fountain, his body cradled in its bowl.

The Golem ran.

More than sixty city blocks lay between her and her destination, and already the sun was crowning over the East River. A few hours earlier, she could've raced in the dark, silent and anonymous. In daylight she would be noticed, remarked upon.

The Golem found she did not care.

She ran, rooftop to rooftop, through the old Germantown tenements, the East River hard on her right. Waking men squinted at her approach; she heard their cries of surprise as she ignored the narrow plank bridges and vaulted over the alleyways below. She dodged chimneys, clotheslines, and water towers, and counted the blocks. *Nine, ten, eleven, twelve.*

Time slowed as she pushed herself. *Twenty, twenty-one, twenty-two.* Union Square fell behind her, then Madison Square Park. Where would he be by now? Fifty-ninth Street? On the carriage path? Was it already too late? She ran faster, trying to keep focus: one misstep at this speed would spell ruin. The wind was a high thin cry in her ears. Children stared from upper windows, and would later tell their friends they'd seen a lady outrun the Elevated. *Thirty-eight blocks. Thirty-nine. Forty.*

At last she could see the park, a distant square of green flashing between the buildings. She clattered down a fire escape, startling sleepers on the landings. And then she was running across the avenues, a plain-dressed woman who dodged the morning traffic like a fish navigating a shoal. A trolley rushed around a corner, and at the last moment she darted past it, ignoring the incredulous fears of the riders who'd seen her coming at them like a cannonball.

She was across Fifty-ninth; she was inside the park. She raced up the carriage drive and then the broad, tree-lined path, feeling the growing things all around her, adding their energy to her speed. Ahead of her, a man in threadbare clothes staggered upright from one of the benches, pressing a careful hand to his head. He straightened, blinking a newly bruised eye, and gaped as she ran past.

Down the stairs, through the arcade, and across the terrace: and even before she was at the fountain she could see him there, curled like a sleeping child beneath the water.

"*Ahmad!*" She jumped the edge of the fountain and plunged in, hooked her arms about him and dragged him back over the side. Water sluiced from his clothing as she laid him on the brick. He was cold, and pale as smoke, and so horribly light in her arms, as though his substance had evaporated. Frantically she tried to dry him, but there was nothing to hand—only her own clothes, already sopping wet.

"Ahmad! You have to wake up!"

There was a man at her side, gripping her arm.

"*Leave me alone!*" she cried, shrugging him away.

"I'm trying to help you!" came the shouted reply, in Arabic.

Saleh's head was pounding.

He winced, scolding himself for not realizing the Djinni would try something like this. Had he thought to simply talk him out of whatever plan he'd concocted? And why, for heaven's sake, was he helping a strange woman save the creature, instead of simply turning around and going home?

Surprisingly, the woman seemed to understand Arabic. She'd moved aside and was now watching with obvious panic as Saleh cupped the Djinni's chin in his hand, turning his head this way and that. He wondered who she was, how she'd known where to find them. *Leave it,* his mind whispered as he examined the too-pale face, felt the chest for a hint of warmth. *Just let the troublesome creature die.*

"Who are you?" asked the woman.

"Doctor Mahmoud Saleh," he muttered and pried open one of the Djinni's eyes. There: a spark. Bare and faltering, but undeniable. "He's still alive," he said. The woman cried out in relief. "Not just yet," he told her. "He's nearly gone."

"He needs warmth," the woman said. "A fire." She began a frenzied search of the horizon, as though she might find a handy blaze nearby.

Warmth, fire. A memory came to Saleh, tinged with ghostly colors. He saw a frost-covered garden, a gigantic mansion of stone set with innumerable gables—and, resting above them, four chimneys that puffed gray-white smoke into the winter sky.

I'd appreciate it if you called on Sophia Winston and conveyed my apologies.

"I know a place," he said. "But we'd have to carry him."

At this the woman scooped the Djinni into her arms, so easily he might have been a sheaf of wheat—and Saleh began to suspect that he was dealing with not one troublesome creature, but two.

"Doctor Saleh," she said. "How quickly can you run?"

27.

On the edge of Chinatown, in a holding cell of the city's Fifth Precinct House, an old man lay motionless, sprawled on the soiled floor.

The officer on duty squinted through the bars as he made his rounds. The old man had been brought in unconscious a few hours before, and he still hadn't stirred. Tiny glass shards powdered his face; his beard and pate were scabbed with blood. *Filthy anarchist*, the lieutenant who'd dragged him in had said, planting a boot in his ribs. But he didn't look like an anarchist. He looked like someone's grandfather.

Various cell mates had come and gone over the hours. A few had tried to pick the old man's pockets but found nothing worth the trouble. Now he lay alone, the last loose end of the overnight shift.

The officer unlocked the cell door and opened it, leaning on the hinges to make them sing. Still the old man didn't move. The light was dim, but as he approached, the officer could make out the rapid rolling of his lidded eyes, the clench of his jaw. His fingers were twitching in rhythmic spasms. Was he having a seizure? The officer took the nightstick from his belt, leaned down, and prodded one shoulder.

A hand shot up and grabbed his wrist.

The human mind is not meant to house a thousand years of memories.

At the moment of contact with the Djinni, the man who'd known himself as Yehudah Schaalman had burst apart at the seams. He became a miniature Babel, his skull crowding with his many lifetimes' worth of thoughts, in dozens of warring languages. Faces flashed before him: a hundred different divinities, male and female, animal gods and forest spirits, their features a blurred jumble. He saw precious gilded icons and crude carved busts, holy names written in ink, in blood, in stones and colored sand. He looked down, saw that he was clothed in velvet robes and carried a silver censer; he wore nothing but chalk, and his hands were clutching chicken bones.

The facts of Schaalman's life began to break apart. His yeshiva friends came to class in silks and soft slippers, mixed their inks in bowls of jade. A prison guard stood above him in a monk's robe and hood, wielding a knotted scourge. The baker's daughter turned dusky and black-eyed, her cries like the rolling of an unseen ocean.

His father lifted him from a wooden cradle. On the man's wrist was an iron cuff, tightly fitted. His mother took him in her arms, put him to a breast of clay.

Yehudah Schaalman thrashed in the current, choked, and went under.

In a moment it would be over, but still he fought. Blindly he reached out—and his fingers closed on a memory that was his and his alone.

He was nineteen again, and dreaming. There was a path, a door, a sunny meadow, a grove of trees in the distance. He took a step, was seized, and held. A voice spoke.

You do not belong here.

The old rage and grief rekindled, as fresh and painful as they had ever been, and turned to a burning lifeline in his fist. He broke the surface, and gasped.

Inch by agonizing inch he battled the current, setting his memories to rights. The silks and slippers fell from his classmates, the robes from the prison guard. The baker's daughter regained her sallow skin and hazel eyes. He reached his own first memory and kept going— back to the self before him, and then the one before that. He traveled each life from death to birth, watching himself worship gods and idols of every stripe. In each life his terror of judgment was all-consuming, and his belief absolute. For how could it be otherwise when each faith gave him such powers, allowing him to conjure illusions, scry futures, hurl curses? His own singed and stolen book, the source of all his wonders and horrors: never once had he doubted that it was the knowledge of the Almighty, the One before whom all others were mere graven images. Did its efficacy not prove that the Almighty was the supreme truth, the *only* truth? But now he saw that truths were as innumerable as falsehoods—that for sheer teeming chaos, the world of man could only be matched by the world of the divine. And as he traveled backward the Almighty shrank smaller and smaller, until He was merely another desert deity, and His commandments seemed no more than the fearful demands of a jealous lover. And yet Schaalman had spent his entire life in terror of Him, dreading His judgment in the World to Come—a world that he would never see!

The further back he went, the greater his anger grew, as he watched all his previous selves toiling in their frightened and fervent delusions. Faster and faster his lives rewound—until at last he reached the source, the mouth of the torrent, where there sat an ancient, filthy pagan named Wahab ibn Malik al-Hadid.

The two men regarded each other across the centuries.

I know you, said ibn Malik. *I've seen your face.*

You dreamed of me, said Schaalman. *You saw me in a shining city that rose from the water's edge.*

Who are you?

I am Yehudah Schaalman, the last of your lives. I am the one who will set things right for all my lives to come.

Your lives?

Yes, mine. You were merely the beginning. You bound yourself to the Djinni without realizing the consequences, and your selves died time and again, never the wiser. I was the one to learn the secret.

Much good it will do, ibn Malik said, *when you die in your turn and the secret is lost.*

I will find a way, said Schaalman.

Perhaps, perhaps not. And the Djinni, what of him? His kind are long-lived, but not immortal. When he dies, we die as well.

Then he must refrain from dying.

So you think to recapture him? Be certain this is not beyond your limits.

As it was yours?

The dead eyes narrowed. *And what are you but myself, dressed in strange clothing and speaking another tongue?*

I am the sum total of a thousand years of misery and striving! You may have given us this broken immortality, but I will be the first to die without fear!

Ibn Malik snarled in anger; but Schaalman was faster. A hand lashed out and caught ibn Malik around the throat.

You cost me any chance at happiness, Schaalman said.

Ibn Malik writhed around his fist. *I gave you boundless knowledge instead.*

A poor second, said Yehudah Schaalman, and squeezed.

The slop-bucket stench of the cell greeted Schaalman as he woke. His ribs felt bruised, and his face burned with tiny cuts. He tried to get up, but a man in a police uniform was collapsed on top of him. Black blood ran from the man's ears; wisps of smoke rose from his torso. Schaalman realized he was holding the man's wrist. He dropped it, and wrestled free.

The door to the cell stood open. Beyond it was a dank corridor, and then the precinct house. He whispered a few words and walked unseen past the handful of officers yawning at their posts. In a moment he was out the open door.

Quickly he walked toward Chinatown's eastern border, and the Sheltering House beyond. His mind still ached with the press of memory, but the threat of dissolution had receded. For the moment his former selves lay quiet, as though waiting to see what he would do next.

It was only five-thirty, but already Sophia Winston was sitting alone at her family's long dining table, finishing her tea and toast. For her first nineteen years, Sophia had never been an early riser, preferring to languish in bed until her mother sent the maid in to wake and dress her. Now, however, she was awake and shivering before dawn. The poor maid was forced to wake even earlier, to build the fire in the dining room and ready her mistress's breakfast. Then the fire had to be lit in her rooms as well—she would retire there after she ate—before the maid could finally return downstairs and fall back into bed.

Sophia had discovered she liked being awake this early, before the rest of the household. She preferred to be alone, reading her father's travel journals, sipping her tea by the dining room's roaring fireplace. The only unwelcome company was the portrait of herself as a Turkish princess, Charles's engagement gift to her. The portrait had been something of a disaster. On the canvas she stood not stately but pensive in her costume, even melancholy, her gaze lowered. She looked less like a princess than an odalisque, captured and resigned. Poor Charles had looked stricken at its unveiling. He'd said little at the supper afterward, only watched her hand shake as she ate her soup. Her mother had ordered the portrait hung in the dining room, instead of the main hall, as though punishing it for failing to meet expectations.

She sipped her tea, and glanced at the clock. Her father liked to wake at six; he would be down soon after for the papers, and then her mother would follow him, to discuss the day's schedule. Little George would evade his governess and run in, demanding morning kisses. As much as she liked her solitude, she appreciated the morning commotion. It was a brief but necessary reminder that they were actually a family.

She had almost finished her tea when she heard hurried footsteps in the front hall. She'd just had time to think that it was early for visitors, and that she had not heard the bell, when she heard a raised voice—it was one of the footmen—and then a woman's answer, forceful and urgent. A shout; and then the dining room door burst open. An apparition filled the doorway. It was one of the tallest women Sophia had ever seen. In her arms she carried, somehow, a full-grown man.

"I'm sorry to intrude," the woman said in an accented voice. "But we need your fireplace."

She strode into the room. Behind her appeared a man in ragged clothing. A footman lunged for the woman, but she was moving too quickly—how was it possible, with the man in her arms? She brushed past Sophia, who'd stood in surprise, and Sophia caught a glimpse of her improbable burden. He was tall, and thin, and soaking wet. His face was hidden in the woman's shoulder. A thick metal cuff circled one wrist; it caught the firelight and flashed like a beacon.

Shock coursed through her, stronger than any chill. She stood, mesmerized, as the woman knelt before the giant fireplace, swept the screen aside, and threw the man into the fire.

The footman shouted in fright, but now the ill-dressed man grabbed him and tried to wrestle him out of the room, saying something in a language Sophia couldn't place. The woman stared intently into the blaze, as though waiting for a sign. The fire had banked at the man's weight, but now it was crackling merrily again, surrounding him with flames like a Viking on his pyre. As Sophia watched, his clothing began to smolder and burn away, leaving his skin whole and untouched.

He'd told her a story once, hadn't he, while she lay half-asleep in his arms? A story about the djinn, fantastic creatures made of fire. And then, in Paris, that all-consuming heat, as though a burning spark had lodged inside her body. It made no sense at all—and yet something whispered to her, *yes, of course. You have always known this.*

Clouds of smoke filled the room, and the stench of burning cotton. The footman broke from his wrestling match and ran into the hall, presumably to raise the alarm. The ill-dressed foreigner scowled in resignation and went to the tall woman's side. He spoke to her in that other language, and she nodded. "Ahmad," she called.

The figure on the fire stirred.

"There!" the woman shouted, joy in her voice. The ragged man said something in reply, hand shielding his eyes.

A commotion from outside; and then the butler strode in shouting, tailed by three footmen and, Sophia's heart sank to see, her father. The woman turned at their approach, her back to the fireplace, as though to shield the man inside. She was bracing for a fight, Sophia realized. Her father was calling for the police. The room was about to break into pandemonium.

"*Everyone please be quiet,*" Sophia shouted.

And indeed the room quieted, in surprise as much as anything. Sophia crossed to the fireplace and bent to see more clearly. "Sophia," her father called, a frightened warning.

"It's all right, Father," she said. "I know this man."

"*What?*"

The man on the fire moved again, convulsing as though in pain. The logs beneath him shifted, and Sophia and the woman jumped backward as he tumbled out of the fireplace in a cloud of smoke and ash. He came to rest curled on the flagstones, his body streaked with soot and embers. The air around him shimmered, and for a moment Sophia thought she saw him glowing like a coal.

Swiftly the tall woman bent over him. The ragged man said something in warning, and she pulled her hands back at the last moment. "Ahmad?" she said.

The man whispered something.

"Yes, it's me," the woman said, and her voice was choked with emotion, though her eyes were dry. "I'm here." She touched his arm quickly, like a cook testing a pan for heat. Apparently finding him cool enough, she rested her hand on his shoulder. His eyes didn't open, but one hand reached up to cover hers.

Sophia looked about the room and might have laughed at the tableau: the most prominent household in New York, reduced to gawking open-mouthed at a naked man on their dining room floor. The servants all hung back, some crossing themselves. Someone whispered to her father, "Sir, the police are in the hall." The woman's head came up at this, her look one of fierce protection.

"No," Sophia said. She moved to stand in front of the three intruders. "Father, send the police away. They aren't needed."

"Sophia, go upstairs. We'll speak later."

"I told you, I know this man. I'll vouch for him, and his friends."

"Don't be ridiculous. How could you possibly—"

"They're my guests," she said firmly. "Send the police away. And someone please fetch this man a blanket." She turned away from them and bent over the familiar figure, who still had barely moved. The tall woman was watching her strangely, as though trying to see inside her. "You know him," the woman said.

She nodded, took the man's other hand in hers. "Ahmad?"

His eyes did not open, but his forehead creased in a frown. "Sophia?" he murmured; and she heard her father draw a shocked breath.

"Yes, it's me," she said, aware of the eyes on her, the too-accurate conclusions they were all drawing. Her cheeks would have burned were she warm enough. "You're in my home. You're safe here." She cast a challenging glance at her father, but he only stood pale and stricken. "What happened to him?" she asked the woman.

"He tried to end his own life."

"My God! But why?"

The woman looked like she would have said more but then glanced about the room, at the frightened and attentive faces. Sophia said, "Perhaps we should discuss this in private. We'll take him to my bedroom. There should be a fire lit already."

A maid entered with a heavy wool blanket; she handed it to Sophia and backed away, clearly terrified. Together the tall woman and the ragged man covered their half-conscious charge and lifted him to his feet, supporting him from either side. Sophia placed a protective hand on the woman's arm, and together, under watchful eyes, the group walked from the dining room. "Father, I'll speak with you soon," she said as they left.

They bundled him into Sophia's bed, and placed a copper foot-warmer under the covers. The ragged man—one Dr. Saleh, it seemed, who spoke only Arabic—set about strengthening the fire, and soon the room was warm enough even for Sophia's comfort. Then Dr. Saleh and the woman, whose name was apparently Chava, talked quietly together for some minutes, with frequent glances at Sophia.

"I apologize for involving you in this," the woman said to her at length, "but we had no choice, Ahmad's life was at stake." A pause. "I take it that you know what he is?"

"I think so," Sophia said. "And you are the same?"

The woman glanced away, suddenly self-conscious. "No," she said. "I'm . . . something else. A golem."

Sophia had no idea what that meant but was unsure how to say this, so she merely nodded. "Please tell me what happened."

And so the Golem related the story. Sophia had a feeling that a number of details were being omitted, but only listened as the Golem described finding the Djinni in Bethesda Fountain. "But that's where I first met him," Sophia said, confused. "And I still don't understand—why would he do this?"

"You may stop talking about me as though I'm not here," a voice muttered from the bed.

The Golem was first to his side—she moved so impossibly fast! "Hello, Ahmad," she said quietly.

"Chava," he said. "You shouldn't have rescued me."

"Don't be foolish. Too much has been lost already."

A harsh laugh. "You say more than you know."

"Hush." She took his hand and squeezed it, as though making certain he was truly there; and suddenly Sophia felt like an interloper in her own bedroom.

The Djinni noticed Dr. Saleh, and said something to him in Arabic, his tone affronted. The doctor responded in kind, gruff and sarcastic, then wiped a hand across his brow. He had, Sophia noticed, gone rather sickly-looking. The Golem asked a question, and he replied dismissively; but it was clear that the heat of the room disagreed with him.

"I'm afraid Dr. Saleh has had a strenuous morning, and little to eat," the Golem told her.

"Of course. I'll take him downstairs, and make certain he's seen to."

A faraway look had come into the Golem's eye. She said, "You might also assure everyone at the foot of the stairs that we're not in fact murdering you, and there's no need to break down the door."

Sophia stared at her. "What, truly?"

"I'm afraid so."

"In that case, I thank you for the warning," she said and resolved to find out what a golem was as soon as possible.

She took Dr. Saleh down to the kitchen, and told the staff in no uncertain terms to feed him, and see to his needs. They stared at her as though she'd grown horns, but nodded and bobbed all the same. Whispers trailed her as she left.

Upstairs she was told that her parents were in the library, waiting to speak with her. She decided she would take this as an opportunity. The servants, she'd tell her parents, were bound to gossip, and her reputation would most certainly be damaged. Why not break the engagement now, before it could end in ignominy? And perhaps it would be best if she traveled for a while, while the rumors ran their course. India, South America, Asia. The warmer climates.

She tried to hide her smile as she opened the library door.

The morning service was already under way when Michael Levy reached his uncle's old synagogue. He'd been wandering the Lower East Side, trying to comprehend the ruin of his life, when he'd realized where his path was taking him. He had no strength left to change his course. He could not stomach the thought of going home. But neither could he go back to the Sheltering House, for fear that she would still be there. He supposed he should be grateful that she'd managed to warn him, that he'd escaped with his life; but at the moment, gratitude lay far beyond his reach.

His uncle's old synagogue had originally been a Methodist church. It was a blandly anonymous worship hall of rough-hewn gray stone, neither imposing nor welcoming, the sort of building that might change hands a dozen times with the neighbors none the wiser. Inside, twenty or so men gathered at the front of the wooden pews. Most were nearing his uncle's age. Michael hesitated just outside the sanctuary, suddenly resistant. He dreaded being recognized by his uncle's old cohorts. They would whisper praises to God on his behalf, claim him as proof that one always returns to faith in times of difficulty.

Well, would they be wrong? He had accepted as truth that his wife was a clay creature brought to life by—what? The will of God? Must he believe in God now, if he was to make sense of this? The thought made him feel petulant, as though he were a child again, being dragged to school against his will. But neither could he unlearn what he'd discovered.

The service began, the men's voices surging and falling. *You have turned my lament into dancing, You loosened my sackcloth and girded me with joy.* They chanted the psalms and praises, and as always the rhythm fastened itself to his heartbeat. It seemed unfair that the prayers could affect him this way, against his will; that he could scoff at the sentiments, yet find himself mouthing along. He imagined himself at ninety, toothless and doddering, unable to remember anything except for the morning prayers. They were his deepest memories, his first music.

He didn't know when, exactly, he'd stopped believing. It had not come on suddenly, nor had he argued himself into unbelief, no matter what his uncle had thought. No, he'd simply noticed one day that God had disappeared. Perhaps he'd never truly believed in the first place. Or else he'd simply swapped one belief for another, loving neither God nor atheism but ideology for its own sake—as he'd fallen in love not with a woman, but the image of one.

Chava Levy, he thought, *you are a hard fact to live with.*

All at once his throat filled with tears. Holding back a sob, he left his spot at the sanctuary door and returned to the street. He could no longer hear the chanting, but his mind took up the thread, leading him unwillingly through the rest of the service as he walked back to the Sheltering House. It was his only true home now, and he supposed if he had a religion, the House was its temple, dedicated not to gods or ideas but living, fallible men. If his wife was there, he would face her.

The House was just waking up when he arrived. The smell of coffee wafted down the hallway; he could hear the ancient pipes creaking in the walls. He braced himself, but his office was empty, the door ajar.

He sat down at his desk and, despite everything, was contemplating starting the ordinary business of the day when he realized that Joseph Schall's sheaf of burnt papers was missing. In his alcoholic fog of the night before, he'd forgotten all about it—had, in fact, forgotten about Joseph.

Frantically he searched his desk. His uncle's notes were still inside the drawer where Michael had shoved them, but Joseph's burned pages were nowhere to be seen. Had Joseph returned from wherever he'd disappeared to and found them in his office? Or had his wife taken them? If he could just locate them and return them to their spot under Joseph's cot, and keep him none the wiser. . . .

A shadow fell across his open door.

"It's strange," Joseph said mildly. "I was just looking for something myself. I think we might have a thief among us." He regarded Michael. "Or perhaps you already knew that."

An icy sweat broke out on Michael's brow. He stood there trapped, painfully aware of his visible guilt and terror.

"I see," Joseph said. He closed the door behind him with a quiet click. His face, Michael saw, was bruised and cut, and his clothing glinted with what looked like tiny pieces of glass. "So. How shall we proceed, you and I?"

"I don't have your papers," Michael said. "They're gone. They disappeared."

Joseph raised an eyebrow. "And did you read them, before they disappeared?"

"Yes."

"Ah, but did you understand?"

"Enough."

Joseph nodded. "Don't think too harshly of your wife," he said. "She was only following her nature, as best she could. A golem is lost without a master."

"I wanted to be her husband, not her master."

"How enlightened of you," Joseph said. His voice had turned flat, its usual drollness gone. "Now. Where is my property?"

"I don't know."

"Hazard a guess."

Michael said nothing.

Joseph sighed. "Perhaps you don't understand after all. I was being kind. I have no need to ask."

An absurd laugh bubbled up in Michael's throat.

Joseph, annoyed, said, "Is something amusing you?"

"I was just realizing that this is who you've been, all this time."

"And what of it?"

"Oh, nothing. Only you really did help them, you know."

"Who?"

"All the men who've come through this House. You helped them find their cots, and gave them good advice, and cleaned up after them. You were a friendly face in a strange city. It must have been torture for you."

"You have no idea."

Michael smiled. "Good. I'm glad it hurt. Though I pity you, I really do. All that power doesn't seem to have gotten you very far."

Joseph's eyes had turned to slits. Michael swallowed and said, "In fact, if you think about it, all those men, the ones you hated helping—

they've all moved on from here, to bigger and better things. You're the one who's been left behind."

"Spare me your pity," Joseph said—and then lunged forward and grabbed Michael by the head.

Michael never lost consciousness as his memories were torn apart. His assailant proceeded in haphazard fashion, grabbing fistfuls of moments in his rage, so that as he died, Michael was bombarded with recollections. He was playing stickball in the street with his friends; he was fleeing down a hallway, running for his life. His aunt cried while he tore up a letter, unread, from his father. A nurse at Swinburne pressed a cool hand to his forehead. He'd skipped school, and now his uncle was bending him over his knee, the half-hesitant slaps betraying discomfort at the task. He was standing in a parlor, watching a tall woman descend a staircase, his heart a joyous, painful weight.

At last, Joseph let go, and Michael collapsed unseeing to the floor.

Schaalman stood a moment, considering what he'd gleaned. Then he stepped to the desk and opened a drawer. There, stuffed in at the top, were Rabbi Meyer's notes on the Golem, right where Michael had left them.

Schaalman leafed through the notes with growing excitement, following the Rabbi's painstaking progress, his discoveries and setbacks. At last he understood why Meyer had stolen those precious volumes from his own colleagues. He'd thought the man to be his nemesis, when in truth Meyer had been building a precious gift for him to find. He had to acknowledge its subtle artistry, so much calmer and more practicable than his own frenzied divinations. The formula's requirement that it be used only with the Golem's permission, for example—that was something he never could have constructed. Though in truth, he would never have thought to try.

An odd irony, to ask that the Golem part freely with her own free will. No doubt Meyer had envisioned a heartfelt conversation with his charge, a solemn and reasoned decision. Schaalman folded the formula and placed it in his pocket, and reflected that in this instance, his own methods would trump Meyer's. After all, a choice made under coercion was still a choice.

28.

The Golem was struggling to comprehend.

For long minutes now, the Djinni had been talking in a low, tired voice, telling her a story of long ago: of a grasping desert wizard and a young girl named Fadwa al-Hadid. He'd described the pain of the binding and the feel of Fadwa's throat beneath his hands, and how ibn Malik had died only to be reborn again and again.

"It seems you know the rest," the Djinni said as she sat, stunned, at the side of Sophia's bed. He was half sitting up now, buried beneath expensive linens, his shoulders against the carved headboard. "Ibn Malik became Yehudah Schaalman."

"Joseph Schall," she murmured. "And you saw his memories." His hand was resting above the coverlet, and the Golem took it in her own, noting that it was beginning to feel weighty again. "So this is why you tried to kill yourself," she said. "To end ibn Malik's life, through your own death."

He was watching her now, sorrow in every line of his face. He expected her to regret saving him, she realized, now that she knew the whole truth. "Listen to me," she said. "This is ibn Malik's doing. Not yours."

"And Fadwa?" he said. "If I hadn't injured her, then none of this would have happened."

"You place too much of a burden on yourself. Yes, Fadwa's injury can be laid at your feet. But ibn Malik was not acting on your orders. And Schaalman has a free will of his own."

"I'm not so certain of that last one," the Djinni said. "I saw his lives, and they all followed the same pattern. As though he could not break free of his own disposition."

The Golem's mouth twisted. "You believe he couldn't choose not to do evil?"

"We all have our natures," said the Djinni quietly.

She wanted to argue, but where would it lead her, except to point a finger back at herself? Frustrated, she rose, paced a few steps. "Yes, you were selfish and careless with Fadwa," she said. "But you cannot accept the blame for the rest, disposition or no. If Schaalman had not existed, then neither would I. Are you responsible for all my actions, the good as well as the bad? You cannot pick and choose, and leave the rest behind."

He gave her a shadow of his usual smile. "I suppose not," he said. Then he sobered. "But do you see now, why I can't keep living?"

"No," she said shortly.

"Chava."

"Didn't you stop me from destroying myself, once? We'll find another way."

He winced but didn't reply, only looked down at her hand still gripping his on the coverlet.

A knock came at the door. It was Sophia, carrying a pile of folded clothing. Servants were hovering in the hall behind her, trying to see in; she shut the door on them.

"Hello, Sophia," the Djinni said quietly.

She smiled. "You're looking better." She placed the folded clothing on the bed. "My father's not as tall as you, but hopefully something will fit."

"Sophia," he said, his voice heavy, and it was clear he was about to apologize—for drawing her into this misadventure, or for something earlier in their acquaintance, the Golem could only guess at the content—but Sophia crisply interrupted. "Dr. Saleh is freshening himself in the guest quarters," she said. "We should join him there soon, if you're feeling able."

The Djinni nodded, abashed.

"I'm afraid we've caused you a good deal of trouble," the Golem said.

"Perhaps," Sophia said, though she seemed oddly unconcerned, even happy. "Even so, I'm glad you thought to come here." She turned to the Djinni, sobering. "You should have told me."

He sighed. "Would you have believed it?"

"No, probably not. Still, you might have tried."

The Djinni hesitated, then said, "Are you well, Sophia?"

It was only then that the Golem noticed the young woman's pale skin and too-warm clothing, the tremor in her hands. Sophia considered her reply, and the Golem sensed a knotted tangle of longings and regrets and, above all, a deep desire not to be pitied.

"I've been ill," Sophia said. "But I believe I'm improving." She smiled. "Now please, put on some clothes. I'll be back to fetch you in a few minutes."

She left, and the Djinni began to sort through the items she'd brought. The Golem sat on a corner of the bed, not sure where to look— watching him dress was somehow more intimate than seeing him na- ked. She went to the young woman's dressing table, idly examining the objects scattered there: a gilded hairbrush, a beautiful necklace of silver and glass, an apothecary's assortment of bottles and jars. Atop a jeweler's box sat a golden bird in a cage, its provenance unmistakable. "You made her one too," she said.

The Djinni buttoned his shirt collar. "Is that jealousy? At least she didn't return hers."

"I couldn't keep it, I was about to marry," the Golem muttered.

Silence hung between them.

"Michael," the Djinni said at last. "He's been caught up in this as well, hasn't he?"

She sighed. "There's something else I haven't told you." And he listened, shocked and grave by turns, as she described finding Michael at the Sheltering House with Schaalman's spells, and her struggle with their contents.

"Where are they now?" he asked.

"Anna has them," she said, and then, at the face he made, "I couldn't leave them at the bakery! She's hiding them somewhere. But I don't know what to do with them."

"Burn them," he said shortly.

"Destroy all that knowledge?"

"Schaalman's knowledge. Ibn Malik's."

"I thought," she said quietly, "that I might use them to free you."

That struck him a visible blow. She watched him turn away, strug- gling with himself. After a moment he looked down at his shirt and started tugging on the sleeves. "Sophia's father has very short arms," he muttered.

"Ahmad—"

"No. You mustn't use this knowledge. Promise me this."

"I promise," she murmured.

"Good." He gave a sigh. "Now tell me, am I presentable to the household?"

She looked him over, smiling slightly: Sophia's father was wider than the Djinni, and the borrowed garments billowed like sails. "More so than before."

He grimaced. "At least they aren't the rags that Arbeely gave me when I came out of the flask."

"You were naked then too? Do you make such a habit of it?"

But he was gazing past her, unseeing. "The flask," he said.

"What about it?"

"Maryam Faddoul still has it. And it's been repaired. Arbeely replaced the seal, he said he copied it exactly." He paused, and then said, his voice strained, "You were right, Chava, there's another way. But you won't like it."

Anna left the Radzins' bakery with her strange package, wondering what exactly she'd been entrusted with. The flat, crackling lump at the bottom of the sack could only be a stack of papers. What was written on them? Someone's secrets? An incriminating confession? Her promise notwithstanding, she almost opened the sack to peek inside—but then she remembered who had given it to her, and the horrors she'd already witnessed. This would be no clandestine love-diary. Best not to know. She would think of a hiding place quickly and be done.

In the end, she chose the dance hall on Broome Street. It was in her mind already, thanks to the Golem—she hadn't been back there since that terrible night and, given its new associations, had doubted she ever would. But when she tried to think of somewhere else, her mind kept circling back. She even knew exactly where she'd hide the sack: atop the old armoire in the back room, where they kept the linens for the tables. All she had to do was to find Mendel the doorman and cajole him into giving her the key. As far as she knew, he still worked at a piecework shop on Delancey, pressing new trousers. Hopefully he'd be there.

Yehudah Schaalman sat scowling at a writing desk in the House parlor, covering a sheet of paper with scrawled and scratched-out lines. The formula to find a lost object should have been easy to remember; he'd used it hundreds of times. But his memories were no longer safe ground. To delve too deeply was to risk rousing his former selves, who might then chime in with their own solutions, deafening him in the cacophony. He had to tread lightly, sidling up to a recollection and examining it askance, capturing the formula a few syllables at a time. It was a slow and painstaking process, and he was in no mood to accommodate it.

A shriek sounded down the hall. He ignored it, ignored the pounding footsteps and the growing sounds of alarm, and tried to concentrate. At last, the formula to find his sheaf of spells was complete. He looked it over—it seemed correct—then braced himself, and spoke what he'd written.

And then he saw—

A flash of a woman's dark workaday skirt, the waist let out to accommodate an eight-month belly. At her side she held a flour sack. The woman—and now Schaalman recognized her, from the tenement hallway—was standing in an open doorway, flirting with a large, sweating boy. She told him something in a teasing voice. The boy's glance darted briefly to her stomach. He said something, a demand. The girl did not look pleased, but finally she nodded. The boy took a string from around his neck; on it hung a door key. He dangled it high, making the girl reach; and as she did he grabbed her and kissed her roughly on the mouth, then reached to grope at her breast. She allowed it for a few moments, then pushed him away firmly, her expression calm. A flash of guilt on the boy's face; then he sniggered at her and went back in. The door closed. Her face crumpled for a moment, but then she composed herself. Clutching the key and the flour sack, she went down to the street. Schaalman took note of the shops, the street corners, saw that she was only a few blocks away.

On Broome, she went to an unmarked door, fitted the key in the padlock, and disappeared inside.

Schaalman came to, his head swimming. He sat as still as possible until his vision was restored and the pounding in his temples had lessened. The pregnant girl—she knew his golem, did she not? Perhaps he had found not only his missing spells, but the bait to snare his golem's consent.

Outside the parlor, the hallway was in commotion. A crowd had formed around Michael's office door. The housekeeper sat on the staircase, sobbing. The cook was talking to a policeman. She saw Schaalman, and her look implored him: *Joseph, see what has happened.* But he was already gone, down the hall and out the door.

The Winstons' hansom, though elegant, was not quite roomy enough for three; but they squeezed in nonetheless, Saleh, the Djinni, and the Golem. The horse tramped smartly through the Winstons' gate and onto Fifth Avenue, only to be stymied in the morning traffic with everyone else. Stuffed into the corner, Saleh started drifting into sleep. He fought it at first, but fatigue and his newly full stomach—the cook had given him a plate of cold meats and a brandied fruit compote, though it was clear she'd rather be shot—soon had him snoring. The Djinni was thankful; it afforded some privacy, without so obvious a tactic as switching languages.

But the Golem, it seemed, was in no mood to talk. Earlier she'd put up surprisingly little protest at his plan, only asking a few practical questions and translating into English for Sophia. Now she seemed conspicuously silent, even for her. She stared at the cabs and carts that idled around them, her face like a stone. In any case, it wasn't as though he knew what to say to her. Everything that came to mind seemed either too trivial or too final. If all went well, if the plan worked, he would never see her again.

"Will it hurt?" she asked abruptly, startling him. "Being in the flask again. Will it hurt you?"

"No," he said. "At least, I don't remember any pain."

"Perhaps it did hurt," she said, her voice toneless. "For a thousand years. And you just don't remember."

"Chava—"

"No, say nothing. I'll go along with this plan, because we must do something to prevent Schaalman from finding you, and using you. But don't think for a moment that I do it gladly. You're turning me into your jailer."

"You're the only one with the strength to put me in the flask. It certainly weakened ibn Malik. I think it might kill someone like Saleh."

"No one is asking him to—"

"Of course not! I only meant . . ." He trailed off, frustrated. "I know how much this asks of you. Leaving New York, going to Syria. The voyage won't be comfortable for you, on a crowded ship."

"The voyage is the least of it," she said. "What if your kin can't protect you from him? What if there aren't any djinn anymore?" He flinched, and she said, "I know, but we must consider it! Am I supposed to just bury you in the desert and hope for the best?"

"Yes, if you must. And then leave me. Go somewhere far away, as far as possible. I won't have you defending me. He may not be your master, but he can destroy you just the same."

"But where should I go? To start over, somewhere else . . . I can barely picture it. I'm not like you. New York is all I know."

"It won't be for long. He doesn't have much time left. A few years at most."

"And after that? Should I search the world for his reincarnations, and murder them in their cradles?"

"I think I know you better than that."

"Oh, do you?"

"Then you could do it? Truly?"

A pause, and then: "No. Even knowing . . . no."

They fell silent. The hansom crept along, finally reaching the southern edge of the park. They cut west, and the air grew heavy with the exhalations of the trees beyond the wall.

At last he asked, "Will Michael be all right without you?" He'd tried, and failed, not to tense at the name.

"Michael will be better off for my leaving. I hope he can forgive me someday." She glanced across at him. "I haven't told you why I married him."

"Maybe I don't want to know," he muttered.

"I did it because you'd taken the paper from my locket. I couldn't destroy myself. I had to live in the world, and I was terrified. So I hid behind Michael. I tried to turn him into my master. I honestly thought it would be better that way."

The self-recrimination in her voice was painful to hear. "You were frightened," he said.

"Yes, and in my fear I made the weakest, most selfish mistake of my existence. So how can you possibly trust me to carry your life in my hands?"

"I trust you above all others," he told her. "Above myself."

She shook her head, but then leaned into him, as though taking shelter. He drew her close, the crown of her head beneath his cheek. Beyond the hansom's window, New York was an endless rhythm of walls and windows and doors, darkened alleys, flashes of sunlight. He thought, if he could pick a moment to be taken into the flask, a moment to live in endlessly, perhaps he would choose this one: the passing city, and the woman at his side.

It was midmorning, the coffeehouse's busiest hour. At the sidewalk tables, backgammon pieces clicked on the boards. Inside, men discussed business in idle tones.

Arbeely sat alone, toying with his coffee-cup. The shop had been too quiet that morning, the silence pressing against his ears. His eye kept straying from his work to the Djinni's unoccupied bench. Arbeely reminded himself that he'd done well before meeting his erstwhile partner, and would do so again. Yet the entire shop seemed to be holding its breath, waiting for the Djinni to come through the door.

Finally he could take no more and went to the Faddouls', to distract himself with the buzz of other people's conversations. He glanced around at the full tables. Maryam traveled about with her coffee and gossip, easily navigating the crowded room. From his vantage he could see how each table grew more lively at her arrival, how each of her smiles was a push to the flywheel that kept the coffeehouse humming. In the kitchen Sayeed ground the coffee and cardamom and boiled the water, in his own practiced dance. Watching them, Arbeely felt a swelling of loneliness.

As if drawn like a moth to his melancholy, Maryam soon angled toward him, concern on her face. "Boutros, are you all right?"

He wanted to ask her, *Maryam, have I been a bachelor too long? Did I miss my chance?* But a shadow fell across the doorway, and the conversations around them paused.

It was the Djinni. At his side was a tall, imposing woman whom Arbeely had never seen before. And behind them was a man dressed like a vagrant, but who held himself like a person of consequence. His features tugged at Arbeely's memory. *Ice Cream Saleh*, someone whispered, and he was shocked to realize that it was true.

The Djinni's gaze swept the coffeehouse until he found Maryam, and then Arbeely next to her. A moment of surprise; but then, undeterred, he cut across the coffeehouse toward them, his companions close behind.

Maryam was staring at Saleh, mouth agape. *"Mahmoud?"*

The dark eyes, newly sharp, threatened tears. "Maryam," the man said, his voice thick. "It's a pleasure to see you."

She laughed, delighted, her own eyes filling in response. "Oh, Mahmoud, how wonderful! But how did this happen?" Her gaze went to the Djinni, and she turned wary. Her husband came to the kitchen door, ready to intervene.

"Perhaps we could speak with you in private," the Djinni said quietly. And then, to Arbeely, "I think you should hear this as well."

And so, after a few quick words with Sayeed, she took them to her home above the coffeehouse, and sat them at her parlor table. Then the Djinni began to talk. In low plain words he uncloaked himself, apologizing for the lies they'd told her, one by one. He explained who the tall woman sitting beside him was, and Arbeely, still reeling from the Djinni's new-found frankness, struggled to comprehend her existence. *Last night I met a woman made of clay*, the Djinni had told him once—and now here she was, a solemn Hebrew giantess, answering Maryam's questions in perfect Arabic while the Djinni listened, his concern for her plain and startling.

"Wait," Arbeely interjected, confused and incredulous. "Are you saying you mean to go back into the flask?" Had this woman coerced him, had she woven some spell? The woman, eyes lowered, murmured something to the Djinni in another language; the Djinni said, "Arbeely, your fears are unfounded. This is my decision alone." Somehow this did not make him feel any better.

Another question from Maryam, and this time Saleh answered, telling of a man who'd come knocking at the Djinni's door. He described the wrenching pain of the exorcism, like a dentist extracting a rotten tooth. And then the Golem and the Djinni both, their comments in counterpoint: *my creator, my master*.

It all sounded like madness. But Maryam listened, and considered. At length she went to the kitchen and returned with the flask, and placed it in the center of the table. They all stared at it, save the Djinni, who looked away, his mouth tight. The sunlight picked out the intricate tracing, the curving lines and loops that wove through one another, chasing their own tails.

"It is yours," Maryam said, "if you want it."

"You believe them?" Arbeely blurted in surprise.

"Must I believe, to part with it? To me it's merely my mother's old copper flask. It's clear that Ahmad values it much more highly." She picked it up and handed it to the Djinni, who took it as though it were a powder keg. "I wish you luck, Ahmad."

"Thank you," said the Djinni. And then, looking around: "Is Matthew . . . ?"

"He's at school," said Maryam.

The Djinni nodded, his disappointment plain. Maryam hesitated; at last she said, "I'll tell him you said good-bye."

They went down to the street, the flask tightly held in the Djinni's hand.

Maryam took her leave and returned to her customers, squeezing her husband's shoulder in passing. The rest of them stood uncomfortably in the noonday light, the sense of urgency straining against a sorrowful reluctance. The Djinni had explained that there was little time; their only defense now was speed and distance, fleeing across the ocean before Schaalman knew to follow. The ship to Marseille would leave in a few hours—Sophia was arranging a single steerage ticket—and before that, the Golem must retrieve Schaalman's spells from Anna so that they, too, could be buried in the desert.

"And you, Saleh?" the Djinni asked. "What will you do now?"

The question had been lurking in Saleh's mind ever since he'd woken clear-eyed on the Djinni's bare floor. Should he go on as Ice Cream Saleh, measuring his life in pennies and turns of the churn handle? Or become Doctor Mahmoud once again? In truth neither name seemed to fit anymore; he suspected he was now something else, something new, but he had no idea what. He'd lived so long in anticipation of his own death that to contemplate his future was like standing at the edge of a cliff, staring into a vertiginous rush of open sky. "I'll have to consider," he said. "For now, I'll content myself with finding my churn." And he too said good-bye, his gaze lingering on the Djinni's face before he turned away.

"Well," Arbeely said, growing awkward. "I'll miss you, Ahmad."

The Djinni raised an eyebrow. "Really? Yesterday you implied otherwise."

Arbeely waved a hand. "Forget all that. Besides," he said, attempting humor, "who will I argue with now? Matthew?"

I'll miss you as well, the Djinni wanted to say; but it was not the truth. The flask would not allow him to miss any of them. Grief squeezed him again, and the beginnings of panic. He clasped Arbeely's hand, then broke away, half-turning his back. "We must do this soon," he muttered to the Golem, "or I'll lose my nerve."

"Chava," Arbeely said, "I'm glad we met. Please, take good care of him." She nodded—and then Arbeely too was gone. They stood alone on the busy sidewalk.

"Then this is it?" the Golem murmured. "It must happen now?"

The Djinni nodded; but then he paused. Something strange was happening. A creeping dimness crossed his vision, and his hearing began to fade. With no warning, the sidewalk vanished and he was wrenched away—

Anna stood before him, holding a stack of crumbling pages. Her face was empty, her features slack. His own hands, veined and spotted, reached out to her shoulders. Slowly he turned her around, stepped behind her, and considered the image they made in the mirrored column, as though posed for a family portrait. Behind them the dance hall was flooded with light. He reached up his hands, and placed them around the girl's throat.

"Bring the creature here," he told his reflection. "And the flask as well. Or I will make you a murderer again."

He felt the Golem's cool skin beneath his fingers. His hands had moved on their own, had grabbed her wrists as though to drag her to Schaalman's side. *The binding,* the Djinni realized. It had never been broken—and now Schaalman could control him, just as ibn Malik had.

Aghast, she said, "Ahmad? What is it, what's wrong?"

What a fool Schaalman was, the Djinni thought bitterly; how little he knew his own creation. Why bother to threaten him, when the Golem would never knowingly abandon Anna, not even to secure a greater good? She would go to him of her own free will—and he would not let her go alone.

His hands were his to move again. He dropped them to his sides and turned away.

"It's too late," he said, toneless. "We've lost."

Saleh's churn was right where he'd left it, in the corner of his basement hovel. He grimaced to see the place clearly for the first time. He nudged his sewn-together blanket with a toe, shuddering to think of the vermin it might be harboring. The churn was the only thing worth salvaging, and even that only barely—the wood was badly splintered, the handle hanging on by a single screw. He had the notion that if he tried to use it now it would come apart in his hands.

Still, he could not abandon it when it had served him so well, and so he lugged it up the stairwell to the street. He was about to take it to the Djinni's room, where he would contemplate his options, when on the other side of the street he spied the Golem and the Djinni hurrying past. The Golem was nearly running, her face set in anguished determination. The Djinni followed behind, looking as though he would give the world to stop her if he could. And Saleh thought, *something has gone very wrong.*

He reminded himself that this was not his fight. For a time he'd been caught up in their troubles, but now that was over. Hadn't he followed them into enough calamity? It was time to decide where he belonged.

Gritting his teeth, Saleh left the churn behind.

29.

The dance hall on Broome Street was as beautiful by day as by evening, but it was a different sort of beauty: not a sparkling, gaslit fantasia, but a warm and golden room. The high, many-paned windows cast squares of light on the dance floor and made the dust glow in the air.

Neither had said a word as they walked to the dance hall, united in their fear, in their knowledge of just how powerless they were. Schaalman could control the Djinni however he wished, and the Golem was his own creature to destroy. He held their lives in his hands; he might use them each against the other, or seal the Djinni in the flask and turn the Golem into dust. Servitude, or else death.

The door to the dance hall stood open a hand's width. They exchanged a grim glance, then went inside.

The tables had been pushed back to the edge of the hall, leaving an empty parquet expanse. In its middle stood Anna, absent and staring.

"Anna," the Golem said, urgently. There was no response; she could feel nothing from the girl. She took a few steps, looked around. The Djinni stood tensed. "I'm here," the Golem called out.

A patch of shadow detached itself from a far corner and resolved itself into a thin old man. "Hello, my golem," said Schaalman. "I'm glad to see you." His gaze turned to the Djinni. "And you as well. You even came willingly. You did bring the flask, didn't you?"—and the Djinni bit back a startled cry as his body moved of its own accord. His arms held out the flask; his feet stepped him forward, covering half the distance between them. He bent and placed the flask upright on the floor, then stepped back again while the Golem watched, horrified.

"Stop it," she said. "We're here, we did what you asked. Let Anna go."

"Golem, you surprise me," Schaalman said. "I thought you would envy this girl. Look at her, just days from the agony of childbirth—but with no cares, no fears, only peace. Is that not a better way to be?" He regarded her from across the dance floor. "You were mastered for so brief a time, but surely you haven't forgotten what it was like. Tell me," he said, his voice sharp. "Do you remember?"

"Yes."

"And how did it make you feel?"

She could not lie, he knew the answer. "I was happy."

"But you would take that happiness from Anna, and give her back her pain." And then, as though he'd reached some limit of endurance, the posturing fell away; in a tone much more conversational, he said, "As it happens, I understand why. I'm merely surprised you feel the same way." He sighed. "I've underestimated you, Golem. I built you with my own hands, and yet you are a mystery."

She said nothing, waiting, tensed. Beside her the Djinni was so still she wondered if Schaalman had frozen him in place.

"And you," he said, to the Djinni. "Look at you. If I said the words that would unbind you, and told you to fly away, I think you would refuse, and stay by her side. I remember a time when you were less considerate to your women. I wonder, is the change ibn Malik's fault, for what he forced you to do? Or can it be laid at my golem's feet?"

"Stop your talking," the Djinni said, his voice cold. "Do what you mean to."

"You're so eager to go into the flask?" He shook his head. "First I want you to understand me. I am not ibn Malik. I want no glory, no kingdoms to rule. I only want my remaining lives to gain some measure of peace."

He turned to the Golem. "To that end, I propose a trade." From his sleeve he withdrew a piece of paper. "This formula binds a golem to a new master. It was written by your Rabbi Meyer. I believe he died before he could use it. Or perhaps he merely didn't have the strength."

The Rabbi? She wanted to deny it, to call him a liar—but then, how often had she felt the Rabbi's nightmares, his fears for her?

"Meyer worked a clever provision into this formula," Schaalman continued. "You must choose to be mastered, of your own free will, for it to take effect. So here is my offer. Anna's life, and that of her child, for your freedom. I would have you truly be my golem," Schaalman said. "My bound servant, as well as my creation."

She looked at Anna, who stood slack as a rag doll, oblivious to the threat. "And what would I do, as your bound servant?"

"Travel the world," he said. "Find each of my future incarnations, each time I die and am reborn. Teach them who they are, and that they have no need to fear death. Shepherd them toward peace, if you can manage it. They will fight you. I would have done the same."

She glanced at the Djinni, saw his growing horror as he realized what she would choose, what she *must* choose. "Very well," she said. "I accept your offer."

"Chava," the Djinni said, aghast.

The Golem turned on him. "What would you have me do, Ahmad? Tell me!"

But he had no answer.

She turned back to Schaalman. "First, let her go."

Schaalman seemed to consider: and then, between them, Anna collapsed to the floor. The Golem ran to her and hauled her to her feet. Anna's muddled gaze landed on the Golem, and then Schaalman. "You," she said. "You're the one who frightened me, in the hallway."

"Get out of here, girl," Schaalman said.

Anna frowned, not understanding. "Go, Anna," the Golem urged. The young woman gave her a confused look, but then hurried to the hallway exit. They heard the door shudder as it slammed.

The Golem had shut her eyes. "Do it," she said.

"As you wish," Schaalman said—and with no more ceremony he uttered the Rabbi's spell.

Hidden in the darkness of the hallway, Saleh held still as the girl ran straight past him and out the door.

It had been slow work, to open the door without it making a sound. And now that he was inside he had little idea of what he was seeing. He'd thought to walk in on some terrible battle—but they merely stood a little ways apart, trading terse sentences in what must have been Yiddish. Until the pregnant woman collapsed, it might have been a business negotiation.

He waited until the door had swung shut, and then crept closer to the end of the hallway. The gigantic room was flooded with light to its farthest corners; once he left the hallway he'd be easily spotted. What could he possibly do, besides run in and be killed? They would not thank him for throwing away his life. Perhaps, he thought, whatever the outcome, it was enough to be there—to witness their end, if it came to that.

Schaalman spoke again; and even at this distance he could hear the power in the words. It prickled his skin, made his hair rise. He watched the Golem stagger, as though struck a blow. The Djinni had turned his back. Whatever was happening, the creature could not bear to watch.

Holding his breath, Saleh took a step closer.

"Hello, Ahmad," said the Golem.

Don't call me that, the Djinni thought. *Not with her voice.*

He made himself turn around. Could he see the difference, or did he merely imagine it? Her eyes were wider, clearer. Some indefinable wrinkle had been smoothed from her forehead. She was smiling, untroubled.

"You could have waited until I was in the flask," he said to Schaalman. "You could have spared me this."

"I wanted you to see, so you might understand," Schaalman said. "*This* is her nature. Not the broken creature you knew."

"It's true," the Golem said. She stretched her arms out before her, as though noticing them for the first time. "I am as I was meant to be. Don't worry," she said to the Djinni's horrified face, "I still remember everything. The bakery and the Radzins, and Anna, and the Rabbi. And Michael." For a moment she seemed focused elsewhere; then she said, "My master ended his life. I'm a widow again." She might have been discussing the weather.

The Djinni stared. "You killed her husband? What possible reason—"

"He said the wrong thing," Schaalman snapped.

"You failed to tell her this before she agreed to your trade."

Schaalman laughed. "You think it would have affected her decision?"

"And I remember you," the Golem said, coming nearer. Her self-conscious hunch had disappeared; without it, she stood taller, more confident. "I never told you how I felt."

"Don't," the Djinni said, desperate.

"It's all right," she said, as though reassuring a child. "I don't feel that way anymore."

"End this," he said to Schaalman. "Put me in the flask."

The man shrugged. "If you wish it."

But it was the Golem, not her master, who bent to pick it up. Of course: Schaalman would not risk draining his own strength, as ibn Malik had. She examined it, then turned to Schaalman. "What must I say?"

Schaalman hesitated, searching back through the years of memories, and then said a phrase in twisted Arabic. The Djinni shuddered to hear it: it echoed in his own memory as well, the words he'd heard at the start of the flask's endless moment.

The Golem lifted the flask and opened her mouth to say the words.

"Wait," said Schaalman quickly. "Not like that. Face *him*, not me."

She nodded, and turned to the Djinni.

"One moment," the Djinni said.

Schaalman raised an eyebrow. "Is that cowardice?"

He ignored the man and stepped toward the Golem. She stood patient, head tilted, watching with cool curiosity as he brought up a hand to touch her cheek. At the base of her neck, the golden chain peeked from the edge of her buttoned collar.

"Good-bye," he told her.

He would have to be quick.

Saleh had crept to the end of the hallway, not two steps from the shadow's edge, and tried to make sense of the tableau. Was Schaalman manipulating the Golem? Or had she turned traitor?

The Golem picked up the flask and asked the old man a question. His answer, when it came, was in Arabic, or at least Arabic of a sort. The words were nonsense, like a child's singsong chant, but spoken with a painful, rasping inflection that grated against the wound in his mind.

For an instant his vision went gray and flat—he felt as though he were trapped and shrinking, his body reduced to a single point—

The moment passed, and Saleh came back to himself, gulping at air. He knew, without a doubt, that the words were the command that powered the flask. He repeated them to himself in his mind, felt again that strange diminishing—and then heard the note of fear in Schaalman's voice as he admonished the Golem, as though, in that moment, she had placed him in danger.

The Djinni reached out to the Golem and touched her cheek, a gesture of deep regret. Then in a sudden motion he yanked something from her throat. It glinted in his hand, and he turned away, taking one running step, two, moving quickly, his hands unfolding something—

The Golem caught him, lifted him off his feet, and slammed him into the floor.

Schaalman was shouting now. Saleh watched, terrified, as the Golem lifted the Djinni again and threw him into one of the mirrored columns. She'd dropped the flask, and it lay on the floor to one side, forgotten.

He was no fighter; he had no weapon. Against Schaalman and the Golem he would be nothing but a momentary irritation. The instant he entered the sunlight he'd be a dead man.

He thought, *I've been a dead man these many years. Let this death be the one I choose.*

Saleh ran out from the shadows.

The Golem stood over her enemy, the one who'd angered her master. He lay motionless, not from injury or pain, but because her master held him with his mind. Above him the column stood cracked, its base askew, its mirror a webbed explosion. She grabbed and lifted him again, reveling in the feel of her body moving, the bunch and release of clay muscles. This was why she'd been built: for this purpose, this moment.

Her master was yelling again, at her now, not the Djinni. His displeasure called to her, telling her to stop toying with her enemy. Her body was speaking as well, saying *keep on, keep on*—but her master's voice spoke louder. Disappointed, she dropped the Djinni to the floor.

"Enough!" her master shouted. "Someone will hear, you'll have the whole city on top of us."

"I'm sorry," she said, eyes lowered. Then she frowned, listening across their binding. "Something is wrong," she said.

"Nothing is wrong," he snapped and turned away. In truth, he was in some difficulty. His past lives were beginning to stir. It was the fault of that Arabic phrase he'd spoken: to retrieve it, he'd rifled too hastily through ibn Malik's memories, and the disturbance had reverberated through all the lives in between. He would need to settle them again, after the Djinni was safely bottled. He looked around. Where was the flask?

There was the noise of running footsteps. He turned, startled, to see a familiar man grab the flask from the floor. But before Schaalman could even speak, the Golem had leapt past him. A single blow, and the man crumpled.

It was the vagrant from the Djinni's building. "Idiot," Schaalman snarled. The Golem grabbed the man by the neck, and Schaalman flinched to see that her eyes were lit once more with joy. He cared little if the man died, but she was on the verge of running amok. Would he have to destroy her?

He closed his eyes, trying to concentrate against the din in his head. The bindings between himself and his two servants were tangling with each other, weaving in and out of his loosed lives. The Golem paused in her assault, confused. The Djinni spasmed on the floor as Schaalman's control wavered.

The memories surged, pulling Schaalman under, dragging him back and back—

In the glass palace, ibn Malik kneeled above him, blood pumping from the wound in his stomach. Schaalman looked down at himself, and saw the same wound tear itself across his own body, opening like a mouth.

Take your immortality, *ibn Malik said, with my blessing. He bared his teeth, a red-stained grin.*

And then Schaalman was in the dance hall, grasping for the shreds of his control. The Djinni had wrestled the Golem to the ground, pinned her arms. Schaalman reeled and saw Saleh crouched on the floor, saw the flask shining in his hands. He tried to shout to his servants—*no, stop him*—but his voice was drowned away as every one of his former selves rose up in a jeering chorus, saying, *you have been undone as we were, conquered by your own folly.*

Saleh faced Schaalman and spoke the words.

With a searing light, the metal came alive. Saleh staggered and fell, his hands still clamped about the flask, feeling it draw the life from him as Schaalman's form began to diminish and disappear. He gave it every ounce that he could, only hoping it would be enough. And as the last of Saleh's strength drained away, he thought he could hear a long and agonized shriek, the sound of a thousand years of thwarted anger, as the copper prison embraced its new inmate.

Epilogue

On a crisp and blue-skied September morning, the French steamship *Gallia* left New York Harbor bound for Marseille, with twelve hundred passengers crowded into steerage. At Marseille many of them would disperse to smaller ships, bound for the ports of Europe and beyond—to Genoa and Lisbon, Cape Town, Cairo and Tangiers. Their reasons for the journey were as varied as their destinations: to conduct business, to bid farewell to a dying parent, to bring back a new bride to the New World. They were nervous for the homecoming ahead, anticipating the changes in their loved ones' faces, and the changes they'd see mirrored there in themselves.

In one of the steerage bunks lay a man listed on the manifest as one Ahmad al-Hadid. He had boarded with little luggage of his own, only a small valise. He was accompanied by a child of perhaps seven or eight years. Something about the duo suggested that they were not father and son—perhaps it was the formal, gingerly way the man talked with the boy, as though he was not yet certain of his role. But the boy seemed happy enough by his side, and took the man's hand as they approached the gangplank.

The man would not be parted from his valise, nor let anyone else touch it, and once aboard kept it beneath his bunk. On the rare occasions when he opened it, to fetch a clean shirt or to check the steamship schedule to Beirut, one could glimpse a sheaf of old papers, and the round, copper belly of what looked like an ordinary oil flask.

It was a cold, storm-wracked voyage. The man stayed in the cramped bunk night and day, wrapped in blankets against the damp, trying not to think about the endless water beyond the hull. The boy slept in the bunk next to his. In the daytime the boy sat by the man, and played with the collection of small metal figurines, cleverly made, that had gained him the envy of every other child in steerage. Eventually he would put the figurines away, and bring out a small faded photograph of an elderly woman in a dark dress, whose gray hair hung in tight curls. It was his grandmother, whom he was going to live with; she'd sent the photograph so that he'd recognize her at the dock. "You have her eyes," the man said, looking over the boy's shoulder. Then he smiled. "And her hair."

The boy returned the smile, but then went back to staring doubtfully at the woman's face. The man reached up from the blankets and placed a hand on his thin shoulder.

The man only went up on deck once, on the fifth day out from New York, during a break in the weather. For a few minutes he sat on a bench, holding the valise in his lap, and looked out over the churning, white-capped steel of the ocean. The ship rocked into a swell, and spray drenched the guardrail nearby. The man shuddered and went back down again.

The ship from Marseille to Beirut was small and cramped, but the route was quicker, the weather warmer. At Beirut they disembarked, and he watched the boy's grandmother give the boy a piece of chocolate before kneeling down to clasp him in her thin, dark-robed arms.

Then it was time for him to leave. The boy clung to him, eyes welling. "Good-bye, Matthew," the Djinni whispered. "Don't forget me."

From Beirut he rode the train over the mountains to bustling Damascus, then paid a camel driver to take him out beyond the Ghouta's green border. The driver, who'd thought the man only wanted to sightsee, was horrified when his customer insisted on being left alone at the desert's edge with nothing but his small suitcase. The Djinni doubled his pay and reassured him that all would be well. Finally the camel driver left. When, an hour later, he thought better of it and went to fetch the man back again, he found no trace of him. The desert had swallowed him whole.

In Central Park the leaves had begun to fall, littering the paths with thin blades of russet and gold. It was a Saturday afternoon, and the park was full of families and courting couples, all determined to enjoy the last of the good weather.

Two women, one noticeably tall, the other pushing a perambulator, walked together on the carriage path bordering the meadow, past the dozen or so sheep that milled nearby chewing placidly on the grass. The women kept some distance from each other, and so far they had spoken little; but now the tall one said, "How have you been, Anna?"

"As well as can be, I suppose," the young mother replied. "The weather's cooling, at least. And Toby's colic is better."

A pause. "I'm very glad to hear it, but I was thinking more of your situation."

Anna sighed. "I know." They walked on for a while. "It's difficult," she said. "I take as much washing and sewing as I can, but Toby takes up so much time! I do get by, though. At least I haven't gone to the streets yet." She tried to say it lightly, but the Golem felt her fear of it, the dread that someday, with nowhere else to go, she would turn to selling herself.

Knowing it was futile, she said, "Anna, if you need anything—"

"That's all right," Anna said crisply, and the Golem nodded. The girl had so far refused all attempts. "We're making do," Anna said, in a softer voice. Then she glanced over at the Golem. "And you? How are you?"

The Golem was silent for a while. "Like you, I suppose," she said at last. "Managing, as best I can."

When it became clear that she would not elaborate further, Anna said, "I hear you're still working at Radzin's."

"Mrs. Radzin would not hear of my leaving," the Golem said. *Go and grieve*, the woman had said. *And then come back. You'll always have a place here, Chavaleh. We're your family now.*

They'd buried Michael in Brooklyn, and this time she'd defied convention and gone to the funeral, braving the stares from his old friends, all of them waiting for her to break down and sob. There had been no shivah; she thought he would not have wanted it. The police had made inquiries—had interviewed her as well, an excruciating experience—and then, as they'd done with Irving Wasserman, relegated the case to the drawer marked UNSOLVED, and turned their attention to greater matters.

It wasn't your fault, Anna had said, but she'd sounded less than certain.

They walked on, Anna cooing at little Toby, who lay fussing in the pram. It wasn't clear how much Anna understood of what had happened that day. *One minute I was hiding that sack you gave me,* she'd told the Golem, *and the next you were telling me to run.* The Golem had given brief, vague answers to her questions. To describe her addled helplessness would only frighten her—and the Golem did not want to feel the girl's terror.

At least that horrible old man is gone, Anna had said; and the Golem had agreed: *yes, he's gone.* Not entirely the truth, of course. Schaalman may have been trapped in the flask, but he was still her master, and they were still bound. In moments of quiet, when the city had gone to sleep—or else here, in the park, with so few minds nearby to distract her—she could hear him: an eternal pinprick of anger, howling on the edge of her senses. At first it had driven her to distraction, but she was growing to accept it as the price of her survival.

Over Bow Bridge's arched ribbon of iron they walked, and down into the dappled hush of the Ramble. Leaves skittered at their feet. The late-summer sun shone down on a ground already turning cool and sleepy. The Golem shivered. It would be a long, difficult winter: the park knew it, and so did she.

There were more courting couples here than on the carriage road, taking advantage of the Ramble's relative privacy. A few had come for more than courting, and she could sense them concealed among the deeply winding paths and dense woods, behind the mossy boulders and rough stone bridges: the forbidden couples, some tentative and others defiant, the illicit and the ill matched, the joyful and the desperate. Their desires rose like sap from the hidden groves.

Anna asked, "Have you heard from him?"

"What?" the Golem said, startled. "Oh. Yes, he sent a telegram from Marseille. And then from Beirut, last week, to say he'd arrived. Nothing else."

"He'll be all right."

The Golem nodded—the reassurance was well meant, if a touch breezy. But she knew better than Anna what the Djinni faced.

"And when he gets back," Anna said, "what will you do about him?"

Despite everything, the Golem had to smile. Most people would refrain from asking a widow twice over such a question, but not Anna. "I thought you didn't like him."

"I don't. But *you* do. And you should do something about it."

"It's more complicated than that," the Golem muttered.

Anna rolled her eyes. "It always is."

Yes, but was it ever *this* complicated? She'd seen the Djinni only once before he left for Marseille, and at first it had felt akin to their earliest encounters: each of them careful of the other, unsure of what to say. They'd walked to the Hudson River docklands, where the stevedores were hauling cargo back and forth under the electric lights. *How much do you remember?* the Djinni had finally asked, and the Golem replied, *All of it*. His face told her it would've been kinder to lie, to pretend not to remember his attempt at destroying her; but she had been down that road with Michael, and she would never go there again. *If I hadn't remembered*, she said, *would you have told me?* And he had watched the stevedores for a while before saying, *I don't know*. An honest answer, at least.

And then slowly, by fits and starts, they'd begun to talk again. He told her more about Saleh, the man's damaged mind, his improbable healing at Schaalman's hands. *Did you know him well?* the Golem asked, and the Djinni said, his regret plain, *no. Not well at all*.

The Golem said, *If I hadn't injured him, then maybe . . .*

The end would have been the same.

You can't know that.

Chava, stop it. Saleh's death wasn't your fault.

But wasn't it, at least in part? Certainly she'd intended to kill him, had attacked him with jubilant, intoxicating abandon. It would've been so much easier to forgive herself, to believe it was all Schaalman's fault, if not for her memory of that joy. And what of Michael? She'd felt such guilt and sorrow at his graveside—but how could she reconcile that with her gladness when she'd learned that her master had killed him? Try as she might, she could not disown the self she'd been in those moments—nor the brief sense that she'd been asleep since Rotfeld died, and had finally woken to her true existence.

At last they'd left the docklands and walked to Little Syria, to an unassuming tenement building, and stood below a wondrous ceiling made of tin. He'd pointed out to her his favorite places, the discoveries of his childhood, the valley where he'd built his palace; and she'd heard his trepidation at the thought of going home. At last he'd said, tentatively, *If my kin are still there, they might know how to free me.*

She'd stood there, absorbing this. And then she said, in a small voice, *I would be very glad for you.*

He'd placed a hand on her arm, said her name; and she had turned into his embrace, his warm shoulder, his lips at her forehead. *This isn't good-bye,* he said. *Whatever happens, I'm coming back. I promise.* A comfort, to hear it—but what sort of resentment would result, if only a promise kept him at her side? She couldn't help thinking that once freed, he would come to regard his life in New York as a dream, the sort a man might wake from with a shudder and a sigh of relief.

In the park, the breeze was strengthening, but the afternoon sun shone on, setting the tops of the trees ablaze. Voices from Bethesda Terrace carried across the water to the Ramble, ghostly conversations in a myriad of languages. In the pram, Toby was drifting off to sleep, his hands curled like shells atop the blanket. He furrowed his brow, small red lips puckering, dreaming of his mother's breast.

They left the Ramble and turned down the park's eastern drive, Anna chattering all the while, mostly gossip about her employers and the sorts of secrets one could learn from a person's laundry. Her cheer was wearing thin, though: the Golem felt her rising discomfort, her longing to be elsewhere, in safer company.

"I think we'll head home," the young woman said at length. "This one will need his supper soon."

"It was good to see you, Anna."

"And you," Anna said. Then she paused. "I meant what I said earlier about Ahmad. You should try to be happy, if you can." And the girl wheeled the pram away, the wind tugging at her thin cloak.

Into the desert the Djinni walked.

He walked for a full day, carrying the valise. Occasionally some creature would spy him at a distance, a *ghul* or an imp, and come to investigate, gleeful at the prospect of a man gone so far astray—but then they'd see what he was, and draw back in fear and confusion, and let him pass. He'd expected no better. Even so, it pained him.

Taken as a whole, the desert had changed little since he'd been gone. He passed the same jagged peaks and valleys he had once roamed, the same caves and cliffs and hiding places. But in its particulars the landscape was entirely transformed. It was as though a millennium of wind and sun and seasons had unfolded all at once, filling in streambeds and eroding hillsides, cracking great boulders into fields of pebbles. He thought of the tin ceiling in New York, and how it was no longer a map but an artifact, the portrait of an ancient memory.

Evening was falling when he neared the outskirts of the djinn habitations, the land of his kin. He slowed his walk, hoping to be spotted. At the border he stopped, waiting. Soon enough he saw them: a contingent of nearly a dozen djinn, flying insubstantial toward him.

A rush of relief: they still lived. That, at least, had not changed.

They came to rest before him, and he saw they were the elders, though none he recognized. The oldest—a female, a djinniyeh—spoke, addressing him in the language he'd thought never to hear again.

What are you?

"A djinni," he told her. "And your kin. I would tell you my name, if I could."

You are kin to us? How is that possible?

"I was trapped in this form a thousand years ago, by a wizard named ibn Malik." He lifted his arm, pulled his dusty shirtsleeve away from the iron cuff—and they recoiled, the nearest ones scattering.

Unnatural! How can you wear that, without pain?

"It is part of the binding," he said. "Please, tell me—can you undo it? Have we gained that knowledge, in a thousand years?"

They regrouped, conferred, their voices a windstorm. He closed his eyes, drank in the sound.

No. We do not have that knowledge.

He nodded, feeling he'd already known the answer.

But can you tell us—need we fear this wizard? Does he still live, to trap and bind us?

"He lives, but you need not fear him." He opened the valise, removed the flask. "He is here, captured as he once captured me. But we are still bound. If the seal is broken in my lifetime, he'll return, to be born again and again."

And after your death?

"Then he may be released, and his soul will go on to whatever awaits him."

A mutter among them. The djinniyeh said, *It is suggested that we kill you, to destroy the wizard. You are already crippled—would it not be a mercy?*

He had half-expected this. "If you are offering me a choice," he said, "then I respectfully decline. I made a promise that I would return, and I would not break that promise."

Once more they conferred, a more heated discussion this time. He looked among them and wondered which were his closest relations. But to ask would be futile, with no way to even tell them his own lineage. And what would the answer signify, when they must remain strangers?

We have decided, the djinniyeh said at last. *Your life will be spared. We will guard the wizard's soul, and ensure its safe protection. It shall be our task, and that of our offspring, until you pass from this earth.*

"Thank you," he said, relieved.

They led him to a clearing within the habitations, and there he buried the flask, the elders watching as he dug into the gritty, hard-packed soil with his hands. He added the sheaf of papers and replaced the soil, and then built a mound of stones, fitting them as tightly as he could. By the time he was finished the entire habitation had gathered to watch. He was painfully aware that he was trusting the care of ibn Malik's soul to the capricious attentions of his own kind. But better this than New York, where sooner or later the flask and the spells would be unearthed, no matter how deeply they were buried, to make way for a new building or bridge or monument. Whereas it seemed that humanity still hadn't conquered the desert.

But how will you live, bound and chained as you are? the eldest djin-niyeh asked him as he stood, wiping his hands. *What will you do, where will you go?*

"I'll go home," he told her. And he left the habitation, a thousand eyes watching as he passed.

His palace was still there, shining in the valley.

There was damage, to be sure. The outer walls were deeply weath-ered, etched by the sand to a milky opacity. The taller towers had crum-bled, littering the valley floor with smooth blue-white shards. In some places the glass was thin as paper. In others it had worn away entirely, leaving curved windows like portholes, open to the elements. He went inside, stepping over rubble. Sand lay in drifts in the corners; the roof was a honeycomb. He saw bird nests, the bones of animal meals.

In the great hall, he found the remains of Fadwa and Abu Yusuf.

The walls of the hall were thick, and the man and his daughter had lain there in peace until the desert air had dried them past the inter-est of the animals. He sat before them, cross-legged on the dusty floor. He thought of Saleh's funeral, a few weeks earlier. Maryam had reached out to Little Syria's small Muslim population and found a man willing to serve as imam. Arbeely and Sayeed Faddoul and the Djinni had all helped to wash Saleh and wrap him in white sheets; and then the Djinni had stood inside the grave to receive the shrouded body. Afterward they had all gone back to the Faddouls' coffeehouse, and he'd listened as they talked about Saleh, sharing what little they knew. *He was a healer*, Maryam had said, and the others had looked at her quizzically; but the Djinni had said, *it's true, he was.* He wished there was someone with him now, so he could tell them about this young woman and her father, the lives they'd led, the loved ones they'd left behind. He thought of Sophia Winston, who was soon to arrive in Istanbul, a relatively short distance away. But he'd only be intruding, and burdening her with sorrows, at the start of her own long-awaited journey.

He wanted to bury Fadwa and her father, as Saleh had been buried, but their remains were too delicate to move. So instead he gathered the shards that had fallen from his palace, and built a tomb around them. He melted the pieces and smoothed them together, shaping first the walls and then a domed cover. It was hard, draining work. More than once he had to go out into the sun, to regain his strength.

At last it was done. He debated whether to carve their names into the glass, but in the end he left the tomb quiet and unmarked. He knew who they were, and why they were there. That, he decided, would suffice.

The sun was setting by the time the Golem returned home, to her new boardinghouse on Eldridge Street. Her room there was no larger than the one the Rabbi had found for her, but the house itself was double the size, and catered to a much more sociable clientele. The landlady was a former actress, and most of her lodgers were drawn from that world: traveling thespians who would stop in New York for a season or two before departing for stints elsewhere. The Golem found she liked her fellow tenants. Their thoughts could be trying, even exhausting; but their enthusiasms were genuine, and they grew to like her as well. She was a spot of stillness in their midst, and a fresh audience for their stories. At some point her skill in sewing had come out, and soon they were all asking her to mend their costumes, even make them new ones: *the troupe's seamstress is just awful, she can't hold a candle to your work.* They paid her if they could, and brought her flowers and petits fours and front-row tickets, and distracted her with cheerful noise. And unlike at her old boardinghouse, they gave no thought at all to lights burning at all hours, or a late-night step upon the stair.

She went up to her room and paused, dismayed. A wedding dress of cheap satin was hanging from her door handle, a gash across its train. Attached was a note from one of her neighbors, thanking her in advance for mending her costume, and promising a bag of chocolate drops or whatever else she might fancy.

She carried the dress inside, lit the lamp, and drew the sewing basket nearer to her chair. Her own wedding dress was folded away in the room's small wardrobe, below her workaday clothes. She hadn't yet been able to part with it.

The mend was an easy one, and soon it was finished. Absently she straightened the sleeves and smoothed the bodice, looking for any small rips she might repair, and thinking all the while of Anna's exhortation that she *do something* about the Djinni. For Anna, that would likely mean a torrid love affair, full of melodrama and broken promises. Perhaps the Djinni could do such a thing—whatever had passed between him and Sophia seemed to be in this vein—but herself? Ridiculous, to picture herself so drunk on passion, so absurdly self-involved, that she could set aside all reason and hang the consequences.

But then, what other option was there? A quiet courtship, then marriage and the domestic life? Almost as hard to imagine. He would go mad with the constraint: the burdens of faithfulness and constancy, of returning home to a tiny room day after day. He would come to blame her, and she would lose him. And even if by some miracle he were willing, would she want to marry again, after Michael? Perhaps it would be better to spend a few years sewing alone in her room. *You should try to be happy, if you can*, Anna had said—but the Golem could not see a way toward it.

A knock came at the door: her landlady was holding a telegram. "Chava? This just came for you." The woman handed it over and closed the door, her curiosity held painfully at bay.

BEIRUT SYRIA 29 SEP

CHAVA LEVY
67 ELDRIDGE ST NY

ALL ACCOMPLISHED EXCEPT STILL BOUND-

She stopped reading and closed her eyes. He'd held out little hope, she knew. And undoubtedly she would have lost him, as wanderlust rose to overtake affection. Even so, she felt a surge of sorrow on his behalf.

She began again:

ALL ACCOMPLISHED EXCEPT STILL BOUND TELL
ARBEELY WOULD LIKE JOB BACK-

At this she smiled.

-WILL RETURN VIA MARSEILLE EXPECT ME 19 OCT
BENEATH YOUR WINDOW.
AHMAD AL-HADID

Maybe, she thought as she fastened her cloak, there was some middle ground to be had, a resting place between passion and practicality. She had no idea how they would find it: in all likelihood they'd have to carve it for themselves out of thin air. And any path they chose would not be an easy one. But perhaps she could allow herself to hope.

She stepped out into the clear, windy night, walked to the telegram office on Broadway, and let him know that he needn't come to her window—she would meet him at the dock.

Acknowledgments

Every book is a group effort, but there are a few people without whom this one would not exist. My indomitable agent, Sam Stoloff, encouraged me to write this novel almost from its conception. My fantastic editor, Terry Karten, has my heartfelt gratitude for her insight and her patience. Thank you also to the many fine people at HarperCollins who helped shepherd this book to publication.

The research process was like a job in itself, and I returned repeatedly to a couple of sources. The books of Professors Alixa Naff and Gregory Orfalea were instrumental for their descriptions of New York's Little Syria. And it would've been much harder to write about 1890s Manhattan from a couch in twenty-first-century California without the help of the New York Public Library Digital Gallery. (Any inaccuracies in this book are, of course, my own.)

My thanks as well to everyone who read portions of this book in earlier forms, including Binnie Kirshenbaum, Sam Lipsyte, Ben Marcus, Nicholas Christopher, Clare Beams, Michelle Adelman, Amanda Pennelly, Jeff Bender, Reif Larsen, Sharon Pacuk, Rebecca Schiff, Anna Selver-Kassell, Dave Englander, Andrea Libin, Keri Bertino, Judy Sternlight, Rana Kazkaz, Dave Diehl, and Rebecca Murray. And a second helping of thanks goes to Amanda Pennelly, for sparking the idea in the first place.

The necessary friendships of Kara Levy, Ruth Galm, Michael McAllister, Zoë Ferraris, Brian Eule, and Dan White kept me sane and motivated, even when common sense told me to stick it in a drawer and call it a day.

Lastly and most importantly, thanks to my beloved family, all my Weckers and Kazkazes and Khalafs—but most especially my mother, father, and husband for their love and support in all its forms. And a final thank-you to my wonderful Maya, who arrived in time for the ending.

About the Author

H elene Wecker received a B.A. from Carleton College in Minnesota, and an M.F.A. from Columbia University in New York. A Chicago-area native who's made her home in Minneapolis, Seattle, and New York, she now lives near San Francisco with her husband and daughter. *The Golem and the Djinni* is her first novel.